MILLION

Also by C.R. Berry

Million Eyes: Extra Time

MILLION EYES

C.R. BERRY

Elsewhen Press

Million Eyes
First published in Great Britain by Elsewhen Press, 2020
An imprint of Alnpete Limited

Elsewhen Press, PO Box 757, Dartford, Kent DA2 7TQ
www.elsewhen.press

British Library Cataloguing in Publication Data.
A catalogue record for this book is available from the British Library.

ISBN 978-1-911409-48-9 Print edition
ISBN 978-1-911409-58-8 eBook edition

Designed and formatted by Elsewhen Press

For Vicky

Shortly after the death of Diana, Princess of Wales, in 1997, royal butler Paul Burrell had a private meeting with Queen Elizabeth II.

Burrell later revealed that the Queen had issued him with an ominous warning: “There are powers at work in this country about which we have no knowledge.”

To this day, Burrell claims he has no idea who she was talking about.

1

July 26th 1100

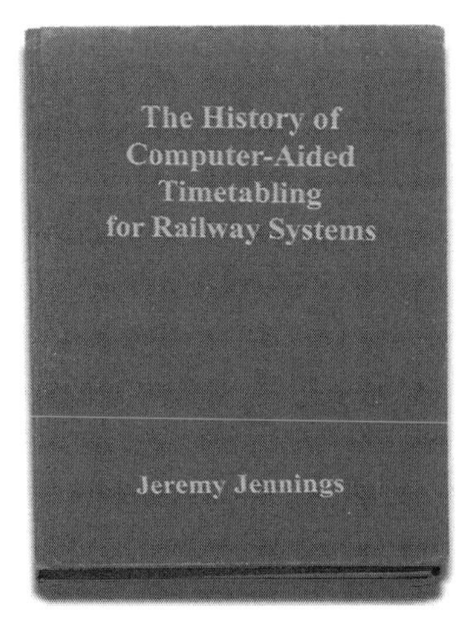

As his servant moored the boat, King William II of England cast his eyes one last time over the unworldly book. Then he closed and fastened the box it was in and slipped it back into his satchel. He climbed out of the boat, boots squelching as he stepped onto the muddy shore of the River Thames.

"Remain here," William said to the servant. "I shan't be long."

The evening dusk thickening fast, William entered the great keep of the Tower of London and climbed the spiral staircase to the second floor, finding his chief minister, Ranulf Flambard, waiting inside the Chapel of St John. With its imposing tunnel-vaulted French stone nave and thick, round columns supporting unmoulded, unadorned arches, the chapel was a stark and uncompromising demonstration of Norman power. One that normally helped William feel in control. Not today.

"Good evening, Your Grace," said Ranulf in his usual rumble of a voice, deepened even further by the cold, impenetrable stone that surrounded them.

"That remains to be seen, Ranulf," said William, opening his satchel and lifting out the box.

"I take it you've made a decision about the book, then."

For weeks the book had brought William nothing but confusion and turmoil. There was so much about it that didn't make sense. Its constitution, for one. It was so cleanly cut and shaped, with thin cover boards dressed in a strange, dark green cloth so fine it was near-impossible to trace the thread, and William could not imagine fingers small enough to have woven it. Its only markings were *The History of Computer-Aided Timetabling for Railway Systems* and *Jeremy Jennings* gold-tooled onto the front and spine, and these were an even bigger mystery. *Jeremy* and *Jennings* looked like names, his experts said, and *The History of Computer-Aided Timetabling for Railway Systems* were utterly meaningless but for a few of the words vaguely resembling some Latin ones.

And if these frightening irregularities weren't enough, what lay beneath the book's covers was worse. Far worse. A part of William wished he'd never opened the damn thing and yet another, bigger, part of him knew that God had endowed him with this knowledge on the understanding that he, the king, would do something about it.

"We must protect it," said William, brushing his fingers over the oak frame and riveted iron bands of the box. "This book is evidence of a serious threat to the kingdom and of those behind it. It is an omen. An omen foretelling a future that God is compelling me to avert."

"Yes, sire. How would you seek to protect it?"

"By hiding it. The prisoner's people must know we have it. They could be here in London right now, waiting for the right moment to come and retrieve it. It cannot remain here."

"I agree," said Ranulf. "They will be coming."

"I am charging you with the task of hiding it, Ranulf. Find

a low-born family of minimal conspicuousness and make sure they understand the importance of the book and its secrets and can be trusted to protect them."

"Yes, sire. I will go tonight."

Though reluctant to part with it, William handed the box to his chief minister, reassuring himself of his decision. Then he reached beneath his cloak and tunic and unhooked a silver chain from around his neck, on which hung a small key. "Here. You'll need this. It is the key to open the box."

Ranulf placed the chain around his own neck, tucking the key into his bishop's robe. "And what of the prisoner? Do you have a plan?"

Oh, how William wished he did. Unfortunately the outlander who was found with the book was but another lingering mystery in an ever-deepening quagmire of them. "Not yet. We must keep trying to ascertain the prisoner's intentions and role in all this."

Ranulf frowned. "But how? We have no way of communicating."

William sighed. "It is a good question, my friend. But I fear, as of this moment, the answer evades me."

"Then perhaps a quiet execution is the most sensible course."

"It could well be. But I must not risk provoking an enemy I do not know how to fight."

"I understand. Will you inform the Council about any of this?"

William shook his head. "Not until I determine who can be trusted. The lesser *curia regis* will meet in two days to discuss Aquitaine. I want the book gone and hidden before then."

William's long-planned invasion of Aquitaine was to be the pinnacle of his reign. He owed it to his father, who had afforded him a great honour by giving England to him instead of his elder brother, Robert. William had enjoyed some successes – securing his hold on England, recapturing Maine, subduing Robert – but none so big as his father's victory at Hastings, earning him the name 'Conqueror'. A fact he was reminded of all too often by the embroidery that hung above the Palace of Westminster's main staircase. A variation of his father's favourite scene from the enormous, ostentatious portrayal of the Norman conquest that adorned the nave of Bayeux Cathedral, it depicted his father astride his horse holding up the crown of England, with defeated Saxon king Harold II lying trampled beneath his horse's hooves with an arrow through his eye.

Aquitaine was to be his Hastings. He would soon replace the embroidery at Westminster with a depiction of his own great victory. The book – and the prisoner – were distractions he couldn't afford.

Ranulf shrouded the box in the folds of his robe, bowed and left the Tower. William wheezed a sigh. He wasn't sure whether it was with relief, doubt, fear – or something else.

August 2nd 1100

It was two days before William was due to leave for Aquitaine with his army and the nights of the past week had not been kind, the book and prisoner still plaguing his every thought. He hoped today's hunt in the New Forest, followed by a riotous feast with singing, dancing and general mischief, would help ease his disquiet and free his body of some tension, if just enough to be able to sleep.

William set out from his hunting lodge with four friends. For a time the five men stayed close, laughing and drinking and swapping war stories. Then William's younger brother, Henry, set his sights on a boar and wandered off on his own. Soon Robert Fitzhamon and William of Breteuil diverged as well. Only Sir Walter Tyrrell, Lord of Poix-de-Picardie and a recent addition to William's court, stayed at his side.

A stag grazing between two elms caught William's eye. With a shining, creamy brown coat with white spots and enormous branching antlers – perhaps the biggest he'd seen – it would be a satisfying kill. He climbed down from his horse and tied it to a tree so he could pursue the stag on foot.

He drew his bow, but the loud crack of a twig behind him prompted the stag to scarper into the trees.

William sighed, lowering his bow and arrow. "Walter, I thought you were a master at this."

His admonishment drew no response. He turned around slowly.

He hadn't suspected Tyrrell could be one of the prisoner's people, not for a second. The big, beefy Englishman didn't seem clever enough to muster such deceit, and yet now William found himself staring at the head of an arrow. Were there clues to his duplicity that William missed?

Though full of doubts, questions and regrets, William put on a mask of calm and confidence, whispering simply, "So you're one of them, then."

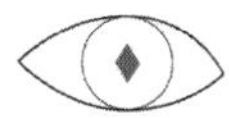

Purkis, a poor charcoal-burner, was leading his horse and cart through the woods. He'd been in the New Forest all morning, collecting fallen wood, stripping it of its bark and loading it onto the cart, ready for burning and selling back home.

The fresh, foggy morning had matured into a blistering afternoon and Purkis was cooking in it. As he headed home, the sun was high and poured its heavy rays over his back, burning through his linen tunic, which was stuck with sweat. He was going to have to start leaving earlier. This heat was too much.

He stopped in a patch of shade to rest, cool and drink. His water skin was nearly empty. His head was beginning to throb.

"Not far now, Samson," he said to his horse. "I'm hankering for a cup of ale. What about you?"

Samson gave a gentle whinny and Purkis smiled and stroked his smooth brown muzzle, saying, "Nice bowl of pottage, too. Cecilia has some fava beans and a carrot, I think. Oh. And a little bit of that nice bread from the market, if there's any left."

Purkis felt a rumble in his belly and rubbed it gently. "Actually, I think we finished it, didn't we?" He looked at Samson, as if expecting the horse to respond and tell him no, there was plenty of bread left. Alas, he just stared with those beautiful amber eyes of his.

Purkis's smile drooped. Food was scarce in his house. Selling charcoal only brought in a small wage, but it used to be enough to feed his family. Then King William raised the taxes, whittling down that wage till his family's dinner table looked more and more bare. As always, peasants like Purkis bore the brunt of the king's greed. But what could he do? He just had to get on with it. Though his wife's pottage was watered down a little more each day and he'd forgotten the taste of meat, there was no use being glum about it. Not while this king lived.

If only someone might rid the kingdom of this selfish foreign ruler.

Purkis swallowed his hunger and tugged the rope round Samson's neck. The faithful horse pushed on. A moment later, he heard the clatter of wood tumbling and turned to see a pile of logs fall off the back of the cart. The cart had rolled over something. He dropped the rope and walked to the rear of the cart. Just a stray root from the beech tree they were passing. He replaced the logs.

He was about to continue on. Then footsteps crackled a few yards away and he froze.

He glanced around slowly. The footsteps weren't loud enough for Purkis to tell what direction they were coming from.

A fallen branch snapped. He flinched. Now his gaze was drawn to the right – and a figure mostly obscured by trees, fifteen to twenty feet away.

"Walter, I thought you were a master at this," said a man with a smooth voice, edged with authority and a touch of annoyance.

A pause. Then the same voice said, "So you're one of them, then."

One of King William's hunting parties? Must've been. Stringent forest laws forbade the killing of deer or boar by anybody other than the king's hunting parties. It was punishable by death.

But the king and his subjects were Norman. Normans spoke French. Purkis couldn't understand a word of it.

This man had just spoken English.

Samson had started to graze on what little grass was available where they'd stopped. Purkis moved closer to the man who had just spoken, hoping for a better look.

He eventually caught the man's bottom half. His top half was still obscured in part by the leafy branches of an oak. He saw the fringe of a thin black cape, elegant blue hose and polished boots, and could just about tell that his blue-sleeved arms were raised.

Purkis moved again. Now he could see that the man was tall, broad-shouldered and formidable. He caught one side of the man's round face and saw why his arms were raised. His bow was nocked, an arrow ready to fly.

He couldn't see the target. Probably a deer. He looked in the arrow's direction and thought he saw a pair of antlers emerge from the shadow of a tree. No. Just a tree branch, missing one side of its bark, pushed by a brief wind into the sun's glare.

"I take it your name is not Walter Tyrrell?"

Oh. The smooth voice wasn't coming from the man with the bow and arrow. There was someone else. But who? The trees were thick here. Purkis moved again.

"No," said the man with the bow and arrow.

Now Purkis saw the owner of the other voice. A short, rotund man with a yellow moustache, flushed cheeks, small eyes encircled by dark rings, and curly, yellow, bedraggled hair sticking out from underneath a red velvet hat trimmed with feathers. He was in a long, dark green tunic with fancy-looking patterns stitched in golden thread, fastened at the waist with a belt encrusted with glistening jewels of different colours, and his thin legs were encased in hose that were the same deep shade of red as his hat.

But that looked like…

No, it couldn't be.

The yellow-haired man said, "Then who – ?"

"That doesn't matter," said Tyrrell, or whoever he was, his voice much deeper and harsher than the yellow-haired man's. "Just give me the book."

The book? What book?

The yellow-haired man seemed equally puzzled. "What book?"

"Don't play games with me, Your Grace. This arrow is pointed straight at your heart."

Your Grace!

Purkis swallowed – it was like forcing down a rock.

He couldn't believe it, yet he knew it to be true. The regal clothes. The golden head. The red complexion that had earned him the nickname 'William Rufus'. For some reason he was using the tongue of the common people, but there could be no doubt. This Walter Tyrrell was threatening to shoot the king.

Purkis felt a tightening in his chest. Just ten minutes ago, he had silently wished the king dead. Could his treasonous thoughts have precipitated this?

"What amusement," smirked the king. "A traitorous pretender accuses *me* of playing games."

Tyrrell just glared down the shaft of his arrow. "Where is it?"

"Safe," said the king, evidently knowing of this book all along. "Hidden. And if you think I'm ever going to tell you where, you may as well shoot me now."

"Fine."

Tyrrell pulled back his bowstring and released it with a twang. The arrow sliced through the air with a faint hiss and thudded into the king's chest.

Purkis clamped his hand over his mouth to suppress a horrified gasp.

The king thumped into a shallow bed of bracken. Purkis moved in a little closer, ducked behind a large gorse bush and peeked over the top.

The king clung to life, fingers clenched around the arrow in his chest, blood spilling over his fist and onto the bracken. Then he wheezed his last, his head drooped to one side, and his gaze froze in death.

Purkis shuddered. A small twig snapped beneath his foot.

Tyrrell reacted, twisting in Purkis's direction.

Damn, he'd heard it.

Purkis stooped low immediately, hopefully obscured by the bush.

No, no, no…

Did he see me?

Purkis could still see the king's killer through gaps in the green, spiny branches and egg-yolk-yellow blooms.

Please, no.

Tyrrell walked forwards, heading in Purkis's direction. As he did, he took out a new arrow.

Purkis stopped breathing, a knot lodged in his throat. He shut his eyes.

Tyrrell's boots crunched over fallen leaves and twigs,

drawing closer and louder.

A sharp sound split the air. Purkis's eyes sprang open. Tyrrell had stopped. It was a bizarre sound – quite musical – and appeared to have saved Purkis from getting shot.

Tyrrell dug his hand inside his tunic, pulled something out.

Now that he was distracted, Purkis moved back to a safer, more distant position, angled so he could see what was going on through a gap in the trees.

Tyrrell was holding something. A flat, black, rectangular object. He tapped it with his finger. The music stopped. Tyrrell lifted the object to his ear.

What was he doing?

"Hello," Tyrrell murmured.

Me? Is he talking to me?

"The king is dead. Did it work?"

There was a silence. A moment later, he continued, "Then I'll continue searching for the book." Another pause, then, "I'll have to lie low for a while, change my identity. I think the king's chief minister, Ranulf Flambard, might know –"

His sentence trailed off, unfinished.

There was a much longer silence, and it was almost as if he was *listening* to the object at his ear.

Was he mad? He certainly seemed it. He finally said, "Are you ordering me to make another jump?" After a pause, "When?"

A further long silence was followed by, "So shouldn't I stick around here, find out if Ranulf Flambard was the one who..."

Another unfinished sentence.

What in the world was going on?

Tyrrell gave a sigh and muttered, "Yes, ma'am. I'll take care of it."

Then he lowered the black object from his ear, tapped the front of it again, and slipped it back inside his tunic. There must've been some holder or small bag that was sewn into the lining.

As he withdrew his hand from the receptacle, something else came with it. Another strange object – small, cylindrical, white. He fumbled with it with both hands. There was a faint click. Purkis peered hard, saw an opening in the top of the object, and recognised that it was a kind of bottle or pot, and

Tyrrell had just removed the lid.

Tyrrell used one hand to tip the bottle into the other and gently shake it. A tiny object the colour of blood – possibly a stone or jewel – rolled out into his palm.

He threw up his palm to his mouth, and the stone was gone, swallowed.

He replaced the lid on the bottle.

Purkis took a breath.

Now what?

His question was answered instantly, as a bright and soundless light – white, hot and painful – seared into his eyes, and made him jump back instinctively.

For a moment he saw nothing but white. He shook his head. The whiteness dissolved steadily to blurry browns and greens and, with a rub of the eyes, solidified to trees and vegetation.

Tyrrell was gone. He could not have walked or run away; Purkis would have heard his footsteps.

He had – impossibly – disappeared into thin air.

Witchcraft?

Purkis waited a minute or so, then stepped forwards through the trees and came upon the body of William Rufus, the king he'd wished dead and was now very much so.

He stared at the body. The king's face was no longer its famous red, rather a spectral grey, since most of his blood had now leaked into the forest floor from the puncture in his chest.

He couldn't just leave him there.

He returned to Samson, still happily grazing. He drew the horse and cart towards the body, unloaded the wood – which he would hopefully collect tomorrow – and lifted the body into the back of the cart. He resumed his journey to Canterton, where he lived, to tell Cecilia that he would be taking the body to Winchester, the capital. It was the least he could do.

Would he tell Cecilia – or anyone for that matter – what he had seen?

No, he decided.

He didn't see anything.

Some things were best left alone.

2

May 29th 2019

HERE STOOD THE OAK TREE, ON WHICH AN ARROW SHOT BY SIR WALTER TYRRELL AT A STAG, GLANCED AND STRUCK KING WILLIAM THE SECOND, SURNAMED RUFUS, ON THE BREAST, OF WHICH HE INSTANTLY DIED, ON THE SECOND DAY OF AUGUST, ANNO 1100.

KING WILLIAM THE SECOND, SURNAMED RUFUS BEING SLAIN, AS BEFORE RELATED, WAS LAID IN A CART, BELONGING TO ONE PURKIS, AND DRAWN FROM HENCE, TO WINCHESTER, AND BURIED IN THE CATHEDRAL CHURCH OF THAT CITY.

Standing reading the inscriptions on the Rufus Stone in the New Forest was Gregory Ferro, a married, bespectacled, bearded, fifty-four-year-old father of two and former history teacher who went grey before his time and, while not exactly fat, was fatter and unhealthier than his doctors wanted him to be.

Ferro was on his way to St Margaret's Church in Highcliffe – a coastal town just south of the New Forest – for an important meeting. Since the events described on the stone were to be the topic of discussion, he had to pay a quick visit. The scene of the crime itself.

Ferro took in the surroundings. The Rufus Stone was next to a quiet country road in a pretty clearing dotted with lush trees, including a sprawling mature oak said to be the direct descendant of the original oak tree off which the fatal arrow supposedly ricocheted. Ferro had always struggled with that account. Glancing off a tree would surely dispel the force required to puncture a man in the chest. But the Rufus Stone, along with most accounts of William II's death, called the shooting an accident, and Ferro struggled with that too. To him it had always reeked of murder. As he listened to the brushing of the trees, Ferro imagined Walter Tyrrell firing his arrow deliberately at an unsuspecting king.

After a few minutes of quiet contemplation, Ferro returned to his clapped-out Rover Metro, for him the biggest hardship of quitting his job five months ago. One hundred pounds it cost him to buy and it surely wasn't worth a penny more. If anything, less. It had a hundred and sixty thousand miles on the clock, made all kinds of concerning noises as it trundled along, had dozens of dents and scratches on the bodywork (already an unsightly yellow), the air vents were broken and it still had a tape deck and manual windows. The old rust-bucket was an unutterably poor substitute for the stunning, silver Suzuki Swift he'd had to trade in.

The car was parked nearby in a little car park for tourists visiting the Rufus Stone. It was a hot day and even though he'd only stopped at the stone for five minutes, the fraying car interior felt hot enough to roast something.

The broken air vents meant that Ferro had to open all the doors and wind down all the windows, which were stiff with age, then stand by the car and wait for the hot air to escape. As he wound down the passenger window, the crank broke and it jammed half-open.

Ferro sighed and exclaimed, "For pity's sake." A couple walking near to his car on their way to the stone glanced at him, thinking he was addressing them. "Don't mind me, I drive a car from the Middle Ages," he said, laughing briefly. They smiled awkwardly back.

Ferro lost patience and got in, sliding into a hot seat and scalding his palms on the steering wheel. The car juddered and coughed into life. The digital clock was also broken – naturally – so he tugged the silver pocket watch from his waistcoat and clicked it open, just to check. The last thing he wanted to do was keep Reverend Thomas waiting.

Closing the pocket watch, he stroked his thumb across the inscription on the front. He always did that – habit. *I wonder what the weather will be like,* it said. His mother's last words before she died, when Ferro was thirteen. The watch was hers, and his grandmother's before her. She'd given it to him when he started secondary school, but it had no engraving then. He had engraved it with her words shortly after her death, and had worn it ever since.

Ferro continued on to Highcliffe, humming along to Mike Oldfield's *Tubular Bells*, aka *The Exorcist* theme tune, crackling out of the car's feeble speakers. It was the only cassette he could find to play in the tape deck, but he was surprised by how much he was enjoying it.

His mind wandered to his impending meeting. He was writing a book about William II, or 'the one after William the Conqueror', as he was probably better known. The king more famous for his death than his life. Ferro had been reaching out to local churches, monasteries and libraries for information, and two days ago Reverend Thomas at St Margaret's Church got in touch. Apparently he had happened upon some enlightening new evidence pertaining to William II's death and was about to hand it over to the British Library when he got Ferro's email. Ferro wasn't sure what to expect.

Ten minutes from Highcliffe, Ferro's phone started buzzing against his leg. He had to burrow into his pocket to get it, not easy while driving but he managed. *Beth calling.* He thumbed the answer button and lifted the phone to his ear. "Hi, love."

"You're not driving, are you, Greg?" she said.

"It's fine. There are no police around," he replied.

"It's not about not getting caught. The law's there for the safety of others, and for you."

"Yes, love, but I've been driving a long time. I'm safer than seventy per cent of the people on these roads."

"Not the point."

Alright, enough now. "Did you call for a reason?"

Beth sighed. "I wanted to know if you're coming home for dinner. We're having steak. Would be nice to see you." That last sentence was both barbed and imploring. Ferro hadn't been around much lately. But he'd always had a tendency to get swept up in his work. His passion was something she loved about him, or she used to.

"Probably not, my love," Ferro said carefully. "I'm following up on an email I got from a church in Highcliffe. I'm heading there now."

"Fine. I won't wait up."

"I'm sorry. We'll go out this weekend, just the two of us. I promise."

"With what money, Greg? You've been unemployed for five months now. We're living on a shoestring."

That wasn't fair. "*Self*-employed, Beth. And a shoestring's a bit of an exaggeration."

"Self-employed people are supposed to make money."

"And I will. As soon as I sell this book."

"And until then, you'll sponge off me."

Ferro said nothing – what on earth could he say to that?

Beth took back her comment at once, "I'm sorry. I didn't mean that."

"I suspect you did."

"No. I didn't. That wasn't fair. You've looked after me when I've been between jobs before. I just… I think the thing is, I had it in my head that we'd spend more time together after you left teaching. You even said that yourself. And if anything, I think we're seeing less of each other. You're always in libraries and churches all over the place. At least when you were teaching, you came home every night. To be honest, a couple of times I've wondered if you're having an affair."

"Beth. Seriously."

"I don't really think that. But I do feel like we're drifting apart."

He really should've told her why he left teaching. She would've been more sympathetic, more understanding, but he was embarrassed. Embarrassed to tell his own wife and children. So he'd kept it from them for eight months – and counting.

It was because they looked up to him. He was the man of the house, the one who was supposed to protect everyone. But if they knew he couldn't protect himself…

The truth was that after teaching history in secondary schools and colleges for thirty years with no real issues with any student, he'd had a nasty, violent encounter with a Year Ten boy, Dominic Flynn, who'd repeatedly punched and kicked him in the school corridor after Ferro gave him a 'D' on a mock exam.

Dominic Flynn was an extremely troubled, angry young

man who lost his mother to cancer at a young age – Ferro could sympathise with that – and whose father had spiralled into alcoholism and depression. Ferro understood, and he forgave the boy. But the incident had destroyed his confidence as a teacher. He was on a knife-edge all the time.

He'd managed to avoid any facial injuries, which made it easier to hide the incident from Beth. These days they rarely had sex, so that wasn't an issue. And although Ferro didn't always wear pyjamas in bed, he made sure he did until the bruising was gone. Meanwhile he told her he was bored and restless and wanted to do something different.

Of course, losing his love for teaching didn't mean he'd lost his love for history, hence the decision to start writing history books. And he'd dabbled in writing before. A couple of unpublished, unfinished novels here and there. It had been an on-off hobby for many years. Why not turn it into something more? Life was short and the pressures of teaching, as much as he used to love it and go with it, had put a good ten years on him. It was time to get a few back.

"I love you," said Ferro tenderly, "and I promise we'll go out this weekend and spend some proper time together. Okay?"

"Okay," Beth murmured.

Ferro saw a sign for Highcliffe and turned left at a roundabout.

"I'll see you later," she continued. "Hope you find what you're looking for."

"Thank you, love. See you later."

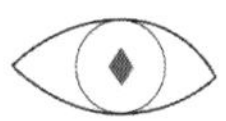

Ferro arrived at St Margaret's Church and parked in the small car park next to the building. He grabbed his phone and messenger bag from the passenger seat and jumped out, welcoming the cooler air and squawk of seagulls that reminded him he was by the coast. The front passenger window was still half-open thanks to the broken crank, but if someone were to break in and steal the car, it wouldn't have been the worst thing. He headed inside the church.

He dunked his fingers in the holy water inside the entrance

door and crossed himself. He'd not been in this church before, so took a moment to appreciate his surroundings. Small and quaint, with parts – he'd read – tracing back to the reign of William the Conqueror, the church had a short nave with half a dozen mahogany pews down each side and a beautiful timber-beamed ceiling arching overhead. Light spilled into the church in a spectrum of warm colours from a large stained glass window behind the altar, which depicted Jesus and the Feeding of the Five Thousand.

There was no one here. Ferro checked his pocket watch – he was on time. He took a seat in a pew near the back of the church to wait. He closed his eyes and prayed.

"Mr Ferro?" a man said gently.

Ferro opened his eyes. A thin man in a black shirt and trousers with a clerical collar stood over him. He looked young, perhaps late twenties, early thirties, but his hair was already receding – poor chap.

"Yes," replied Ferro, standing up to greet him.

"Hi, I'm Reverend Thomas. Welcome. Thank you for coming."

They shook hands.

"Thank *you*. This is a beautiful little church."

The reverend smiled. "Yes, it is. A lot of history too. More history, in fact, than we thought."

"Yes, so I understand."

"Come with me, please."

Ferro followed Reverend Thomas into the vestry, a tiny room with a kitchenette, storage cabinets, a table and two chairs in the centre, and another door, probably leading to a toilet.

"Take a seat," said the reverend. "Cup of tea? Coffee?"

"A peppermint tea, if you have one, please."

Reverend Thomas prepared drinks and placed them on the table. Then he unlocked one of the storage cabinets and removed a clump of old-looking papers, loosely held together with frayed string, with a brown leather bookmark sticking out of the top. He handed them to Ferro.

"We found those papers during renovations of the crypt, hidden in a secret compartment in the wall. A compartment that we suspect nobody has opened since the 12th century."

"What are they?"

"The chronicles of a Benedictine choir monk called Father Jerome. He was writing during the reign of Henry I, William II's successor, from Canterton Priory in the New Forest, a monastery that fell victim, sadly, to Henry VIII. I've been studying them. They provide a fascinating insight into what life was like for monks in that period. But when you get to February 1105, that's when things become rather more disturbing, surreal even. In fact, Father Jerome stopped writing immediately after, which is when he must've hidden the manuscript. I've bookmarked the relevant section. You said you can read Latin?"

"I can, yes."

"Then by all means. I'm keen to hear your thoughts."

Ferro removed the string and went to the section that was bookmarked.

This evening, after Vespers, I was called to the village to administer the Last Rites to Purkis the charcoal-burner. It was an extraordinary and deeply troubling conversation.

Purkis believed that our Lord was punishing him. That was why He saw fit to take away his wife, Cecilia, and his daughter, Eva. That was why Purkis himself now lay on his deathbed.

I asked what Purkis could have done to warrant such punishment and he confessed to being responsible for the death of King William II, brother to the present king. I asked him how. He told me that one afternoon, five years ago, he wished the king dead. That same afternoon, the king was killed.

I asked Purkis if he shot the fatal arrow himself. He

said no, but that he had seen it happen. He had been collecting wood nearby and witnessed a confrontation between His Grace and a man who used a false name, 'Walter Tyrrell'. Strangely, both spoke the common tongue and Purkis was able to understand their conversation.

According to Purkis, this man, Tyrrell, questioned His Grace about a book. The king pretended, at first, to know nothing of this book, but later admitted otherwise and said he had hidden it. Tyrrell demanded to know of the book's location. His Grace refused and Tyrrell released his arrow, piercing the king through the breast and killing him.

Afterwards, Purkis described Tyrrell removing a flat, black, rectangular object from his tunic, placing it to his ear and talking to it, or himself, about having killed the king. What he did next was even stranger. He removed a small pot from his tunic, opened it and took out a tiny red stone, which he proceeded to swallow. A white, silent light burst from where he stood, blinding Purkis momentarily. When his eyes could see again they searched for the man who had killed the king. But he was, by some heinous spell, gone. Purkis said he would have heard footsteps if Tyrrell had walked or run away, but he did not. It is Purkis's belief that Tyrrell used a dark and forbidden magic to make himself disappear.

Purkis is dead. I must now decide what to do with the knowledge he has bequeathed to me. My hope is that the Lord will guide me to a right and just decision.

Ferro felt a rush of adrenaline. This was huge. He knew it in his bones.

He placed the papers on the table. His throat was dry. He drained his cup of tea, the peppermint crisp and cold at the back of his throat.

"So, what do you make of it?" said Reverend Thomas. "It almost sounds like Tyrrell was talking on a phone! Which is impossible, I know."

"Yes." Ferro picked up the papers. "Can I borrow these?"

"What for?"

"I want to get some tests run on them to prove their age."

"Won't the British Library do that?"

"Yes, but I can do it faster. I have a friend who can do it."

"Mr Ferro, these are important historical records. I'm sure you can appreciate that, being a history tutor. I'm uncomfortable handing them over to someone I just met."

"You have my word that I'll return them."

"Yes, but with respect, I don't know what your word is worth."

Ferro sighed. "Alright. What if I made a donation to your church?"

"I'm listening."

"Five hundred pounds, and I'll return the manuscript to you in three weeks – maximum."

"Make it a thousand, and you have yourself a deal."

Ferro chewed on this, leaning back in his chair, sighing heavily. He had to walk out of there with those papers, and Reverend Thomas could tell how much he needed them. But all he kept thinking was, *Beth will eat me for breakfast.*

He stuck out his chin, scratched his beard and extended his hand for a handshake. "Deal."

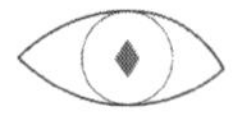

Ferro decided, driving home, that he wasn't going to tell Beth. He'd transferred the money from some savings he had – she'd never know. And now, tucked up safely in his messenger bag on the passenger seat, was a manuscript that could change everything.

Stopping for a late dinner at a service station, he got home at gone eleven. Beth and his two teenagers, Maggie and Ryan, were all asleep, or at least he thought they were. Walking past his daughter's room, floor creaking as he went, he heard Maggie say quietly, "Night, Dad."

He whispered loudly, "Night, sweetheart," and creaked into his bedroom.

Beth stirred as he undressed and climbed into bed. He kissed her cheek with a soft, "Goodnight, my love," and lay down next to her. Not that he was expecting to get much sleep with the implications of Purkis's deathbed confession turning over and over in his head.

"Did you find what you were looking for?" Beth replied sleepily.

"I think I found the first piece," Ferro murmured.

"The first piece of what?"

"Something big."

3

September 12th 2019

It had been a long day at Actuate Solutions, a call centre in Deepwater, Hampshire. Jennifer Larson's bum was numb, her back ached, the ridges of her ears stung from the clumsily designed headset pressing into them, and her stomach burbled with a good six or seven mugs of coffee.

She'd spent the last hour watching the clock, which snailed painfully towards the end of her shift. Still another hour to go. Another hour of sleepwalking through scripted courtesy calls about how much the customers of car dealerships were enjoying their newly purchased vehicles.

A couple of months ago she was partying, having sex, bingeing on old *Doctor Who,* reading, getting high and basically making the most of her last few weeks at university. Now… *this?*

She looked out of the window. A grey day had become an even bleaker night, rain spitting at the glass, strong winds coursing through trees, rattling gutters and bins, and whipping up swirls of dead leaves and litter. What a perfect reflection of her mood.

"Good evening. Could I speak to…?"

Nope, she couldn't. *"Welcome to the Vodafone Voicemail Messaging Service."*

What on earth was she doing here? She had a history degree that was completely and utterly going to waste. Monkeys could do this. But then, she'd never really formed a career plan. She still hadn't. The here and now was her speciality. The future – not so much. She'd gone to uni for the experience, studied her favourite subject from school, and the plan was – make a plan while she was there. But each time she tried, shots of tequila interfered.

And then suddenly it was all over. Over – and no plan. Her friend Martin recommended the job at Actuate Solutions and she took it because it was easy and she was bereft of other ideas.

The calls went quiet, so Jennifer did a bit of job hunting, looking for roles related in some way to her history degree. There had to be something out there better than this.

She could only do job hunting for so long, though. It was boring. After ten minutes of not getting anywhere, like always, she found herself checking her emails instead. A keen reader, she followed a lot of blogs, particularly ones related to history and her other love, sci-fi, so there was always a stack of new posts in her inbox each day.

Yay. There was a new post from her current favourite blogger, Gregory Ferro, a former history teacher – or so he said. He didn't post that often but it was always a treat when he did. She'd found the blog a couple of months ago, saw that he'd posted an article called *William II was murdered by a time traveller.* It was a thrilling read. William Rufus's murky death in the New Forest was the highlight of her Norman England module at uni. Scores of historians were unconvinced by the official verdict – that Sir Walter Tyrrell's arrow was intended for a deer – and Jennifer remembered learning about all the people who had motives for murdering the unpopular king. His younger brother, Henry, the French king, the Church. But she'd never heard anyone suggest that he'd been killed by a time traveller. As a *Doctor Who* nut she was hooked in immediately.

Apparently this time traveller was pretending to be Walter Tyrrell and was looking for an unnamed 'book' that the king had hidden. He then shot the king, talked to someone on what Ferro had interpreted as a mobile phone, and swallowed something that caused him to vanish into thin air. These events, purportedly witnessed by Purkis the charcoal burner who conveyed William's body to Winchester, were detailed in the chronicles of a choir monk and secretly buried in the walls of the crypt at St Margaret's Church in Highcliffe, Dorset, for over nine hundred years. And according to Ferro, the papers were written in authentic medieval Latin and had been carbon-dated, proving that they really did originate from the 12th century.

It was fascinating stuff, if totally bonkers. Ferro had included some rather fuzzy, low-res photos of the alleged chronicles with the article. The bits of Latin Jennifer had been able to make out looked authentic, but in all honesty it was probably just hokum cooked up by Ferro himself for shits and giggles. That was normally how these things went.

She followed the blog anyway, for entertainment value. Subsequent articles chronicled Ferro's search for more evidence of these time travellers, as well as lots of theorising about who they were and what this mysterious book they were chasing could be.

Now there was a new one, much shorter than the previous few, published this morning and titled: *Time traveller who killed William II present during the Black Death?*

This was loads more fun than roboting through courtesy calls and hunting for jobs…

I've been meaning to write about the big discovery I made two weeks ago, but life, as it so often does, overtook me. Now that I have a spare few minutes I can reveal all. After months of having my head buried in books about William II, I came upon on a little-known 14th-century history of England written by historian and priest Simon of Stonebury, which spans the reigns of William the Conqueror through to Edward III.

Studying it, I found a description of a rumour that circulated at the time of the Black Death about a malevolent doctor who, in the autumn of 1348, interrogated plague sufferers in London about a book. Not just a book, in fact, but a 'book with a strange title'. Stonebury writes that the doctor threatened to exacerbate people's conditions if they failed to satisfactorily answer his questions and that, interestingly, all those he questioned shared the same surname – 'Godfrey'. Most significantly of all, Stonebury writes that the doctor was seen sneaking into an alleyway, talking to a strange device at his ear, and disappearing into thin air shortly after. Just like the man who killed William II.

My apologies for the brevity of this blog but I have a lot of reading and cross-referencing to do. This is the first piece of new evidence I have found that William II was killed by a time traveller and my first important lead in ages. A book with a strange title? What could it be?

I will write again soon with more details.

Jennifer thought of something to challenge Ferro's notions of time travellers talking to each other on phones in the 12th and 14th centuries, and decided to leave a comment at the bottom of the article. It looked like hers was going to be the blog's first. None of Ferro's previous articles had attracted any comments, likes or shares, and the *Follow this blog via email* widget said that Jennifer was one of just seven followers.

She wrote: Hey there Ferro! Great blog! There's just one little problem with the idea of time travellers talking to each other on phones in the Middle Ages… I'm pretty sure there were no signal towers back then!

A sharp *beeeep* smacked her in the ears. After a good twenty minutes of no calls, the system had found a customer, and a new script flashed up in front of Ferro's blog.

Jennifer switched on her telephone facade, "Good evening. Please could I speak to Mrs Winters?"

"Who is calling, please?" replied a rather posh female voice.

She continued through her script, "My name is Jennifer. I'm calling on behalf of Macey's Motors. The reason for my call is to see –"

"Do you realise what time it is, young lady?" the woman interrupted.

Not patronising at all.

Jennifer broke script to answer matter-of-factly, "Yes, it's 7.45pm."

"And do you think it's appropriate to cold call someone at this time of day?"

"This isn't a cold call, ma'am. This is –"

"Don't answer back, girl."

Jennifer clenched both hands around her coffee mug and pushed through gritted teeth, "I'm just explaining –"

"What you should be doing is apologising for bringing me to the phone unnecessarily, and taking my number off your records immediately."

"Yes, Mrs Winters, I'll do that."

"Good. And I have some advice for you, young lady. Why don't you get yourself a proper job instead of annoying people with unsolicited phone calls."

"Thank you for the advice. Mind how you go when you next sit down."

"What? Why?"

"Because of the enormous stick up your arse."

Mrs Winters' voice rose like a gathering storm, "I beg your pardon – what did you just say to me?"

"Sorry, I didn't realise you couldn't hear me." She scornfully upped her volume. "There seems to be an enormous stick up your arse, Mrs Winters! Best get it checked asap! Bye!"

Jennifer hung up.

Woah. Her hands were shaking.

She'd heard the gasps of her colleagues the moment she had made the stick comment, caught their shocked expressions in her periphery. Now she felt everyone's eyes on her, and, oh dear, her manager, Melissa Jones, was standing at the end of the communal desk where Jennifer sat. Staring, wide-eyed, lips parted.

A second later, Melissa calmly approached.

"Jennifer, can I speak to you in my office for a moment, please?"

Shit, she'd done it now.

As Jennifer stood up and followed Melissa to her office, she already knew the outcome.

"Jennifer, I cannot have my staff talking to customers like that," Melissa said immediately as they sat down.

"Do you want me to explain what happened?"

"It doesn't matter what happened. In this business, the customer is always right. If they are rude to us, we just have to take it on the chin."

"I don't see why we should have to put up with being spoken to the way that woman spoke to me."

"This is a call centre. That goes with the territory. You've clearly demonstrated that it's not territory you can cope with."

She didn't want to sound too pathetic, but she needed the

money. "Give me one more chance."

"This is the second time this has happened in two months. I'm sorry, Jen. You're fired."

Jennifer sighed. She was in her probationary period – no point fighting the decision. "That's fine. I understand. But to be honest I don't regret what I said. That woman needed bringing down a few pegs."

"You won't get very far with that attitude."

"Maybe not here. But I don't plan to make my career working in a call centre." Shit! As Melissa cocked her pencilled eyebrows, Jennifer realised what she'd said. "Sorry, no offence." Melissa had been a call centre manager for a good ten years.

Melissa stood up. "You don't have to stay until the end of your shift. We'll pay you for today."

"What about my notice period?"

Melissa looked at her coldly. "Gross misconduct gives me the right to summarily dismiss you."

"And you think that was gross misconduct?"

"You told a customer she had a stick up her arse. Yes."

Jennifer felt like arguing further, but it was probably futile. She murmured, "Fine," and left Melissa's office. She gathered her things, trying to hold a dignified smile as she said goodbye to her colleagues. Her friend Martin congratulated her for having the guts to stand up to a customer.

She texted her best friend, Adam Bryant, as she left the call centre. Balls, balls, balls. Just got fired.

Why didn't she bite her tongue? Now she was without a job, and Actuate had paid rather well. Yes, call centre work was tedious, but it was money. She didn't want to live with her mother forever.

Getting pounded by fierce winds and rain as she walked home didn't help matters. She did own a car, but since Actuate was a ten-minute walk from her house, she thought it best not to waste her petrol. She really wished she'd driven today, particularly as her coat wasn't waterproof and cold wetness was seeping through to her skin.

"Fucking weather."

A car hurtled past at sixty miles per hour through a wide, deep puddle in the road, kicking a mini tidal wave all over her. She stopped, screamed "*Fuuuck!*" for about five seconds and walked on.

She turned into The Birches, the cul-de-sac where she lived, named after the silver birch trees that towered over the houses. She passed beneath a short-circuiting streetlight that had turned the surrounds into a feeble, moist disco with no beats. Reaching her house, number thirty-five, she saw that her sister Jamie's car, normally parked next to hers, was gone. She and her boyfriend Tom had recently turned into conjoined twins, so the odds were pretty solid that she was at his place.

As Jennifer walked up the path to her front door, the rain stopped. How typical, since she was already as wet as the sea. Probably best to write today off.

"Hello love," said her mother as she walked in. She was sitting in front of the TV watching *Coronation Street*, but turned her head and saw that Jennifer was drenched and shivering. "Oh, Jennifer, why didn't you take an umbrella?"

Jennifer shrugged. In truth it was because her umbrella was flimsy and cheap and even negligible winds turned it inside out, let alone the bloody great gale that was blowing out there right now. She needed a new umbrella, a new coat, a new job. *A new life.*

Her mother stood up and walked over to her. "Go and get out of those clothes before you freeze to death. I'll make you a nice cup of tea."

Jennifer smiled with that awfully British feeling of warmth when someone offers you a cup of tea. "Thanks, Mum." She started upstairs.

"How come you're home early today then?" her mother called from the kitchen. It was 8.15. Jennifer's shift was supposed to finish at nine.

Jennifer stopped to reply, "Oh, urm... there weren't many calls this evening, so they let us go early." She wasn't in the right frame of mind to face a tirade of criticism about her hot-headedness tonight. Best to postpone the firing story till the morning. She carried on upstairs to her bedroom.

She peeled off her soggy clothes and put on her dressing gown. She looked at her phone. Adam had replied to her message about getting fired. I'm coming over. She wasn't going to argue. She could use the company. She texted back.

Okay, thanks. Don't say anything coz I haven't told Mum.

She went downstairs to get the tea her mum was brewing, at which point she noticed the fresh-looking bunch of flowers sticking out of the kitchen bin.

"Are those from Phil?" Jennifer asked.

"Yup. Special delivery earlier this evening. He just text me to see if I got them."

"Did you text back?"

"Yep. I told him to shove his flowers up his arse."

Jennifer smirked. It was clear where she got her temperament from. Perhaps Mum would've understood her reaction to Mrs Winters? Maybe, but Mum had learned to put up and shut up when money was at stake. She would've expected Jennifer to do the same.

"Are you sure you want to do this?" said Jennifer. "I thought you two had a good thing going. Better than some of the others anyway."

"It was never that great, darling," said Mum as she dropped Jennifer's teabag into the bin. "A few sparks at the beginning, but they died out pretty quickly if I'm honest. And I've had a lot better in the sack, I can tell you."

"Mother! TMI."

"What's TMI?"

Jennifer sniggered. "You need to get down with the kids, Mum. Too Much Information."

"Oooh." She laughed as she handed Jennifer her mug. "Sorry!"

Her mother had not been lucky in love. Although Jennifer had no memory of her father – being two when he had an affair and Mum kicked him out – she certainly remembered the long line of men that followed in his wake. More misses than hits. But Jennifer got on well with several of them, which made her wonder whether Mum was the one with the problem. Much of Jennifer and Jamie's childhood had consisted of toing and froing between different childminders because Mum – a marketing executive – was working flat-out to pay the mortgage and provide for the family. She had no time for a relationship. But things weren't as desperate as they were back then. The mortgage was paid off. Jennifer and Jamie were grown up and fending for themselves (well, except when they were getting fired). Yet Mum remained career-driven. She could've made time for a man if she wanted to, but Jennifer wasn't convinced she did.

Phil had been on the scene for nearly a year – longer than usual. He'd even moved in – another rarity. He was a personal injury lawyer and a good decade older than Mum, and his career meant a lot to him too. A good match, Jennifer had thought. But for some reason in the last few months, their relationship had grown stale. And unfortunately, Phil, one night they were out for dinner, had gone off on Mum for allegedly flirting at the bar with an old friend she'd not seen for years. It was the straw that broke the camel's back and she kicked him out. An overreaction by some people's standards, sure, but she had zero patience for jealous or proprietary men. As far as she was concerned, as long as she wasn't cheating, she could do whatever the hell she wanted with whoever the hell she wanted. Anyone who said otherwise could piss off.

Jennifer was about to go back upstairs with her tea when the doorbell rang.

"Can you get that, love?" said Mum, who'd seated herself back in front of *Coronation Street.*

"Yeah, it's probably Adam."

She opened the door.

"Evening!" said Adam brightly. Bless him, he'd brought a bottle of wine. He murmured quietly, "Thought you might need this."

She smiled as he came in.

"Hi, Kerry," Adam called to her mum.

"Hi, Adam. You okay?"

"Yes, thanks."

Jennifer got them a couple of glasses and she and Adam headed upstairs to her bedroom.

"So what happened?" he said immediately after slumping onto the chaise in the corner.

Jennifer parked her bum on her swivel chair at her desk. "Oh, this woman just really riled me. She thought I was cold-calling her, which I wasn't, and was super-pissed off that I'd called her at the unholy time of 7.45. So, er, I might've given her a piece of my mind."

"What did you say?"

"Told her she had an enormous stick up her arse."

Adam laughed. “Yep, that’ll get you fired. So what you gonna do now?”

“Not work in a call centre.”

“I think that’d be wise.”

She smiled. She already felt better. Funny how Adam always managed to do that without really doing anything. He never failed to make her laugh, even when laughing was the last thing she felt like doing. He was, in all honesty, the most dependable friend she’d ever had.

Not that it had always been like that. In fact, in secondary school where they met, they hated each other. Jennifer thought Adam was goofy and a weirdo and Adam thought Jennifer was a bitch. She had a “right nasty streak” back then, Adam had told her. (She did have an attitude but liked to stress that Adam was a bit of an oversensitive soul in those days too.)

But then they ended up at the same sixth form college, minus all their friends, who’d either left school and started apprenticeships or gone to the tacked-on sixth form at their secondary school. Not knowing anyone meant they hung around together occasionally, got talking, realised they had stuff in common. Neither of them – unbeknown to the other at the time – had had a blast at school. With his floppy hair, short stature and unconventional good looks, Adam was an easy target for bullies. And while Jennifer wasn’t bullied as such, the girls she’d surrounded herself with never understood why she liked *Star Trek* and *Doctor Who* and offbeat indie bands instead of Beyoncé, boys and makeup. And her distance from them grew when she came out. All of them were straight and literally obsessed with guys, and a couple of them acted weird around her, like she might hit on them at any time (not untypical adolescent behaviour).

So to be honest, Jennifer didn’t really get them either. The fizzling out of those friendships-that-weren’t-really-friendships was best for all. And now the guy she’d so casually dismissed had turned into one of her favourite people.

Talk about misjudgement.

“So what’s the latest with Phil?” Adam also knew when to change the subject.

“They’re definitely over. Was just talking to her about it

before you arrived."

"That's a shame. I quite liked him."

Jennifer sipped her tea. It was super-hot and burned her mouth slightly. Her mum never put enough milk in. "Me too."

"What happened exactly?"

"I don't think she was ever that into him, to be honest."

"Even though he moved in?"

Jennifer nodded. "Yep, they got more distant after he moved in. Think she regretted it. She likes her own space. He did make a bit of a tit of himself, though. That was the trigger."

"What did he do?"

Jennifer told Adam about the flirting incident.

"Ah, yes, I can see your mum not taking that too well," said Adam.

"She certainly didn't. I don't think I would've thrown him out over it, though."

"That's true. If a girl had done that to you you'd probably have punched her in the eye."

She laughed. "Shut your face."

Her phone buzzed. She checked it. An email telling her that her comment on Gregory Ferro's blog about there being no signal towers in the Middle Ages had been responded to. She'd almost forgotten about all that.

The email linked through to the blog, and the new comment.

It was Ferro himself. If these people can travel in time, which most scientists believe impossible, I'm sure they can manage phoning each other without needing signal towers.

Actually, a very good point.

She said so. Good point!

"Who is it?" said Adam.

"Just this guy whose blog I was reading at work. He thinks time travellers are messing with our history."

"Sounds right up your street!"

Ferro replied. Who is this?

Jennifer. I'm a history graduate. Love this kind of thing.

"Shall I leave you and Mr Time Travel alone?" said Adam, both of his bushy eyebrows raised.

"No, hang on. He just asked me who I am, probably because I'm the only one who's posted on his blog so far."

"Well, don't tell him. He could be a psycho-killer-rapist."

She laughed. "I've just told him my first name and that I'm a history graduate. I'm being polite."

"Okay." Then, "Are you drinking that tea? Because I'm going to pour some wine."

"Go ahead."

She read Ferro's reply to her comment. There's so much more going on here. I just discovered something else today that will blow your mind. It's certainly blown mine. I live in Norton Hill, Hampshire, in case you're near there. If you're interested, I'd be happy to show you my work.

For goodness sake, this guy lived round the corner! Norton Hill was like a twenty-minute drive from Deepwater, if that. What were the odds?

Weirdly enough, I'm not far from you. But as fascinated as I am by all this, I'm not really one for meeting up with randoms I talk to online.

Ferro replied. I'm a fifty-four-year-old writer and father of two who used to be a teacher. I promise you I have no plans to chop you up and bury you in my walls. The offer's there. I would only be willing to meet you in a public place anyway because, for all I know, YOU might have plans to chop me up and bury me in YOUR walls.

Jennifer laughed. It was tempting. It really was. She wanted to know if these manuscripts were genuine, because if they were, this was huge. Well, potentially huge.

At the same time, what if he was, as Adam put it, a psycho-killer-rapist and this was just his way of grooming her?

At twenty-two, she was a big girl. She could handle herself. And if they met in a pub or something with people around, he wouldn't try anything. And if he was as nutty as a fruitcake, he'd probably make good entertainment for an hour or so.

Fuck it, why not?

LOL. Okay, well there's a pub in Deepwater I like called The Kipper and the Corpse. We could meet there if you want.

I don't know it but I'll look it up. When would you like to meet? Tomorrow at midday?

Her schedule was pretty clear now that she was

unemployed. Yep, that works for me. See you then. And just to warn you, if you try anything funny I'll kick your arse.

I promise I won't.

Adam handed her a glass of red. She decided to skip the tea.

"Cheers to no more shit call centres," said Adam. They chinked glasses. "Onwards and upwards."

"Thanks, mate," she said, and took a sizeable sip.

She debated whether to tell him about the meeting she'd just arranged with Gregory Ferro.

Nah. She'd tell him about it afterwards. He'd only worry.

4

November 3rd 1348

While her husband worked and her children played, Catherine Hawthorn made her way to Holy Trinity Church in the City of London with a trowel. Stopping in a small wooded area some thirty feet behind the church cemetery, she looked around and checked for witnesses. All clear. She lowered herself to her knees, drove her trowel into the ground and dug.

It took fifteen minutes of heaving thick mud out of the ground – still sodden from last night's rain – to reach it. Out of the hole she lifted a tired-looking oak box with rusty iron bands. She used her gloved fingertips to brush off the mud and confirmed once more that she was alone with a glance in all directions. She then retrieved a tiny drawstring pouch from her satchel, tugged it open and tipped a key into her palm. She unlocked the box and lifted the lid and there it was. The impossible book – *The History of Computer-Aided Timetabling for Railway Systems*. Next she took a letter, fastened with a wax seal, from her satchel and placed it on top of the book. She closed the box, locked it, replaced the key in the pouch, placed the pouch and the box in her satchel and used her trowel to slovenly refill the hole she'd just dug, before hurrying away from the church.

She returned to the streets and hitched a ride in the back of a cart belonging to Mr Hughes, a wealthy merchant going to Westminster to deliver goods to the king. As she went, her heartbeat got faster and harder till she could feel it at the base of her throat and wanted to gag. She tried to swallow it back down but it didn't budge.

Be calm, Catherine. This is *the right course.*

Thirty minutes later, the clatter of rickety wheels and horse hooves eased to a peaceful silence. They had arrived at the palace, the home of King Edward III and his court. The king's secretary, Sir Mortimer Tully, stood waiting for Catherine at the gates. Mr Hughes had arranged the meet on her behalf as a favour to her husband, Peter, a cordwainer who had provided Mr Hughes with fifteen years' worth of fine leather boots.

Catherine climbed down from the cart and approached Sir Mortimer. Mr Hughes drove the cart to a different entrance of the palace to offload his goods and collect payment.

The frowning secretary stood still and straight as a post. Catherine took a succession of deep breaths in an effort to quieten her heart and hoped the sweat collecting beneath her wimple did not send any stray beads down her face.

"I do not have long, madam," said Sir Mortimer.

"Then I shall not keep you," said Catherine, lifting the box and the pouch from her satchel and handing them to him. "Please get these to the king immediately. There is a letter inside the box that explains its contents. The key to open it is inside the pouch. I must be so bold as to humbly request that you do not open it yourself, nor let anyone see you with it. The contents of the box are for the king's eyes alone."

"You *are* bold," said Sir Mortimer. "And why should any of this be of interest to His Grace?"

"I can only ask that you trust me when I say that it will be of *great* interest to him."

Sir Mortimer raised a disapproving eyebrow. "It is lucky you are a friend of Mr Hughes."

Catherine bowed her head. *Yes. Very lucky indeed.*

Sir Mortimer shrouded the box and the pouch in his cloak and strutted inside the palace. Catherine sat down on the steps before the gates and waited for Mr Hughes to return with his empty cart to escort her home.

December 1st 1348

The Great Pestilence had come to Cordwainer Lane in the City of London. The workshops had closed and the street sellers were gone. Residents were either stuck up in their homes caring for loved ones or begging God's forgiveness at the church. If there were people on the street, they were most likely to be plague doctors or body collectors. A fog of death and depression hung over what used to be a place of thriving commerce, a fog that seemed destined never to lift.

In one of the houses on the lane, a visiting plague doctor was about to confirm Catherine Hawthorn's worst, though expected, fears.

"I'm sorry, madam. You have the Pestilence."

He would have removed his wide-brimmed black hat as a mark of sympathy, but it was a shield from infection. So was his mask, which had glass eyepieces and a large, arched, stork-like beak, filled with herbs and spices to fend off the evil smells of the Pestilence. Gloves, boots and an ankle-length overcoat completed the ominous costume, designed to leave not an inch of his body exposed to the air.

Catherine's eight-year-old daughter, Beatrice, sitting on the edge of the bed where her mother lay festering in sickness, crumbled in tears.

"Beatrice, it's all right. Be strong," said Catherine softly, knowing full well that there weren't any words capable of consoling her. First the Pestilence had taken her little brother, Nicholas, then her father. Now it was about to take her mother.

"Drink the herbal mixtures I have recommended," the doctor instructed.

"I will. Is there anything else I can do?"

"Yes, madam. You can pray. I will come by again tomorrow."

Praying didn't work when her son and her husband was lying here. The Lord God saw fit to take them anyway.

After the plague doctor left, Beatrice and Catherine prayed together. It was more for Beatrice's benefit than Catherine's. Catherine knew that these were her last days and she knew why. Hers was the first house on Cordwainer Lane to be afflicted with the Pestilence and it was because she had delivered *The History of Computer-Aided Timetabling for Railway Systems* to King Edward. God was punishing her for relinquishing her responsibility.

But why couldn't He understand the logic of what she'd done? The impossible book that predicted an ominous threat to the realm, given to her ancestor Thomas Godfrey in the summer of 1100 by William II's chief minister Ranulf Flambard, would not stay hidden, buried near Holy Trinity Church. Not when mass graves were being dug everywhere for victims of the Pestilence. The Godfreys had guarded the book for two and a half centuries; the people they were protecting it from were probably long gone. It was high time to discharge the burden the Godfreys had carried for generations and for the king to take responsibility for the book once more.

Catherine's pain worsened as the bright sunlight pouring through the window began to grow dim. It wasn't night, just gloom. Maybe it was just the sickness stepping up its attack on her body, or maybe the sunlight really did take the edge off the pain. She remembered the agony endured by her husband seemed worse when dismal weather set in.

She must've dozed off. She was a fifteen-year-old newlywed again, making love to Peter in their favourite spot by the River of Wells when no one was around – but then a loud knock at the door wrenched her from the dream. A moment ago her body was youthful and nimble; now it was weak and withered again, heaving with buboes the size of eggs, lodged in her thighs, beneath her arms and on her neck, and filling up with black infected blood, making walking, talking and breathing a painful and exhausting experience.

O Lord, am I really so deserving of such cruelty?

Beatrice was still sitting on the bed praying. The rings around her eyes suggested she was fighting her own fatigue to keep watch over Catherine. At the sound of the knock, she rose from the bed and bolted downstairs to answer the door.

A few minutes later, Catherine heard two sets of footsteps coming up the stairs. She recognised her daughter's – dainty and quick – but the other set were loud and stomping.

Beatrice entered, followed by the looming shape of a plague doctor. Could've been the one who visited earlier. She couldn't tell. They all wore similar costumes.

"Doctor's here to see you, Mother," said Beatrice.

"Are you the same doctor who came by earlier?" Catherine murmured weakly, straining to sit up.

"No, Mother," Beatrice answered for him. "He's come to offer a second opinion. He says there is hope!" There was jubilation in Beatrice's high voice, but Catherine was dubious.

"I see," Catherine said. Something warm trickled over her shoulder and down her arm – the bubo on her neck was bleeding again, from where the previous doctor had cut it open. She used a damp cloth to dab the wound.

"I'll leave you to examine her, Doctor," said Beatrice, turning and leaving, shutting the door behind her.

For a moment the plague doctor just looked at Catherine with his vacant, inert, stork-like face, every inch of his real expression hidden. A chill knifed her in the small of the back.

"So what is this hope you are teasing my daughter with?" she asked.

"I'm not teasing her with it." His voice – partly muffled by his mask – was thick and rough, lacking in warmth, but she felt a twinge of relief nonetheless. *So you are alive under there.*

"Then tell me," she insisted.

"Are you Catherine Godfrey?"

"I – er – Godfrey was my maiden name. My husband is – *was* – Peter Hawthorn. Please, sir. What is this hope you bring?"

"A cure."

"I'm sure. I have heard of plague doctors who offer erroneous alternative cures for fees over and above what the city is already paying them. If you presume to con me, sir, know now that it will not succeed. My mind remains sharp despite the failure of my body."

"This cure is not erroneous," said the doctor.

"Oh, is it not? Then you are a worker of miracles?"

Catherine coughed, then silently scolded herself for being so bold. He might just have been trying to help. She sighed, "I apologise, doctor. I fear this plague is eating away at my manners."

The doctor was silent for a moment and Catherine wished she could see his expression through that ghastly mask. Then he continued, "This cure is real. I can free your body of the Pestilence and I'm not demanding extra fees."

Catherine raised an eyebrow. "I sense a 'but' approaching."

"There's one condition."

"What?"

"Tell me where the book is."

She felt a tightening in her chest. "I'm sorry, what book?"

The doctor produced a sheet of parchment from inside his overcoat. "This," he said, holding it up.

When she saw it, it was like a spear had been driven through her belly.

On the parchment was a picture, more detailed than any painting she'd ever seen. It showed the cover of the impossible book that told the future. The book with the unmistakable title: *The History of Computer-Aided Timetabling for Railway Systems* by *Jeremy Jennings.*

"I know of no such book," Catherine lied.

"Did you hear what I said? Give me want I want and I can free you and your daughter of this disease."

"My daughter?"

"Your daughter has it. Her symptoms aren't showing yet, but they will. If you help me, I can save her."

He was probably telling the truth. These were powerful people. The power to detect and to cure the plague was no doubt one of many unfathomable capabilities.

But what would Catherine be if she helped them? A traitor. That's what she'd be. A traitor to her king and her country. Beatrice wouldn't have wanted that.

"Please, sir, look around you." Catherine gestured weakly with her left hand, indicating the small, simple room they were in. There was the bed Catherine lay on and shared with Beatrice (and previously Peter and Nicholas as well), which was a large, lumpy bag of hay over a lattice of rope straps housed in a basic wooden frame. The only other items were a small round table with a jug of water, a cup and a candle on it; a large chest of clothes by the wall beneath the window; and a chamber pot in the corner. "I am the widow of a cordwainer. A simple tradesman who could make ends meet but little more. Do you really think we would possess as rare and expensive a commodity as books?"

The doctor lunged, gripped both of her arms in his gloved hands and pinned her to the bed. She flinched, banging her head against the wall behind her linen pillow. He stooped close to her face, and she could smell the perfumes coming from inside his beak. He rasped in her ear, "Catherine, I'm losing patience."

"Please, sir," Catherine choked. "I'm telling you the truth.

You've got the wrong Godfrey."

The doctor stared at her, motionless. Did he believe her?

Moments later, he released her arms and straightened. She felt a warm, steady flow on her shoulder and down her arm again. The bubo on her neck.

The doctor reached beneath his overcoat, this time pulling out a tubular device that was transparent, possibly glass, with a dark liquid roiling inside and a tall, glinting needle jutting out of the top.

"What is that?" Catherine asked. "Is that the cure?"

"No. It's an enhanced form of your disease. You have about a day to live but if I inject you with this, you'll have minutes. And they'll be horrible. The worst pain you can imagine."

Please God, don't let this happen.

She refused to give in. "Please. I promise you. I know nothing about this book you speak of."

The doctor lifted the device, his thumb against the rounded top of a rod that extended from the other end of the tube. She reasoned that it was a kind of hand-operated pump, the rod a piston for pushing the liquid up the tube.

"Last chance. Tell me where it is."

"I'll scream. I'll scream so loud that all of London will hear."

"Do that and I'll go downstairs and stick this needle in your daughter. Actually, maybe I'll just go and do that now."

The doctor turned to leave. Catherine felt a stab of panic. "No! No, I'll tell you."

The doctor stopped at the door, turning slowly to face her.

"Please don't hurt her." Her breathing became heavy, the bubo on her neck throbbing and bleeding, reducing her voice to a whimper. "I'll tell you where it is."

"So you had it all along. You lied."

"Y-yes." She coughed.

"Well? Where is it?"

She took a breath. "I-I g-gave it t..." Her voice trailed into a feeble mumble.

"What?"

"I... I g-gave it t-to..."

The doctor sprang towards the bed, yelling, "You gave it to *who?*"

Channelled by desperation, which took the form of a sharp and almost otherworldly bolt of strength, Catherine shot up, thrust her arm towards the doctor and snatched the tubular device from his grip. She went to stab him with it, but he jerked out of the way and she missed. So she plunged the needle into her own arm. As he lunged to retrieve it, her thumb was on the piston, thrusting it up the tube, pumping the dark liquid into her blood. By the time he grabbed it back, she'd emptied it.

"Stupid bitch!"

"Beatrice, get out of the house!"

"M-mother?" she heard Beatrice call from the bottom of the stairs. "W-what's hap –"

"He'll kill you! Run! Get out of th –"

The words stuck in her throat as the doctor's gloved hands closed around her neck in a painful grip. The bubo on her neck burst, warm blood and pus wetting the bed beneath her. As her arms shot up to try to grapple with him, she saw that both were turning purple, her fingers blackening. She felt a warm flow trickling across her face from her nose, and then another from the corner of her mouth.

"You're dying," the doctor whispered, tightening his grip on her throat. "I can stop it. If I inject you with the cure you'll recover."

Not even tiny wisps of breath could get past the doctor's grip. She tried to dig her blackening fingers beneath his, but as she bent them, acute pains ripped through them, rippling up her arms as if someone was peeling off her skin. The rising agony took over, whittling away at her strength. She couldn't fight him. Vision blurring, heart pounding in her ears, she let her throbbing limbs fall to the bed.

"Just tell me where it is."

She opened her mouth to speak, the doctor's grip loosened, and she channelled everything she had left to her voice, spitting, "Burn in Hell."

The doctor's bird-like face fell inside a blanching haze, growing ever more indistinct. She saw him jerk, and then a quick, hard blow to her left cheek flung her head to the side.

She couldn't help but smile as her eyes met the rapidly disappearing window. Her limbs were paralysed and all the pain had turned to numbness. She welcomed the release. She hoped to God that Beatrice had heeded her words, but as she'd not called for her again, or come up the stairs, Catherine satisfied herself that she had.

Then, as the window rolled into the thickening mantle of white, shimmering flecks of golden light were all around her.

Heaven?

Please God, let me have that.

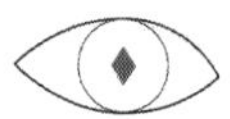

When Robert Skinner went back downstairs to the room that served as a living space, a kitchen and a shoemaker's workshop, Catherine Godfrey's daughter was gone. He made a quick exit, sloshing through the mud puddle at the front of the house and hastening up the plague-ridden street, passing a couple of body collectors who were replenishing their cart with the occupants of the house next door. The fumes from the open sewer ditches running along both sides of Cordwainer Lane gave way to a stench of dead, diseased flesh so strong that it penetrated Skinner's clove and cinnamon-filled beak.

He sneaked into a narrow alleyway leading to some cart sheds, then stopped for a moment to catch his breath.

How would he find that fucking book now?

He walked past the cart sheds, through another alley, coming out onto a different street, home to a rather sedate marketplace that had obviously been sapped by plague and was not as bustling as it should've been. Squawks of "Sheep's feet, hot sheep's feet," and "Three pies for a halfpenny," came from a young lad behind him, carrying a tray laden with bowls of misshapen pies and unappetising-looking hooves. Skinner saw a fishmonger with hay-filled crates of glistening mackerel and cod and a couple of barrels of live crabs, farmers selling chickens and sacks of wheat, and a couple of men selling furs, cloth, horseshoes, candlesticks, faggots and tableware made from pewter.

Skinner weaved through, catching a few stares from the peasants, valets and tradesmen who were shopping here. He passed another plague doctor buying a pound of fresh ginger from a spice-seller, perhaps to top up the perfumes in his beak.

He rounded a corner onto the next street, walking in no particular direction. He just needed to think. He needed a game plan.

He'd have to go back for the daughter. After weeks of interrogating Godfrey families across London he'd finally found the right one. Now that Catherine was dead, the daughter was his best – his only – lead. Would Catherine have shared knowledge of the book with her daughter? Who the fuck knew. But he was going to find out.

Struck by dizziness, he stumbled against the wall of a closed-down baker's, a pain shooting from his abdomen to his throat and triggering a cough. Steadying himself, he straightened and inhaled deeply, filling his lungs with cloves and cinnamon. The dizziness abated.

Was it the jumps? He knew that time travel could have side effects, but they were rare and only affected a small percentage of travellers. Skinner never thought he'd be one of them, but figured that even if he was, he was a big guy and could handle it. Now he wasn't so sure. Something was wrong. Something *felt* wrong – inside. How the hell was he going to be able to pull this off if he was getting sick?

There was an easy answer to that. *Because I have to.* Skinner's own life had been rewritten, and that was on him. Karen, his darling wife. Carly and Shannon, his two beautiful little daughters. It was his fault they were never born. He had to put it right. And he wasn't about to let a few stomach cramps get in the way.

His ringtone pealed from his pocket. *Shit!* He thought he'd put his phone on silent. He did a fast turn into another alleyway. He pulled his phone from his pocket and removed his mask.

He felt a bite of nervousness in his throat. He decided he wouldn't tell her. He'd just say he was still looking. Then he'd have to think of something. He composed himself, cleared his throat with a forced cough, and answered confidently, "Yes, ma'am?"

"Report, Mr Skinner."

"Nothing yet, ma'am, but I will find it. I just need a bit more –"

"Please don't say *time*."

Skinner swallowed the word. A foolish thing to say, given

the circumstances. He reiterated, "I promise, I *will* find it."

"No, you won't. Not there, anyway. You're done with 1348."

Oh no. She wanted him to jump again. *Great.* "What do you mean?"

"I have a new lead."

5

September 12th 2019

Ferro had heard of a museum in the market town of Portphilly in Snowdonia, North Wales, that was home to a collection of archaeological finds and historical texts thought to be apocryphal. Wall-to-wall with fake artefacts, unreliable manuscripts, and books about UFOs and conspiracy theories, it was said to be the place where bad research and discredited ideas went to die. Historians whose assertions had been proved inaccurate, fraudulent or based on dubious sources often found their work on the shelves of Portphilly Museum. Not surprisingly its nickname was the 'Museum of Bad History'.

A lot of people thought the Bible belonged there. Ferro could see why, but he just didn't – *couldn't* – agree. Even though he was a history teacher accustomed to testing the historicity of everything he read and encouraging his students to do the same, he believed the Bible – despite being of anonymous and non-contemporaneous authorship – an exception to the rule. He always had, and it had brought him comfort on a lot of very dark days. Still, he recognised the contradiction.

Opening in 1922, Portphilly Museum was held in much higher regard in its early days, but as time wore on, its contents became increasingly controversial. Although the museum continued to present itself outwardly as credible and legitimate, it was said that the curators were aware of the nickname and quietly perpetuated its low-brow reputation. After all, the museum attracted scores of ufologists, conspiracy theorists and fringe researchers, many of whom were willing to donate large sums of money to keep the place going.

Ferro was starting to wonder why he was here. He thought himself sensible, level-headed. He wasn't someone who believed in wacky conspiracy theories like the Royal Family being alien lizards in disguise or the Earth being flat or Paul McCartney having died in the 60s and been replaced by a lookalike. Yet he was surrounded by books that propagated these ideas.

Having said that, that was the point. He'd come here hoping to find more evidence to support Purkis's deathbed confession, which suggested that William II had been murdered by a time traveller. Most people would think that a pretty wacky theory, one that flies in the face of modern science. Having visited a whole bunch of libraries and museums up and down the country, he wondered if Portphilly Museum – home of cold-shouldered history – could hold some ignored and overlooked clues.

He spent his first day studying the three books the museum had on the Normans but turned up nothing about Walter Tyrrell or the 'book'. He used his dwindling savings to book a night at the cheapest bed-and-breakfast he could find and, in the morning, used the free WiFi to publish an article on his blog about the Simon of Stonebury text he came upon in the Parker Library at Corpus Christi College, Cambridge, two weeks ago. He opened by saying that 'life' had prevented him from writing about his findings earlier, which was true. The collapse of his marriage and breaking up of his family was making it difficult to concentrate on much of anything. After barely leaving the house for two weeks, he'd decided that the best source of distraction would be to resume his search for the truth about William II's killer, so he'd forced himself to get in the car and drive to Wales.

After posting his article and refuelling with a generously portioned full English breakfast – was it called a full Welsh over here? – Ferro checked out of the B&B and returned to Portphilly Museum. On arrival he asked the curator if she knew of any books they had relating to the Black Death, to see if he could find anything to corroborate the Simon of Stonebury-cited rumour about the plague physician who interrogated people about a 'book with a strange title', and was seen using a phone-like device before disappearing.

The curator directed him to a 1977 book by Edith Starkey, *Secrets of the Great Pestilence*. The only one they had on the Black Death, she told him. He sat down in a quiet corner to read it, with a rather tepid peppermint tea he'd purchased from the museum's tiny cafe.

'Great Pestilence' was one of several medieval names for the scarier-sounding Black Death, one of the most devastating pandemics in history. Across Europe, fifty million people – sixty per cent of the population – were killed. In some places, whole communities were wiped out. It changed the course of European history completely.

Most of Edith Starkey's book, though written with enthusiasm, talked about things Ferro knew, things that were already well-documented.

But then, and honestly it was like winning the lottery, he came to a section titled, *Legend of the Evil Plague Doctor.* It mentioned how Ralph of Wallingsworth, writing in 1358 about the arrival of the Black Death in London ten years earlier, recorded the story of an evil plague physician. Similar to what Simon of Stonebury wrote, it was said that a mysterious, malevolent man dressed as a plague doctor was visiting homes and questioning people on their deathbeds, threatening to make their sickness worse if they refused to cooperate. He was only interested in talking to families with the surname 'Godfrey' and was seeking the location of a 'book with a strange title'.

There it was again – the book with the strange title. What in the world could it be? Would Ferro ever find out?

Unlike Stonebury's account, there was no mention of the doctor being seen on a phone-like device and disappearing into thin air in an alleyway. But Starkey went on to say…

> Whether there is any truth to the story of the evil plague doctor and the 'book with a strange title' is unclear, but some historians have linked it to another legend from that time, that of the 'Godfrey letter'. According to the legend, the Godfrey letter was written to Edward III by a woman called Catherine Godfrey and enclosed with a book. Of particular note is that Catherine wrote the majority of the letter in Middle English, except for the title of the book, which she wrote in Modern English. She gave it as 'The History of Computer-Aided Timetabling for Railway Systems by Jeremy Jennings'.

What?

Ferro stopped, went back and read that paragraph again. And again.

He blinked hard and carried on.

Some believe that 'The History of Computer-Aided Timetabling for Railway Systems' was the very same book that Ralph of Wallingsworth was referring to, the 'book with a strange title'.

Strange title? Try impossible title!

In her letter Catherine explained that the Godfrey family had been looking after the book at the request of King William II since 1100. According to her, the book warned of a terrible oncoming threat to the realm and yielded an otherworldly power that nobody could understand. She said it was no longer safe in her possession, hence why she had decided to discharge her family's burden and pass it back to the king.

Ferro shut the book, keeping the tip of his index finger in that section so he could return to it, and looked at the back for any hint that author Edith Starkey might be having a laugh. The blurb was like a million others he'd read on the backs of history books.

But this was unbelievable. Totally unbelievable.

He returned to where he was in the book and continued reading.

Unfortunately, the Godfrey letter, reportedly once held at the Tower of London, has never been traced or verified. Today, most historians believe it to be a myth.

Ferro got out his phone and used the museum's WiFi to google *The History of Computer-Aided Timetabling for Railway Systems* by Jeremy Jennings.

The plot thickened.

There it was. Boring-looking book, long out of print, just a couple of copies available on Ebay. Hardback, basic green cloth binding, with gold foil lettering on the front and spine in Times New Roman – the world's dullest font – but no other distinguishing features.

But the publication date was 1995. Ferro double-checked the publication date of *Secrets of the Great Pestilence.* As he thought. 1977. Which meant *The History of Computer-Aided Timetabling for Railway Systems* was published eighteen years after it was cited in Edith Starkey's book.

Astonishing. Just astonishing.

Evidence of real time travel.

A book from the future, stuck in the past, chased by time travellers.

Had he stumbled into a science fiction movie?

Needless to say, Ferro bought a copy of *The History of Computer-Aided Timetabling for Railway Systems* immediately. He then went and asked the curator if he could take Edith Starkey's book away with him. She said no – he could make copies of the relevant pages only. That would have to do. He could always buy a copy of her book online too if necessary, if copies were available.

The curator led him to the room with the photocopier. Just as he was about to start copying, his phone rang.

It was Beth's solicitor, violently yanking him back to reality. "Mr Ferro, have you received my letter about the divorce?"

The word 'divorce' made him wince. Like a knife in the heart. He still couldn't believe it had come to this.

"Not yet, no," Ferro lied. He received it yesterday. A parting gift just before he headed off to Wales. He wasn't sure why he lied. Pretending he hadn't received it was only delaying the inevitable.

"Can you let me know tomorrow if you haven't, please?" the solicitor asked.

Oh, get off my back. "Yes, alright."

"Thank you." She reeled off a list of procedural points and Ferro was struck by the indifference in her tone. Not a single thought for how hard this was for him.

"Yes, yes, I know all that," he said, interrupting her.

"I'm just making sure."

"Please can you get Beth to call me?"

"Mr Ferro, my client does not wish to speak to you."

He winced again. 'My client' made it sound like they'd

done a bit of business together and were in dispute over it, not that they'd been married twenty-three years.

"Can you just ask her for me?" said Ferro. "Please?"

"I'll mention it next time I speak to her."

"Thank you."

"And I must advise you, again, to retain your own solicitor."

He'd heard that before as well. He didn't have the money. "Yes, fine, thank you." He just wanted her to go now.

"I look forward to hearing from you when you've received my letter. Goodbye."

She was like a robot. He echoed, just as coldly, "Goodbye."

He hung up and copied the pages he needed from Edith Starkey's book. Then he left the museum and began his long journey home to an empty house.

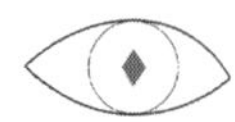

After a tedious five-hour drive, Ferro was back home in Norton Hill, sitting in a chair in his lounge with a glass of Merlot, looking at a framed photo of him, Beth and the kids and fingering the inscription on his pocket watch. A tear splashed the glass in the frame, blurring Maggie's face. His chest ached.

It was all his fault, he knew that. He'd been ignoring Beth for months, ignoring the kids. Never at home, always at this library, that museum. His love for them all never changed, never faltered, but his research had become an obsession he couldn't shake. Didn't *want* to shake. He had to know what was going on. He'd pleaded with Beth to be patient, told her the things he'd found, but she wasn't interested.

He remembered their last exchange two weeks ago, every word of it burned into his memory, like a video on continuous playback.

Beth's ultimatum.

"We've had enough," she had said, catching him off guard as he walked in the front door with some shopping, finding her, Maggie and Ryan in the hallway with suitcases.

"What are you doing?" he asked.

"Giving you a choice, Greg," Beth said. "You can choose

this preposterous mission you're on. Or you can choose us. Your family."

At that point he'd just discovered the Simon of Stonebury text – new evidence that time travellers were tinkering with history. He couldn't stop there. He just couldn't.

"Beth, I'm getting closer to the truth every day," he'd said. "These time travellers –"

"I don't want to hear another word about time travellers, Greg. It's nonsense. I feel like I'm married to David Icke."

"I'm not crazy. I promise. This is real."

"Whatever, Greg."

Ferro looked at Maggie and Ryan. Maggie was crying. Ryan looked like he was trying to hold back tears. "Is this how you two feel as well?"

Ryan answered, it felt like, for both of them, "There's no point us being here at the moment. You're never around. You never do anything with us. I asked for your help back in June with some of my exams and you kept promising you would, but that's when you'd just found out about William II and the, erm, time traveller" – there was derision in the way Ryan said it – "and you were always too busy. So Dad, do what you've got to do. We still love you. But it's clear you don't want us around right now."

Ryan was so grown-up. Seventeen going on thirty. And hearing him say that was a real punch in the stomach. Of course Ferro wanted them around. They were his family.

But he was trying to have his cake and eat it. He knew that. Expecting them to be there for him when he wasn't there for them.

"I do want you around," Ferro insisted. "I love you. All of you." He wiped Maggie's tears with his thumb, then looked at Beth. The look on her face was cold, hard, like she'd already let go.

If only she could understand how important this was. To them. To everybody.

"Beth, please don't do this," he said. "Please don't make me choose."

"You already have, Greg."

And that was that. Beth and the kids moved out and went to live with her mum. A few days later, Beth instructed that delightful divorce lawyer.

Sniffing, wiping his tears with his palms, Ferro replaced the photograph on the side table by his chair. He'd not checked his emails since Portphilly so he dug out his phone.

In amongst some uninteresting marketing emails was one telling him he'd had a comment on his blog, on the article he wrote this morning at the B&B.

A small twinge of excitement eased his heartache. He'd been publishing the odd article about his findings and theories since his trip to the New Forest in May, just in case anyone else in the world knew anything. Unfortunately his blog didn't get much traffic and only had seven followers. Now, at last, he'd had his first comment.

The twinge of excitement diminished somewhat when he saw the username of the commenter: 'WibblyWobblyTimeyWimey'. Not expecting a particularly intellectual discussion, he clicked through to the comment.

Hey there Ferro! Great blog! There's just one little problem with the idea of time travellers talking to each other on phones in the Middle Ages… I'm pretty sure there were no signal towers back then!

Ah, okay. He was wrong. WibblyWobblyTimeyWimey had raised a sensible point that others might be wondering about too. While he didn't profess to have the answer, he typed back a quick and obvious counter-argument about time travellers being able to phone each other without needing signal towers because they're… time travellers.

Ferro was about to put his phone away, but WibblyWobblyTimeyWimey commented again immediately. Good point!

Ferro thought he may as well ask who he was.

WibblyWobblyTimeyWimey answered, Jennifer. I'm a history graduate. Love this kind of thing.

Oh, that surprised him. He'd assumed it was a man, though he wasn't sure why.

In any case, 'Jennifer' sounded interested. What the hell. It would be nice to share his work with someone who might actually appreciate it. So Ferro typed back telling her that he'd discovered something new today, mentioned living in Norton Hill in case she was nearby, and suggested meeting to show her his work.

After posting the comment, he suspected he might've

scared her off. Oh well. No harm in trying.

Jennifer responded saying she actually wasn't far from him, but wasn't one for meeting up with someone she'd just started talking to online. Fair enough. Very sensible.

Ferro thought he'd put her mind at rest anyway, commenting that he'd only meet her in a public place, because for all he knew, *she* might be the crazy one.

It worked, surprisingly, so she was obviously quite keen to hear what he had to say. LOL. Okay, well there's a pub in Deepwater I like called The Kipper and the Corpse. We could meet there if you want.

Ferro didn't know Deepwater or its pubs that well but said he'd look it up and suggested they meet at midday.

Jennifer rounded off their conversation with a warning that she'd kick his arse if he tried anything funny. He might've said the same were he in her position. He promised he wouldn't.

At least tomorrow he could talk time travel with someone who was prepared to listen. He'd been on his own with all this for months now.

He downed the dregs of his Merlot and went to bed.

6

September 13th 2019

Jennifer arrived at the Kipper and the Corpse five minutes late. She was, admittedly, a bit nervous. Let's face it. What she was doing was pretty random and potentially a little stupid. After a five-minute conversation online, she'd agreed to meet up with a bloke more than twice her age who was potentially off his rocker. If it was her own daughter doing this, well, she wouldn't be. (Not that Jennifer had told her mum – that would be dumb. She would've blown a gasket.)

Having said all that, she *had* done a bit of due diligence. As in, she'd googled Gregory Ferro last night. She didn't find much. Good sign, really. No news articles about a 'Gregory Ferro' getting convicted of murder or anything. She did find a seven-year-old article with a photo of a Gregory Ferro posing alongside some A-Level History students at Reading College, the history department having won an award. This Ferro had grey hair, glasses and a short beard – she guessed he was mid-fifties. Whether it was the one she was meeting, who knew. He hadn't put a photo of himself on his blog for her to be able to compare, but he did say he was a former history teacher.

Jennifer entered the pub and scanned the large main lounge at the front. There was one man sitting at the bar with a lager who didn't look like he was waiting for anyone, and a man and a woman eating sandwiches in one of the booths. She went through into the back room that had the fireplace. A man sat in the corner, sipping a cup of tea, a box file on the table in front of him.

It was him. Same man as in the picture she'd looked at last night. A few details had changed. He was larger, his glasses rounder, and he looked like he was trying to go the full Father Christmas with his beard.

"Gregory Ferro?" Jennifer said, approaching his table.

He stood up, held out his hand to shake hers. "Yes. Jennifer, is it?"

They shook hands. "Yes, pleased to meet you. What do I call you? Gregory? Greg?"

"Ferro, actually. Everybody calls me that." He smiled, "Apart from the wife and kids, of course."

Okay, good. He'd already said online that he was a father of two. Now she knew he was a husband. Very normal so far. She wasn't sure what to make of the crucifix around his neck. Normally that meant the wearer was religious, but not always. Could've been a family heirloom.

"I'm just going to grab a drink," said Jennifer. "You want anything?" A few inches of something yellowy remained in his cup, and the cool tingle of peppermint had hit her nostrils when they shook hands.

"No, thank you."

Jennifer got a cider from the bar and returned to the table.

"Pretty freakish coincidence, this," she said, sitting down opposite Ferro. "You and I living this close to each other."

Ferro gave a small smile but didn't say anything. If there was anything Jennifer hated it was an awkward silence, so she took a sip of her pint and continued speaking. "I've been following your blog for a couple of months now. Really interesting stuff. I loved studying William II, particularly his mysterious death and all the people who had a motive to bump him off."

Finally he spoke – "What did you make of it all?"

"Of what? Your blogs about it?"

He nodded, "Yes."

Jennifer wondered if he was trying to suss out if she was genuinely open to his ideas. Honestly, Jennifer wasn't sure on that herself yet.

"It's a fun idea. Great plot for a movie. Do I think William II was actually shot by a man who talked to someone on a mobile phone, then disappeared? Not really." Jennifer smiled, sipped her pint. "Unless you can prove it to me."

"Let me show you proof, then," Ferro said, opening his box file and lifting out a folder of papers, which he handed to her.

Jennifer put down her pint and opened the folder. She found some pictures of the Rufus Stone, colour photocopies of the Latin manuscript he'd posted the fuzzy photos of on his blog, some white pages on which he'd typed up an English translation of the Latin, and a report detailing the results of a radiocarbon dating test.

He explained, "Those photocopies are of the chronicles of Father Jerome, a Benedictine choir monk from Canterton Priory in the New Forest, writing in the early 12th century. They were discovered recently, buried in the walls of the crypt at St Margaret's Church in Highcliffe."

"Yes, you talked about these on your blog," said Jennifer.

"Correct. And as you know from my blog, in February 1105, Father Jerome detailed a deathbed confession from Purkis, the man who took William II's body to Winchester and, we know now, also witnessed the king's death."

"Do you have the original manuscript?"

"I did have, but I was only allowed to keep it for a few weeks. I got some tests done on it and copies made in that time. You can see there the results of the carbon dating test, proving that it originated in the 12th century. The original's been sent to the British Library. Have a read of the papers that are in English. I've translated the Latin. And any expert will tell you that it's a near-perfect translation."

"Fortunately I have a pretty good grasp of medieval Latin myself." Jennifer had read a bit of the Latin in the photos on Ferro's blog, but not a lot since they weren't very good images.

"You do?" said Ferro.

"Yes. I learned Latin as part of my history degree."

"Even better, then. Just read the photocopies. You'll see that I'm not fabricating any of this."

Would she, though? There were tons of clever ways of hoaxing historical manuscripts, and Jennifer was only looking at photocopies, not the original text.

On the other hand, Ferro had told her that the original was at the British Library, so she could just look it up there if she doubted him.

She read the copies. At points, she compared them to Ferro's translation. Pretty spot-on.

And yes, according to Father Jerome, Purkis had described

on his deathbed seeing a man falsely calling himself Walter Tyrrell shoot the king after questioning him about an unnamed book. He then had a conversation with a *flat, black, rectangular object* that admittedly did sound like a phone, before swallowing a red stone and vanishing.

Jennifer finished reading and said coolly, "Okay."

"Do you see what I mean?" said Ferro. "Seems obvious to me that Tyrrell was talking on a mobile phone. And this little red stone that made him disappear… I suspect it was a time travel device of some kind."

Jennifer played devil's advocate. "But you're reading something written in the 1100s through modern eyes. There could be hundreds of rational explanations for what Purkis saw."

"Alright." Ferro sat back in his chair. "Such as?"

"Oh, I don't know. Maybe instead of being on the phone, Tyrrell was just talking to himself and scratching his ear. This object, if there really was one, could be anything. A stone, a piece of wood, an item of clothing. We don't know how far away Purkis was standing, or how good his eyesight was. And maybe the little red stone he ate was just a berry or a nut or some kind of medicine – they did have pills back then, just not ones like ours. And instead of disappearing into thin air, Tyrrell could've ducked behind a tree. Or have you considered that maybe Purkis hallucinated the whole thing on his deathbed? Or lied? This is just one account, told through Father Jerome, so it's not even first-hand. And there's nothing backing it up, which I know, because I studied William II's death."

"Quite the sceptic," Ferro said, smiling. "I respect that. But there's more."

Ferro lifted something else from his box file and handed it to her. Copies of Simon of Stonebury's *History of England.* "This is just an extract showing the section I talked about in my blog, the bit about the plague doctor. I sourced it from the Parker Library at –"

"Corpus Christi College, Cambridge," Jennifer answered for him. "History graduate, remember."

She skim-read the extract, but she already knew – from reading Ferro's blog – what she wanted to say. "Okay, but this isn't really anything," she said, handing it back to him.

"What do you mean?"

"Well, it's a rumour, isn't it? Rumours aren't evidence."

"And the fact that this is, once again, about a book? The fact that the plague doctor was seen talking on a device held to his ear, before vanishing? Just like Tyrrell?"

Jennifer said flatly, "Coincidence."

Ferro frowned.

"And it's a rumour that 'someone' saw the plague doctor doing all that," she added. "There aren't any named witnesses here."

Ferro sighed. Jennifer wondered if she was being too hard on him. He dug some more papers from his box file. "Alright, take at look at these, then. This is what I discovered yesterday, the thing I mentioned last night."

He handed her some more photocopies, this time pages from a modern history book, *Secrets of the Great Pestilence* by Edith Starkey, published in 1977. As well as the title, copyright and contents pages, he'd copied a section called *Legend of the Evil Plague Doctor,* relaying an account from Ralph of Wallingsworth that virtually mirrored Simon of Stonebury's.

Jennifer then read about the 'Godfrey letter', swallowing a laugh when she read that the 'the book with a strange title' the evil plague doctor was chasing was supposed to have been called *The History of Computer-Aided Timetabling for Railway Systems*. Was this whole thing a giant leg-pull?

She looked at Ferro, trying her hardest not to smile. "This is a joke, right? *The History of Computer-Aided Timetabling for Railway Systems?*"

"I suspected as much when I first read that. But no. It's no joke."

"Where did you find this Edith Starkey book?"

Ferro was hesitant, then said quietly, "Portphilly Museum, North Wales."

Jennifer rolled her eyes. That explained it. "Portphilly? Also known as the 'Museum of Bad History'? Surely you know about that place. No self-respecting historian would rely on anything in it."

"I know its reputation. But I also think it's exaggerated. Not everything there is bogus."

"That's not what I've heard."

"Look. The main thing to take from this is a matter of simple fact. Edith Starkey is talking about a book by Jeremy Jennings called *The History of Computer-Aided Timetabling for Railway Systems* in 1977. I googled this book yesterday and it is real. But it was first published in 1995, eighteen years *after* it was cited in Edith Starkey's book. You can look it up for yourself. How do you explain that?"

Jennifer sat back in her chair. "Mmm." Admittedly, that had stumped her a little bit.

At the same time, she still couldn't trust anything to come out of Portphilly Museum, and this – all of it – was just too far-fetched for her to accept. Yes, okay, so there was one puzzling detail to this story that she couldn't (right now) explain, but evidentially, Ferro's case for time travellers messing with history was about as strong as a wet noodle.

"I'm sorry, Ferro. I just don't buy it. It's a great story. I love a good time travel story and it sounds like something out of *Doctor Who*, which I also love. You probably guessed that already from my username."

Ferro looked blank.

"Wibbly wobbly timey wimey?"

Still looked blank.

"You know, when David Tennant calls time a 'big ball of wibbly wobbly timey wimey stuff' when he's talking about paradoxes?"

Ferro maintained his blank look, now marked with a hint of *get to the damn point.*

"Guess not," said Jennifer. "Anyway, while I love a good science fiction story, I never lose sight of the fact that it's science *fiction*. Time travel's impossible."

Ferro took back his papers and closed his box file. "Okay. Fine." He was pissed – she could tell. "I'm starting to feel like you think I'm delusional. Like I'm a fantasist or something."

Jennifer nearly vocalised, *Well, aren't you?*

"I'm not," Ferro said. "I'm fully aware of how implausible this sounds but that doesn't mean it's not real. I *know* that I'm onto something big here. I can just feel it."

"I'm sure you can."

Ferro frowned. "What do you mean by that?"

"Well, you're religious, aren't you?" Jennifer pointed at

Ferro's crucifix.

"I'm Catholic. What does that have to do with anything?"

"It means you're inherently more willing to believe in nonsense."

His voice rose a touch in volume, pinched with irritation, "I beg your pardon?"

Jennifer tried to clarify. "I just mean that you're more suggestible, easier to persuade." Okay, that probably made it worse. "More gullible." *Jen, shut up now.*

Ferro gave her a piercing glare. If looks could kill, she'd be dead, buried and fully decomposed.

"I think we should leave it there," Ferro said, noticeably holding back. He stood up and started gathering his things.

"I'm just trying to help," said Jennifer.

Ferro's eyes widened. "Help?"

"I'm just trying to give you a little perspective. You've clearly gotten a bit obsessed with all this. What do your family think?"

Ferro's glare returned and sharpened, and his tone went from irritated to angry. "*Don't* psychoanalyse me, and *don't* talk about my family." He took a breath and said more calmly, "This was a mistake. Goodbye, Jennifer."

He took his stuff and left the pub.

Jennifer finished her pint, reflecting on what she'd said. Definitely shouldn't have called him gullible. Or obsessed. Or brought up his family. She'd only just met him. That wasn't cool. But it wasn't the first time her wayward mouth had got her in trouble. Yesterday, case in point.

She felt guilty now. She hadn't meant to upset him.

She'd been extremely unbending in her scepticism too. What if he had a point? Was discounting all of his research as a bunch of meaningless coincidences short-sighted? Naive, even?

Then again, if she accepted what Ferro was saying, she'd be accepting that time travel was real.

She couldn't do that, could she?

7

June 5th 1482

"W-what is the meaning of this?" cried Edward IV, bolting upright in bed, startled awake by the clatter of his bedchamber door swinging open and striking the wall.

Orange light punctured the darkness, but his sleepy eyes caught only a blur of it. He blinked, several times, his vision clearing to reveal a tall, well-built man holding an oil lamp, the excited flame illuminating his face in a dance of shadows – a face he did not recognise.

"Who are you?" Edward demanded.

The man placed the oil lamp on Edward's writing table and replied, "Where is the book?"

Dear Lord! Did he mean…?

Edward tried to conceal a reactionary swallow. He felt a tingling in his cheeks and around his eyes. He said nothing, and the man just stared at him.

"I have just about had enough of this." Edward threw off his covers and swung out of bed wearing just his shirt and braies.

The intruder charged forwards to block his path and Edward saw the glint of the small, black-handled dagger in his other hand.

Edward slid back onto the bed, backing against his gold-plated headboard.

"Move again and I'll kill you." The man's voice was gruff and firm. "Tell me where the book is – now."

Despite a painful heat in his chest, Edward remained outwardly calm. "To which book are you referring? There are many."

The intruder's glare deepened. He inched forwards, arching

over the bed and pointing his dagger at Edward's face. "*Don't*, Your Grace. I've had enough. I just need to..." As his words faded, his features loosened and Edward saw a deep anguish and despair in his eyes.

It was only for a moment, though. The intruder cast aside his suffering with a flick of the head, a furious grimace re-forming. "You know what book I'm talking about. *The History of Computer-Aided Timetabling for Railway Systems.* By Jeremy Jennings."

Edward knew it. He knew they would come for it eventually. But even as there was a blade just inches from his eyes, he wasn't going to give in. "I don't understand what that means, so I am afraid I cannot help you."

"You're lying."

"I cannot tell you what I do not know."

"Stop... *lying!*" In an instant, the intruder's voice was like a great tree splitting in two, scraping the walls. He screamed so loud he made himself choke. Coughing, he stumbled against the wall.

A chance to escape. Though Edward wasn't as nimble as he used to be, a fire at the pit of his belly propelled him. He dived forwards, scrambling across the bed.

The intruder's coughing ceased immediately and Edward knew that his escape was not to be. He felt an iron grip on his shoulder and a powerful force yank him backwards. He fell against the headboard, cracking his head. For a moment it was like the back of his head was on fire, then the trickle of warm blood was on his neck.

The next thing he knew, the intruder was virtually on top of him on the bed, restraining him, and Edward's throat met the cold bite of his blade.

The intruder spoke with a strained voice, face red and twisted with what looked like both fury and pain, "If you don't tell me where the book is right now, I'll take your fucking head clean off."

Edward's heart raced. His neck stung as the blade pressed deeper and harder, and he could feel the blood struggling to squeeze past it. Any moment now and it would penetrate his flesh; that blood would come spilling out. Expecting to die, he spoke his last words as coolly as he could, "I will not help you."

"*Fucking tell me!*" The furious scream caused the intruder's fragile voice to shatter in another guttural cough. He doubled over, falling to the side of Edward's bed, the dagger with him. Edward's hands were immediately on his throat, checking that the skin wasn't broken. It hurt, but nothing ran warm over his fingers – his neck was intact.

Hacking and convulsing, the man toppled against the wall, knocking a portrait of Edward's sons.

His choking went on longer this time, and Edward seized the moment, diving to the other side of the bed and leaping off, unhooking his longsword from the wall and returning quickly to where the intruder was bent over coughing.

Wasting no time, Edward impaled the man in the back, penetrating through his chest. It was like slicing into a soft fruit. The man's coughs stuck instantly in his throat and his body shook, making the hilt of the blade tremble in Edward's hand. The dagger fell from the man's hand, hitting the wood floor with a small clunk.

Edward withdrew the sword. The intruder collapsed, turning as he fell, landing with his back partially propped up against the wall. Within seconds there was blood everywhere, dripping from the point of Edward's sword onto one of the ornate golden rugs that dressed the wood floor, seeping from the man's back and chest, forming an expanding puddle around him, escaping into grooves and cracks in the planks, and spreading around and underneath Edward's bed, chasing the gentle slope in the floor.

Edward had killed men before. But it had always been in battle. Fast. Mad. Busy. No time to dwell on it, normally because he had to turn his attention to the next man who was attacking him.

Right now, it was just Edward, the intruder and God. The air was still, no low winds rustling the trees or whistling through the eaves. Even the insects were quiet tonight. And as Edward stood there, he found himself oddly transfixed by the rippling red flow draining from the man.

He wasn't quite dead. Slumped against the wall, gargling and spitting blood, he reached stiffly inside the green cloak he was wearing over his tunic. Edward watched, sword poised in case he was about to draw another weapon.

"I… I have to…" the man choked out.

Instead of a weapon he took out a small pot. Edward watched him breathlessly remove the lid, pluck a tiny red object – a stone or some odd kind of pill – from inside and lift it to his mouth.

"Have to… have to save them…"

His eyes went blank, just before the thing touched his tongue. His hand dropped away from his mouth and fell limp at his side, and the little pill rolled onto the floor. His chin flopped against his chest.

Edward had barely a chance to process what had happened before the dead silence of the room gave way to an unusual and tuneful melody coming from the intruder's body.

Edward investigated, following the sound to a pocket in the inner lining of the man's cloak, probably the same one he'd taken the pot of pills from. Edward thrust his hand in the pocket and took out a slim rectangular object.

Lord have mercy.

The curious melody was emanating, somehow, from the object, which was trembling as though it was alive. On its flat, shiny face was an array of colourful shapes, symbols, lines and words Edward couldn't understand. He went to touch it but hesitated out of fear. It took a moment for his kingly courage to return and push his finger against one of the larger shapes, a green circle with a bone-like symbol inside it. The melody and trembling stopped, and a transcendent magic compelled all the words, shapes and symbols to fly about the surface of the object in a dizzying display. He closed his eyes – tight. Was he losing his mind? Possibly. He opened his eyes a crack and saw that the words and shapes had rearranged themselves.

Then a tiny voice started speaking. Edward brought the object closer to his ear so he could hear.

"Skinner?" A woman's voice.

What did *Skinner* mean? Unsure what was happening or how to respond, Edward just listened silently.

After a short silence, the same mysterious woman spoke again, "Mr Skinner! What the hell are you doing?"

Despite the vulgarity of her language, it was a good question – what was he doing?

"What sorcery is this?" Edward said finally. He knew these people had powers beyond his comprehension, but it was worth trying for an explanation.

"What? Who is this?" the woman asked.

He saw no reason to hold back his name. "You are speaking with King Edward IV of England. What is your name, madam?"

There was a loud thud, then the woman cried, "Jesus!"

A heinous lie. Edward flared, "You dare to impersonate our Lord Jesus Christ? You must be one of Satan's apostates."

The woman confessed, "Yes. That's right. I am. And I have great power, too. So I suggest you do as I say or I will release a plague of…" She paused for a flicker of a moment, then said, "… cats upon you."

Cats. The Devil's favourite animal. A witch's familiar. This woman was truly evil, but Edward stood firm against her threats, refusing to succumb to fear. "I am not afraid. I serve the Lord, and Him alone. Whatever power you possess is no match for Him."

"Don't be so sure. Where is the owner of the device we are using to speak?"

Edward glanced at the intruder's bloody corpse. "You mean the man I just killed?"

"Fuck!"

There was a moment's silence, then a shrill squeal sliced into his ear, not unlike a bird being throttled. He lowered the black object from his ear and looked at it. Suddenly it was transparent and rippling like water. He blinked hard, did a fast head shake. It made it no difference and he wondered if his vision was failing. Then he glanced around his bedchamber, dimly lit by the oil lamp. Everything was clear.

He closed his fingers around the object. He couldn't *feel* it anymore. His fingers fell right through it. He opened his palm again and could see it, hazy as it was, but it had no mass.

How was that possible?

He tried to touch its surface with his other hand. By the time he did, it wasn't transparent anymore. It was gone. Vanished.

Caught in a wave of dizziness, Edward grabbed a post at the foot end of his four-poster bed to steady himself. In a moment, the feeling passed. The back of his head still throbbed from where the intruder had thrown him against the headboard, but the bleeding had stopped. He would need to see a physician, but there was no time for that now.

He had to move quickly.

He called a servant in the next room to summon Sir Lionel Frensham, one of his favourite and most trusted courtiers, from his bed. Then he dug his legs into a pair of hose and pulled a doublet over his bloodied nightshirt, tying it with a broad leather belt encrusted with gold buttons. He retrieved a key on a silver chain from beneath his mattress and placed it around his neck.

Though he lived on the other side of the palace, Sir Lionel was at the door of Edward's bedchamber in a matter of minutes, gasping as he entered and cast his eyes on the corpse in the corner, swimming in blood.

"As you can see, I need your help," said Edward.

"What happened, Your Grace?" Sir Lionel asked.

"Somehow this man got past the guards and found his way into my bedchamber."

"He threatened you?"

"Yes. He wanted something. And I fear others may follow in his wake."

"How can I help?"

"I need you to dispose of this man's body and get this bedchamber cleaned up. But before you do that, I need you to arrange for a carriage to take me to the Tower. I have something urgent to attend to."

"Now, Your Grace?"

"That is what I meant by urgent, Sir Lionel."

Sir Lionel's cheeks flushed. "Yes, Your Grace."

As Edward tugged on his boots and draped a fur-trimmed brocade cloak across his shoulders, Sir Lionel inspected the intruder's body. "Your Grace, what shall I do with this?" he asked, facing Edward with the intruder's pot of strange red pills in his hand.

Edward approached him. "I'll take it," he said. Sir Lionel handed him the pot and he placed it in a pocket inside his cloak.

Sir Lionel gave a gentle frown. "Your Grace, may I ask what it –"

"No," replied Edward. "Please have the carriage pick me up from the front gates."

"Y-yes. Very good."

"Oh, and Sir Lionel," Edward added, just as he was about to depart.

"Yes, Your Grace?"

"Speak to no one about what has transpired here tonight."

8

October 17th 2019

Ferro's Rover Metro was dead. Its engine had packed up and it was going to cost way more to get it fixed than the car was worth. Ferro certainly couldn't afford another right now. He was making ends meet by helping out at Sanjay's, the corner shop at the top of his road, but it was loose change, not real money. Still, he was trying not to let it hamper his quest. He was getting closer. And if he had to skip a few meals and otherwise live on jacket potatoes and beans for a while, so be it. He needed to lose a couple of stone anyway. The little he earned was much better spent on books and train tickets.

Today he was returning home from Oxford having spent the day at the Bodleian Library studying an exciting new lead: the journal of Sir Lionel Frensham, a courtier to Edward IV. His brain was so bustling with new ideas, new theories, that at 11pm when his train stopped at Basingstoke, he barely noticed Jennifer – that girl he hoped never to see again – step aboard the train.

Small world. *Too* small.

Ferro ducked down a bit lower in his chair and faced the window, staring into the thick darkness beyond his reflection.

Damn. He could see in the corner of his eye that she was coming this way. Even though there were plenty of seats on both sides, rotten luck or fate or perhaps even God's will brought her straight to him.

He continued to stare out the window, pretending not to have seen her and praying she didn't see him.

"Ferro?"

God hates me today.

Ferro turned his head and looked up at her, unsure at first

how to respond. Last time they met she'd insulted his faith and called him gullible and obsessed, and he'd got out of that pub as quickly as possible to avoid saying something he'd regret.

At the same time, he wasn't angry anymore. She was just a stupid kid. Well, not a kid. A history graduate. And she wasn't stupid, she was clever. Perhaps too clever for her own good. A part of him admired her pragmatism. He just couldn't abide unnecessary rudeness.

He figured the best thing to do was be polite. "Hi," he said. "I didn't expect to see you again."

Jennifer looked sheepish, lips pulled into a flat, uneasy smile, cheeks flushing ever so slightly – perhaps she felt guilty. "Me neither." She glanced at the seat opposite Ferro, which was free. But it was late; most of the seats were free.

Please don't sit there.

"Do you mind if I sit here?"

Ferro's heart sank but he maintained his polite veneer, if with a pinch of animosity, replying, "Of course. I don't own the train."

Jennifer sat down, placing her handbag on the seat next to her. She was wearing baggy, dark green cargo trousers with half a dozen pockets and a jacket that was open over a white sweatshirt with a picture of the TARDIS from *Doctor Who* and the tagline from *The X-Files* beneath it: 'I Want To Believe'. Ferro held back a grin.

"So… how are you?" said Jennifer, a tad awkwardly.

"Fine, thanks," said Ferro matter-of-factly. "You?"

"Yeah, good. Just been for some drinks in Basingstoke with my friend Adam. Couldn't go too crazy though. Work tomorrow."

That didn't really warrant a response, so Ferro forced a smile and turned his gaze back on the window, even though all he could see was the illuminated carriage – and Jennifer – reflected in the glass.

"So, er… how is the research going?" she asked, needlessly prolonging this uncomfortable exchange.

Ferro replied simply, without looking at her, "Well, thanks."

"Have you learned anything new?"

"Yes. Several things."

"I'd love to hear about them."

Ferro faced her. "But I'm the obsessed and gullible Catholic. Why would you want to hear any more of my – how did you put it – *nonsense*?" Okay, perhaps he wasn't totally over the things she'd said.

Jennifer turned even redder. "Alright, fair one. I'm sorry about that. I shouldn't have said those things. I just… I have a bit of trouble with… religion."

"And with religious people, it seems."

"No. It's not that. It's the nature of religion as a whole. It just isn't logical to me – believing in things you can't prove."

"Says the woman wearing a sweatshirt with 'I Want To Believe' written across it."

Jennifer looked down at her sweatshirt. "That's just the *X-Files* tagline."

Ferro smiled, nodding, "I know. I'm just pointing out the irony. In any case" – he wondered if he was going to regret getting into this with her, but decided to take the risk – "you're right. There is a certain illogic in it. But my religion isn't about logic. It's about faith."

Jennifer squinted sceptically. "Yes, but – respectfully – that's a copout. Faith is just a label. A way of ducking out of a rational argument. It's… lazy."

"So I'm lazy now, too?"

Jennifer sighed heavily, grabbed her handbag and stood up. "Look, I'm sorry, I – I'll just go and sit somewhere else. I don't want to upset you – again."

Ferro laughed softly, "It's fine, sit down. You haven't upset me. I understand where you're coming from."

Jennifer stopped in the aisle. "You do?"

"Of course I do. I'm not stupid."

Jennifer sat back down as Ferro continued, "I accept that my faith isn't particularly rational. But I can't just wish away my beliefs. I've had them all my life. Grew up with them. Organised religion has its flaws, but it's also brought me a lot of comfort. If I'm wrong and there's no God, no pearly gates, no everlasting life – fine, I'm wrong. But I'm not going to stop believing."

Jennifer smiled warmly. Even though there was no chance of a meeting of minds on this subject, perhaps she admired his fortitude.

She diverted at just the right time, "And what about time travel? Do you still believe in that?"

"Wholeheartedly. But don't worry, that's not a case of 'believing in things you can't prove' because I *am* proving it. The evidence is starting to stack up."

"Will you tell me about it? I promise I won't be as dismissive this time."

She certainly seemed genuine. Ferro decided there was probably no harm in having another go at convincing her. He opened his messenger bag on the seat next to him, took out some photocopies of handwritten papers in the Chancery Standard of English and handed them to her.

"What are these?" she asked.

"Did you read the article I posted on my blog yesterday?" She was still one of his blog followers, but whether she read all his articles, he had no idea.

"Oh. No. I missed that one," she admitted.

"Okay. It was about a journal written by Sir Lionel Frensham, one of Edward IV's courtiers. Those are copies of it. I've just been at the Bodleian Library studying the original. For centuries the journal was in the possession of Frensham's descendants, buried amongst old deeds and records in the cellar of a medieval country manor still owned by the family. One of the descendants discovered it in 2017 and handed it over to the Bodleian Library, who commissioned carbon-dating tests to verify its age." Knowing Jennifer was a stickler for the evidence, he handed her a folder, saying, "Here's a copy of the report."

Jennifer briefly cast her eyes over the report, then looked at Ferro as if waiting for further explanation.

"Go ahead," Ferro said. "I've bookmarked the relevant sections of the journal. I figured you'd prefer to read it yourself. Straight from the horse's mouth and all that."

"*We are now approaching Litchmere,*" said the automated woman over the tannoy.

"Mine's the next stop," said Jennifer. "Any chance you can give me the headlines?"

"Okay. Frensham says that one night in June 1482, he was summoned by the king from his bedchamber in the early hours. The servant who fetched him let slip that he'd overheard the king arguing with someone, and that whoever it was had questioned the king about a 'book'. Frensham attended as ordered, discovering that the king had killed the man he'd argued with. Frensham was ordered to make arrangements to dispose of the man's body and described finding a small pot of 'strange red pills' in the intruder's hand. The king took the pills and Frensham never saw them again. He was also asked to make arrangements to convey the king to the Tower of London for an unknown purpose that very night."

"I see." She wore a squinted frown, now looking more intrigued than sceptical.

"That's not all," said Ferro. "Near the end of the journal, Frensham recounts that when Edward IV was on his deathbed less than a year later, he asked Frensham to deliver something to his son, the twelve-year-old Prince Edward. A package. It was sealed and Frensham, though curious, didn't ask any questions about what was inside. He just did as his king commanded and delivered the package."

Ferro could see the cogs turning in Jennifer's head. "Prince Edward... He was... Wait. Wasn't he the elder of – ?"

Ferro answered for her, "The Princes in the Tower, yes. Britain's most famous missing persons case. How much do you know about them?"

Jennifer sat back in her seat and entwined her hands. "Well I know that Prince Edward was king for a matter of days before his uncle, Richard III, nabbed the throne for himself. And I know that Edward and his younger brother were sent by Richard to the Tower of London and disappeared. Probably murdered by Richard himself but nobody knows for sure."

"Yes. Murder's always been considered most likely, particularly after the skeletons of two children were found buried under a staircase in the White Tower in 1674."

"Oh. Don't remember hearing about that. Was it them?"

"No one knows. The bodies couldn't be identified at the time, so they were buried at Westminster Abbey. They were re-examined in 1933 but the results were hardly conclusive. We don't even know if the bodies were male or female. Historians have pushed for a re-excavation to identify the bones using DNA testing, but the Queen needs to grant permission for that. She hasn't."

"Mmm. So… this 'package' Frensham delivered to Prince Edward. What do you think it was?"

"I don't know yet. But if Edward IV's attacker was after a book…" Ferro was in speculative territory at this point and restrained himself. Jennifer wanted evidence, not assumptions.

"Do you think it's connected somehow to the princes' disappearance?"

"Possibly," he said cautiously. "I have some books about the Princes in the Tower to go through and see if I can find references to this package. We'll see."

"We are now approaching Deepwater."

As the train slowed, Jennifer opened her handbag and pulled out her phone. "Let me take your number. I'll call you and we can meet up again, go through all this properly. If you want. I completely understand if you'd rather not."

Ferro smiled. "That's fine with me." He gave her his number and she punched it into her phone.

"Great. I'll check my diary and call you tomorrow sometime."

Ferro nodded. "Speak then."

Jennifer made her way to the doors and stepped off the train, immediately disappearing into the darkness of the platform.

As the train resumed its journey towards Norton Hill, Ferro couldn't help but feel quietly elated that he was on the road to converting the uber-sceptic.

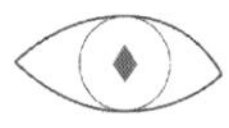

When Ferro got home, his high spirits dipped the moment he saw the divorce petition on his kitchen table. It had arrived two days ago but he was ignoring it. He had five more days to respond and planned to wait until the very last minute. Virtually everything had been agreed, but he still held out a sliver of hope that Beth might change her mind. Doubtful, but possible.

It was gone midnight but he poured a glass of wine and settled for a bit in the lounge to check his emails.

At the top of his inbox was an email sent a couple of hours

ago by someone called Sophie Rousseau. The subject line read: *Please can we meet.*

He'd never heard of a Sophie Rousseau. Could've been junk – some foreigner offering him millions of dollars if he handed over all his personal details – but his spam filters were normally quite good at catching those. He opened the message to shed some light.

Dear Mr Ferro

I hope you don't mind me emailing you, but I have just been reading your blog and your theories about time travellers and I have some information. There are some striking similarities between the things you have discovered in your research on William II and the Black Death and something I witnessed myself twenty-two years ago.

I would rather not divulge anything more over email or phone but would like to meet you and explain. I live in France but can be in London next Monday. Can we meet at St Pancras station at around noon?

I look forward to hearing from you.

Regards,

Sophie Rousseau.

Ferro's deflated spirits rose again. Without thinking, fingers itching with excitement, he typed back a reply that, yes, he could meet her at St Pancras station at noon next Monday.

9

August 30th 1997

Sophie Rousseau, devoted wife of a surgeon and mother to three children, lived in the small town of Lagny-en-Brie in the eastern suburbs of Paris. Sophie's children had grown up and moved away, the last one having left the nest nearly a year ago. Finding herself alone for long stretches, husband Frédéric working increasingly demanding hours, Sophie decided six months ago to buy a gorgeous liver and white Basset Hound – Kimmy – to ease her loneliness.

Today Frédéric was working an all-day-all-night shift so Sophie embarked on a highly productive day in his absence. She walked Kimmy, cleaned the house, took a fresh bouquet of lilies to her mother's grave, sewed up all the Kimmy-chewed holes in Frédéric's socks, cooked dinner, fed Kimmy, walked Kimmy again, then settled finally to rewrite the penultimate chapter of her novel.

As always, work on her novel took place in a different time stream, one in which the minutes passed at twice their normal speed. It got to 1am and, right in the middle of a pivotal scene, Kimmy started whining.

She got up from her desk and saw Kimmy standing by the front door. "Seriously? You need to go out again?"

Kimmy barked and did a three-hundred-and-sixty-degree turn on the spot. A yes.

"Good job I love you." It was late anyway; she could resume in the morning. Some fresh air would be nice, actually. She went to get Kimmy's lead. The pup had an aversion to doing a number one or a number two in the garden, meaning she always had to take him down to the woods near the house.

They headed out. It was a warm, clear night and that lovely smell of mowed lawns was still in the air. As usual Sophie went at Kimmy's pace rather than her own and her continual instructions to heel were lost on him.

When they got to the woods, Sophie let Kimmy off the lead, switched on her torch and rubbed the ball of her shoulder from where Kimmy had been trying his utmost to pull her arm off. She stood and waited while he did a wee and investigated some new smells. Despite not knowing how to heel, he was a good boy in the woods and didn't stray too far, particularly if it was dark. He liked to stay close to Sophie and her torchlight.

Except for tonight. Sophie saw Kimmy scamper behind some trees. A few minutes later she still couldn't see him. She walked forwards, scanning the area with her torch, but Kimmy was beyond its reach. She stopped, waited a minute longer. When he'd still not come back to her, she called, "Kimmy? Kimmy, where are you, boy?"

She whistled to him, waved her torch. Nothing. No sign of him. Her heartbeat quickened. Where had he got to?

She walked forwards again, deeper into the woods than she'd wanted to go. Then she saw something. A flicker in the bushes ahead, caught in the periphery of the torchlight. She cast the full glare of the torch over the bushes but they were still. She heard rustling in a different direction and hoped to God it was Kimmy and not… well, something else.

She walked in the direction of the rustling, then stopped. In the near distance she heard the low hum of a car engine, the crackle of tyres over gravel.

She switched off her torch. Someone else was here.

Not wanting to draw attention, she lowered her voice to a whisper and called, "Kimmy…"

She moved forwards carefully, stepping lightly and using her feet to feel for large twigs and clusters of leaves so she could avoid them.

An old streetlamp began to ease the thick darkness of her path. Then, fifteen to twenty feet ahead, half-hidden in foliage, was a little creature with a prominent head and huge, curtain-like ears, softly silhouetted against the streetlamp's dim, orange glow.

There you are.

Kimmy sat watching something intently, panting. Sophie gently approached him. She followed his stare through the trees to the narrow, overgrown, disused road that wound through the woods, flanked by the streetlamp that no longer served a purpose but was helpful to dog walkers.

There on the road was a white Fiat Uno, engine now off. A tall, hulking man in a dark suit was standing next to it, looking around.

Why would someone bring a car through here? The road met a dead end, where the woods literally absorbed it. There was nowhere to go.

And so late? She checked her watch – it was nearly half one.

Curious but worried she might be seen, Sophie quietly clipped Kimmy's lead to his collar and ducked down beside him, her arm arched over his back.

The man stuffed his hand into the left inside pocket of his blazer and took something out. It was flat and rectangular and the man started tapping the front of it with his fingers before lifting it to his ear – it was obviously some kind of mobile phone.

Sophie peered hard and listened. She was about a hundred feet away and Kimmy was panting in her ear, but she just made out, "Yes, ma'am, it's done."

His voice was deep and heavy and he spoke in English, with an English accent. There was a general air of menace about him that made Sophie shiver.

"The book is destroyed," the man said.

Intriguing – what book?

"Yes, ma'am. It can no longer harm us." After a short silence, "I'll wait for your call."

Sophie's ear popped as she swallowed. The man lowered the phone from his ear, tapped it and slipped it back into his blazer.

Then he bent down and Sophie caught the outline of a huge metal can near his feet. He picked it up, unscrewed the lid and tipped its contents over the Fiat Uno. She figured the clear liquid gushing from its neck was petrol. After wetting the roof and windows, he opened the doors and doused the seats.

It was then that she noticed a dent and large slash of black paint across both passenger doors, and saw that the tail light was smashed. Perhaps the white car had collided with a black one?

The man lit a match, tossed it through the open driver's door, and stepped back. Flames erupted from the car, but they were like nothing Sophie had ever seen. *Green*. The fire was bright, fluorescent green.

What on earth?

Kimmy started whining. Both of them could feel the heat of the blaze. Sophie shortened his lead and tightened her arm around his back, in case he tried to run off. Fortunately the coarse roar of the fire masked his whines.

Then the unfathomable started happening. Whatever was in that 'petrol', it was powerful. The car's entire structure was caving in on itself, crumpling like a cheap children's toy. Dark green smoke swamped the air and Sophie was hit by a whiff of chemicals that made her eyes water and the back of her throat sting. She wanted to cough but swallowed the feeling and threw her hand over her nose – not that it did much good.

In mere moments, the powerful green fire had devoured the car and, well, *disintegrated* it. What sort of liquid could do that? It was like something off the TV.

When there was nothing left to burn, the fire withered to crackling green embers.

I really should go.

There was a very faint buzzing, then the man took out his phone again and answered, "Yes, ma'am, did it work?"

Sophie was hankering to know what this woman was saying to him. But all the man said next was, "Understood," and hung up again. Sophie was no closer to the truth.

The man replaced his phone in the left inside pocket of his blazer, then stuffed his hand into the right one and took out a small white bottle, pills rattling inside. Medication? After what she'd seen, Sophie wouldn't be surprised if it was more than that.

She was sweating, the heat from the fire lingering. Kimmy had stopped whining, thank God. The man might've heard him now the fire had stopped raging. But his panting escalated and whines would soon follow if she didn't head back soon.

She couldn't though. She was aching to see what he did next. So she hugged Kimmy, stroking his back and rubbing his ears to try and calm him, and waited a little longer.

The man unscrewed the bottle, took something out and placed it on his tongue.

Oh, so perhaps it was just medic –

A startling burst of light shocked the sight from her eyes. She toppled from her crouched position, landing on her backside, legs sprawled out in front of her. Yanking the lead from her grip, Kimmy charged away, paw steps rustling furiously into the distance.

The mantle of white that hung over Sophie's eyes gradually fragmented and fell away, her eyes readjusting to the darkness. She climbed to her feet to see what had happened.

The man was gone. Whatever that bright flash of light was, it had taken him with it.

Sophie switched her torch back on and scrambled through the trees, calling out for Kimmy. She couldn't see him anywhere. That light must've really spooked him.

Perhaps – *hopefully* – he had run back to the house. He knew the route well.

Thank God. She got home and found Kimmy circling the porch, panting and shaking, lead dragging behind him. She cuddled and stroked him. "It's alright, baby, it's alright. The scary man's gone." The words were a comfort to herself as well as the dog. "Come on. Let's get you inside."

There was a wheeze in her breathing, she noticed. She needed her inhaler – the last half-hour's events had irritated her asthma.

As soon as the front door opened, Kimmy bolted into the kitchen, leapt into his brown tweed bed and slipped beneath his blanket to hide. Sophie dug her inhaler from her handbag in the hallway and took a couple of puffs. Her breathing steadied and she brought Kimmy some doggy treats.

After a short while, Kimmy calmed down, came out of hiding and ate his treats. He made his bed on Sophie's lap as she settled in front of the TV. It was gone 2am now. She really ought to have gone to bed, but she knew she'd dream about the sinister disappearing man, the green fire and disintegrating car, and the 'book' – she needed to fill her brain with something else.

A film she saw years ago, a musical, was playing. She liked musicals, and this one was quite good, although she couldn't remember the name.

She fell asleep with the TV on and woke up in a ball on the sofa, Kimmy in his bed, at – she checked her watch – 5.05am.

Sleepily, she stretched her limbs and rose to her feet. She went to turn off the TV.

What?

Her tired eyes sprang open and she dived to grab the remote control and ramp up the volume on the news.

There had been a car crash. Bad one. In the centre of Paris.

Diana, Princess of Wales, was dead.

10

October 23rd 2019

The moment the clock on her phone hit 13.00, Jennifer was up and out of her chair, scurrying out of the office as if flames were licking her ankles. When she was at Actuate Solutions she watched the clock out of boredom. Now, at Dunbar & Associates, the corporate law firm in Reading where she'd been working for the last four weeks, she watched it out of desperation.

'Like a rat out of a cage!' That's what one of her bosses – Gloria Dunbar – would've said if she'd caught Jennifer leaving the office for lunch with such haste. She'd said it once about the secretaries when they bolted for the door at half five on the dot, no more enthusiastic about being there than Jennifer was.

If you didn't make it feel like a cage, perhaps everyone wouldn't be so desperate to leave, Jennifer thought at the time.

She walked out of the building onto Oxford Street in Reading town centre and was hit by a squall of cold air that was actually quite refreshing. The place was heaving with harassed-looking men and women in suits on their lunch breaks, diving in and out of cafes and bakeries as if time was always against them, and Jennifer realised, miserably, that she wasn't far off becoming one of them.

She began her usual circuit. She wasn't even that hungry. She just needed air, freedom, and to vent to someone. She took out her phone and called Adam.

"Hey!" he answered jovially.

He was always so happy, the lucky bastard. "Are you on lunch?"

"Yup. What's up?"

"I'm seriously considering murdering my employers."

Adam laughed. "Ah. Are they – ?"

"Still arseholes? Oooh yeah."

"What have they done now?"

"Hitler had another go at me" – that was Jennifer's nickname for Caroline Ward, the partner she most despised – "this time for not using a tray when I was carrying the tea. Even though I'm twenty-two, apparently I'm not capable of carrying a cup of tea without spilling it on their precious carpet tiles."

Dunbar & Associates was the latest job to have fallen into Jennifer's lap. Just days after losing her job at Actuate, her old college friend Alison Fawke – the long-suffering trainee solicitor at the firm – messaged her saying they had an opening for an admin assistant. Jennifer had no intention of getting into law long-term but while she was still short of a career plan and waiting for a light bulb moment, the job paid well and was more interesting than being a call centre agent.

That was how she felt after the first day, anyway. It dawned on her pretty quickly the sort of place it was. The partners – Gloria Dunbar, Michael Herrington and Caroline 'Hitler' Ward – were walking corporate lawyer stereotypes. Rich, old-fashioned, authoritarian snobs who treated their staff like naughty children. The kind of people who'd greet you first thing in the morning not with, 'Good morning, how are you?' but with, 'Is that report finished yet? I need it – hurry up.'

"Are you going to stick it out?" asked Adam.

Jennifer sighed. "For a bit longer, yeah. It's good money. And I need to make up my mind about what I want to do with my life before I chuck in another job. It's just getting harder and harder to bite my tongue."

"They do sound like dicks. But you don't wanna get fired again."

"I know. How's your day?"

"Yeah, same old. Hasn't been that busy in-store, so I've been able to be geeky and fiddle about with some software on my MEc." 'MEc' meant 'Million Eyes computer'. Adam was an IT technician for Million Eyes, now the biggest computer company in the world after purchasing Apple at the beginning of last year. Adam worked at the 'MEstore' in Basingstoke.

"Glad one of us is having fun," Jennifer said. "Fancy a pint down the Kipper tonight?"

"Sounds good to – shit!"

"What?"

"I've just seen Hannah go into WHSmith. I'm gonna go chat to her."

"Wait – is Hannah the one you're banging or the one you want to be banging?"

"The one I *want* to be banging. Rachel's the one I'm banging."

Jennifer rolled her eyes. "Rachel. Of course. How could I forget?"

Adam had changed so much since Jennifer first knew him. Back in school he was timid, shy, awkward and more likely to sprout a new head than chat up a girl. But college, uni and a close friendship with Jennifer (or so she liked to think) had brought Adam out of his shell – far out of his shell. He was a lot more confident now. Too confident in some cases.

Not that confidence equals aptitude. His chat-up lines were straight out of the 1980s and he still had moments of old-Adam-awkwardness, normally at the least opportune times. He also needed the odd pep talk from Jennifer as to the way women's minds worked. She wondered if any of these were the reason this Hannah girl still wasn't sleeping with him.

"I've gotta go," Adam said. "Kipper tonight then? Say eight?"

"Eight works," said Jennifer.

"Cool. Try and have an okay afternoon."

"I won't. But thanks. You too. Good luck with Hannah. Try not to say anything stupid."

"I won't!"

Jennifer hung up and popped into the nearest newsagent for a sandwich. She still wasn't hungry, but she needed sustenance if she was going to get through the rest of the day. She picked up an egg mayonnaise and cress baguette and sat on a bench to eat it.

She checked Facebook and her emails. She saw that Gregory Ferro had posted a new blog. He was writing a lot more lately and had posted several blogs since she saw him on the train last Thursday. She'd not read all of them, but this one caught her attention like a smack in the face. It was called *Princess Diana was murdered by time travellers.* What on earth could he have found this time?

Curiosity itching, she clicked through to the article. Ferro said he'd spoken to a witness with information about the white Fiat Uno that had fleeting contact with Princess Diana's Mercedes during the crash, but had never been traced by the authorities. Having read Ferro's blog, this witness, unnamed in Ferro's article, believed that the car belonged to the same time travellers responsible for the death of William II. She said she'd seen it being disposed of in some woods by a 'man in black', who talked on the phone to someone and mentioned a 'book', before taking a pill and vanishing in front of her eyes.

Having met him twice now, Jennifer didn't think Ferro would fabricate this woman. The question was whether *she* was doing the fabricating. There were plenty of fantasists, hoaxers and con artists out there, cooking up wild stories with the intention of corroborating a conspiracy theory.

Still, her interest was piqued. What if this woman really did see those things in the woods? Over twenty years had passed since Diana, her partner, Dodi Fayed, and their driver, Henri Paul, were killed in the Pont de l'Alma tunnel in Paris in August 1997. Jennifer had learned a lot about it from journalists, authors, filmmakers and Wikipedia. The French had concluded that it was an accident, but many people still believed she was murdered. In 2007, a coroner's inquest concluded that there was no conspiracy, the final verdict being that Diana was killed by the grossly negligent actions of Henri Paul, allegedly three times over the French blood-alcohol legal limit, and the paparazzi pursuing her at the time of the crash. Scores of people – both hardened conspiracy theorists and 'normal folk' – didn't buy it. Jennifer was on the fence.

She searched her contacts for Ferro's number and called him. He answered after two rings, "Hello?"

"Ferro! It's me, Jennifer. I've just read your Diana blog!"

Ferro laughed briefly. "I thought that might get your attention. Weren't you supposed to call me last Friday?"

"Shit, yeah. Sorry. Had a lot going on." A bit of a white lie.

In truth she'd been persuaded not to by Adam. After discussing with him what Ferro had told her on the train – about Edward IV and the Princes in the Tower – Adam fired off a load of technobabble about the physical impossibilities of time travel, arguing that while Ferro himself might be for real, the evidence he'd found was most likely a collection of hoaxes. Having seen some of the evidence herself, Jennifer wasn't entirely sure she agreed, but Adam's arguments were enough to persuade her that these unlikely stories about time travellers hundreds of years ago probably weren't worth getting sucked into.

Now Ferro was saying that time travellers killed Princess Diana. That changed everything.

"So – Diana," Jennifer said. "Is this woman legit? The one who saw the man in the woods?"

"I believe so," said Ferro. "She has nothing to gain from lying to me, particularly as she won't let me publish her name. What do *you* make of it?

A good question. What did she make of it? She hesitated before answering, "Well, I'd need to know exactly what she said. But if she really is legit, this is huge. A game changer for sure."

"Okay. Well I have a recording of our meeting. Would you like to hear it?"

"Definitely!"

Jennifer could hear the smile in Ferro's voice. "Great. Are you free tonight?"

She remembered her drinks plans with Adam, but they weren't till eight. "I have a bit of time tonight, yeah. Meeting a friend at eight."

"Okay. Do you want to come to mine? I have your number now, I can text you my address."

She remembered that he lived in Norton Hill, which if memory served was only about half an hour from Reading. "Sure. I finish work at half five, so I'll come straight from here. Should take about half an hour, depending where you are in Norton Hill – and traffic."

"Wonderful. See you then."

"Cool. Bye!"

Jennifer glanced at the clock on her phone as she hung up. Time was getting on – she needed to get back to the office or else face the wrath of her overlords, ahem, *employers*.

Heading back, she felt her phone buzz. It was Ferro. 12 Cavalier Road, Norton Hill, DP13 7RS. See you later.

She got back to the office with three minutes to spare – just enough to brew herself a coffee.

As soon as she'd sat down at her desk, Hitler approached her.

"Jennifer, I need you to proofread this document," she said, laying a slim bundle of papers on the desk. "It is a business purchase agreement. Our client is a small technology company called Cyberware, which is being bought out by Million Eyes."

Of course it was. Million Eyes were basically taking over the world, absorbing every competitor – big and small – into their vast empire.

"It's all finalised," said Hitler. "I just need a second pair of eyes on it before our client signs it. Please try and be more thorough than you were last time."

Because of one missing comma Jennifer failed to notice last week. The condescending cow.

Alison Fawke shot Jennifer an awkward glance. Hitler's comment was – of course – in earshot of everyone in the open-plan office. Jennifer smiled uneasily, "Yes, will do."

"And before you do that, tidy up your desk. You might choose to live in a pigsty, but I don't want you turning our office into one."

Wow. Jennifer's desk had three piles of papers, neatly stacked, one client file, a textbook, a document she was working on earlier and yesterday's mug, which she hadn't yet taken to the kitchen. If this was a pigsty, Hitler would've had a heart attack at the sight of Jennifer's bedroom.

"Yes, sorry, I'll do that," said Jennifer, feeling her cheeks redden. The temptation to throw coffee in Hitler's face was huge. She resisted.

"Good. And don't dawdle. I want to get that agreement over to the client in an hour for signing." Hitler strutted back to her OCD-immaculate office.

The money's good, the money's good, the money's good, Jennifer reminded herself throughout the afternoon.

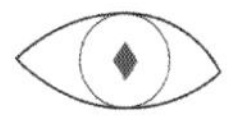

At half five Jennifer was out the door, pretending not to hear Hitler's disapproving tut as she breezed past her. She got in the car and popped Ferro's postcode into Google Maps. She wasn't worrying about dinner; she'd just grab something at the pub with Adam.

She got stuck in the usual traffic before snailing behind a tractor for five minutes thinking, these really should be banned from being on the roads during rush hour, or maybe just banned full stop. At 6.16pm she pulled into Cavalier Road. Ferro's house was about three hundred yards up. She saw only one car on his large driveway and space for her to park next to or behind it, but his wife and kids could've had cars (she wasn't sure how old Ferro was, but presumed his kids were grown-up), so Jennifer just parked on the road.

She took in the house as she walked up the driveway. A decent size, detached and Victorian – bay windows, patterned bricks, dormers and a gable-roofed porch. Nice. She wasn't really sure what she was expecting, but somehow it seemed to fit.

She knocked on the smartly painted front door.

"Hello, Jennifer," said Ferro as he opened the door, his unfetching cardigan and old man slippers making him look more grandfatherly than normal.

"Hi," she replied. "You alright?"

He nodded and welcomed her inside. She took off her shoes in the large hallway, noting only one pair of shoes on the mat and one coat hanging on the coat rack.

His wife and kids must've been out.

Ferro showed her into the lounge. It all seemed fairly pleasant and normal-looking. Floral wallpaper a bit dated. Sofas a bit worn. The room was dotted with photos of Ferro and his family. He had a boy and a girl, both teenagers. The boy looked about sixteen, seventeen, the girl a bit younger.

The room was pretty tidy apart from the papers, folders and a stationery box covering the coffee table, plus a dictation machine on top of one of the piles. Ferro motioned for her to take a seat and offered her a cup of tea or coffee. She said no.

He disappeared into the kitchen for a minute to pour himself one. She suspected it was peppermint again when he came back in and she glimpsed the yellowy liquid in his cup. Jennifer hated herbal teas. English breakfast all the way.

Ferro sat in the armchair close to the coffee table so he could handle the papers.

"Your wife and kids not in?" said Jennifer.

"No," said Ferro, a tad sharply.

She couldn't help herself – she wanted to know where they were. "Oh, okay. What are they up to?"

Ferro raised an eyebrow. "Er – that's not really any of your business."

Shit – she'd touched a nerve. "God, I'm sorry, you're right. It's none of my business. Sorry for prying." Then, realising what she'd said, "And sorry for saying 'God'."

Ferro sighed, a faint smile appearing and disappearing on his lips. With a long blink and a shake of the head he said, "No. I'm sorry," then admitting, to Jennifer's surprise, "My wife is divorcing me. She and the kids have moved out. It's still a little raw at the moment. I don't mean to take it out on you."

Jennifer could see the pain in his eyes as he said it. "Honestly, don't mention it. I… I'm sorry about your family." She wasn't sure what else to say. His honesty had caught her off-guard.

"It's my fault," said Ferro. "Too busy chasing these bloody time travellers."

It was the way he said it. It told Jennifer he didn't actually *want* to be chasing them. Rather, he felt he had no choice. And from the sounds of it, he was regretting ever finding out what he had.

"Maybe when you prove that these time travellers are real, they'll come round." Jennifer was just trying to make him feel better, but probably shouldn't have used the word *when*. She wasn't quite there yet.

"I don't think so," Ferro murmured sadly, staring off into space. A moment later, he shook his head like he was flicking away the pain and said, "Anyway. Princess Diana. Let's talk about her."

Jennifer smiled. "Yes, let's."

"So on Monday I met a woman called Sophie Rousseau

who claims to have seen someone disposing a white Fiat Uno in the woods on the night Diana was killed. I made a recording of our conversation, as I mentioned. Do you want me to play it?"

"Absolutely."

Ferro pressed play on the dictation machine on the coffee table.

Jennifer listened to him and a woman he identified at the start as Sophie Rousseau, clearly French from the sound of her accent, talking about the night of Princess Diana's death. Sophie was walking her dog in the woods in a town called Lagny-en-Brie at about 1.30am and saw a heavily built man in a dark suit standing next to a white Fiat Uno. He was on the phone to a woman he kept calling 'ma'am', and Sophie remembered him saying "the book is destroyed" and "can no longer harm us."

After Diana's death, forensics found white paint scratches on her Mercedes and bits of broken tail light on the road near the crash site. They determined that the paint and the tail light had come from a Fiat Uno, but it was never traced and the driver never came forward. Sophie said that the Uno she saw had black scratches on its passenger side and a broken tail light, which was why she believed it to be the one involved in the crash, the one that many people thought was used to block the road in front of Diana's Mercedes, causing it to swerve and crash in the Pont de l'Alma tunnel.

Sophie said that after his phone call, the man doused the car in some kind of strange liquid and torched it. Apparently the fire was green, like nothing she'd seen before, and appeared to dissolve the car until there was nothing left. She then watched him take a pill she thought was medication, but instead caused him to disappear right in front of her in a blinding but fleeting burst of light.

Ferro asked why Sophie didn't come forward at the time. She said it wasn't until she heard about the involvement of a white Fiat Uno in Diana's crash that she realised the implications of what she'd seen, and that she was too scared of going to the authorities because of all the people saying that MI5 or the Royal Family had orchestrated Diana's murder. She didn't want to become a target. When she read Ferro's blog, she realised how huge the conspiracy really was and decided it was high time she talked to someone.

Sophie certainly didn't sound like she was lying. That said, many liars and loons didn't.

"So there you have it," said Ferro after the recording ended. "Thoughts?"

Jennifer blew a sigh, unsure how to respond. "I… I don't really know, to be honest. It sounds just crazy."

"Yes. It does." He handed her a folder. "Here. These are the materials I showed you at the pub, in case you want to have another look. The copies of Sir Lionel Frensham's journal are in there too."

Jennifer leafed through them, turning first to Frensham's journal, which she'd not had time to look at properly that night she met Ferro on the train. She read Frensham's description of Edward IV's bloody confrontation with a man after a 'book', the pot of red pills Frensham found in the man's hand, the mysterious package Frensham delivered to Edward V, the older Prince in the Tower, a year later. Then she reread Purkis's deathbed confession, Simon of Stonebury's description of the book-seeking plague doctor rumour, and Edith Starkey's elaboration on the rumour and description of the 'Godfrey letter', which revealed the name of the book as *The History of Computer-Aided Timetabling for Railway Systems* by Jeremy Jennings – a book that didn't exist when Starkey was writing about it. It was the piece of evidence that had stumped Jennifer more than anything else.

Jennifer had to admit, Ferro was onto something here. These weren't just coincidences, *couldn't* be. There were just too many of them. A collection of hoaxes? That was unlikely too. It would require a bunch of different people, centuries apart, with no obvious connection to each other, to have concocted the same story.

She couldn't believe she was actually thinking this, but she was – time travel was starting to look more plausible.

"Did you find out anything more about this book – *The History of Computer-Aided Timetabling for Railway Systems*?" Jennifer asked.

Ferro perched on the edge of his chair and leaned forwards, opening the stationery box that was on the opposite side of the coffee table. He lifted out a stack of papers scrawled with lists of words, letters and numbers along with diagrams trying to link them all together – he'd been doing some code-breaking, it looked like. Underneath was a small hardbound book with a gold-tooled title, the only thing on the green cloth cover. Ferro handed it to Jennifer.

There it was. The most boring-looking-and-sounding book she'd ever seen. Jennifer opened it, scanned the opening pages, in particular the publication information on the copyright page.

Published in Great Britain in 1995 by Bradley & May. First edition. © Jeremy Jennings 1995.

"It's an interesting read," said Ferro.

Jennifer looked up, disbelieving eyebrows prodding her forehead. Ferro had a slight smirk.

"I'm joking," he said. "It's the dullest book I've ever read. As it sounds, it's everything nobody wanted to know about the development of computer-aided timetabling for railways, written with all the personality of a houseplant."

Jennifer chuckled. She continued flicking through it. The chapters were long, the paragraphs thick, the words tiny. "If this really is the book these time travellers have been chasing, do you think they're just worried about people in the past having information about the future? About railways and computers, things that don't exist yet?"

"I don't know. But would they really go so far as to kill people, including important historical figures, over a book about railways and computers? Plus, in the 1100s everybody in England spoke Old English or Norman French or Latin. Nobody then would understand a word of something written in Modern English. By the 1400s they were speaking Middle English so they might be able to make out some of it, but they're not going to have a clue what a computer or a train is."

"Mmmm. You're right. And if it's to do with future tech, how does Princess Diana factor in? She was killed *after* the book came out."

"Exactly. Wouldn't make sense. I wonder if there's more to this book than we realise."

Jennifer glanced at Ferro's attempts at code-breaking. "I

take it you've been looking for secret messages in the text?"

Ferro sipped his tea. "I have, but I've not found any. Not that I'm an expert, mind you. I bought another copy of the book – last one left on Ebay – and sent it off to a friend of mine who's a cryptographer. If anyone can crack its code – if there is one – she can."

Jennifer shut the book. "What about the author, Jeremy Jennings? Have you looked into him?"

"One of the first things I did. But he's dead. And there's very little information about him on the internet."

"The publisher, Bradley & May?"

"Yep. Nothing on them either, only that they closed down in 1999. I also looked into Edith Starkey, since *Secrets of the Great Pestilence* is currently the only source I have linking the time travellers to Jeremy Jennings' book. I literally can't find *anything* on her. I don't even know if "Edith Starkey" is her real name. No other books have been published under that name. And just like with Jennings' book, the publishers of *Secrets of the Great Pestilence* no longer exist."

"So you're at a dead end."

Ferro sighed. "Yes, sadly."

"Still, there's got to be a shit-ton of stuff on Princess Diana's death out there. Maybe they'll be some mention of this book?"

Ferro nodded, "That's what I'm hoping for. I have a lot more to go through yet. I'm still looking for references to this package Frensham talks about in his journal. Next I have some books on Diana's death to go through."

Jennifer hesitated for a moment, wondering if she might regret what she was about to say. *Fuck it*, she decided. It wasn't as if she had more important things going on in her life right now. "Is there anything I can do to, you know… help?"

Ferro's eyes widened. "Really?"

Jennifer swallowed. "Really."

Ferro stood up and walked over to the bay window. Hands behind his back, he stared out at the night-darkened street, deep in thought.

"There is, actually," he said, turning round.

Oh God – what is it?

"You can say no."

Will I want *to say no?* "What is it?"

"Well I've been thinking about going to this town – Lagny-en-Brie, near Paris – where Sophie Rousseau saw the man and the Fiat Uno. I thought I would go and do a little investigating, see if I can find some evidence of what happened there, maybe collect some specimens for testing. I also thought I'd knock on some doors in the area, see if anyone else knows anything. You could come with me… if you want."

Jennifer thought about this for a moment. A jaunt to France to hunt for Princess Diana-murdering time travellers was not your everyday travel invitation.

"You know what – why not," she said. "We can pretend we're Mulder and Scully." She thought immediately – *which is apt because Scully's the sceptic who has to rein in Mulder's flights of fancy.*

"Great," said Ferro, smiling. "Well, money's a bit tight right now so I won't be able to book anything for a couple of weeks. But as soon as I'm in a position to, I'll give you a call."

"Sounds good to me."

"And if you happen to change your mind in that time, that's fine too. There's no pressure. I just thought two heads might be better than one."

"No worries." Jennifer checked her watch – it was nearly twenty past seven. She was cutting it fine to meet Adam at eight. "Shit. I better get going or I'm gonna be late." She stood up and got ready to leave.

"Yes, of course. You're meeting a friend, aren't you." Ferro showed her out. "Thank you for coming round, Jennifer. And for… listening."

"Don't mention it," Jennifer said, and did a fast walk to her car.

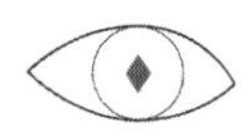

Robert Skinner sat in a tinted-windowed black Lexus opposite Gregory Ferro's house, Ferro and Jennifer Larson's conversations flowing crisply into his earpiece. As Larson prepared to leave, Skinner texted his wife, Karen. Think I might be late home tonight, babe. There's a security incident I need to deal with.

It wasn't a lie, but it may as well have been, since he knew Karen would be imagining him behind a computer, inputting and analysing data. She had no idea what his work for the Information Security Department actually entailed.

Karen texted back. Okay. I'll save you some ravioli.

Thanks. Love you. Give the girls a kiss for me.

Larson made a hurried exit and Skinner rang his CEO, Erica Morgan. Normally she wouldn't get involved in something like this, but as soon as Ferro started looking into Princess Diana, Miss Morgan decided to personally oversee the operation.

Skinner didn't like this one bit. He was much happier dealing with the head of Information Security, Pete Navarro. And it wasn't just that Miss Morgan was the CEO, or that she was uncompromising and quick to anger like many CEOs were. It was something else. In all the years Miss Morgan had worked for the company, nobody had learned anything about her, not really. And Skinner had always thought there was something *empty* about her – like you could stab a puppy in front of her and she wouldn't bat an eyelid. She was probably a sociopath, although perhaps she needed to be, given her position. And maybe Skinner was just being a pussy.

"Yes, Mr Skinner?"

"Miss Morgan, Gregory Ferro just met with the Larson girl again. He played her the recording of his meeting with Sophie Rousseau. She's come round to his theories – I think she's going to start helping him. They're planning a trip to France to find evidence of the Fiat Uno involved in Diana's crash."

Skinner heard the clank of a china mug slamming against a coaster. "I've already let this go too far. If those two dig any deeper, we're in real danger of being compromised."

"What do you want me to do?"

Miss Morgan let out a low, ragged breath. Skinner heard rustling and crinkling and the metallic twang of a lighter. Familiar sounds. Miss Morgan was a chain-smoker.

"Kill Ferro," she said finally, her command falling effortlessly off a deep inhalation. "Kill him and destroy his research."

"And Larson?"

"Kill her too."

11

July 7th 1483

In a few short months Richard Plantagenet had gone from Duke of Gloucester to Lord Protector of the Realm to King of England. His power had been cemented by a glorious coronation ceremony at Westminster Abbey and though his road to the throne had been long, bloody and at times underhand, he was finally at the end of it, about to start a new one. One, he hoped, with a little less death on it.

The morning after his coronation, Richard awoke to find cloudless skies outside his window and fragrant summer air wafting into his bedchamber. Moments later, his queen, Anne Neville, stirred.

He gazed at her. She really was perfect. Could a man like him be this lucky?

Anne said nothing, just smiled, lust in her eyes, which seemed as blue as the sky. She placed his crown back on his head and climbed on top of him for a repeat of last night, and was again the untamed animal that exhilarated him so.

But, in the middle of their lovemaking, Richard found his mind wandering. He kept thinking about his crown, how he wasn't used to it being there, and wasn't sure he liked it. It was heavier than he'd expected it to be. He remembered the ache in his neck yesterday after he'd been wearing it all day. Now that ache was back and he couldn't help but wonder if the Lord was trying to tell him something. Namely, that his crown was only as heavy as the price paid by others for him to wear it.

Richard couldn't believe the Lord was punishing him, though. That wouldn't make sense. The Lord wanted this. The Lord put him here.

Didn't He?

As soon as they'd finished, they untangled themselves from the sweaty bed sheets, breathless, hearts pounding. And as Anne leaned on Richard's chest, brushing her fingertips across the jewels in his crown, gazing into his eyes, he found himself questioning even her love for him, too. That is, how a woman as perfect as she could be in love with a man with so much blood on his hands the skin was stained red.

Why was he so full of doubts this morning? Perhaps it was all the wine from last night; it had certainly left his head woolly.

Still, he was compelled to ask, "Do you truly love me, Anne?"

"A foolish question," Anne said, dabbing the glistening sweat on her cheeks and forehead with her spindly fingers. "You know I do."

"In spite of what I have done? All the things I have done to be able to wear this crown?"

"My king, I do not love you in spite of them. I love you *for* them." She leaned closer to his face, kissing his cheek and then his lips. "I married you because you have what I look for in a man: ambition, strength, ruthlessness."

"I fear – maybe too much."

"You can never have too much of those things. But compassion – you *can* have too much of that. Compassion is what threatens to lead you astray, my king. You must remember to vanquish such feelings as soon as they emerge. Clean hands may as well be cut off."

So she liked his stained hands. Good. Still, when were they too red even for her?

"But Anne, when is it too much? How far is too far? If the people knew what I had done, they would turn against me in a moment. I would go down in history as England's most despised king."

"Your Grace, do not speak such folly. The people are sheep. Helpless, feeble-minded sheep. They need a strong guiding hand and you are it. You are their shepherd."

"Only because I have cheated them. Because I have murdered my own brothers. Imprisoned both my nephews and used false pretences to rescind their claims to the throne. Because I have permanently silenced all their guardians and allies. Lies, deceit and bloodshed are how I won England's throne."

"Enough!" She slapped his face. Her lips were clenched, her eyes inflamed.

Please don't be angry. Richard felt his eyes water. He reached to cover his stinging cheek with his palm.

"Do not become weak and pathetic now," said Anne, her voice as sharp as his arming sword. "I will not allow it. Everything we have done has been for the good of this country and you know it. Your brother George was an imbecile. Your brother Edward was an ailing, ineffectual king – a puppet of those insidious Woodvilles – and his sons are cut from the same stone. This country needs rulers who are strong if the wars that so burdened the beginning of your brother's reign are to be prevented from reigniting. The white rose of York must continue to flourish. The red rose of Lancaster must never bloom again."

"You are right, my love," Richard whispered. He remembered why she was so important to him – she always knew how to allay the confusion in his head. "I apologise. Unreservedly. I fear my conscience sometimes betrays my logic."

Anne, even as she lay naked in bed, breasts exposed and hair in disarray, was the embodiment of confidence. "Do not let it. You should refrain from looking inward for advice. You have me for that. And I have some for you now."

"What advice is that, my queen?"

"Your task is not yet complete. You have the crown of England, but it does not sit securely on your head while your nephews remain in the Tower. We may have convinced Parliament to declare them bastards, but those boys will remain a threat to you as long as they are alive. Your enemies will use them as a cause for rebellion and fight in their names."

He paused and looked deep into her eyes. He knew what she was saying, but couldn't bring himself to think it, so he asked her anyway, "Anne, what is it you're suggesting?"

"Fool!" She slapped him again, harder. "My words could not be plainer. If you do not have those boys killed, our crowns could be taken from us. Do you want that? I know that I am not prepared to lose mine."

Richard's cheek throbbed and his lips quivered. He felt winded, more by her words than her strike. He had hoped he'd reached the end of his bloody road to the throne. But Anne was right. There was another mile to go. He shook his head, saying, "It must be the air this morning. You are right, of course. I will make certain that neither of us lose the crowns we have fought so hard for."

"Good." Her glare thawed to a soft smile. She leaned towards his face, nipples grazing the matted black hairs on his chest, and kissed him softly on the lips. "Forgive my outburst, Your Grace. I live to serve. I dreamed of us in the small hours and I fear it has only intensified my passion."

"Tell me."

"I dreamed that we had been king and queen of England for many peaceful, prosperous years. Our faces were lined and jaded, our hair grey, and we died in each other's arms, of old age, beneath a starry sky. Weary but content. My king, I am certain that it was a vision. A message from God that our reign shall be long and distinguished. Perhaps the most illustrious that the kingdom of England has ever seen. We have to make sure that we do not stray from the path God has laid for us."

It was strange that Richard's dreams were quite the opposite. He'd thought since he was a boy that he would meet a grisly fate at a young age on the battlefield. But then he trusted his queen implicitly. The moment she said it, he knew her vision was real and his own doubts and fears were mere tricks of the Devil.

He could see quite clearly now that this *was* God's plan. And the next stage of that plan – as distasteful as it was – was to dispose of his two nephews in the Tower.

"I love you, Anne," he whispered, wrapping his queen in his arms. "The princes will die today."

12

October 23rd 2019

After Jennifer left, Ferro went into the kitchen to make another cup of peppermint tea, excited to have found a companion in his, thus far, lonely quest. And even though he had no money to book anything yet, he was going to start planning their trip to Lagny-en-Brie, working on the assumption that Jennifer wasn't going to change her mind.

Damn. No teabags. He needed his last one of the day or he wouldn't sleep. Sanjay's would still be open. He'd pop in there.

He threw on his coat and shoes and headed up the road. Sanjay was in the process of closing early – his daughter wasn't well – but he was kind enough to let Ferro buy his teabags first, particularly as Ferro was not just a customer of late but an employee as well.

Walking back, Ferro noted the stillness of Cavalier Road. It was often like this. Peaceful. It was probably because most of the residents were retirees.

But the stillness meant he could hear everything – including, as he neared his house, the very faint crunch of footsteps that weren't his.

He stopped and turned around. The sound had come from behind him, but there was no one there.

Did he imagine it?

He glanced in all directions. Nothing and no one. Maybe it was just the trees. He continued on to his house.

He went inside, reboiled the kettle and brewed himself a cup.

Planning to spend a few more hours in his study before bed, he piled all the materials he'd gone through with

Jennifer into his arms and switched off the downstairs lights.

It was as he turned off the lamp in the dining room that he caught a flicker of movement through the French doors to the garden. He walked over to them and looked out.

The garden was dark and still. Probably just next door's cat again.

He shivered. For some reason he felt on edge tonight.

He took his tea and research materials upstairs to his study, where ordered chaos reigned. Books, printouts, photocopies, translations, maps, diagrams, handwritten notes, post-its and stationery were everywhere, like a burglar had ransacked the place searching for something. Still, Ferro liked it that way. As much as it didn't look like it, he knew where everything was. And this way, he had everything to hand. If he started filing away notes, papers and books into drawers, vital pieces of the jigsaw he was assembling might fall away, forgotten.

The moment he sat down to start planning his trip to Lagny-en-Brie, his phone rang, and he was hit by a twinge of hope that it was Beth calling to say she wanted to cancel the divorce proceedings and come home.

He felt that twinge of hope every time it rang, but, to be honest, it was getting weaker. He had (reluctantly) acknowledged receipt of the divorce petition within the seven days stipulated. He'd hoped she might withdraw the petition before that, but she didn't. And she still wouldn't speak to him. Not properly. Not unless it was to do with Maggie and Ryan, or via solicitors. She seemed to have no desire to entertain the prospect of a friendship with him. Admittedly, things hadn't been right between them for some time, but were twenty-three years of marriage not worth *anything*?

He looked at his phone's touchscreen. *Private number calling.* He answered with a tentative, "Hello?"

"Is… is this Gregory Ferro?"

His heart sank. It was a man's voice, slightly muffled. One he didn't recognise. "Yes. Who's this?"

"I – I need to tell you…" The man was slurring and breathing heavily, his words trailing off.

"Yes?"

"It's about… about the people I work for. I've learned… things."

Ferro repeated, "Who is this?"

"You need to know. Everybody needs to know." The caller paused, swallowed and took another deep breath. "Mr Ferro, the people I work for… are the people you're looking for."

This astonishing phone call lasted three and a half minutes. Afterwards Ferro stood motionless in the middle of his study, not sure what to do, what to think.

Jennifer.

He searched his contacts for Jennifer's number and called her.

Damn. She wasn't answering. It rang eight times and went to voicemail, so he left her a message telling her everything.

A door creaked downstairs. Ferro stopped mid-sentence, froze.

It must've been the dining room door. It was the only one with squeaky hinges. Ferro had been meaning to put some WD-40 on them for months, just hadn't got around to it.

A draught? But there were no windows open. It was October.

Ferro turned out of his study onto the landing. He stood at the top of the stairs, looked down at his dark hallway for any sign of movement in the shadows.

"H-hello? Is… someone there?"

No answer. Ferro started down the stairs, slowly, left hand squeezing the banister, right hand holding his phone, voicemail still recording.

"Beth, is that you? Maggie? Ryan?" They were the only ones with keys.

The moment he was down, he switched on the hallway light. No one there. The dining room door was half-open. As he'd left it. As he *thought* he'd left it. He went in, switched on the light, glanced around. He did the same in the kitchen.

Then he entered the lounge. The bright light from the other rooms had already thinned the darkness and Ferro could see, reflected dimly in the black of the TV screen, the broad silhouette of an uninvited guest standing a couple of metres behind him.

Ferro lifted his phone to his ear, eyes locked on the silhouette.

A shadowy arm rose.

Ferro swallowed, whispered fast into the phone, "Jennifer, they know."

A bolt of green light surged across the room and something hard and heavy slammed into his back. The agony ripped through him and was gone, replaced almost instantly by numbness and a faint sense that he was falling.

But that too only lasted a moment.

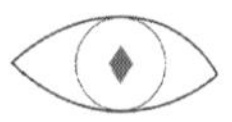

Ferro fell forwards, dropping his phone, which skimmed across the hardwood floor. The dead weight of his body smashed into the coffee table, which collapsed in a small explosion of snapping wood. He came to settle on his back at the foot of his armchair, face stuck in a wide-eyed look of shock.

Robert Skinner holstered his disruptor. One down, one to go. He took out his phone and called Miss Morgan.

Her silky voice shivered down the phone, "Is it done, Mr Skinner?"

"Gregory Ferro's dead. I'm about to destroy his research and go after Larson."

"So you've done *half* of what I asked you to do. And you're ringing me for… what? Words of encouragement?"

"N-no, ma'am." Skinner felt his cheeks redden. He should've been more direct. "There's something else. Ferro just left Larson a voicemail, telling her all about us."

"What? How did he know?"

Skinner had wiretapped Ferro's phone, too. He'd heard everything but it had taken him a few minutes to disable Ferro's burglar alarm and get into the house – by the time he had, Ferro was already spilling the beans to Jennifer. "One of ours, ma'am. Stuart Rayburn. He didn't give his name but I recognised the voice. Somehow he obtained information way above his clearance level and decided to tell Ferro everything, including about our role in Princess Diana's death."

The sound of glass smashing against a wall made Skinner wince. Miss Morgan returned to the phone a few moments later, her voice low, rippling with barely suppressed fury, "Stuart Rayburn will be dealt with. You need to hurry. Find Larson before anyone else hears that voicemail."

"Yes, ma'am. I'll take care of it."

Miss Morgan hung up. Skinner picked up his bottle of paraffin, launched upstairs to Ferro's study and poured two thirds of the bottle over his desk and computer, plus a few splashes over the carpet. He took a box of matches from his pocket, struck one and threw it onto the desk. A blast of heat hit Skinner's face as a blanket of roaring flames instantly draped itself across the desk, ferociously devouring Ferro's research. Skinner backed out of the study as the computer started hissing and crackling, flames leaping excitedly onto the carpet and curtains and scrabbling towards the door.

Skinner hurried downstairs and used the last third of the paraffin on three blankets in the lounge, igniting them and throwing them into different corners of the room. The fringe of one blanket landed on Ferro's leg. A procession of blue flames danced up his trousers, turning orange as they burned into the material. Skinner glanced at the three pillars of fire burgeoning from the corners of the room before turning out of the lounge, into the dining room, and slinking out of the house through the French doors.

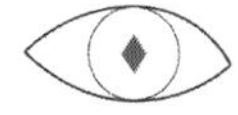

Arriving ten minutes late, Jennifer sat down with Adam in the garden of the Kipper and the Corpse. Adam was still wedded to his fag habit, which was why they were in the garden in October. Fortunately the pub had outdoor heaters.

"Sorry I'm late," said Jennifer. "I kinda met up with Gregory Ferro again."

"What?" said Adam, screwing up his face and nearly choking on his cigarette. "Why?"

Jennifer sipped her cider. "In all seriousness I think he's onto something."

"Wait. So you actually think time travellers are messing about with history in pursuit of some book about railways?"

"As wacky as it sounds, yeah, I'm starting to. The evidence is pretty compelling when you look at all of it together."

Adam stared at her, wide-eyed and silent.

"What?" said Jennifer.

Adam's silence broke to, "Seriously?"

"Yes."

He frowned. "*Seriously,* though."

"Yes!"

Adam sighed and sipped his Guinness. "Next you'll be thinking the Royal Family's a bunch of alien lizards."

Jennifer cocked her left eyebrow, smirking, "They are."

Her phone buzzed in her pocket. She took it out.

A message from who? Fabienne? And that wasn't her wallpaper. It was a picture of Tom, her sister's boyfriend.

"Fuck balls, I picked up Jamie's phone," Jennifer said. She remembered now. It was on the kitchen table. Jamie was in there in cooking pasta. In a rush, Jennifer just grabbed it, but now she suspected that hers was still in her work trousers, strewn across her bed. They both had the same phone and same-colour case – she'd told Jamie not to get the same case as her.

Jennifer sighed. "Sorry, mate," she said to Adam. "I'm gonna have to run back home."

"Oh, what? You need your phone that bad?"

"*I* don't, no. But Jamie will whinge and whine at me for a week, particularly if, heaven forbid, Tom tries to call her while I've got her phone."

"Fine." Adam hated sitting in pubs on his own. Always said he got funny looks from everyone, but Jennifer was convinced that was him being paranoid.

"Really sorry. Be back as quick as I can."

"I'll look after your pint."

"Thanks."

Jennifer launched out of the pub garden's outdoor gate and sprinted down the road.

After a few minutes, she crossed to head down Witney Lane, the residential road that led to The Birches and her house.

Tyres screamed. An engine roared.

What?

She'd thought the road was clear.

She spun towards the roaring engine, but didn't see a car. Only headlights.

Thwack.

The car's front bumper took out her legs and tossed her in the air like a doll. She slammed against the bonnet, hard and cold, the *crack* of her own body ripping through her.

It was the most pain she'd ever felt – and then there was no pain at all.

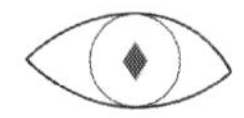

The thumping of Jennifer Larson's body as she tumbled over the bonnet and windscreen of his Lexus reminded Skinner of when he killed that deer a few years back. He rammed his feet against the brakes, skidding for several yards.

There was very little time and he needed to avoid being seen. He dived out of the car and rushed over to where Larson's body was sprawled face-down in the road. He checked her neck for a pulse – nothing. Then he shoved his hands into the pockets of her bloodied jeans and yanked out her phone. In order to ensure that no one would hear the voicemail Ferro had left for her, he shot the phone with a narrow beam from his disruptor and kicked the scorched, broken pieces into a nearby drain.

Then he hurried back to his car and drove away.

13

July 7th 1483

Standing tall and proud on the north bank of the River Thames was England's great bastion of royal authority: the Tower of London. Despite its name it was not one building but many, circled by two fortified curtain walls and a deep moat. At its heart was the huge, square White Tower, the original Norman keep built by William the Conqueror, with ninety-foot walls of whitewashed Kentish rag-stone defended on the corners by three square towers and one round one.

Majestic and intimidating to all who saw it, the Tower of London doubled as a royal residence and a prison. For Richard III's nephews, twelve-year-old Edward and nine-year-old Richard, it was supposed to be the former, but each day felt more and more like the latter.

The boys had recently been moved from their royal lodgings in the White Tower to the Garden Tower, one of the mural towers along the inner curtain wall, close to the river. It overlooked the Constable's Garden where they played together, but now they weren't allowed out, and sentries kept watch at the entrance to the Garden Tower to make sure. For some time Edward had sensed that something was wrong. Although their uncle never visited, Edward had been assured by all the visitors they did have that he would be crowned on June 25th. Almost two weeks later, all of their visitors, including Edward's physician, Dr Argentine, had stopped coming – and still he had no crown.

On the morning of July 7th, Edward woke abruptly, rocking the bed he shared with his brother and striking the little table at his bedside with his arm. His cup fell off the table, landing with a clank, spilling water over the floor and startling

Richard awake.

"Brother!" Richard cried. "Are you all right?"

Edward lay back down, chest heaving, throat dry and sore. His pillow was sodden with sweat and cold against his head. "Just a nightmare," he replied. He couldn't even remember what it was about.

"You keep having them, don't you?" said Richard.

"Sometimes." An understatement. He'd been having recurring nightmares about horrible things happening to the two of them in the Tower, the kind that caused him to wake up in a panic. Most mornings he did remember them, though he always pretended he didn't for Richard's sake. This morning he appreciated the memory loss.

Edward tumbled out of bed, the stone floor like ice against his bare feet. He approached the mullioned window. Yellow sunlight poured through, painting hot gold bars on the opposite wall. In a few hours when the sun had moved, the room would be dark and chilly again. Edward looked out over a deathly quiet Water Lane, the thoroughfare in the outer ward that ran parallel with the Thames, and St Thomas's Tower – the castle's river entrance – directly opposite. The river wrinkled by beyond it, but the tower and the outer curtain wall blocked it from sight.

From the corner of his eye, Edward caught his brother's rapt stare in his direction. "Richard, what is it?" he asked.

"When do you think they are going to let us out of here?"

Edward faced his brother and shook his head, "I do not think they are."

"What? Why?"

"Come on, Richard. I know you are two years younger than me, but surely you cannot be blind to what is going on here."

"What do you mean?"

"Think about it. I am the king, or at least I am supposed to be. And yet I am confined to this room as though I have done something wrong. The people who bring us food are our only visitors, and they always come when we are asleep. It is as if Uncle Richard is pretending I do not exist. When he sent you here, brother, he said it was so you could keep me company. That is not the true reason. I think it was because, after me, *you* are next in line for the throne. And I think our power-hungry uncle wants the throne for himself."

"You mean, he put us here to get rid of us?"

"Yes. And I suspect he is not done yet."

"What does that mean?"

"Well, he can't leave us in here forever, can he? If he wants the throne, he is going to have to kill us."

"What? No! He can't!" Richard threw off his covers, leapt out of bed and hastened to the door. He shook the handle, pulled it, but the door was locked from the outside. Desperate, he pulled it again, harder, with more urgency, but the door barely moved, the lock banging defiantly. Richard shrank back, his whole body wilting in defeat.

"Richard, do not be disheartened," Edward said softly. "These past few days, I have been thinking. I have been thinking about something Father gave me. While I was at Ludlow Castle, Father sent me a package, shortly before he died, and there was a letter from him accompanying it."

"A package? You never told me. What was in it? What did the letter say?"

Edward walked over to the Gothic elm chest that housed their clothes. He opened the chest and dug past their garments to retrieve a leather satchel wrapped in a tunic at the bottom. He opened the satchel and pulled out two items – a little white pot with writing on it and a ragged-looking oak box with riveted iron bands that were scabbed with rust – and placed them on the table where they ate.

"What are those?" Richard asked.

Edward returned his hand inside the satchel, pulling out a large, folded sheet of parchment which he unfolded to read.

"Is that Father's letter?" said Richard.

"Yes. Let me read it to you. It will help you make sense of what I am about to show you."

Richard nodded and Edward started reading.

Edward, my dearest son and heir, if you are reading this now, the Lord God has answered my prayers and this package has reached you safely at Ludlow.

My son, please do not fear, but I am not long for this world and soon you will be made king. Your kingship is a gift I had not intended to bestow on you this early but if it is our Lord's will, so be it.

With kingship come fine rewards and weighty burdens. There is a burden I have been carrying that I must now pass to you. In the package you will find four objects. The first is a box, the second a key to opening it. The third you will find inside the box: a book, like none you have ever seen. For one it tells the future. Its pages predict a serious threat to the Crown and the Realm that will occur centuries from now. For another it yields a strange, unworldly power that has led prior custodians to name it the 'Impossible Book'. I call it the 'Book That Listens'.

In 1348, the book was given to my great-great-grandfather, Edward III, by Catherine Godfrey, the wife of a cordwainer. Catherine explained that it was given to her ancestor, Thomas Godfrey, by the chief minister to the Norman king William II, and that her family had been instructed by King William to keep it safe, hidden and secret. At the time London was ravaged by plague and Catherine decided that her family could no longer discharge the burden that King William had put upon them.

It is not clear where or when the Book That Listens originates, nor how it came to be in King William's possession. What is known is that King William had the box that houses it specially made to guard against its power.

Edward glanced at his brother. A deepening frown was on his brow. Edward could not blame him. He carried on.

Edward III kept the box with the Royal Treasure in the Tower of London and the key on his person. The kings that followed him were told of it and did the same. We all pledged to keep it safe.

The final object you will find in the package is a pot of unusual-looking red pills –

"Pills?" said Richard.

"Yes," said Edward, retrieving the pot from the table, lifting its lid and handing it to Richard.

Richard pinched a pill from the pot to look at it. "W-what are they?"

Edward held up their father's letter and resumed reading.

This is something that came into my possession last year. A man forced his way into my bedchamber and threatened to kill me if I did not surrender the book. I was able to overpower him and thrust my longsword into his back. As he lay dying he removed this pot of pills from inside his cloak. He opened it, took a pill and went to place it in his mouth. Before the pill touched his tongue, he was dead.

It is plain that the architects of the Book That Listens have powers beyond imagination. That is why I am certain that these strange little pills are enchanted. I have wondered if they possess the power to transport he who swallows them to another place and if the intruder meant to use them to escape.

After my encounter with him, I moved the book and the pills to a new hiding place here at Westminster. Unfortunately whatever is killing me is doing so with haste and, with you still at Ludlow, the book and the pills will soon be unguarded. Henceforth I have sent them to you there so that you can continue to keep them safe.

There is little time and much to do, so let me finish by saying that I love you. I know that you

> have been working hard at Ludlow and I am sorry that we have not been able to see each other more. I am making your uncle, Duke Richard, Lord Protector of the Realm until you come of age, and with you and your uncle together, I know that I leave England in good hands.
>
> Farewell, my son. Look after your brother, your mother and your sisters.
>
> Your adoring father and king.

Tears dangled on his brother's eyelashes. A couple fell. "I miss him," Richard said, sniffing.

"I know," whispered Edward, squeezing his brother's shoulder. "I do too."

"Father trusted Uncle Richard. That much is clear."

"Yes. He clearly did not know what Uncle Richard would do the moment his blood was cold."

Richard placed the pot of red pills on the table and picked up the box. "Can I see it?"

Edward tucked his hand into the collar of his nightshirt and unhooked a silver chain with a key from around his neck.

"You sleep with the key?" said Richard.

"Yes. Ever since I received the package."

He handed the key to his brother. Richard turned but Edward put his hand on his shoulder to stop him and warned, "Be careful, brother."

"Why?"

"Because walls do not have ears. But books do."

Edward released his shoulder. Face contorted in a deep, confused scowl, Richard sat down in his chair, the box in his lap, eased the key into the small, rickety lock and turned it, making a series of small clinking sounds. He opened it and lifted out the Book That Listens.

"*The History of Computer-Aided Timetabling for Railway Systems* by *Jeremy Jennings*. What in the world does that mean?"

"No one has been able to determine that yet."

Richard examined the cover, stroking his fingers over the dark green cloth binding. "What do you mean... *ears?* And why did Father call it the Book That Listens?"

Edward took the book, opened it to the last page of text, and handed it back to him.

Richard shot to his feet, the box tumbling off his lap onto the floor with a thud. "*What*?" He looked up at Edward, shaking his head with disbelief. "But… it can't be. How? How can it – ?"

Richard returned his eyes to the book and gasped. He threw it down on the bed in horror.

"No! I don't believe it. It's… impossible!"

"Yes, brother. Hence – *the impossible book*."

Richard sat down on his side of the bed, gripping the edge of the feather mattress with both hands, trying to get a handle on what he had just seen. A moment later, "Wait. Father also said it told the future. How? What future?"

Edward walked over to the bed and picked up the book. He opened it to the beginning and showed Richard. He saw the pallor in his brother's face thicken to that of a corpse as he read about *them*.

"I… I do not understand what this means."

"It means they are coming, brother. And we must play our part in stopping them."

"But they're not coming for centuries! What are we supposed to do?"

"Just as our predecessors have done. Protect the book, now the pills too. But Richard, there is another reason why I have chosen this morning to show you these things."

"What is it?"

"You heard what Father said in his letter about the pills. He thought they were enchanted and might present a means of escape. So what if we could use them to leave the Tower?"

Richard stood and gestured wildly with his arms, crying, "Father was speculating! He had no idea what the pills are capable of." Edward could tell by his brother's increasingly high pitch and animated delivery that he was becoming agitated.

Edward replied, calmly as he could, "You're right. We cannot presume to know what might happen if we swallowed one of these pills. But if our uncle means to do away with us, they could be our only chance."

Richard rasped, "Uncle Richard may yet let us go free."

"You keep believing that."

He folded his arms and sat back down. "Perhaps I will. You're not always right about everything, you know." He pulled a sullen, pouty face, the one he made when he took exception to his elder brother telling him what to do, and Edward half-expected his customary retort, 'You're not king yet, brother,' but Richard just sulked silently.

Edward decided not to push him. He hoped he'd instilled enough fear and uncertainty in Richard that he would come to the realisation on his own. He changed the subject, tried to talk to Richard about other things, but got little response.

Hours passed. Edward tried to read. Richard stared out of the window, his face drawn with worry. Every now and again, a tear rolled down his cheek. Eventually he lay down on the bed and slept, or tried to. He was so alone and Edward didn't know how to comfort him.

If only their mother were here. Richard really needed her, as did he.

Edward went to the window. The blue sky was darkening to a lavender-grey. Another night was drawing in. Another night stuck in this room. It had started to occur to Edward that the room was a little bit smaller each day, that the walls were closing in, an inch at a time.

Or perhaps he was losing his mind.

His belly made a noise. He was hungry. The paltry amount of bread and fruit left inside their doorway each day was never enough.

For a moment, he contemplated an alternative getaway. In the small hours someone would come before either of them were awake, open their door and leave the food and a jug of water before closing and locking it again. If Edward resolved to stay awake, he could make a move when the food-bringer arrived. Spring for the open door, push the food-bringer down the stairs, breaking his or her neck, and then he and Richard could make a run for it.

But what if he failed? What if the food-bringer was a sentry, a huge tree of a man who could snap him and his brother like twigs?

As time wore on he couldn't shake the feeling that the next person to visit would not be a food-bringer anyway. He would be their killer.

It was while these thoughts lingered that the sound of a

door scraping open at the bottom of the tower startled both of them.

"Who's that?" Richard shrieked, leaping off the bed.

The night was young and neither of them were asleep. Couldn't have been their food-bringer.

The decision was made. "Come here now," Edward said. "We're doing this."

"But brother –"

"There's no time to argue. I'm your elder brother and you will do as I say." Edward had been trying to cut back on the bossiness, but this wasn't the moment to worry about appeasing his little brother. He needed to assert his authority – now.

"What if they're coming to let us out?"

Now the heavy stomp of approaching footsteps was throbbing through the walls.

"They're not."

Both of them were dressed, as they were every day, just in case they had a guest. All Edward needed was the satchel with the book, now locked away in its box again, and the pot of red pills. He grabbed the satchel and flung it over his shoulder, plunged his hand inside and pulled out the pot. Then he grabbed Richard's wrist and tipped a pill into his palm before tipping one into his own.

"We'll do it together on three," Edward said, immediately continuing, "One, two, three."

Though his eyes were glazed with uncertainty, Richard followed Edward's lead. In unison they placed the pills in their mouths. Edward swallowed. He saw the small undulation in Richard's throat as he did the same.

They stared at each other, waiting for something to happen. The stomping footsteps were now so close the visitor was a mere moment from being in the room with them.

But then…

A loud and constant humming sound buzzed through Edward's ears, like a hive of bees swarming around in his head. It drowned out everything else, including the footsteps. His brother looked confused and frightened. His mouth formed the word *brother* but any sound that came out was engulfed by the humming.

Dizzy, Edward felt his eyes fall shut in a slow blink. When

they reopened, the room was suddenly heaving with people. People that were hazy and transparent like ghosts. There were men, women, children and persons whose genders he couldn't easily discern. They were wearing the most peculiar of garments and were all around him, crossing the room, walking into each other, *through* each other. His eyes couldn't process it. If he'd tried to count, he could've counted hundreds, maybe thousands of people in their bedchamber all at once – except that that defied all manner of possibility.

He was dreaming. He must've been. Only in dreams could this kind of absurdity occur. He was obviously still ensnared inside the nightmare from this morning and none of this last day had really happened.

Light-headed, he was compelled to shut his eyes again.

He opened one a crack. Ghosts everywhere – still. And it wasn't just the people that were transparent. So were the walls. Edward could see through them, beyond them. The sky was visible through the ceiling. All the furniture was see-through. Their four-poster bed. Their chest of clothes. Their table and chairs. In front of him was a large burgundy leather chair he'd never seen before. And the ghosts walked straight through all the furniture just as easily as they walked through each other.

Were the princes dead? Had the red pills killed them? Was this... *Heaven*?

The humming persisted. Richard clasped his hand around Edward's wrist and squeezed. He was the only solid thing in the room.

Richard spoke again. This time Edward heard his voice, but only faintly. A soft murmur nearly lost in the whirr, "Edward, w-what's happening...?"

Edward couldn't feel the floor. He looked down to check it was still there. It was but it was see-through like everything else. Edward could see into the lower chamber, also flooded with ghosts in strange attire.

He blinked hard, shook his head, but nothing changed. He stepped forwards and found he could walk as normal, but it was as though his feet were numb or he was floating. He felt Richard's fingers slip off his wrist. He crossed the room, passing through – literally through – the ethereal figures that filled the space around him.

Edward floated towards the window and looked out. Water Lane was no longer deathly quiet. Well, not quiet anyway. It thronged with ghosts – hundreds of them – all blurred into one, so 'deathly' was actually quite apt. St Thomas's Tower and the outer curtain wall were still there, but they were transparent too. Edward could see the river, jammed with dozens of unusual phantom ships all passing at once.

A couple of people caught Edward's attention, running through Water Lane. Two ghostly soldiers in red tunics, armour and bronze helmets with neck and cheek guards and huge red crests, carrying red, half-cylindrical shields adorned with yellow painted lightning bolts and eagles' wings.

Romans? How could that be?

Then, beyond the curtain wall, a bizarre sort of carriage went past. Huge, red and rectangular, it rolled along the bank of the Thames on thick, black wheels, the passengers inside on two levels. But what was most disturbing was that the carriage was driving itself... Where in the world were the horses?

And then Edward noticed the dragons. Not that they looked like dragons, or at least how Edward imagined one. Huge, frightening creatures with dome-shaped bodies, stumpy legs, long, tapering necks and tails, small heads, and no wings, wading through the river.

This wasn't Heaven. This was Hell. But what had they done for the Lord to punish them like this?

Edward was about to pull away from the window, then his eyes were drawn to the spectre of a sad-looking woman in a broad, green gown and gold-trimmed bonnet. He concentrated his gaze. As he did, her ghost started to lose its transparency and become clear. The hundreds of ghosts in Edward's periphery appeared to be fading away as this woman and the people accompanying her looked as real and solid and tangible as he and his brother were.

Maintaining an unblinking stare, Edward watched her climb the slippery steps from the water gate beneath St Thomas's Tower, flanked by guards. Then she dropped to her knees at the top of the steps, sobbing. Her sobs began to pierce through the humming.

As a guard went to lift her to her feet, she snapped her head back, face fierce and wet with tears, and swiped his arm away, roaring, "Do not touch me!" The humming was low now and her voice was clear.

The same guard stooped to grab her arm again. This time he was able to hook his sizeable arm in hers before she could swipe it away, and haul her to her feet. "Please, milady," he said, "do not resist."

"*Milady?*" the woman screamed. "I am the queen. You will address me as Your Grace!"

The queen? Edward had never seen her before, and the only woman in the country who could lawfully call herself queen was his mother.

"Edward, what are you looking at?" Edward heard his brother's voice over the woman's protests. He turned his head. Richard had moved to the window and was standing next to him. When Edward returned his gaze to the woman, she was a transparent wraith again, blurring into the melee of people and creatures that overwhelmed the Tower and the river. And the humming was back.

If he focused on something, it became clear, while everything else started to fade away.

If he lost concentration, the chaos returned.

The key to their escape?

Edward faced his brother and took his hand. He was about to focus his gaze on one of the spiral-shaped walnut posts of their bed – something familiar – when something else drew his eye. A framed painting on the wall beside the bed. Like several other items in the room, he'd never seen it before.

Edward peered through the crowd of ghosts. Initially dim and transparent, the painting sharpened and the humming began to fade.

Two boys in black tunics and hose and gold livery collars, looking frightened and huddled together on a four-poster bed much like their own.

Lord have mercy. It's us.

Edward's stare persisted and before long, the painting of the two boys had solidified completely, the humming was gone, and the blur of people in Edward's periphery had fallen away.

Then everything turned white.

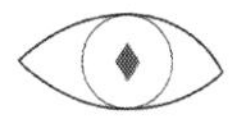

A burst of light flashed underneath the door to the princes' bedchamber just as two of Anne Neville's guards were unlocking it.

"What was that?" said the taller guard.

"No idea," said the shorter guard. "Just go in. Let's get this over with."

They opened the door to an empty room, silent as a crypt.

"What?" said the taller guard. "Were they moved to a different room?"

"No. Upper chamber of the Garden Tower. That's what the queen said."

They checked beneath the princes' bed. Nothing. They looked behind their clothes chest, then inside it, pulling out every garment in case either of the boys was hiding inside.

"Someone must've let them out," said the shorter guard.

"What are we going to tell Her Grace?"

"She'll blame us. I know what she's like. She wanted their hearts. She'll have our heads on spikes for this."

"What should we do?"

"Well I'm not losing *my* head, so we'll just have to find some alternative hearts."

"What if the princes come back?"

"If they know what's good for them, they won't. If they do, we'll finish the job."

14

October 24th 2019

A sliver of light. Jennifer's eyelids peeled open slowly, stiffly, like they'd been stuck down with glue. She felt an uncomfortable pull and tickle around them, but nothing else. She was a disembodied pair of eyes.

Her brain connected with the rest of her. She was lying on a bed with a thin cover draped over her. She still had limbs, still had a waist and back, still had fingers and toes. But everything hurt. Her head throbbed and spun. She felt bruised all over. She felt like she'd been at the gym and overdone it, seriously overdone it, so that all the muscles in her body, even the littlest ones, were torn. She shifted her head slightly. *Shit.* Her neck twinged and forced a low murmur from her lips.

"Jennifer?"

Eyes now open, the sliver of light had become a blur of different light sources, white and grey shapes, and eventually, when she gasped at the pain in her belly, a bit of a blurry face leaning into her periphery.

"Jen?"

The voice was miles away, echoing down a long tunnel, even though the person was next to her.

"She's waking up!"

The voice was nearer now. The person leaned over the left side of her bed, face now at the centre of her watery vision, but still a pinky blur, patchy with brown.

Jennifer's normally perfect eyesight began to return and she traced hazy but familiar lines and curves across the face. She knew who it was even before his green eyes, brown crew cut and designer stubble sharpened into view.

Adam.

"Kerry! Nurse!" he shouted. "She's waking up!"

"Jennifer?"

Jennifer heard her mother's voice and the familiar clack of her heels, getting louder till she was standing over her, gently stroking her face. "Jennifer, my darling, thank God."

A nurse was close behind – Jennifer could see him checking monitors and adjusting drip bags in the corner of her eye. He said to her mother, "If you could just step out of the way for a moment, ma'am." Mum stepped back.

"Miss Larson, can you hear me?" said the nurse, adjusting her drip bags.

"Y-yes, I can hear you," Jennifer croaked weakly.

The nurse leaned over her, smiling. His name was Tim, Jennifer could see from his name badge. "How are you feeling?"

"Been better."

"I'm sure. I'll go and get your doctor. She'll examine you and explain everything. Okay?"

"Yep. Sounds good."

As Tim left her bedside, Jamie arrived, clutching three small vending machine coffees. "Sis, you're awake!"

"Hey Jamie," Jennifer wheezed. She shifted her gaze to her mother. "What happened?"

"Just rest, darling," Mum said firmly. "We'll talk about it later."

"But – but how did I get here?"

Then came her motherly scold, "I said, rest. Let's wait until the doctor gets here. Alright? The main thing is, you're alive, you're safe and you're awake."

Last thing Jennifer remembered was heading to the pub to meet Adam; everything after that was hazy.

Dr Liz Royan arrived minutes later and examined her. While doing so, she explained that Jennifer had been in Deepwater Hospital since last night. She'd been in a road accident, but Dr Royan wasn't specific about what kind or what had happened. She'd suffered bruising, cuts and abrasions, two cracked ribs and some minor head trauma, and she'd been unconscious but responsive since she was brought in. She was in the Medical Assessment Unit so they could monitor her, but Dr Royan was confident – certainly now she was awake – that Jennifer would be able to return home in a few days. She was lucky, Dr Royan said.

Then, as Dr Royan shone a small torch into her eyes, the bright light triggered something. She saw a flash. A burst of light. Two lights. *Oh my God.* She saw the glare of two headlights rushing towards her face.

The doctor's words faded into the screech of tyres, the roar of an engine, the blood-curdling crack of Jennifer's own bones against a bonnet. She felt her whole body tighten, then loosen sharply in a shudder.

"Are you alright?" asked Dr Royan.

She saw her mother and sister step closer to her bed.

"I know what happened…" Jennifer whispered. "I remember…"

"What do you remember?" said Dr Royan.

"Someone ran me over."

"Mmm. A hit-and-run, it looks like. There are some police officers here who need to speak to you – when you feel up to it."

"Okay." Jennifer wasn't prepared to talk to the police yet. She needed to process it all first. She wanted to be clear on what happened.

"Get some rest," said Dr Royan. "I'll come and check on you again a bit later."

Dr Royan left. Adam, Jamie and Mum sat with her. They chatted, all three of them making every effort not to mention the accident. They were clearly brimming with questions about it but instead made semi-forced small talk about work, TV and the frostiness of some of the hospital staff. Mum probably thought talking about it so soon after might upset her, or perhaps Dr Royan had said something.

They were probably right to avoid it but Jennifer could think of nothing else. She had a feeling she couldn't shake. A feeling that it wasn't an accident, that the car that hit her was… aiming for her.

Later, Mum and Jamie returned home for dinner. Jennifer asked Adam to stay a while longer. She said she wanted him to be there till she dropped off, but in reality, she wanted to talk to him without her family present. She didn't want to worry them.

"I think someone tried to kill me," she said when the coast

was clear.

Adam frowned, "What? No, don't be silly."

"I'm not."

"Jen, the guy was a probably a drunk idiot who panicked. Completely cunt-ish, don't get me wrong. But I doubt he was *trying* to kill you."

Jennifer sighed. She really didn't know what to think.

She caught Adam's awkward expression. "What is it?"

"I wasn't sure when to mention this," he said.

"Mention what?"

"It's… er… it's Gregory Ferro."

Jennifer's heart skipped a beat. "What about him?"

"He's dead."

Somehow she knew it was coming. It was the look in Adam's eyes, coupled with the dread that was rising inside her as she thought more and more about the 'accident'. It didn't lessen the impact, though. For a second the words didn't go in, just washed right over her. When they did she felt winded, like something had sucked the air from her lungs and she couldn't breathe. A wave of dizziness hit her between the eyes.

"Jen? You alright?"

She found her breath, and the dizziness lifted – slowly. "How? W-when?"

"There was a fire at his house. Last night, sometime. I saw it on the news this morning."

Murmuring between breaths, "But I was… I was there."

"You were where?"

"At Ferro's house. That's where I met him yesterday, before I came to meet you."

"Fuck."

"Do the police know what caused the fire?"

"Not yet, no. They're investigating it. Maybe you can ask the officers that are due to speak to you. They might know. But try not to think about all that now. You'll only work yourself up and you need to get better so you can get out of here."

Jennifer couldn't believe it. Dead. Actually dead. She was only talking to him yesterday – now he was gone. Just like that. Ferro was the first person she knew who'd died. She hadn't even lost any grandparents like a few of her friends had, because both her mother's parents had died before she was born, and she had no contact with any of her father's family.

It just felt so… weird. Weird and wrong. She didn't even know him that well, yet a part of her felt like crying. She thought of his two kids, his estranged wife. They'd probably be beside themselves with regret given how they'd all left things.

"I just remembered something," Adam said, bending down and picking up Jennifer's handbag and a large brown paper Primark bag from beneath his chair. He placed both bags in her lap. "We brought you some stuff you might want. Some clothes, toothbrush, latest edition of *Doctor Who Magazine*, and your phone."

Phone…

Phone! She left her phone in her work trousers on her bed. She remembered now. She took Jamie's by mistake. That's why she was hurrying back home from the pub, to give Jamie her phone back.

"So where's Jamie's phone?" said Jennifer.

"Good question," said Adam. "It wasn't found where you were hit."

"That means someone took it."

"Who could've taken it?"

"Same person who tried to kill me, I expect."

Jennifer looked at her phone. She had five or six texts from friends wishing her a speedy recovery; Adam told her that her mum had put the news out to as many people as possible on Facebook. Among them was a text from Alison Fawke, wishing her well and reporting on Hitler's latest rant about the dreadful untidiness of the office after finding a stray post-it note on the floor.

And she had a voicemail. The timestamp on the message was yesterday evening at 7.43pm, not long after she left Ferro's.

She pressed to listen to the message, swallowing hard as the voice of Gregory Ferro rippled into her ear.

"Jennifer, we need to talk. Urgently. Someone just called me. He wouldn't give his name but said he'd hacked into some encrypted emails that implicate his company in Princess Diana's death. The emails also made reference to

the company having secretly invented a means of travelling through time."

"What is it?" Adam asked, frowning. "Who is it?"

Jennifer didn't answer.

"And that's not all," Ferro continued. *"He managed to override the company's security and discover a lot more. It turns out it has secret departments that ninety per cent of the workforce know nothing about. And these departments have undercover operatives everywhere – inside the police, the security services, the armed forces, even... Parliament. He thinks... Jennifer, he thinks the UK government is accountable to it. He thinks the company is manipulating everything that goes on in our country – and has been for a long time."*

Jennifer's heart raced. Who? What company was he talking about?

Finally Ferro answered her question, *"I don't know if I was surprised or not when he told me the company's name. It's Million Eyes."*

She looked at Adam. He'd been working for Million Eyes for the last two years.

"Jen, who the hell is it?" Adam asked, wide-eyed.

"This proves we can't trust anyone," Ferro continued. *"We need to meet and work out wha –"*

Ferro fell silent mid-sentence. Jennifer couldn't even hear him breathe. She glanced at the screen of her phone – the voicemail hadn't ended. She returned the phone to her ear, waiting.

"*H-hello? Is... someone there?*" Ferro's words were shouted but far away. She realised he wasn't addressing her.

"Beth, is that you? Maggie? Ryan?"

Further silence.

Jennifer waited, chewing her bottom lip.

Suddenly Ferro whispered fast, phone at his mouth again, "*Jennifer, they know.*"

A piercing hiss crackled down the phone, followed by a crash and a thud. Jennifer jerked, startled, and the phone slipped from her hand.

"What the fuck was that?" Adam asked. He'd heard it as well. It was so loud that the patient next to Jennifer probably heard.

She brought the phone back to her ear.

The voicemail had ended, followed by the usual recitation: *"To listen to the message again, press one. To save it and move on, press two."*

Jennifer sunk her teeth into the skin around her thumbnail. "Shit. Shit, shit, shit."

"Jen, for fuck's sake, are you *going* to tell me what's going on?"

Fired by urgency, Jennifer flung off her covers and lifted her legs – which felt like they had five-kilo dumbbells attached to them – out of bed. Her bare feet stung when they hit the freezing hospital floor.

"Hey! What are you doing?"

"You have to help me." She examined the two IVs in her arm and hand and – as carefully as she could – pulled out the needles. She groaned as sharp pains knifed through her body and blood dripped to the floor from the wounds.

"Jennifer, stop! I'll get whatever you need as soon as you get back into bed."

"No, I can't. I'm in danger here. Someone deliberately tried to kill me. Same person who murdered Ferro."

"What are you talking about? *Murdered* Ferro? You don't know that he was murdered."

"Yes, I do."

"What exactly was in that voicemail?"

She couldn't tell him. Not yet. Not till she'd worked out a plan. Million Eyes were his employers. If she told him anything, she'd be putting him in danger as well.

"It doesn't matter," she said. "I just need to get out of here. They'll be back for me."

"Right. Jen, stop being a crazy person and get back into bed – now."

"No, I can't. I have to leave. I have to get out of Deepwater."

"Out of Deepwater?"

"Yes. It won't be long before they realise I'm alive. If I stay here – or go home – they'll find me. I need to – *aaahh!*"

Jennifer was bending down to fetch her handbag from the floor and instantly her chest was on fire with the pain. She doubled over, falling against the side of the bed.

"Jen, you've been hit by a fucking car and you have two

cracked ribs. Get back into bed. I mean it. You're perfectly safe here. It's a hospital."

"You – you don't understand –" She had to push her words through gasps for breath.

"I do understand. I have no idea what spooked you in that voicemail, but this is Deepwater, not an episode of *24*."

"But –"

"Nope. You're not going anywhere." Adam helped her back into bed. At this point, she was in no state to resist.

"Everything alright in here?" said a nurse passing Jennifer's bay. She noticed the blood from where Jennifer had removed her cannulas. "What are you doing, Miss Larson?"

"It... it was an accident," Adam lied.

"Ah ha," said the nurse dubiously. She was probably used to patients pulling out their IVs. Having tubes sticking out of your veins was one of the most unpleasant and uncomfortable feelings ever.

The nurse unhooked the clipboard of notes from the end of Jennifer's bed and flicked through them. She had heavy lips, large breasts and a mole on the left side of her nose. Not really Jennifer's type, but clearly Adam's – his eyes were stuck to her every curve. He dipped his head so he was in eyeline with her name badge and said, "Katie. That's a pretty name."

"Thank you," she replied flatly, either oblivious to Adam's interest or deliberately ignoring it. She replaced the IVs in Jennifer's arm, which involved puncturing two new veins. Jennifer was starting to feel like a pin cushion.

"Can I get you anything?" Katie asked. "Cup of tea? Coffee?"

"Your phone number?" Adam chimed in.

Jennifer gave a pained smirk and murmured weakly, "Sorry about him, nurse."

Katie looked at Adam with a coy half-grin, blushing slightly. "That's alright."

"And no," replied Jennifer to her earlier question, "I'm good on the drinks front, thanks."

"No worries. Make sure you keep drinking your water. You need to stay hydrated. And try not to have any more" – Katie raised her eyebrow disapprovingly – "accidents."

Katie left and Adam's eyes followed her gently wiggling arse up the corridor. "Jesus, there are some hot nurses here. Any chance you can get run over more often?"

That should've made Jennifer laugh. Adam's ability to make light of the most horrible situations was one of the things she loved most about him. But – as unbelievable as it sounded – the world's most powerful computer company had just murdered Gregory Ferro and tried to murder her. And now her own injured body was trapping her in this hospital. It was difficult to see the funny side.

Adam kissed her forehead. "It's late. You're tired. I'm tired. I'm gonna go home and get some sleep. And you're gonna get some sleep as well, okay? I'll be back first thing."

"Okay…" she whispered sleepily.

"Good. And no more panicking about people trying to kill you, alright? No one's out to get you. I don't think anyone would dare mess with Jennifer Larson. Not if they know what's good for them." He sniggered.

Jennifer uttered a small, breathy murmur in reply. Through half-shut eyes, she picked up a dim image of Adam grabbing his jacket and leaving.

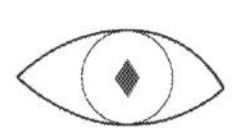

Staff Nurse Katie was standing near the main entrance of the hospital as Adam made his way out. She caught his eye and he switched on that playful smile from earlier as he started to approach her.

She had her phone to her ear, but it looked like he was going to come talk to her anyway. She said sweetly into the phone, "I love you too, baby," loud enough for Adam to hear.

Adam's smile straightened, eyes flickering with chipped pride. He plunged his hands into his pockets and veered off his path towards her, heading for the hospital car park instead.

"What was that about?" said the man at the end of the line.

"Oh, this guy was about to come over and hit on me," said Katie. "I wanted to ward him off."

"Right. I take it you're calling 'cause you've found Larson?"

"Yes, sir. I just paid her a visit. Larson was brought in to Deepwater Hospital last night. She was pretty beaten up, but the doctors are saying she'll make a full recovery."

Her boss, Robert Skinner, replied with a not-surprising note of worry, "I'm hoping you're going to change that as soon as possible."

"Yes, sir," she said confidently. Skinner had promised to wangle a nice big promotion for her if she finished his job for him. "She'll be dead before the end of the night."

15

August 30th 1888

With a crack, the uncrowned boy king, Edward V, fell on his knees against a hard stone floor. His arms and legs were weak, tingly, his ears ringing. He couldn't breathe. His chest and throat were burning and he saw nothing but white.

Then, thankfully, his throat opened a fraction and he drew in as large a breath as he could.

The ringing faded. A moment later, "Edward… Brother, are you there? Edward, w-what happened…" Richard's voice, but quiet, gurgling and undulating, like Edward was underwater.

Slowly the whiteness dispersed and he could see his hands, his white fur cuffs and black sleeves, his hose-covered knees, and the floor beneath him. The burning in his chest softened to a dull ache, his throat opened wider, permitting him more air, and the muffled voice of his brother sharpened.

Edward lifted his head. Richard was next to him, also on his knees, head in his hands. Edward was near enough to extend his arm, stiffly, and touch his brother's shoulder. Richard looked up, met Edward's gaze, a dazed expression on his face.

Edward rose awkwardly to his feet, legs like lead pipes. He checked that he still had his leather satchel. He did. It hung from his shoulder, the box and the pot of red pills still inside.

"We're alive," he whispered.

He scanned the room. Definitely the same room. Same shape, same fireplace, same mullioned window. All the ghosts – thank the Lord – were gone. But so was all the furniture, including their bed, chest and the table where they ate. It was bare, but for a single wooden chair and unlit candelabra. And hanging near where their bed used to be was the painting of the two frightened boys in royal finery. The one Edward had seen while they were among the ghosts and thought looked like him and his brother. Other paintings dressed the walls, ones that weren't there before, all depicting the same two royal boys.

"Father's speculations were right," murmured Richard, pulling himself to his feet and nodding towards the door. "Those red pills have effected our escape."

Edward looked. The door was open. Richard sprang for it and began hurtling down the narrow staircase that corkscrewed to the bottom of the Garden Tower.

"Richard, wait!" Edward, disconcerted by what had happened, had no choice but to follow his eager brother.

At the bottom of the staircase was the guardroom, empty. Edward followed Richard into the tower gateway. All looked much the same.

A raven skipped towards them and cawed, flicking its head. Edward noted that its slick black feathers and charcoal eyes had a slight orange glow about them, the light of sunset washing through the Tower.

Sunset? It was night when they ate the pills. The sun was definitely down. How long did they spend in the realm of ghosts? Was this a different day?

Edward looked through the gateway into the inner ward. The White Tower was still there, but several buildings behind and around it Edward had never seen before. And high above the White Tower, some unsightly distortion of England's flag waved in a light breeze, the red cross of St George encroached upon by blue triangles and red, diagonal stripes.

"Come on," said Edward, taking his brother's hand. "I think we should go."

They passed underneath the raised portcullis in the gateway. It looked rusty and old – more so than when Edward last saw it – but its nasty iron spikes could still skewer a person into the ground.

At least all the ghosts were gone from here too. No Romans or dragons or giant red carriages that could drive themselves. No mysterious woman calling herself queen.

Stepping onto Water Lane in the outer ward, Edward slowed and glanced around. He noticed the grey plaque on the exterior wall of the Garden Tower, just above the arch of the gateway. The plaque displayed the words *Bloody Tower*. Edward knew the word 'bloody' but 'tower' was unfamiliar.

"Edward, come on," said Richard, yanking his arm. Now it was Richard who was anxious to leave.

They walked up Water Lane – then someone shouted something behind them.

They whirled round.

A sentry had rounded the curve of the Wakefield Tower and was staring right at them, clad in a peculiar uniform: tall, wide-brimmed hat, shiny shoes and a knee-length tunic that was dark blue with scarlet trimmings, the letters *VR* embroidered across the chest. He was wielding some kind of spear and shouting something in a language Edward didn't recognise.

Foreign sentries? At the Tower?

Perhaps there had been an attack. The city captured. That could explain the flag on the White Tower, too.

But captured by whom? And how could they have changed everything so quickly?

This wasn't the time to find out. Edward grabbed his brother's hand. "Run!"

They hurtled up Water Lane to the Tower at the Gate. The gateway was open – they were able to run straight through.

Edward hesitated. The wooden drawbridge to the Middle Tower was gone, replaced by a stone causeway that traversed a waterless moat now covered with grass.

This doesn't make sense.

He glanced back to see if the sentry was pursuing. He was.

They ran across the causeway to the Middle Tower, itself substantially reshaped. Again, they were able to pass straight through the open gateway.

What?

They found themselves on a road, ahead of them a building with signs displaying the words *Ticket Office* and *Refreshment Room*. What in the world was a 'ticket office' and a 'refreshment room'? And where was the Lion Tower? The semi-circular building that was home to the Royal Menagerie was apparently no more, pinched from existence in the blink of an eye.

To their left, the River Thames was busy with boats, far

more than there used to be. Odd-looking sailboats mostly, and boats with tall, round chimneys billowing out smoke – extraordinary! On the other side of the river, countless new buildings and structures made dramatic and menacing silhouettes against the setting sun, which was bobbing behind them like a fat blood orange. Edward found himself entranced by two enormous, rectangular towers climbing into the sky from both sides of the river, each tower consisting of beams and columns that appeared to be made from metal, the tops resembling the long snouts of two dragons reaching to sniff each other.

"Edward, come on!" cried Richard, pulling Edward in the direction of some kind of entrance gate.

They raced through the gate, across another road and onto a street that was bustling with bizarrely-dressed people and remarkable horse-drawn vehicles quite unlike those they were used to. There were strange-looking houses all joined together in rows and the streets remained lit even as the sun was going down, courtesy of curious metal poles mounted with glass lanterns that had been fixed to the sides of roads.

Realising that their pursuer had either lost them or given up, they slowed to take it all in.

"Edward, this is not the London I remember," Richard murmured. "Not at all."

"No," Edward agreed. "No, it is not."

The sun finally sank, spots of pink and orange light rippling across the sky. Clouds rolled in, threatening rain, though none fell. The air was still and humid.

Edward didn't want to draw attention from the exotic populace so they huddled together in the porch of a house at the end of a row, out of sight. The house was dark, quiet, its occupants either out or sleeping. In case it was the latter, the princes made sure to keep their voices low.

Richard whispered, "Do you still have the red pills?"

"Yes," said Edward.

"Let's use them again. I think we should leave this place."

Silently agreeing, Edward pulled his leather satchel across his lap. He reached inside for the pot of pills. As he pulled it out, his arm was shaking fiercely.

"Brother? What's wrong?"

As Edward tried to steady his trembling arm, which he

supposed was some after-effect from the pills, the satchel slipped off his lap and tumbled down the porch steps, the box lurching from inside onto the pavement.

"No!" Edward cried, bolting to his feet.

A man with a long face, pointed nose, and bushy patches of facial hair that stretched from his hairline to his jaw was walking along the pavement in front of the house. He stopped when he saw the box slide in front of his feet.

The man's clothes were as eccentric as his facial hair. Loose grey hose, black, scuffed boots, some kind of brown, knee-length coat buttoned over a white shirt and strange necktie, and a brown hat with a bowl-shaped crown.

The man bent down and picked up the box with gloved hands. He said something in another language, his chevron moustache twitching as he spoke. Another foreigner, no doubt. Perhaps he hailed from the same place as that sentry at the Tower? It was looking ever more likely that London had been captured by invaders.

The man brought the box to his ear and shook it, realising something was inside. He tried to open it. He couldn't, of course. Edward had the key round his neck.

Edward furtively handed the pot of pills to his brother – he didn't want the man to see that as well – and started down the steps from the porch, commanding, "Hand that back to me at once."

The man looked at him, gibbering something incomprehensible.

"What did he say?" said Richard from the top of the steps.

A few of the man's words seemed familiar, but his accent was thick and impenetrable. "A foreigner," Edward replied. Then to the man, "We do not understand what you are saying."

The man grunted a reply and held out the box towards him.

"Yes." Edward reached the bottom of the porch steps and approached him. "Hand it to me please."

The man lunged abruptly at Edward. Edward twisted away but the man formed an iron grip around his wrist using his free hand, flapping his alien tongue with increasing volume and waving the box in front of Edward's face.

"Unhand me. I am the king!" shrieked Edward. He struggled but the man was too strong. Though he continued to vomit words Edward couldn't understand, his objective – by the way he was waving the box – was clear. He wanted to get inside it.

But Edward had sworn to protect the book. There was no way he was giving it up. He'd die first.

Richard scrambled down the steps and charged at the man, screaming, "Let him go!" The man turned and kicked Richard's spindly legs hard with his right foot, and Richard collapsed on his side on the pavement.

"Stop this!" screamed Edward.

Still holding Edward's wrist, the man yanked him towards Richard. Evidently dazed, his brother hadn't had time to get to his feet before the man's boot was on his neck.

"I am your king and I command you to stop!"

Richard started to choke as the man pressed down on his neck, crushing his throat.

"Very well – here – take it. Just stop!" Edward might be willing to die for his oath but he wasn't about to sacrifice his little brother. He used his free hand to pull the neck chain out from under his tunic. The man's dark eyes lit up with fiendish intent as they settled on the key. He lifted his foot from Richard's throat and Edward sighed with relief as his brother coughed and spluttered over the pavement.

The man kept a hold of Edward's wrist and thrust the box towards him, shaking it as a gesture that meant *open it,* more foreign words pouring from his mouth. Edward acquiesced, lifting the chain over his head, pushing the key into the lock, turning it and lifting the lid.

The man's eyes narrowed in confusion, his top lip curling in disgust. He finally let go of Edward's wrist so he could take the book out and examine it. He read the cover aloud in his obscure accent, one eyebrow arched. Then he tossed the box away and stuffed the book into his coat.

Edward followed as he started to walk away, pleading, "You must give that back to me. You do not know what it –"

The man spun round and clouted Edward across the face with the back of his hand. Edward fell to his knees, his brother, now recovered, rushing over to him, wrapping both arms protectively around his middle.

As Edward watched, stunned and shaking, the man fished a small device from his pocket, put it to his lips and blew, making an awful, shrill wail. The noise appeared to summon a two-wheeled, one-horse carriage from an adjacent road. The carriage clacked towards the man, splashing through puddles, then the driver, sitting behind the vehicle on a high seat level with the roof, tugged the reins and stopped the horse a few feet from where the man was standing. The man and the driver exchanged words in the same unknown language.

"Give me the book," barked Edward. "Please. You do not understand its importance."

The man ignored him and climbed inside the carriage.

"Stop – I must have that book!"

The man rasped something in reply, flashed a sardonic grin and gestured strangely, lifting his hat up, revealing his forehead and a tuft of hair, then lowering it again. Some kind of vulgarity, no doubt. The driver cracked his whip and the horse trotted away.

Now what?

"Are you all right, Richard?" Edward said.

"No," said his brother honestly, rubbing his reddened throat. "I want to go home."

A light flickered on in the house whose porch the princes were sitting in before the altercation. The din of it had woken someone. A woman appeared in the window holding a candle, illuminating her hunched frame and a mouthful of broken teeth. She bawled through the glass something unintelligible – did anyone here speak English?

Whatever she said, just her tone and volume were enough to tell Edward that they had to go. Edward stooped to grab his satchel, flung it over his shoulder. He left the box upturned in a puddle – what use was that now? Hand in hand they dashed away from the house, slowing to an urgent walk as they started up a different street, heading in no particular direction.

"I swore to guard the Book That Listens with my life," said Edward, shaking his head. "I failed."

"There's nothing we can do about it now," said Richard. "Please, brother. This doesn't feel right. This place. These people. None of it feels right. Let's just use the pills and get out of here."

Looking around, Edward wondered if this nightmarish corruption of the place they knew was the consequence of a foreign invasion, or if they'd been dead all along, since first eating the pills, and this perverse, misshapen London was a plane of Hell or Purgatory or a vicious trick of the Devil.

Either way, escape was desirable.

Edward stopped, nodding at his brother. Richard dipped his hand into the pocket that hung from his belt, pulled out the pot of pills and handed it to Edward. As Edward went to open it, he found, looking down, that he'd stepped on a large, damp, ripped sheet of parchment. He moved his foot and stooped to pick it up. It felt unusually thin and brittle, so he handled it carefully as he sought to read the words that weren't faded or smudged or lost through tears. Some were familiar, some just looked misspelled, some were completely unreadable. The parchment's title was *The Daily Telegraph* – whatever that meant. And just below the title was the date.

THURSDAY, AUGUST 30, 1888.

A wave of clarity washed over him, the knots in his head untangling, the fog lifting. Finally it was all making sense.

They *were* still in London. But they had moved – *in time.* They had come forwards four hundred and five years. That explained the city's dramatic transformation. The princes were looking at over four centuries of change.

"Richard, I think –"

"Brother, please. I don't want to stay here a moment longer." They were attracting ominous stares from passers-by and Richard had grown pale and anxious, a shimmer of sweat on his brow.

Edward knew now that they would have to use the pills again. They couldn't just stay where – or rather when – they were. Somehow they had to get back to their own time.

"All right, let's try this again," said Edward, placing his hand on Richard's shoulder, who was shaking. It was a warm, still night so it couldn't have been with cold.

Edward removed the lid from the pot and they each took a pill. As they swallowed them, Edward encircled his brother in his arms.

"Take me home to Mother," Richard murmured.

"I'll try, baby brother," said Edward. "I'll try."

16

October 24th 2019

After Adam left the hospital, Jennifer fought insomnia. Though drowsy, a jumble of nasty thoughts and scenarios was tumbling around in her head, stopping her at the brink of sleep.

Her bay in the Medical Assessment Unit became quieter and quieter. Visiting hours were over and many of the patients were settling down for bed. The nurses had turned the lights down and bathed the room in a gentle orange glow. The clatter of shoes tapping, trainers squeaking and heels clicking as people went up and down the busy corridors next to the ward was gone, as was the incessant drone of voices. Now Jennifer's ears were being treated to the heavy breathing of the patient next to her, overlaid with some light percussion from the-lady-who-hiccups-in-her-sleep in the bed opposite, and – completing the chorus – the pig-like sounds coming from the snoring man in the corner of the ward. Even if her brain was allowing her to sleep, this bunch was the next obstacle.

Lying there, her thoughts kept returning to Ferro, time travel, Million Eyes, Princess Diana… and Adam.

Could Adam have known about Million Eyes? He'd worked for them for two years. Could they have told him anything?

No, Jen, don't be stupid. Million Eyes had over five hundred thousand employees and Adam was way too low down the food chain to know about any of this. He was just an IT technician at their Basingstoke store.

Now wide awake, she grabbed her phone and listened to Ferro's voicemail again, shivering as he said, "*Jennifer – they know*," flinching as she listened to the sound of his murder.

The moment Million Eyes discovered she was still alive, they would come after her again. You see it all the time in movies. And right now, lying in a hospital bed, injured and attached to IVs, she was at her most vulnerable.

She couldn't go to the police. Not after that whistleblower told Ferro that Million Eyes had operatives inside the police.

All she could do was run. Hide. Work out what she was going to do next.

She needed to go. *Now*.

Mind made up, she carefully pulled out her IV cannulas for the second time that evening. She used the bed sheets to dab the blood that leaked from the wounds – there wasn't as much this time. Then she slipped quietly out of bed, conscious that she didn't want to wake anyone or alert any nurses. She changed into some of the clothes Adam had brought her: jeans, a green hoody and Ugg boots.

She checked that her purse was in her handbag – it was. She looked inside to see how much cash she had. Twenty-three pounds and a few silvers. Not enough, but there was a cash machine in reception. She left her bag – it was full of crap she didn't need – and tucked her phone and purse into the front pocket of her hoody. Then she walked lightly away from her bay. A couple of nurses were talking a little further down the corridor, but had their backs to her. She sneaked out of the Medical Assessment Unit and, increasing her pace as soon as she was out of sight, followed signs to the main entrance.

The adrenaline of the moment had deadened the pain in her body. All she knew was that she had to get out of the building, fast. She scrambled down a stairwell to the bottom floor, then headed up another corridor. This led to the hospital café and shop – both closed and cloaked in darkness. Ahead of those were reception, the main entrance and freedom.

The cash machine was outside the shop. She used it to withdraw three-hundred pounds – all the money she had. She wasn't going to use her bank cards after that as Million Eyes might be able to track her. Stuffing the bank notes into her purse, she hastened towards the automatic doors at the entrance.

"Jennifer?"

She stopped and spun towards the direction of the voice. Staff Nurse Katie was standing in reception behind her. "Where are you going?" Katie asked.

"I'm sorry," Jennifer said. "I can't explain why, but I've got to go."

Katie approached. "Let's get you back to the ward."

"No. I'm leaving. I'm leaving now." Jennifer turned and continued towards the entrance.

"No. You're not."

There was something different in Katie's tone. It was sharper, colder, her friendly facade gone.

Jennifer stopped, turned around slowly, found herself staring down the barrel of a gun.

You imagine these kinds of things never happening to you – until they do.

"So you're one of them?" Jennifer said. "Million Eyes?"

Gesturing gently with her gun, Katie just repeated calmly, "Let's get you back to the ward."

"And if I refuse? You're going to shoot me right here? Wake loads of patients, alert loads of staff?"

Katie gave the same half-grin she gave to Adam earlier, but this time there wasn't anything demure about it. Her soft voice, stony eyes and remarkably still hand – the one wielding the gun – all demonstrated one thing. Confidence.

"You are gravely underestimating how powerful we are," Katie said.

Jennifer took that to mean that, yes, Katie was willing to shoot her in the middle of reception. Even if she attracted attention and caused a mess, it was a mess she was quite sure she'd be able to clear up.

"Then you'll have to shoot me." The words just tumbled freely from her mouth. "Because I'm walking out that door."

A part of her said, *Jen, what are you doing?* But Katie was going to kill her anyway. She just wanted to do it *her* way, with the least hassle. Jennifer had no intention of making it easy for her.

"Fine," said Katie, deadpan.

The two were locked in an unyielding stare, motionless.

Just do it, Jen.

She sucked in a breath and held it, about to turn –

"Everything alright out here?" said a male security guard, entering reception behind them.

Katie's head jerked to the left, her eyes off Jennifer momentarily.

Jennifer's survival instinct kicked in. She lunged at Katie and thrust open palms into her chest. Katie flew backwards, limbs flailing, and landed with a smack on the hard vinyl floor.

Jennifer wanted to grab the gun, but it never left Katie's hand, even as she went down. The security guard charged forwards to restrain the gun-toting nurse, but Katie's recovery was instantaneous. She rolled onto her front and pointed the gun square at his chest.

Jennifer was expecting a bang and a bullet. Instead, a beam of florescent green light shot out of the muzzle with a hiss, surging into the security guard's chest and tossing him in the air like a doll. He slammed so hard into one of the partition walls that he went straight through, fragments of plasterboard flying.

Run. Run now.

Jennifer sprang for the automatic entrance doors just as Katie spun onto her back to refix her aim on her real target.

The glass doors were only partly open as Jennifer launched through them. Green light reflected all around her, another beam from Katie's gun. It blasted through the doors, barely an inch from Jennifer's shoulder. A flurry of shattered glass rained down over her like hailstones.

No doubt Katie was on her feet by now but Jennifer didn't look back. Bruises pounding, chest on fire, she ran only as fast as her battered body would allow. She crossed the ambulance bay into the car park, running half-stooped between the smattering of parked cars for as much cover as possible.

A car exploded behind her. Mid-run, she glanced over her shoulder. Car alarms blared, triggered by the explosion. Katie was outside the front of the hospital, shooting maniacally in her direction. Her gun was a frighteningly destructive force – the cars weren't cover at all.

Jennifer tried desperately to pick up her pace.

Another car exploded, this one just metres from her. The hot blast wave punched her in the side and she face-planted the tarmac. Everything was black and quiet for a second, but her body revived quickly, spurred by surging adrenaline. She wasn't going to let this bitch kill her. Urgency rerouted her brain from her badly grazed face and jolted cheekbones and the fresh pounding taken by her ribcage – and she was up on her feet, running again. Now half a dozen car alarms were screaming.

The car park ended at a grassy incline with a road at the bottom that wound past the hospital. On the other side of the road was a large wooded park, thick with darkness and stretching beyond her line of sight. A bolt of light from Katie's gun blasted a lamppost flanking the car park, just as Jennifer raced past it and plunged down the incline. Glancing back as she ran into the park, she saw the top half of the lamppost toppling towards the ground, its midsection pulverised by the beam. Moments later, the crash of metal rang out.

She ran and ran, weaving between trees, nearly colliding with a couple of picnic benches. About four or five hundred metres into the park was a clearing with a large pond, reflecting the bright, near-full moon in its waters and painting the edges of the trees with pale grey light.

Jennifer couldn't hear Katie behind her. Did she see her run into the park? Did she follow her?

She ran around the edge of the pond to a denser section of woodland. The impenetrable darkness made it virtually impossible to tell one tree from the next, so she couldn't run for fear of smacking into one. Walking as fast as she could, she then felt her pain coming to the fore, forcing itself on her. Everywhere throbbed and stung. Her ribs, her limbs, her face… The pain and exhaustion from running forced her to stop and gather herself.

Leaning against a hefty oak, she shoved her hand in her pocket and took out her phone. Once she'd caught her breath, she rang Adam.

"I need you to come and get me," she wheezed quietly, voice weak and trembling.

"What? Why?" said Adam.

"That nurse you were flirting with – she's trying to kill me."

"I – I – *what*?"

"Adam, move your arse and come get me. I ran from the

hospital. I'm in a park right by it. There's a pond and loads of woodland."

"I – I don't understand. Have you called the police? Where's the nurse now?"

"I don't fucking know! But she's looking for me. She's got this crazy ray gun like something out of *Star Trek* and I've already seen her kill someone. And I can't call the police. I can't explain why, I just can't. Please, just come now!"

"Okay, okay… The park next to the hospital is Queen Victoria Park. I don't know which direction you're going in but if you keep on heading through –"

Jennifer noticed clicking on the line while Adam was talking. Quiet, in the background, a bit metallic in tone. Each click was at approximately two second intervals. She interrupted Adam, "What's that?"

"What's what?"

"That clicking. Do you hear that?"

"I don't hear anything. Do you want me to come and get you or not?"

Shit, they'd tapped her phone. They were tracking her with it. "I need to dump this phone – now."

"Jennifer, calm down. You're not making any sense."

Was he trying to keep her on the phone? So that Katie could find her?

"Adam, I'm sorry. I've got to go."

"Jen – wait –"

She hung up.

She was about to chuck the phone and carry on through the woods when it vibrated. She'd turned it on silent earlier so she could try and sleep. Thank fuck she did that.

She looked at her phone. A text message from Adam. Running and hiding is pointless.

What! She took a fast intake of breath and it wedged in her throat.

She typed back, OMG, please don't tell me you're in on this!

She waited, mashed her trembling bottom lip between her teeth.

A few seconds later, Adam replied, WTF?

The text you just sent!

I didn't send a text!

Jennifer couldn't believe that Adam had anything to do with this. She just couldn't. The guy wasn't that good an actor.

She replied, Then they must've hacked your phone too. I've gotta go. Don't trust anyone.

The phone vibrated again. Another text from Adam. Hahahahahaha! No, don't trust anyone Jen – especially not your best mate! Fooled you again. This is fun.

Her stomach lurched. She couldn't breathe. When she tried, her lungs burned.

Fuck this shit.

The light from her phone's screen reached into the thick darkness for a metre or so, faintly marking out the contours of the oak tree's large, sprawling roots. Jennifer set her phone down on a flattish section of the roots, picked up a stray rock and smashed the phone to pieces. Smash, smash, smash. Each hard swing of her arm jarred her chest and made her cracked ribs cry out, but she smashed through the pain.

After all, the pain in her body was nothing compared to the thought that Adam had betrayed her.

But had he? She left the remnants of her phone in the dirt and carried on weaving through the trees. Perhaps those texts were a ploy by Katie and her cohorts to keep her on the phone, so they could track her.

Yes. It must've been a trick. Adam wouldn't do that to her. He wouldn't. It was that fucking bitch Katie.

Jennifer hoped that by dumping the phone, she'd thwarted her.

But these woods… they seemed to be never-ending… Where the fuck was civilisation?

A twig snapped loudly some distance behind her.

No. God, no.

She froze, stopped breathing. She moved her head slowly but nothing else. She looked behind her and saw heavy darkness relieved only by a trace of moonlight.

Bushes rustled lightly. Something was moving nearby.

She was partly shielded by another fat oak tree, but if someone was coming, she wouldn't be for long.

Please be a fox.

The rustling continued, closer now. Louder.

Torchlight glanced off nearby foliage. Seconds later, Jennifer saw the dark shape of the torch's owner.

Katie.

Shit, shit, shit.

Katie had her back to her, but they were only metres from each other. Before long, Katie would turn in Jennifer's direction and she'd be exposed.

But these woods were so dense with vegetation that there was no way Jennifer could make a run for it without causing a bush-rustling, leaf-crunching, twig-snapping racket.

Only one option.

Without thinking, Jennifer charged at Katie while she still had her back to her.

The crunch of Jennifer's footsteps alerted Katie immediately. She swung round, gun and torch poised, but Jennifer slammed into her left side before she even saw her coming.

Katie hurtled to the ground. This time both the torch and gun went flying out of her hands, but the darkness was so thick Jennifer didn't see where they landed.

Hopefully neither did she.

Jennifer turned and ran.

A hand clasped her left ankle and yanked. Jennifer yielded to gravity, plunging into shrubbery. Her head spun towards Katie, still gripping her ankle. With all the might that was left in her broken body, she slammed her right Ugg boot into Katie's face.

Ankle free, Jennifer launched to her feet and took off through the trees as fast as she could without colliding with them.

Yes!

The rev of a car, a short distance away. Civilisation at last. Gradually orange streetlamp light began scoring through the darkness. Within minutes, she was out of the park and on a pavement in a residential road.

She hastened up the sleepy road, crossing several interconnecting residential streets and cul-de-sacs, all unfamiliar. She kept looking back – no Katie. Her run soon slackened to a fast, painful stagger, two separate inflictions of car-related injuries taking their toll. But at this point, if she didn't keep going, she knew she'd stop for good.

Eventually she stumbled onto a main road and small bells of recognition chimed.

Yes. Station Road. She knew where she was: about fifteen minutes from Deepwater train station.

She hurried to the station, arriving just as the heavens opened. The rain quickly seeped through her hoody, wetting her bare skin. But it wasn't cold or unpleasant. Her wounded body had been in overdrive and overheat mode for ages, making her forget that it was October. The rain was soothing.

She used the cash in her purse to purchase a ticket from one of the machines. The last train of the night was ten minutes away. She would arrive in Brighton at nearly 1am.

Hers was the furthermost platform – four. She crossed the bridge over the railway track and hid in the waiting room between platforms three and four. When the train was a minute away, she emerged.

She stared down the track for the first sign of lights. Then the tracks and adjacent trees in the distance glowed, and two glaring lights crept around the bend and speared into her eyes, making her squint. Metal roared and brakes squealed as the train pulled into the station – empty – and ground to a stop. She leapt through the doors the moment they opened.

Oh my fucking God.

Sitting down, she saw through the window Katie hurtling down the stairs from the bridge, face covered in blood.

Her hands were empty – she obviously hadn't found her gun – but that didn't make Jennifer feel any better.

If Katie were to get on the train, it would be a fight to the death – and Jennifer wasn't strong enough.

Go, train, please.

GO!

Katie charged onto the platform. Her eyes connected with Jennifer and her bloody face hardened with fury. She sprang for the train doors.

YES!

The train rumbled forwards. Jennifer saw Katie rebound off the doors. She was too late.

Jennifer kept her eyes on Katie's bloodied face as the train pulled away from the station. She looked pumped with rage – eyes wide and bulging, lips pursed, hands balled into fists. She looked ready to take on a whole army singlehandedly.

Fortunately Jennifer didn't have to look at the bitch for long.

17

As Jennifer sat on the train, entire body throbbing, she couldn't shake Katie's crazed face from her mind. What would she do next? This train had a handful of stops before Brighton – would she try and get to the next one before Jennifer got there? What if she had a dozen operatives waiting to ambush her at each station?

She should've killed her in those woods.

What was she saying? *Killed her?* A few hours ago Jennifer hadn't known anyone who'd died, let alone killed anyone.

This was all too much. How the fuck did she get into this?

She tucked her hair into the neck of her hoody and pulled the hood up to hide her face. She decided to get off at the first stop, Crossmore, a tiny village in the South Downs. She'd then get a taxi to Brighton. Safest thing to do.

With only darkness outside, for most of the journey she saw nothing through the window but her own reflection and that of the well-lit train. Nothing to take her mind off the night's events, so she just kept replaying them over and over.

Thirty minutes later, the train pulled into Crossmore. Jennifer hadn't moved for that long, so everything twinged unbearably as she dragged herself to her feet and hobbled off the train.

The station was quiet and empty. Good. Her body really couldn't take any more Hollywood chase scenes tonight.

She limped from the station onto a road lined with old country houses. At the end of the road was a pub – the Coach House – and on the corner was one of those famous red telephone boxes you barely see anymore.

Please be working.

It was, and as was customary in telephone boxes, had a board of useful numbers (and ads for phone sex lines). Jennifer dropped a bunch of 20ps into the coin slot – something she'd never done in her life having grown up in an age of smartphones – and called one of the taxi companies on the board.

She waited by the phone box and, fifteen minutes later, a taxi pulled up next to the Coach House. Hood still up, she avoided looking at the driver and got straight in the back, keeping her head low.

"Can I go to Somerfield Street in Brighton, please?" she murmured.

"Somerfield Street? No problem."

Jennifer realised as they drove to Brighton that she probably looked really suspicious. Lots of people thought ill of young people in hoodies, particularly folk from nice villages in the English countryside. Ones who deliberately tried to obscure their faces looked even dodgier. Jennifer engaged in small talk to put the driver at ease.

Before long a valley of lights swept across the pitch-black expanse of the South Downs. Brighton, the seaside city of exuberance, diversity and hopefully refuge for Jennifer, beckoned.

The driver took her into the city centre. Students filled the streets. Music boomed from clubs and pubs, a blur of noise. The roads seemed as busy with cars and taxis now – just gone 1am – as they probably were by day. The route to Somerfield Street took her past the Royal Pavilion, its ornate, onion-shaped Indian domes and minarets lit up and looking beautiful; and briefly onto the bustling seafront, where the illuminated Brighton Pier made its way out to sea, painting the waters around it a shimmering orange; then onto streets full of cute cafes, lively-looking bars, and shops selling comics, sci-fi merchandise and sex toys. It surprised Jennifer that she'd only been to Brighton once, given that it was the UK's gay – and geek – capital. It was just her kind of place.

Her taxi arrived on Somerfield Street. She paid the driver and got out. As the taxi drove away, she approached number twenty-three, which she hoped was still the home of Becks Shayes, the last place in the world anyone would expect her to go.

She rang the doorbell. It was 1.15am – Becks was probably in bed. She rang it again and knocked. A couple of minutes passed. Then Jennifer heard movement inside. Somebody switched on a light. It shone through the two frosted glass panels in the front door.

Becks would've checked who it was through the security peephole. Chains and locks rattled. First good sign. At least Becks had seen it was her and was still opening the door.

"Hi Becks," said Jennifer awkwardly.

Becks was obviously still an enormous Disney fan. Her pyjamas were covered in Pascals, the chameleon from *Tangled.* But her expression as she greeted Jennifer wasn't as cheerful as her attire.

"What the hell are you doing here?" she said, top lip curling in disgust. "And what the hell happened to your face?" Jennifer could tell from her voice that she was asking out of curiosity, not because she cared. But that was to be expected.

"I'm so sorry to come here like this," Jennifer said. "But you're the only person who can help me."

Her hackles went up. "I'm sorry – *help* you? You expect me to help *you*?"

"No, I don't expect anything. I'm just hoping. Hoping that you might."

"Really?"

"There are people after me. People who are trying to kill me. Last night I was hit by a car – deliberately. Left for dead. Then one of them tried to finish the job at the hospital, but I got away and came here."

"Are you high?"

"No. I'm being serious."

"I don't believe you."

"Why would I lie?" *Jen, what a stupid thing to say.*

Becks didn't need to answer anyway. Her expression of *did you seriously just ask that?* was enough.

"Okay, you're right," Jennifer conceded. "There's no reason why you should believe me. No reason why you should help me. Particularly after what I did to you. All I can say is, I think these people will keep looking for me and I came here because this is the last place anyone would expect to find me."

Jennifer met Becks at the University of York, one of the top universities for history. Their chemistry was immediate but Becks was, on paper, straight. It soon turned out Becks just thought she was straight when Jennifer, aided by some tequila slammers, coaxed her into bed. They were a couple for a few months but eventually Jennifer realised that they were on different pages of different books. Becks was talking marriage and babies and Jennifer wasn't interested in any of that – not with her, anyway.

The nice, decent thing to do would've been to break up with Becks there and then. But Jennifer took a far more cunt-ish option and got drunk and slept with a hot, tattoo-covered goth whose name she couldn't even remember. Overcome with shame, she kept it from Becks – till a mutual friend admitted to Becks that he'd seen Jennifer making out with Goth Girl on the dance floor, forcing Jennifer to come clean. In the heat of the moment Jennifer made it worse by blaming Becks for pressuring her into a commitment too soon and pushing her to cheat.

Becks broke it off and apart from seeing each other in passing on campus, they never spoke again. She'd heard that Becks had gone back to live with her parents in Brighton after uni. And here she was.

"So what do you want from me?" Becks snapped.

"A place to stay. Just temporarily, while I sort myself a job and somewhere else to live. Then I promise you'll never have to see me again. And once I've got money, I'll pay you some rent. Please, I'm begging you."

She shook her head and sighed with exasperation. "You bitch. I don't believe or care what you say but you're obviously beaten up. And if I turn you away and you wind up dead, I'm going to be the one saddled with guilt, aren't I? Guilt *over you.* So I don't really have a fucking choice."

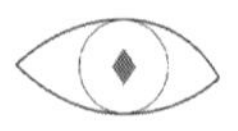

Later that night, Jennifer lay in bed in Becks's parents' spare room, staring at the ceiling and tracing the creases in the artex, listening to the distant whir of voices, music, traffic and seagulls that was occasionally sliced into by blaring sirens.

She kept imagining her mum and Jamie reacting to her disappearance. Jennifer and Jamie weren't as close as they used to be, not since Jamie had been revolving her life around Tom, so she'd probably be nonchalant about Jennifer's vanishing act at first. Still, they were sisters and they loved each other. As soon as the reality hit that Jennifer wasn't coming back, she knew Jamie would be upset.

Not as upset as Mum though. Neither Jennifer nor her mum were hearts-on-their-sleeves sorts of people, but that didn't mean they weren't close. Their bond was a deep, unspoken, unchanging one – which was why Jennifer now felt like vomiting at having left her. She was doing this to protect her and Jamie from Million Eyes, too, but she just kept picturing her mum raging because she didn't know where her daughter was, blaming the police for doing such a shit job finding her, but secretly crying herself to sleep each night.

And what about Adam? When she last spoke to him, she was being chased, telling him that her pursuer might be tracking her. Now that she was running away, would Adam think that Katie found her – and killed her? Would he tell her mum and sister that?

Assuming Adam really was the friend she thought he was. Those texts had really screwed with her head.

Jen, stop it. It *was* a trick. It had to be. Adam was her best mate.

And she was leaving him too.

She couldn't let Mum and Jamie and Adam think she was dead. What could she do? She couldn't call them. Million Eyes would see that coming. They'd probably tapped their phones as well.

A letter. She could send them a letter. Million Eyes were a computer company. They could tap phones and trace bank cards – anything technological. But they probably didn't monitor the Post Office as well.

Probably.

Yes, that's what she'd do. She'd write to them – soon – and let them know she was safe, but that she needed to stay hidden, at least till she'd worked out a plan.

The question now was simple, yet harder to answer than ever before.

What the hell was she going to do next?

18

August 30th 1888

James Rawling would never openly question Miss Morgan's decisions, but he was convinced that sending Robert Skinner to retrieve the book and restore the timeline was the wrong call. He understood that this gargantuan shitstorm was Skinner's fault and Skinner's responsibility to fix, but he'd not travelled in time before and, more to the point, he'd already proved himself incompetent – why put the future in his hands?

What's done was done. Skinner had failed again, this time by getting himself killed by a medieval king, and Rawling, who would've been a more sensible choice to begin with, had taken his place in the hunt for the book. It was time to get history back on track.

A while ago the small, round spectacles Rawling was wearing – not for seeing better but for extracting information – picked up trace chronoton particles, which was strange. Chronoton particles meant time travellers. He himself would've been emitting them, but he should've been the only one doing so.

The mystery was solved quickly. Having tracked the particles to a spot in what would one day be the Tower Hamlets area of East London, Rawling now stood across the road from a man called John Snider and, of all people, the Princes in the Tower. He double-checked the facial recognition software in his spectacles and yes, it really was them. Edward V and Richard, Duke of York, to be exact. *They* were the time travellers.

Thinking about it, that made sense. Miss Morgan said that Skinner had been killed by Edward IV, who must've given

Skinner's chronozine to his sons. Did that mean he'd given them the book as well?

Snider and the boys were having some sort of altercation. They were shouting and Snider had a hold of Edward V's wrist, waving a small wooden box in the boy's face. Rawling got close enough to hear – but not too close. He found a shadowy spot between two streetlamps, removed his spectacles and slipped them into a pocket, and watched.

"Come on then, open it, you little weasel," said Snider. "Show me what it is you've stolen."

"Unhand me. I am the king!" screamed Edward.

"I told you I don't speak your foreign prattle. Just open the damn box, boy."

Four hundred years of language change were preventing Snider and the princes from understanding each other. To Rawling they all spoke Modern English, but that was because of his cognit and the psychic field it was generating, translating everything he was hearing. It was the main reason Rawling couldn't get too close. If he did, the psychic field would get into Snider's head, get into the princes' heads, and they'd all be able to understand each other. At the moment Snider thought the boys foreign thieves in fancy dress. Rawling wasn't about to risk further damage to the timeline if Snider were to find out that they were the famously long-missing Princes in the Tower after having time-travelled from the 15th century.

Rawling saw the younger of the princes, Richard, race down some porch steps and charge at Snider, who took out his legs. The boy fell flat on the pavement, then Snider dragged Edward over to him and placed his foot on the boy's neck.

Despite Edward continually asserting his kingly authority, albeit in a child's squall, Snider pressed down on Richard's throat, demanding that he open the box. Finally Edward relented, removing a key from around his neck, and Snider freed his brother and ordered him to unlock it.

The box open, Rawling dug his fingers into his palms. Could the book be inside?

Snider let go of Edward's wrist and lifted something suitably book-like from the box, reading the front of it aloud, "*The History of Computer-Aided Timetabling for Railway Systems…*"

Yes! He'd found it.

"Sounds fascinating," said Snider, hurling the box and stuffing the book into his coat, quite happy, it seemed, to steal from thieves.

Edward pleaded for it back and the arrogant son of a bitch whacked him across the face. As the brothers huddled together on the ground, Snider used a whistle to summon a horse-drawn carriage, which click-clacked noisily over to him.

"Good evening, sir," said the driver.

"Take me to Whitechapel," said Snider as he climbed into the carriage.

In response to Edward's continued pleas, Snider rasped, "Away with you. Go back to the boat you stowed away on," and scornfully tipped his hat to the boys.

As his carriage rolled up the road, an occupant of the house the princes were standing outside shouted through the window, "Oi, you noisy tykes, sling yer 'ook!" and frightened them away.

Rawling was torn. He had to go after the book but at the same time he couldn't just let two missing royals from the 15th century continue wandering about 19th-century London. Their being there was Million Eyes' doing.

He decided he'd catch up with Snider later and went after the boys. He saw them stop soon after running from the house. He couldn't hear what they were saying anymore – he was too far away. He saw Edward pick up a stray sheet of newspaper and examine it.

A minute later, he saw them each take another chronozine pill and pull together in a tight embrace. A flash of light – white, blinding and silent – blazed from where they stood, lighting up the whole street for a split-second.

Gone.

The white flash had drawn confused looks from passers-by. A couple of people stopped, glanced around and moved on, slightly more haste in their step. Rawling hoped no one had been watching closely enough to actually see the princes vanish in front of their eyes.

One problem at a time.

It was still only a matter of minutes since John Snider had departed for Whitechapel with the book – Rawling could still catch up. He put on his spectacles and did a quick scan of the princes' point of dematerialisation: *out of temporal radius*. That meant wherever the princes had gone, it was beyond the ambit of his chronode, the chip in his head that allowed him to read time and select time zones after taking a chronozine pill. Its ambit was ten thousand years in the future and ten thousand years in the past. Rawling hoped the princes' destination was sometime beyond the former – then at least there was no chance of them fucking up the existing timeline (which was messed up enough as it was).

Well… no changes yet.

With nothing left to do but go after Snider, Rawling hurried over to another carriage that had just pulled into the street. This one, unlike the vehicle he'd watched Snider get into, had four wheels, two horses and the driver sitting in front.

"Good evening, sir," Rawling said to the driver. "Please kindly take me to Whitechapel."

"Of course, sir. And a good evening to you too." He seemed surprised by Rawling's politeness. Perhaps Victorian Londoners were just as rude as 21st-century Londoners. Rawling climbed inside the carriage and closed the door. He heard the soft snap of the driver's whip and the carriage rocked forwards.

He retrieved his phone from his waistcoat pocket and rang Miss Morgan to update her.

"Yes, Mr Rawling?" she answered sharply.

"I've found the book, ma'am," he replied.

"You have it?"

"Not yet. A man called John Snider has it. I'm pursuing him as we speak."

"Do you know how he got it?"

"Yes, ma'am, I do. He took it from… from Edward V and Richard, Duke of York."

A pause, then, "So they had Skinner's chronozine. Edward IV must've given it to them. And the book."

"Yes, ma'am."

"Where are the princes now?"

"They used the chronozine to travel in time again."

"To when?"

"Out of temporal radius."

Rawling could tell her teeth were clenched as she spat,

"For fuck's sake," through them, but her exasperation tailed off quickly, probably as she realised its uselessness. Sighing deeply she echoed his earlier sentiment, "One problem at a time. Just get that book back, Mr Rawling. We have less than two hours till the Shield fails."

Then it would be over. Rawling would be trapped there, with no future to return to. "Yes, ma'am. Understood."

Miss Morgan's anxiety-flecked voice cut to three short beeps, then silence. Rawling slipped the phone back into his pocket. Immediately worried that he wasn't going to catch up to Snider, he opened the window and called to the driver, "My friend – any chance you can go a bit faster? I have an urgent engagement."

"Yes, sir." His whip snapped loudly and the horses sped up.

Shortly after, the carriage pulled into Whitechapel High Street and, a stroke of luck, Rawling caught sight of Snider walking up the road. His carriage must've been particularly slow, or Snider had got waylaid somehow. Rawling climbed out of his carriage, paid the driver and discreetly followed Snider.

Rawling checked his watch – 11.15pm. He saw Snider wander up Osborn Street and onto Brick Lane and followed, walking about a hundred metres behind on the opposite side of the road. Up ahead, prancing down his side of the road and swinging her hips inelegantly was a plump, unsightly woman in a rugged, red-brown overcoat, ample brown frock, black boots and a black bonnet. Hanging from her shoulder was a tatty-looking brown bag, shoddily woven from frayed, flimsy strands of rope. Her features lit up with excitement at the sight of Snider and she ran across the road to him.

Ah. Could this be her?

Rawling retrieved his spectacles and put them on.

Mary Ann Nichols. DOB: 25/08/1845.
Commonly known as 'Polly'.

It was her. The woman destined to hand the book to Queen Victoria – which Rawling was there to prevent.

He stayed back, watching them embrace. Snider clasped Nichols' face in his hands and buried his tongue in her mouth for such a length of time that it looked like they would both suffocate. Her hands slid up his back and her fingers bent into claws as she dragged them down again, her fingernails looking like they might rip the broadcloth of his coat.

They broke away at last. Nichols took Snider's hand. She led him inside the front door of a house a little further up the road, shutting it behind them. Rawling waited in a shadowy alleyway between two houses and watched. He saw a low light flicker in an upstairs window.

He waited.

Fifteen minutes later, the front door opened and Snider and the woman emerged looking flushed and a bit dishevelled. With a parting kiss, they walked off in opposite directions, the woman towards the Frying Pan public house on the corner of Brick Lane and Thrawl Street, Snider towards Rawling.

Rawling wasn't sure what to do. Had Snider given the book to Nichols? Or did he still have it?

Snider was crossing onto Rawling's side of the road. Any moment now he would pass the alleyway. Rawling was going to have to confront him.

Snider walked briefly out of view, blocked by the house Rawling was hiding behind. Rawling listened for the tap of his shoes against the cobbles.

Rawling's stomach churned. He'd known that he might have to resort to violence to recover the book. He just hoped it wouldn't come to that. He'd been in control for years now. Everything that happened – it was in the past. And it was going to stay there. There was no way he was going to lose it now.

Snider's footsteps now clear and loud, Rawling stepped into his path, standing about a metre in front of him.

Snider stopped, frowning. "Do I know you?"

"No," said Rawling. "Do you still have the book?"

Snider shook his head, looking confused. "Book? What book?"

Please don't do that. Rawling hated liars. Time-wasters. "You know very well I'm referring to the book you stole from the two boys. Give it to me, please."

"Sorry. I don't know what you're talking about."

Snider tried to walk around Rawling – Rawling blocked him.

"Get the fuck out of my way."

"Not until I have the book."

Snider barged past him but Rawling clamped his hand on his forearm.

Snider's eyes flared at Rawling's gall. He jabbed Rawling's cheek with his free fist.

Rawling bounced back quickly. He was tougher than he looked. *Why does everybody fucking underestimate me?* Something hot and fast surged through his body and propelled him at Snider. He grabbed him by both shoulders and yanked him hard into the alleyway.

Snider fell face-first onto the ground, smashing his chin, and his bowler hat flew off. As he twisted round, mouth open, eyes darting about in panic, throwing up his hand to collect the blood dripping fast from the gash in his chin, Rawling arched over him, smothering him in his silhouette.

Rawling's fingers were tingling. Why did the fucker have to provoke him like that? "Where is the book?" Rawling demanded one more time.

"Go fuck yourself!"

I haven't got time for this.

Rawling dived to his knees, fastened a grip on Snider's throat and squeezed, Snider's chin wound bleeding all over his brown leather glove. Snider's hands shot up and clawed at Rawling's, desperately trying to prise open his fingers.

"Please don't make me ask again," said Rawling, trying to remain as calm as possible.

When Snider still refused to speak, Rawling closed his hand around his neck another centimetre. He could feel the fast throb of Snider's blood through his glove, labouring through the veins that he was crushing. Purple tinted Snider's face.

Something familiar stirred in Rawling. It rose from the pit of his stomach, rippled all the way to his fingers. The rush was back. The one he'd not felt in years. The life slowly fading from Snider's eyes made him feel like he was waking from a dream. He didn't want to let go. He'd missed this. Oh, how he'd missed it.

With no voice, just a sliver of breath, Snider finally choked, "Okaaay," and stuffed his trembling hand into the left side of his coat.

So he *did* still have it.

Although the excitement coursing through him was difficult to part with, Rawling forced himself to loosen his grip slightly. He didn't want to – he had to.

Snider's eyes flickered with panic. He pulled out his hand – empty – and shoved it inside the right side of his coat. He withdrew his hand – still empty.

He didn't have it. *Fuck.* Rawling released his throat. He couldn't just pluck this man out of history. He was there to fix things, not fuck them up. He was better than that idiot, Robert Skinner, and he was going to prove it.

Snider doubled over, heaved for air, coughed and spat blood. Rawling must've burst something. "S-she… she must've… stolen it from me," he spluttered.

Rawling left Snider sprawled on the cobbles and headed for the Frying Pan pub.

What just happened? He removed his bloody gloves and tucked them in his pocket. *What did I just do?*

He'd closed that door a long time ago. And it wasn't a door that was easy to close. If what he'd just done had reopened it, he knew he'd never close it again.

Keep it together, James. Keep it together…

Reaching the Frying Pan, he gazed through the grimy window. He didn't go in, just scanned for Nichols. Prostitutes loitered around men playing cards, swigging beer and occasionally making provocative gestures at them with their tongues and fingers. There she was. Standing slanted at the bar as though one of her legs was much shorter than the other, clutching the edge of the counter to stop from toppling.

Her shabby rope bag was swinging from her shoulder. Rawling peered hard to see if he could make out the dark green binding of the book through the bag's loose weave. He couldn't, but it was probably shrouded by the other things she had in it.

When Nichols moved away from the bar, she stumbled over an empty chair and let a good inch of her cloudy pint splash over the shoulder of one man's frock coat. She laughed hysterically. The man was pink with rage and shot an obscenity at her, but she was already halfway across the pub, falling all over a bunch of people who appeared to be her friends.

Rawling waited for her to part with the bag, but she didn't let it off her shoulder. Perhaps she'd realised the book's importance and wasn't letting it out of her sight.

He waited outside until half-midnight when Nichols left the Frying Pan, lurching and swaying down Thrawl Street, utterly wasted. Rawling was on the opposite side in a furtive pursuit, the street too busy and open to apprehend her. He watched her go inside a common lodging-house marked *Wilmott's*.

Once again he waited. He would've waited till morning if he had to, but nearly an hour and a half later, the front door to Wilmott's opened, Nichols stumbling out. "Sorry, Nichols," said a man from inside. "No money, no room. I ain't running no charity here."

"Never mind!" Nichols squealed in reply. "Save a bed for me, will you? 'Cause I'll soon get my doss money." She pointed at her hat, "See what a jolly bonnet I've got now!"

The front door slammed and Nichols turned, staggering along Thrawl Street. It would've been easy to pounce on her and snatch her bag, given the state she was in, but Rawling couldn't have done it without someone seeing. So he bided his time, maintaining a careful distance as she continued at a stop-start pace, occasionally colliding with walls, onto Commercial Street. It was even busier here, mostly with prostitutes looking for trade, along with a few pedestrians and the odd carriage. Victorian London didn't sleep any more than 21st-century London.

Rawling watched Nichols knock on the doors of several more lodging houses and get turned away. She turned left up Whitechapel High Street, tried another lodging house – to no success.

She reached the corner of Whitechapel High Street and Osborn Street, spotted someone she knew and made every house around aware of that fact with a jubilant scream, "Emilyyyy!" She floundered towards her, arms flailing like spaghetti, legs barely attached to the rest of her.

Emily looked like another prostitute but by her symmetrical walk was clearly less intoxicated. She was almost overturned when Nichols plunged into her arms.

"God, Polly, how much have you had?" Emily said, freeing herself from Nichols and propping her up against her hands.

"Only a couple," Nichols lied, unleashing that loathsome, piercing, wince-inducing giggling sound she kept making at the pub.

This woman was getting on Rawling's last nerve.

"Best get back to Wilmott's, before you do yourself a mischief," said Emily.

"Naaaah. Can't, can I. Bastards kicked me out." She continued to sway from side to side as she leaned against Emily's hands.

"Why?"

"Couldn't pay 'em. Made me doss money three times over today" – she hiccupped – "but I drank it aaaaall away."

"Oh, Polly, what d'you go and do that for?"

"It's fine. I'll make it again. Won't be long before I'm back."

"Where you going now?"

"Work the streets, I guess. Got a new bonnet, see. They're all gonna want some of this!" She did a graceless pelvic thrust as she said 'this'.

"You be careful. Pickings are slim tonight. And it's almost" – the bells of a nearby church chimed at that very moment – "no, it's *exactly* half two in the morning."

Nichols murmured as they parted, lips struggling to shape the right words, "Don't you worry about me!"

Emily turned up Osborn Street, and Nichols continued her meandering course up Whitechapel High Street. Rawling resumed his pursuit.

He followed her to a narrow street called Buck's Row. *At last* a road that was bare of people. The smell of stale urine that was common all around these parts was even more pungent here. To Rawling's left were some warehouses, to his right the grim edifice of a school, with a stable yard and a row of dreary terraced houses just ahead of it, the only light on the street coming from a single gas lamp at the other end.

No time to lose. Rawling saw Nichols stumble against the brick wall just next to the gateway to the stable yard. She was too drunk to notice the clap of his hard leather boots against the cobbles as he advanced towards her.

He couldn't give her a chance to scream. There were houses right there. So he clamped his hand around her left arm and spun her against the wall, then slammed his fist square into her face. Knocked out, she crumpled to the pavement.

He dropped to his knees and yanked her bag from her shoulder. He rifled through raggedy bits of clothing, a rank facecloth, stained pocket handkerchief, comb, broken slab of mirror, ripped, stained papers, a chunk of stale bread and some loose, partly shrivelled grapes, and there it was. *The History of Computer-Aided Timetabling for Railway Systems* by Jeremy Jennings. He tossed the bag and its contents, and stuffed the book into the large inside pocket of his suit jacket.

Nichols moved her head, started to murmur. She was coming around.

Go, James. Run. You have what you came for. Run before she sees you and wakes everyone in a square mile with her screams.

But a part of him wanted her to scream. Then he'd have no choice.

He stared down at Nichols. Waited. Found himself reaching into his other pocket for his knife.

No, James. Don't.

He released the clean, silver blade from its leather sheath, caught a flicker of himself in the metal. The blade shone orange in the low light from the gas lamp at the end of the street.

Nichols' eyes opened a crack, saw him and the blade hanging over her, then sprang open like mouse traps. Her body heaved and she opened her mouth to scream.

Rawling swung the blade, carved through her throat like a cake. Blood squirted the cobbles. Nichols' intended scream turned into a guttural cough, blood erupting from her throat like a malfunctioning fountain, spraying Rawling in the chest.

The thrill he'd felt earlier was back, just ten times stronger. Warm, tingly, gratifying. He remembered this feeling so well. A hundred times better than all his best orgasms. He looked up, breathed in deeply, closed his eyes. He was exhilarated, like he'd been set free. His whole body throbbed with it.

He opened his eyes, returned them to Nichols. She was spluttering silently, arms flailing about her open throat, which spewed a continuous flow of blood onto the pavement.

His lips trembling, he swung the knife again, deeper. *Fuck.* This time he felt the scrape of bone against the tip of the blade – her spine. Instant tingling in his fingers.

The life went out of Nichols' eyes like snuffed-out flames. Her head drooped to one side, arms flopped beside her, and she was still. A steady trickle of blood leaked from the corner of her mouth like an unfastened tap. He ran his bloody knuckle along his lower lip, leaving a droplet of blood which he licked away.

Wow.

Feeling more alive than he had in years, he buried the knife deep in Nichols' abdomen, dragged it through her flesh. *Sshlunk.* Took it out, stabbed again. *Sshlash.* Again, again, again.

He heard something. Rustling. He had to stop. *Damn.* It was like pulling out before finishing. He stood up straight, breathless, and looked around.

Meeoow.

A small tabby cat, fir marbled with white, greyish-brown and a little black, slinked towards him, tail curling.

He looked down at Nichols' body. *James, that's enough. What have you done?* He wiped his bloody hands and knife on Nichols' frock and picked up the leather sheath he'd tossed aside. He replaced the knife in the sheath and returned it to his pocket.

The soaring pleasure was gone, replaced by confusion, fear.

He'd lost control. And now his past had come hurtling into his present.

The tabby cat meowed again.

Rawling lowered to his knees and the cat climbed into his arms. He cuddled it, stroking the ball of its head. "You look just like Bella," he murmured, a picture of his mother's cat flashing through his mind.

Instantly his thoughts were on his mother, on telling her what he'd done. What would she think? He supposed he wouldn't need to worry about that. Mother had dementia and couldn't speak. He'd still tell her – he told her everything, always had. But he never knew how much she understood because she just stared blankly at him like an imbecile. It infuriated him sometimes.

Suddenly – nearby footsteps. Someone was about to turn down Buck's Row.

"I've got to go, little one."

He set the cat down on the cobbles. It crept towards Nichols' body, sniffing the blood that was congealing beneath her. Rawling turned and sprinted up Buck's Row.

He veered onto a road called Brady Street and sneaked into an alleyway. He waited for his heaving chest to relax. Then he took out his phone and called Miss Morgan.

"I have the book."

A small breath of relief. "Good. Destroy it. Destroy it now."

"Yes, ma'am. Then what?"

"Wait for my call."

"Yes, ma'am."

Miss Morgan hung up.

Rawling pulled the book from his pocket. He reached for his disruptor, holstered beneath his jacket on his hip.

"Bastard!"

Rawling's fingers never touched the disruptor. Somebody slammed into him from behind, two hands gripping his arms, and he thumped onto the cobbles, the book yanked from his grip. In his periphery, Rawling saw it plummet into a storm drain some metres ahead.

His attacker was on top of him, screaming, "You killed her, you bastard!" Rawling squirmed to face him, saw a red-faced John Snider pull back his arm and swing his fist.

Rawling thrust out his hand to block the punch, clamping it round Snider's wrist. He swung his other hand, fist connecting with Snider's jaw with a *thwack*.

Snider dazed, Rawling grabbed both of his shoulders and rolled, flipping him onto his back, both hands going straight for Snider's neck. This time he wasn't letting go. As Snider tried to grapple with him, Rawling squeezed. Without gloves, every laboured ripple of blood through Snider's throat was tangible.

"I... know... w-what's in that... book..." Snider choked. "I know... what you're... planning..."

Rawling squeezed harder, tighter, as Snider thrashed and clawed for air and freedom, mouth stretched open awkwardly.

Pleasure tingled through him once more, becoming stronger and more gratifying the tighter he squeezed, the more purple Snider's face became.

Snider's eyes rolled backwards in their sockets, his thrashing growing aimless, feeble. Then his arms flopped to his sides, his movements weakening to a twitch.

Then nothing.

Rawling released his grip, release sweeping through him. He took a long deep breath and climbed to his feet. His hands were red-raw.

As the sensation passed, rational thought returned.

He was supposed to recover the book. That was it. Miss Morgan said nothing about killing anyone.

Now he'd killed two people. Snatched them from the timeline. Could he have done more harm than good? Who knew. Alright, so Mary Ann Nichols was just a prostitute. Her impact on the timeline would've been minimal. Well, probably minimal. John Snider – Rawling was less sure about him. He wasn't poor, judging by his clothes and manner. Rawling had no way of knowing his importance.

He could only hope that history wouldn't miss him.

Rawling left Snider's body in the alleyway and walked over to the storm drain that *The History of Computer-Aided Timetabling for Railway Systems* had fallen into. He looked through the gaps in the grate but couldn't see anything in the water below.

Damn.

It was as good as destroyed though, submerged in London's drainage system – Rawling hoped.

A phone call from Miss Morgan was imminent. Either she would order him back to the future, the timeline restored, or there would be a further loose end to tie up somewhere or somewhen.

Rawling wasn't ready to go. Not yet. He felt higher than he'd ever felt his whole life. He'd been walking round like a zombie for so many years. Finally he was alive again. Alive – and powerful. He needed to feel this again. He needed to.

The door *was* open. And it would stay open. He should never have fucking closed it.

He tweaked the temporal alignment on his phone so that by the time Miss Morgan called, it would be a couple of months later for him. One of time travel's perks.

Then he left the alleyway and walked up Brady Street. He would walk the streets for the rest of the night, waiting for the sun to rise. After about ten minutes it started to rain. Rawling lifted his face into the rain and let the water fill his mouth and eyes and pour down his open suit jacket and bloody shirt, diluting it pink.

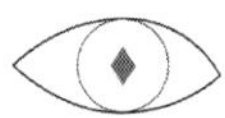

James Rawling was right about one thing. John Snider was not a man destined for the history books. Still, had Rawling not just strangled him to death, he would have gone on to father a son with his wife in 1891: Arthur Snider. Arthur Snider in turn would've fathered a son in 1927: Christopher Snider.

Christopher Snider would've been a wayward child and a hateful, unhinged adult. Instilled with his family's prejudices, he would've become a founding member of a far-right terrorist group with a fierce anti-Muslim agenda.

That agenda would've led him and his cohorts to Saudi Arabia in 1957 to commit a mass shooting in a shopping centre in Riyadh, Saudi's capital.

One of the casualties would've been Hamida Ibrahim, wife of Mohammed bin Laden, at the time eight months pregnant with a son.

A son she was planning to call Osama.

19

June 23rd 2020

After a long shift in the warehouse at Tesco, Jennifer was heading home. Home was a just-big-enough room in a house she shared with four very loud Sussex University students. It wasn't all bad. They were nice people who she'd happily befriend were it not for her new commitment to a people-free life. Her job as a warehouse operative wasn't all bad either. She did the night shifts, typically, which involved long periods of alone time. That worked for her.

The morning sun was wading through a thin mist lingering at the tops of the buildings as Jennifer strolled through Brighton's still-sleeping bohemian quarter, the North Laine. This former slum had kooky-looking bars, shops and theatres that did their damnedest to coax her out of her self-imposed solitary confinement whenever she walked by.

As she passed Mrs Mistle's flower shop, her thoughts returned to her mum. It was her birthday today. Jennifer had arranged for a bunch of gerberas to be delivered to her at home this morning, before work. Big, ostentatious ones with bright orange, yellow-tipped petals, just the kind she loved, with a note to reiterate that she was okay and she loved her.

Jennifer felt a sharp pang in her chest. Wasn't enough. She wanted to speak to her. She hadn't heard her warm, slightly husky voice in eight months. She wanted to know if she was okay, how work was going, if she was seeing anyone new since Phil, if Jamie hated her. She'd written to the both of them shortly after she arrived in Brighton. She was honest – to a point. Told them what she'd told Adam about people trying to kill her and that she'd had to run away. And she wrote a separate letter to Adam, just to let him know she was safe. She promised them all she'd be back and that she had a plan, but that was a lie. She had no plan. *Time* was her plan. Let enough pass and hope that Million Eyes would move on, forget about her. Maybe then she could return home.

The sun had mopped up what remained of the mist by the time she passed the Grindstone, the tiny pub on the corner of her road. Right now she had two sanctuaries in the world – her bedroom and the Grindstone, where she could drink in peace since only about three or four locals were ever there, and always too drunk to notice her. Sticky floors, peeling wallpaper, gross toilets and a gruff barman with a sweat problem all did a brilliant job of fending off the masses.

Her front door opened just as she went to insert her key. It was one of her housemates. Amy – she thought. Or was it Chloe? One of the two. Amy/Chloe said brightly as she walked past Jennifer, probably on her way to a lecture, "Oh, hi Vicks."

Eeek.

There it was, like always. The invisible flinch she did each time someone called her Vicks or Vicky. Would she ever get used to it?

Changing her name was one of the first things Jennifer had decided to do after coming here. She didn't go through the proper legal process, of course; she wasn't about to get flagged up on any government databases. Instead she found a guy in the city who was a dab hand at forging identities. Understandably never giving his name, just calling himself the Facechanger like some Marvel character, he helped Jennifer assume the identity of Victoria Moore, complete with an elaborate fictional backstory. His skills weren't cheap, though, and Jennifer was without funds. Fortunately (or unfortunately, depending on how you looked at it), the Facechanger revealed himself as your average pervert and was willing to accept a blowjob instead. Jennifer was still working on burying it in the deepest, darkest recesses of her memory; heavy drinking was helping with that.

She used her new identity to land the job at Tesco, which enabled her to move out of Becks Shayes' spare room and leave the poor girl alone. From that moment on she was on her own. Nobody knew her, but that was the point. Jennifer had been clinging to the fiction of Victoria Moore's life like a security blanket ever since.

Jennifer climbed to the first floor and was hit by a wall of heat as she entered her bedroom. Her room got the first of the day's sun and her flimsy cream curtains did next to nothing to keep any of it out. Definitely time to invest in some blackouts. She dropped her handbag next to the leaning tower of laundry in the corner, switched on her fan, threw open her window as wide as it would go, got naked, and plunged onto the bed.

She tried to sleep – couldn't – and it wasn't just the heat. It was everything. She had days like this. Low days where all she could think about was her mum and how she'd die for a cuddle. There was no one who cuddled like her mum. She was a proper squeezer, would hold you so tight that the folds and textures of your clothes would dent your skin, like she was protecting you from a bomb. On a low day, a cuddle like that instantly took the edge off.

Now Jennifer got cuddles off no one, ever.

There were times when she thought, *You know what? I am willing to die for a cuddle.* That she was going to jump on a train to Deepwater and go home to Mum, and stick two fingers up to Million Eyes along the way by telling everyone on her path everything she knew about them. She didn't have a scrap of evidence but that didn't matter. All she needed to do was get enough people asking questions, and sooner or later they'd crumble under the weight of them.

But it was all talk. That kind of thing would take bravery, not something Jennifer had in abundance. She did what she had to, to survive, but that was about as far as it went. If it was fight or flight she'd always, if she could, choose the latter – hence her current situation. She was a coward, really. Million Eyes had scared the shit out of her, and she'd run away.

Maybe she was being too hard on herself. She wasn't just protecting herself from Million Eyes. She was protecting her mum, her sister, Adam. Going home for a cuddle would put them in danger as well. It wasn't just cowardice that stopped her packing her things and getting on a train. It was them.

Thing is – had she protected them? Were they safe? Getting away had always seemed like the best way of keeping them safe, but what if Million Eyes had gone after them anyway?

Mum, Jamie and Adam had heard from her but she hadn't heard from them. Not for eight months. So who the fuck knew?

She sat up, swung her legs off the bed. *Oh God.* She gagged and clutched her chest as her every worst fear hit her at once.

She leapt off the bed. There was something she'd thought about doing for a few months now, these fears surfacing more and more. But each time she'd almost gone through with it, she'd stopped on account of the risk and drowned her fears in a bottle of cheap rum.

But today she had to know. She had to know they were okay – *now*.

Before she could talk herself out of it, she went to grab some fresh underwear from her chest of drawers and, realising that every sock, bra and pair of knickers she owned was in her laundry pile, put back on the ones she'd worn at work last night. Then she pulled on loose shorts and a t-shirt, closed her window, switched off her fan and went downstairs. She grabbed a bottle of water and left the house.

The nearest train station was London Road, a ten-minute walk. Jennifer got there and bought a ticket to Eastbourne. On the forty-five-minute journey she thought about what she was going to say. She'd have to keep it brief, which meant choosing her words carefully and not letting emotion overcome her – which, she knew, was going to be fucking hard.

She got off the train in the town centre. It was a five-minute walk to the second-hand phone shop she'd looked up earlier, where she purchased an old Nokia and stuck a tenner's worth of credit on it.

She found some quiet-looking public gardens and parked on an empty bench, as far away from anyone else as she could get. She took out the phone she'd just bought, glanced over both shoulders to check she was alone, and rang her mum at work.

She heard ringing and swallowed. She felt her breath quicken, her heart begin to pound.

It rang for some time. It was her mum's direct dial, but maybe she was in a meeting?

Or maybe she was… Jennifer cut off the thought. She

wasn't going there. No fucking way.

Please answer. Please, please just –

"Hello, Kerry Larson speaking."

Even if she hadn't said her name, Jennifer would've known from the word 'hello'. She'd know that voice anywhere. Oh, that wonderful, warm, perfect voice. She'd never appreciated how comforting a sound it was until this moment. She felt a rush of God knows what, like a deep emptiness inside her was suddenly filling back up.

The rush made her hand shake so hard she thought she might drop the phone. She gripped it with both hands and tried to blink back the tears that were filling her eyes.

Keep it together, Jen. Don't waste this.

"Hello?" said Mum. "Is anyone there?"

Jennifer had to take a deep breath to form the words but still they came out small and shaky, "Happy birthday, Mum."

Her voice cracked. "Jennifer?"

"Yeah."

"Oh my God. Jen? Is it… is that really you?"

"It's really me."

Mum's quick breaths turned to sobs. It made Jennifer crumble too. "Mum, I'm sorry. I'm so, so sorry."

Mum was able to push some words through her sobs. "Jen… where are you?" Then, with more urgency, "Where the *hell* are you?"

"Safe, Mum. I'm safe, I promise. Did you… did you get my flowers?"

"Yes. I got them. But I don't want flowers. I want my daughter."

"I know."

"I've been worried sick, Jen. I got your letter. You said there are people trying to kill you. Who?"

"It doesn't matter."

Her voice sharpened with anger, "Are you joking? It matters to me! You're my daughter." Her voice cracking again, "Why won't you just tell me where you are?"

"Mum, I… I can't. I don't want to put you in danger."

She took a breath and hardened, instantly, with motherly conviction, "Jen, listen to me. Whoever's after you, we'll face them together. We'll go to the police – together."

"No, Mum. These people have operatives everywhere,

including inside the police, which means I can't trust anyone right now. I need to find another way."

"But Jen – !"

"Mum, please! Let's just talk. Please, I just wanna talk to you. I've missed you… so much." She rubbed away fresh tears.

Her mum started crying again too. "Oh, sweetheart…"

"Are you okay? You know, generally?"

"You mean apart from my eldest daughter abandoning me?"

Jennifer clutched her forehead. "I'm sorry, Mum. I just… I just want to know how you are."

Mum sniffed and took a breath, "I'm alive, Jen. That's as good as it gets."

Jennifer's hands were shaking. She didn't know what to say or do to put this right. Was there anything?

"Is Jamie okay? Does she hate me?"

"She's your sister, Jen. She loves you. We both love you."

It wasn't something Jennifer and her mum said to each other often. They didn't need to. But this was different. This couldn't be more different. Million Eyes had ripped them from each other without so much as a goodbye. They *both* needed to hear it.

"I love you too." Jennifer felt her heart throb as she said it.

"We tried to find you, you know."

"You did?"

"Yes. Me, Jamie and Adam got together, messaged as many of your friends as we could think of."

Two thoughts hit her at once. It was a good thing she went to Becks – a part of her life she pretended never happened. And… *Adam*. Relief pinched her gut. "Adam? You've spoken to him? Is he okay?"

"I've not seen him in a while. I told him to move –"

"Wait." The air vanished from Jennifer's lungs. She heard something. *Clicking*.

"Jen, what is – ?"

"Ssshh."

She listened. *Tker-tker. Tker-tker.* It was quiet, metallic, in the background. Two second intervals, or about that. Just like when Katie was after her and she was on the phone to Adam.

Then it stopped, and all she could hear was her mother's

ragged breathing. She didn't remember it stopping before.

"Jennifer, what's going on?"

Maybe it was nothing.

Tker-tker. Tker-tker.

Shit, it was back. Jennifer's stomach rolled with dread.

They're listening. They've tapped Mum's phone.

"Shit! Mum, I've gotta go."

"What? No. You can't. Please, sweetheart."

"I'm sorry."

"Please don't." Quiet sobbing overtook her again. "You're breaking my heart."

Jennifer shook. Those words had just broken hers.

"I love you, Mum."

She hung up and got to her feet, drawing in a long, steadying breath and swallowing a wave of emotions. She'd deal with them later. She glanced around and hurried to the gardens' exit, dropping the phone into one of the many sculpted stone fountains along the way.

This was her intention from the get-go. It was why she'd come all the way to Eastbourne. If Million Eyes really were listening in on that call and were able to trace it, they'd trace it here, and Jennifer would be long gone. Yes, it was a risk. But it was worth it to hear Mum's voice, to know she was… well, okay was generous, given that Jennifer's disappearance had utterly broken her. *Alive.*

Jennifer hastened to the station and caught the first train back to Brighton. She stared mindlessly out of the window at a blur of greenery, Mum's broken voice in her ear – "*You're breaking my heart*" – over and over again like a succession of cuts. By the time she was back in Brighton she felt nothing. Just numb. Numb and cold, despite it being thirty degrees outside.

She walked languidly to the Grindstone and ordered a double rum and coke, followed by another a few minutes later, and another after that. It worked. Her mother's voice started to fade away.

She was staring at the bottom of an empty glass, no concept of what the time was, when a bunch of girls barrelled into the pub, laughing loudly. Jennifer glanced over. There were four of them, all attractive twenty-somethings, not the sort you'd expect in the Grindstone. But then, their volume and posture suggested they probably weren't all that aware of where they were. It was a pub, it sold booze. Hell, that was enough for Jennifer – why not them?

She ordered another rum, hoping they wouldn't stay long and she could go back to drinking in silence. By the time she'd paid, the prettiest and soberest-looking of the four friends was at the bar next to her, about to order.

"Could I get a porn star martini, gin and tonic, Jack Daniels and diet coke, and, erm…" Fish, the barman, frowned as she scanned the beer taps. "A pint of Stowford Press for me, please."

Hmm, a fellow cider drinker. Stowford Press was Jennifer's drink of choice when she wasn't trying to get shit-faced as quickly as possible. She found rum much better for that.

"Anything else?" said Fish in that annoyed-sounding growl of his.

The girl looked over at her mates at the round table in the corner. "Fuck it. Four Jägerbombs as well, please."

Jennifer feared a further increase in these girls' volume. Perhaps if she drank more as well, she'd be able to drown them out.

As Fish fetched their drinks, Jennifer could sense the girl looking at her. *Please don't talk to me.*

But she was 'one of those' – confident and quite happy to start chatting to a random. "You alright over here on your own?"

Without looking up, "Fine, thanks." Biggest lie of the day thus far.

"You don't look it."

Jennifer looked up, cocked an irritated eyebrow at the girl. *Wow*. She really was pretty. Stunning, even. Silky brown hair with blonde highlights, thin lips, arresting blue eyes. Jennifer pretended not to notice. "And how do I look, stranger?"

"Like shit."

Jennifer mustered a half-hearted bitchy look and resumed staring at her drink. She couldn't be too offended. It was the kind of directness she dished out herself. Well, back when she had people to dish it out to.

"Hey, I'm just saying what I see," the girl persisted. "You look like you could use some company."

Jennifer faced her again. "When are you gonna finish telling me what I look like?"

"About – now?"

"Good answer."

She held out her hand, but quickly lowered it again when Jennifer didn't reciprocate. "I'm Toasty."

"Come again?"

"Toasty."

"So you're warm. Or a sandwich."

She laughed. "Yeah, I get that a lot. My parents were drunk when they named me."

"Your parents were mean."

"You got a name?"

She almost said 'Jennifer'. The alcohol was to blame for that. "Vicky."

"Nice to meet you, Vicky. Do you wanna come join us?" She gestured to her friends. "You might not get much out of Trish and Nina – they're steaming. But me and Sarah are pretty coherent." A girl with bright red hair, probably Sarah, saw Toasty and Jennifer looking over and waved.

Jennifer thought about it. 'Toasty' – *what a name* – was right. She could use a bit of company right now.

"One drink," she said.

Toasty smiled. "Sure."

Fish finished preparing the Jägerbombs and placed them on a tray with Toasty's other drinks. "Actually, make that five Jägerbombs," she said, winking at Jennifer.

Jennifer's stomach fluttered. She felt a smile coming on for the first time in ages.

Fish prepared the last drink – huffing with apparent irritation as though he'd rather not have the extra business – and Toasty paid. Then she picked up her packed tray of tipples and did a slow, careful walk to the table. Rum and coke in hand, wondering if this shitty day might end a bit better than it started, Jennifer followed.

20

November 9th 1888

Unfortunately eleven-year-old crossing-sweeper Harriet Turner and her mother, Emma, were going to have to huddle together beneath a blanket on Whitechapel Road for the second night in a row. The last few days had been less than lucrative, so after buying a small pie from Mr Bradshaw's bakery for their supper, Harriet had nothing left for a bed in the doss-houses.

It was Miss Mayhew's fault. Lovely Miss Mayhew had not come by for several days now. She was a regular customer of Harriet's, always needing to cross Whitechapel Road for this, that or the other. After Harriet cleared the mud and horse dung from her path so she could cross without dirtying those magnificent dresses of hers, she was not only more generous with her coins than other folk, she'd often compliment Harriet on how thorough she'd been.

Harriet hoped to God that Miss Mayhew was all right. Whitechapel was a dangerous place right now. There was no telling what Jack the Ripper would do next.

Talking of whom – "Can I read it yet?" Harriet tugged on her mother's arm.

Her mother lowered the newspaper, a copy of *The Whitechapel Evening News* that a passing gentleman had dropped. It had an article about Jack the Ripper's latest victim, Mary Jane Kelly, murdered last night in her doss-house room on Dorset Street. Word on the street was that hers was the most horrific yet.

"You certainly cannot," Mother replied.

"What, not at all?" said Harriet.

"Not at all."

Sometimes Harriet wondered why her mother had taught her to read in the first place. She sulked for a bit, but it was always futile. Once Mother's mind was made up, no amount of pouting was able to change it.

"Are you going to eat your pie?" said Harriet. She'd only broken off a third of it for her, as asked for, but that third was still in Mother's lap, untouched.

"You have it, love," said Mother. Harriet was afraid she'd say that. "You need it more than I."

"Are you not hungry?"

"Not particularly. Not this evening."

Or yesterday evening. Or the day before. Or the day before that, come to think of it.

Her mother's appetite had been dwindling for weeks. All right, so Emma Turner – everybody knew – was not a well woman. Hadn't been for some years now. She used to be a costermonger, selling fruits and vegetables on the streets, earning a reasonable living. People liked her. She was known for having the shiniest, reddest apples and for being well-spoken, confident, smart and possibly the only literate coster around. But that's because she had a whole other life before the streets. She didn't like to talk about her family, so all Harriet knew was that her grandparents were well-to-do folk who'd banished her from the family home for getting pregnant with Harriet outside the bonds of marriage. A great sin, certainly. Harriet knew that. But it saddened and infuriated her that they could so readily disavow their daughter without giving her the chance to repent, and forsake their granddaughter in the process.

When she was five, Harriet started school. It was compulsory now – had been since 1880, her mother said. Children aged five to ten, rich and poor alike, had to go. Not that all of them did. Many went to work instead. Harriet herself was only in school a year – less than that, in fact. She left when her mother got ill. Suddenly her mother was tired and in pain all the time. It got so bad she couldn't make it to the wholesale markets anymore and her street-selling business crumbled. She and Harriet ended up, for a time, at the South Grove Workhouse, a ghastly place where they were separated in different wards and forbidden from talking to each other. They only went there for the free medical care and even that turned out to be useless. The doctors didn't know what was wrong, so they accused her mother of being lazy and feigning the pain.

And that was that. For the last year Mother had only been able to walk a few yards – with Harriet's help – and was always exhausted afterwards. Their home now was Whitechapel Road and occasionally its many crowded doss-houses, when allowed by the meagre living Harriet earned from keeping people's clothes clean.

Her mother's diminishing appetite was a new development, a worrying one. Harriet had tried to convince her to return to the workhouse – she refused. Harriet wondered if something had happened to her there, but of course Mother never said. She wouldn't, always trying to protect Harriet from the horrors of the world.

Alas, with Jack the Ripper stalking the streets since the summer, there was no hiding from them anymore – for anyone.

"May I go to the church, Mother?" said Harriet after finishing both shares of the pie.

"The hour is late, Harriet. This is when he prowls. Pray here tonight."

"Mother, please." Harriet felt much closer to God at St Mary's than on these mucky streets. She felt like her prayers had more chance of being heard.

"No, Harriet."

Harriet waited till her mother was asleep and decided to go anyway. As foul as they were, the streets were her home. Jack the Ripper wasn't going to scare her away from them. And anyway, St Mary's was only up the road. She had her knife, the one she took everywhere, if she ran into trouble. She'd be fine. Harriet needed God to hear her prayers tonight – she was concerned about Mother.

She plucked *The Whitechapel Evening News* from beside her sleeping mother and read the article about Mary Jane Kelly, entitled *Latest Ripper murder is the worst one yet*, on her way to the church.

> Another ferocious murder has shaken Whitechapel, this one more sickening than all those that came before. Earlier this morning, Mary Jane Kelly was found torn to pieces in her room at Miller's Court, on Dorset Street, her death presenting the hallmarks of the previous murders committed by the maniac known as Jack the Ripper. It is understood that Inspector Frederick Abberline of Scotland Yard is on the case.
>
> The following details have not yet been confirmed, but it is said that the mutilation of Miss Kelly's body was more wild, wanton and ghastly than in all previous Ripper cases, perhaps because it took place indoors instead of on the street. We understand that her throat was cut from ear to ear, right down to her spine. Her face and breasts were cut off and her chest and abdomen torn open. Most of her internal organs were removed and spread around the room. We're also told that her heart was taken, which is similar to previous Ripper victims Annie Chapman and Catherine Eddowes. Chapman's body was missing her uterus, Eddowes was missing both her uterus and left kidney. It is possible the Ripper takes them as trophies...

Harriet dropped the newspaper and gagged. A bead of vomit scuttled up her throat. She forced it back down and took some deep breaths.

What a way to die. How could a human being do something so horrendous?

Mother was right. She shouldn't have read it. Now she wouldn't sleep for days.

She tried to shake it away, think about something else.

Her mood changed as soon as she entered the church of St Mary Matfelon, standing on the site of a long-gone 13th-century church that was known to locals as the 'white chapel' for its bright, whitewashed finish. It was the root of the district's name. Harriet always liked telling people that. Surprisingly few people knew.

She took in her surroundings and felt instantly at ease, as if what happened to Miss Kelly was only a dream. Grand pointed arches, columns crowned with sculpted stone flowers, and an abundance of statues of cherubs and saints watched over her. Beautiful stencilled patterns dressed the walls and richly coloured stained glass windows twinkled in the candlelight. It never failed to fill her with awe, even though she'd seen it a thousand times. There was no question that she was nearer to God here, cut off from the physical and moral filth of the outside world, its dangers and degradations seeming so far away.

St Mary Matfelon was her sanctuary.

This evening Harriet noticed she wasn't alone in her desire for comfort at such a late hour. Halfway down the left side of the long nave, a man in dark clothes sat in one of the pews, looking like he was deep in prayer.

Not wanting to disturb him, Harriet tiptoed into a pew near the back and lowered herself onto the kneeler. Elbows on the pew in front, she clasped her hands together, closed her eyes and began addressing God.

Lord, my mother continues to suffer, yet has repented many times over for her wicked fornication. Can she not now be forgiven? Please Lord, make my mother well again...

A sound intruded on her prayer and the quiet of the church. She opened her eyes.

The man further down was breathing heavily, noisily and fast. An occasional moan slipped into each breath.

Curious, Harriet crept silently out of her pew and slunk along the north aisle flanking the nave towards the man. She had no shoes – that helped.

The man had his back to her, head down, but she could see he was a thin, small-framed man wearing a smart black suit and top hat. Stooping low to the ground, she sneaked between the pews behind him, tiptoeing in his direction.

Repetitive sounds added to the man's deep breathing and moaning – the fast swish of material rubbing together, the persistent click of a belt buckle. The man's left arm was juddering rapidly.

Surely not. Surely he can't be doing... *that.*

Harriet moved out of the pew into the central aisle next to him. As she came around to his side, she saw that his mouth was open, his eyes squeezed shut and, confirming her fears, his trousers were open and he was moving his hand up and down his penis with increasing speed.

"What are you doing?" Harriet blurted out, the stony echo of her voice swirling around the arches.

The man's hand froze. Harriet looked away as he tucked his penis back into his trousers. Then he stood up, faced her and tipped his hat, saying as if they'd just passed each other on the street, "Good evening, ma'am."

His boldness baffled her. She examined his face. Long, but not unsightly. Dimple in his chin. Green eyes. A smile that girls would melt for.

And yet he'd just been fetching mettle inside a church. Not just *a* church. *Her* church.

Harriet thought she'd left the filth and degradation outside but here it was, standing in front of her, casually defiling her sanctuary.

"Do you not realise you're on hallowed ground?" said Harriet. "How can you be so bold as to do *that* in our Lord's house?"

"It's quiet here," said the man, looking around, completely unrepentant.

Harriet was dismayed. "Who are you?"

The man gave a smile that at this point couldn't be anything but eerie. "Van Deen. Henry Van Deen. And you are?"

She wasn't sure whether to give her name or not, but in the interests of gleaning more information from this vile heretic… "Harriet."

"Pleased to make your acquaintance, Harriet." Mr Van Deen held out his left hand to shake hers – the one he'd been using to masturbate.

She recoiled in disgust. Was he making a sick joke? Or had he simply lost his mind?

"Do you not fear God's judgement, sir?"

He lowered his hand and mused on this. "There are other things I fear more."

"More than God?"

"More than God."

Harriet didn't understand him at all. "I will pray for your soul, sir."

He smiled softly. "Thank you."

This was clearly an ill man. One that didn't grasp the gravity of his sin. Harriet thought it best to leave him be.

Then she noticed his briefcase. It was tall and made from a light brown leather and was on the seat next to him. Her attention was drawn, in particular, to the dried bloodstains around its rim.

"What's in the case?" she asked.

The man shook his head. "You don't want to know."

"There's blood on it. Why?"

"I reiterate what I just said."

But she did. *Curiosity killed the cat,* her mother would say if she were here. *Yes, but cats have nine lives,* Harriet would always respond.

"Tell me or I'll scream," she said.

Mr Van Deen shrugged. "Fine. Look for yourself." She stuck her unblinking eyes to him as he lifted the case and approached her, her hand in the pocket of her pinafore, fingers clenched around the handle of her knife.

He held out the case to her. She bent forwards slightly, carefully, unstuck her eyes from Van Deen's slender frame and peered inside.

An acrid odour assaulted her nose. Her eyes met a collection of body parts. Shrivelled, wrinkly sacks of yellowy-green flesh mottled with black, and one that was pink and bloody, fresher than the others. Harriet spun away from the briefcase, unable to quell the upsurge of vomit that erupted from her throat and splashed across the floor tiles.

"I did warn you," Van Deen said.

Doubled over, leant against the nearest pew, Harriet took long breaths, eyes tracing the lines around the tiles, mind racing.

Organs.

Trophies.

Trophies from his victims.

Lord have mercy.

She straightened her back and faced Van Deen, pulling her knife from her pocket and pointing it at him, chest pounding. "You're him… You're… Jack."

"What?" He frowned. He seemed surprised. "I'm who?"

"Don't play dumb with me. I'm not stupid. I know exactly who you are. You're Jack the Ripper."

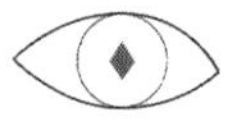

Jack the Ripper?

James Rawling froze, staring blankly at Harriet. Perhaps he should've been reading the newspapers.

Rawling knew precious little about Victorian history and hadn't brushed up on it because there was no time. He'd heard of Jack the Ripper, though. Of course he had. But he had no idea who he murdered, how many, or when.

What had he done? He'd been killing prostitutes – nobodies – because they were the safest bet, unlikely to be of importance to the timeline. But he was kidding himself. Jack the Ripper was Britain's most notorious serial killer. The whole fucking world knew about him. People *studied* him, for God's sake. How could he have been so reckless?

Rawling's heart started to race. *What will Mother think?* She loved him no matter what, he knew that. And once he'd explained the situation, she'd understand. Surely she would.

A more pressing concern was Miss Morgan. She was counting on him to fix the timeline, not fuck it up more. He was supposed to be proving himself to her, after Skinner had failed her so miserably. Talk about getting carried away.

Wait a minute.

Jack the Ripper was in the history books long before Rawling got here, long before this crisis even started. If Rawling really was *the* Jack the Ripper, that meant his actions in 1888 were supposed to happen.

Shit.

Everything was starting to make sense.

Rawling wasn't changing history.

He was becoming part of it.

"How could you?" shrieked Harriet, eyes wide. "How could you do that to those women? It's unspeakable!"

Rawling felt his phone vibrate in his pocket. Once Harriet had finished shrieking, its buzzing was audible to both of them in the silent church.

"What's that?" she frowned.

"I have to go," said Rawling softly. "Lovely talking with

you, Harriet."

"You're not going anywhere. I'm fetching a policeman."

She hurtled down the nave of the church towards the doors. After she was gone, Rawling took out his phone. Miss Morgan. Hopefully she was calling to tell him that the timeline was restored and he could return home.

"Mr Rawling, are you still in 1888?"

There was an irascible edge to her voice. That meant one of two things. A loose end connected to *The History of Computer-Aided Timetabling for Railway Systems* – last seen hurtling into a storm drain – needed tying up. Or Rawling's trickery with his phone hadn't worked. Over two months had passed for him, but only minutes should've passed for Miss Morgan – if he'd got the settings right.

"Yes, ma'am," said Rawling quietly. "Shall I return to the future?"

"No."

Rawling felt a tightening in his stomach. "Is this timeline still…?"

"Fucked? Yes."

It seemed his temporal tinkering had worked, but he wasn't out of the woods just yet.

"What do you ne –" Rawling started.

"Where's the book?"

He paused, unsure how to respond.

"Rawling, I know you failed to destroy it. So where is it?"

Shit, she knows. But how much? He swallowed. "I was attacked by the man who stole it, and it" – he took a nervous breath – "it fell into a drain."

She dryly repeated his words, "It fell into a drain."

"Yes, ma'am." An attempt at mitigation, "So it's as good as destroyed."

"No, Rawling, it isn't. Someone has it."

It was official. He'd screwed up. Worse than Robert Skinner? Maybe. Miss Morgan would definitely send him to the Room for this.

Then she said, "Fortunately for you I know who."

A reprieve?

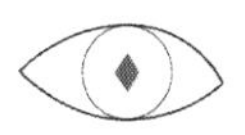

As soon as she'd launched out of the church, Harriet realised that she ought to watch where Henry Van Deen was going. The police would only lose him if she didn't give them some idea of his direction.

She turned and went back through the outer doors into the small vestibule that exited onto the nave. She ducked down and peeked through the glass panels in the inner doors.

Mr Van Deen was still standing where she'd left him, but he was holding a slim, black, rectangular object to his ear and talking to it.

"Yes, ma'am," he said. "Shall I return to the future?"

Harriet gasped. *The future?*

"Is the timeline still…?"

Harriet tried to wrap her mind around what she was seeing and hearing. She'd read about those new machines – telephones, she thought they were called – that could transmit people's voices across vast distances. Could Van Deen's device be something like that? Was somebody else talking to him *through* it? She'd seen a couple of pictures of people using these telephone things but Van Deen's looked nothing like them.

More importantly, what did he mean by 'timeline'? And how does someone 'return to the future'?

With the device still pressed to his ear, Van Deen continued talking. He mentioned being attacked by a man who'd stolen something and that this something had fallen into a drain. It really did seem like Harriet was hearing one half of a conversation.

Van Deen asked for instructions. After apparently receiving them, he lowered the device from his ear, tapped it with his finger and slipped it back into his pocket.

He glanced around, picked up his case of body parts and skulked through one of the arches flanking the nave, disappearing into the church's south aisle.

Compelled to follow, Harriet quietly pulled open the inner doors and tiptoed into the south aisle. She couldn't see him. She walked up the aisle, heading for the large room at the end where relics of the old church were displayed. Suddenly a bright white light flashed from inside the room, quick as lightning.

She froze. Her head was telling her not to go any further.

Her feet had other ideas.

Heart racing, she walked slowly into the room.

Huh?

There was nobody there – which didn't make sense. The room had no other door and there was no way Van Deen could've crawled out of either of its slim windows.

So where in the world did he go?

Harriet turned and ran from the church to Leman Street Police Station, telling policemen there that she had found Jack the Ripper and that they needed to come quick. The police were sceptical but they carried out a search of the church and the vicinity anyway, unwilling to leave any stone unturned.

As Harriet feared, they found nothing. They accused her of wasting police time and said that next time they'd arrest her.

After that, Jack the Ripper stopped killing. The police continued to investigate his crimes but he eluded them at every turn.

Harriet couldn't help but wonder if she was the only person in the world who knew why. She remembered Van Deen's words in the church. His talk of the timeline and returning to the future. And how could he have got out of that room? It was like he'd vanished into thin air.

Or perhaps to another point in time.

Eventually Harriet convinced herself that the reason the police hadn't found him was that he was gone, not just from Whitechapel, but from 1888.

Jack the Ripper had gone back to the future.

21

October 13th 2021

"*Fuck*," said Jennifer, as Toasty Clements slid up her naked body and poked her head out of a thick, damp cloud of duvet, before dropping down next to her on the bed. Her whole body weak and tingly, Jennifer stared at the ceiling and waited for her heart to slow. Then, turning to Toasty, "Can you do that again?"

Toasty smiled lovingly and kissed her lips, then looked past her to the clock on Jennifer's bedside table. Playfully, Jennifer threw her hand over Toasty's haunting blue eyes. "No, don't look at the time. Let's just stay here and do that all day. Yeah?"

Toasty chuckled. "Wouldn't that be fabulous? Unfortunately, you know… *life*." Toasty sat up and swung her legs out of bed.

Jennifer sighed, conceding inevitable defeat. "I know. Boring fucking life ripping you away from me. And that fucking magnificent tongue."

"You can have it back later." Flashing Jennifer her bedroom eyes, she stood up, skipped into the en-suite bathroom and hopped in the shower.

Jennifer rolled out of bed, walked over to the window and pulled back the curtains, squinting as a wave of light crashed over her. These were decent, thick curtains that actually darkened the room, not like the ones in her last place. She looked out over Trafalgar Rise, a residential road in Kemptown where she and Toasty had been living for nearly five months. It was a narrow, one-way street full of dips and potholes, with cars parked on both sides, where any car that dared to squeeze down it was in danger of shearing off dozens of wing mirrors. They were a stone's throw from Kemptown's amenities and at the bottom of Trafalgar Rise was Brighton's seafront. Jennifer couldn't see the sea from the window but she could hear it, just. And when the window was open she could smell the salt on the air. Sometimes, when Toasty was working late, she would go and sit alone on the pebbles at the water's fringe, dip her feet in the froth, or walk to the end of Brighton Pier and just stare across the endless waters. The sea made her feel safe. Free. It soothed her, something she was often in need of these days.

The house was a two-bedroom rental with a damp problem in the middle of a long terrace. The rooms were small and a bit beat-up, it had no front or back garden – just a tiny, high-walled rear courtyard – and there was nowhere to park; there weren't any permits left for the road so Toasty had to park her car ten minutes away. Still, it was a far sight better than the shared house setup Jennifer had had before. Warts and all, this house was theirs.

Of course, if Toasty had had her way, it would've been theirs for a lot longer than five months. It was after only three months of dating that Toasty first mentioned the idea of them moving in together. Jennifer had put it off as long as she could but Toasty eventually wore her down. Okay, that wasn't quite true. Jennifer *did* want to live with Toasty. She just didn't want to rush into anything. Even though she'd been called impulsive since she was a kid, that impulsiveness had never extended to relationships. She'd always been a bit more tentative when it came to those. More cautious. Daddy issues, perhaps.

Million Eyes had only made it worse, turned her into a full-on commitment-phobe. Convincing herself that Toasty wasn't a secret Million Eyes operative was the first hurdle she'd had to get over. And even though she believed that Toasty was 'clean' – as they say on TV – even now something made her want to be careful and not get too close.

Jennifer heard the yelp of the shower tap, bringing the splatter of water to an end. A moment later Toasty called, "Shower's free."

Jennifer went into the bathroom, saw Toasty bent over, her beautiful naked arse on display as she towelled her lower legs. Jennifer felt an irresistible urge to stroke it.

"Oi, that's my bum," Toasty smirked.

"Damn fine one at that."

Jennifer got in the shower as Toasty finished drying herself and brushed her teeth.

Then, as she started out of the room, Toasty said hesitantly, "Vicks…" which Jennifer barely heard over the shower.

"Yeah?"

"We do need to talk. About… you know, what we talked about last night."

Shit. They'd drunk a lot of wine last night. Now the memory of one particular conversation came back like a punch in the tit.

The 'B' word.

"Yeah," said Jennifer. "We will. Give me a couple of days to get my head together on it, then we'll talk."

Basically, Toasty wanted to know where Jennifer was on the subject of babies. Not that she wanted to have them right now, but Toasty – who was three years older – had felt the need to talk seriously about the possibility of having them in the future. It was something that had caused the wine to start flowing faster into Jennifer's glass last night, and it wasn't long before a potent mix of alcohol and sex had shelved the discussion before Jennifer could think too deeply on it.

The simple fact was that Jennifer didn't know. She'd always thought she'd have a baby some day, but not like this. No way. Her whole life was a fake. What she had with Toasty was real, but it was the only thing that was. And Jennifer wasn't willing to lie to her own child.

Plus, was it even fair to bring a child into this world? A world in which Big Brother was real and took the form of a time travelling global computer company that secretly controlled the government and was quite willing to kill people – past and present – to further its goals?

Having a baby wasn't an option, not till she'd dealt with Million Eyes and got her life back. And even though it was two years since she'd run away, she still hadn't a fucking clue how she was going to do that.

So, Jennifer *did* know exactly how she felt about the prospect of having a baby. What she didn't know was how to tell Toasty.

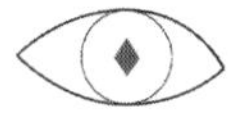

Just before 9.00am, Jennifer arrived at Willow's Antiques, a ten-minute walk from her house. There she worked as a retail assistant with her now friend, Sarah Myers. The manager/owner was Willow Hopkins, an ageing eccentric who'd been an antique dealer since – as he regularly reminded them – Jennifer and Sarah's mothers were in nappies.

Sarah was awesome. She was Toasty's friend from uni, the red-haired hottie Jennifer had met in the Grindstone on the same night she met Toasty, although Jennifer liked to think that Sarah and her were now equally as close. That night Sarah had mentioned working in an antique shop in Kemptown and that her boss was looking for a second shop assistant, having just extended the shop into the empty retail unit next door. Before the excruciating phone call with her mum earlier that day, Jennifer had been content with her lonely warehouse job at Tesco's, but after, she realised she needed people, distraction and perhaps a little bit of affection in her life. Toasty and Sarah came along at just the right time – probably saved Jennifer from a nervous breakdown. Sarah got her an interview with Willow (a pretty weird experience; the guy spent the whole half hour talking about his extensive collection of mustard pots) and the rest was history.

"One Klingon hot chocolate. Extra sugar." Having arrived a few minutes after Jennifer, Sarah set down a large paper cup next to Jennifer's cash register. On the side of the cup was the three-pronged emblem of the Klingon Empire from *Star Trek.*

Jennifer cocked an eyebrow. "Where did you get that?"

"It's Vortex today, remember," said Sarah. "I walked through it on my way here, saw three Klingons selling coffee… You know, the guys with the foreheads from *Star Trek.*"

"Yeah. I know the ones. Thanks honey."

Of course Jennifer knew what a Klingon was. Before Million Eyes turned her life into a science fiction movie, she was an ardent geek. *Doctor Who, Star Trek,* the Marvel films, *Black*

Mirror, The X Files – you name it. Vortex, the annual sci-fi, fantasy and horror festival that took place on the seafront, was the sort of thing she'd take a day off work to attend. Not anymore. She particularly couldn't handle anything with time travel in it, which meant saying goodbye to her favourite of the lot: *Doctor Who.* Her entertainment diet now consisted of frivolous comedies and gentle dramas that didn't require too much brain power, and she told everyone she met that sci-fi and its offshoots weren't her thing.

It was a shame. Sarah was probably the biggest girl sci-fi buff Jennifer had met. In different circumstances she'd love to wax lyrical with her about Klingons and the like.

"How are things?" said Jennifer as Sarah went to hang up her coat.

"Peachy. Had another barney with Gloria this morning." Gloria was the mad and unfriendly old spinster who lived next door to Sarah.

"Does she still think you're stealing her WiFi?"

"Yep."

"Mad old bat."

"That's what I said."

They started setting up the exterior displays on the pavement outside the front of the shop. "What about your date last night?" Jennifer asked, clutching a pair of 19th-century fruitwood farmhouse chairs, one under each arm. "How did it go?"

Setting down a huge Chinese vase and some old baskets, Sarah pulled a face. "Pfft."

"Ah. Not good then."

"Sex was good."

"Did he stay over?"

"Shit, no. We banged, then I kicked him out."

Jennifer laughed. "You player."

Sarah looked innocent. "What? I've got more charisma than him in my big toe."

"But you still slept with him."

"He was hot."

Jennifer started piling up old suitcases next to the farmhouse chairs. "Isn't that a bit… mean?"

Sarah sighed. "Well… yeah. I guess. But guys have done it to me loads."

"Yeah, but you're better than them."

Sarah beamed. "Aww, honey! That's sweet. I guess I just really needed to get laid last night. Having said that, I don't think Mark – no, wait – Mike? Shit. Whoever he was, I don't think he was complaining."

They laughed.

As they went back inside the shop, a customer in her fifties in a smart, charcoal skirt suit, hair drawn so tightly into a bun it was stretching her face, asked Jennifer how old the grandfather clock in the next room was. Jennifer checked the database on one of the store's Uzu laptops – the only technology brand left that wasn't Million Eyes or Million Eyes-affiliated – and advised that it was circa 1720.

She turned her attention back to Sarah, who'd started attaching price tags to a range of antique cigar cases that had just come in. "Hon, can I ask you something?"

Sarah looked up. "Course."

"Do you want kids?"

Her eyes widened. "Geez. Nine o'clock in the morning and she asks a question like that."

Jennifer grinned. "You know me. I like to keep you on your toes."

Sarah contemplated her answer, then said, slightly scrunching her face, "Mmmm, to be honest… no, probably not. I don't think I'm maternal enough. Or patient. I'd rather be a kick-arse aunt. Why?"

"Toasty wants a baby. Not right this minute, but she definitely wants one."

Sarah rolled her eyes. "Tell me something I don't know. Her uterus skips a beat every time she sees a baby. Has done since uni."

"I know," said Jennifer. "We were talking about it last night. Thing is" – she didn't want to sound like she'd already decided, even though she had – "I'm not sure how I feel about it."

"About having a baby?"

"Yeah."

Sarah turned on her serious face. "Okay. Have you told her that you're not sure?"

"I told her to give me a couple of days to get my head together."

"Well all I'll say is that if you're leaning towards not wanting kids, you need to end things. Before they get too serious."

"Things are already serious. We're living together."

"I know. And I know Toasty rushed you on that. She's totally besotted with you, you know. And if you give her a wishy-washy 'Yeah, maybe I'll want kids one day,' she'll stay with you and she'll wait. And if you then decide, nah, you don't want kids, you'll basically shatter the girl."

Sarah was right. There was no way Toasty was going to change her mind about having kids. Jennifer could either lie to her – tell her that a baby was a definite possibility even though it wasn't – which wasn't fair on either of them, or she could put an end to the best thing that had happened to her in ages.

There was another option, of course. She could be honest, tell Toasty everything. Her real name, her life before Brighton. Million Eyes.

Except that wasn't *really* an option. She grown accustomed to living this lie. It was comfortable, safe. She wasn't going to risk destroying everything.

So what now?

This really was a bit heavy for nine o'clock in the morning. Jennifer lightened the tone, "Of course, the real question is – if things don't work out between me and Toasty, who gets you in the divorce?"

Sarah laughed, "Ha! Well, that's a tricky one. I was obviously friends with Toasty first."

Jennifer grinned. "But I'm amazing."

Sarah nodded in agreement, "But you're amazing," and rubbed her chin thoughtfully. "We might have to let a court decide."

"A custody battle? I'm game."

The woman with the tightly wound bun brought a Victorian era pewter teapot to the cash desk and Jennifer went to serve her while Sarah continued labelling new items. After she'd gone, Jennifer remembered talking to Toasty about inviting Sarah round for dinner. "Before I forget – dinner tonight at our place?"

"Who's cooking?"

"Toasty wants to."

Sarah formed a pained expression. Jennifer chuckled, "I know, I know, but I've been teaching her. Her culinary skills are improving."

Sarah nodded. "Alright. I'll risk it. What time?"

"About seven?"

"Sounds good."

Jennifer took a swig of her hot chocolate. "Oh – and let me pay you for this."

"Nah, it's on me."

"Bollocks. You got us Starbucks yesterday." Jennifer walked over to where she'd hung her handbag and took out her frayed and rapidly-falling-apart purse. As she went to unzip the coins pouch, her bank card, key card, Brighton travel card and various supermarket points cards slipped through a hole in the side, the stitching finally giving up the ghost.

"Oops," said Sarah. "Jesus, Vicks, get a new purse."

"Looks like I'm going to have to."

Sarah bent down to help her pick up her cards, now strewn across the floor. In amongst them, Jennifer realised too late, was a small photograph. It had been tucked between old supermarket cards she hadn't used for so long that she'd forgotten it was even in her purse.

Sarah picked up the photo and looked at it. "Awww, who's this?"

It was a photograph of Jennifer and Jamie, taken at London Zoo when they were kids, but now it basically depicted two strangers.

"My… my sister…" It just slipped out.

"Sister? I thought you were an only child."

Jen, don't fall apart! She was normally so good at the lies, but the wave of emotion she'd felt at the sight of the photo ripped her out of the fiction she'd been living.

Thinking quickly, she took advantage of it, turned it into a new lie. "It's because she… she's…" Her voice cracked and a tear rolled down her cheek.

"Shit, Vicks." Sarah cupped her hand over Jennifer's. "I'm so sorry."

"I'll be back in a minute." Jennifer pulled away and hastened to the staff toilet.

She shut herself in a cubicle, sat on the toilet lid and

sobbed. The small photo – a selfie Jamie had taken with a giraffe arching into shot above them – fluttered in her quivering fingertips. A moment in time she yearned to have back.

Slow breaths, Jen. Calm down.

By the time she returned to the shop, her emotions were safely boxed away and the shop had got busier, which meant there was thankfully no real opportunity for Sarah to mention her sister. Willow arrived soon after and tasked Sarah with driving to a place in Lewes to pick up some new pieces.

No doubt Sarah would bring up the subject again, though. She was like that. Even though common sense might tell you that Jennifer didn't want to talk about it, Sarah would want to make sure that was the case by raising it again and asking, giving her ample chance to open up. Jennifer wasn't sure if it was prying or caring. Maybe a little of both.

In any case she'd be ready to deflect Sarah's questions, whenever they came.

She hated lying to her, though. Hated it.

But she wasn't going to stop.

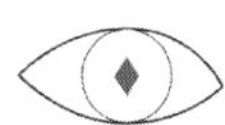

After work, Jennifer arrived home to find a large cardboard box in the hallway. Toasty was home too; she could hear her chopping vegetables in the kitchen. Toasty shouted, "Hi, muffin," but Jennifer was crouched over the box, examining it, and didn't answer.

When she saw the logo on the side, she heaved, like someone had slammed a fist into her stomach. Outline of a human eye. Red diamond for the pupil.

Million Eyes.

Furious, she hollered, "What the fuck is this?"

Toasty came into the hallway. "It's our new TV. The METV 808-Elite. Shit-hot model."

Jennifer shot Toasty a pointed glare. "You're kidding, right? You know I don't use Million Eyes *anything*."

"Yeah but these are the best TVs out there. It's got this cool new tech that –"

"I don't give a monkey's, Toasty." Jennifer had to put up

with Toasty using a Million Eyes laptop and phone, but she wasn't about to make one of their products the centrepiece of her lounge. "I don't want one."

Toasty frowned, "Jesus, Vicks, chill out. It comes with a thirty-day free trial so I thought we'd try it."

"Well you should've asked me, because I would've said no."

"That's why I didn't ask you! I don't understand this weird resistance you have to technology."

Not technology. Just Million Eyes. Although the two weren't really mutually exclusive anymore.

"I just thought you might open your mind the tiniest, weeniest little bit," said Toasty.

Jennifer shook her head. "I'm not trying it – ever."

"Christ, okay! You're the fucking boss. I'll take it back tomorrow." Toasty stormed into the kitchen.

Jennifer went upstairs to change. It didn't take long for her anger at Toasty for ignoring her wishes to ease into guilt at reacting like that. As much as she hated to admit it, Million Eyes devices were generally the top choice for anyone who didn't know they were murderous time travellers using consumer electronics as a smokescreen – which Toasty didn't. Jennifer's aversion to everything Million Eyes wasn't going to make an ounce of sense to her.

Oh, Jen. This was the second time today that she'd let buried feelings re-surface.

After changing, she switched on the TV in the bedroom and lay down on the bed to get a hold of herself. As bad timing would have it, the Million Eyes Annual Tech Summit – basically a live, two-hour-long, internationally televised advertisement for all things Million Eyes – was on. She'd caught bits of them in the past and they consisted of speeches about the latest innovations, demos, and interviews with consumers and businesses who piled praise on Million Eyes like brainwashed lemmings.

She grabbed the remote control to change the channel, then saw that the host was welcoming on stage the CEO of Million Eyes, Erica Morgan, to give the summit's keynote speech.

Jennifer lowered the remote.

She watched Miss Morgan strut onto the stage wearing a

pale blue knee-length skirt with tiered ruffles, a matching blouse and a loose, dark grey, checked blazer buttoned at the waist. Her silky, coal-black hair spilled over her shoulders like a tap running with ink. Jennifer had seen her before, but she was known for keeping a low profile, avoiding public appearances and rarely giving interviews, certainly not keynote speeches at televised events. Having checked her out, Jennifer had found out hardly anything. Her Wikipedia page was sparse; nothing was known about her family, her background or her jobs and achievements before she suddenly became CEO of Million Eyes in 1998. It was rumoured that she'd worked for Million Eyes for some time before that, but nobody seemed to know what she did there. Even her date of birth was unknown; people had been trying to guess her age for years. If Jennifer had to hazard a guess she'd say mid-fifties, but something told her she might be a lot older and just looked really good for it.

Thunderous applause winding down, Miss Morgan addressed the crowd in a soft but confident voice, "Friends, good evening. Thank you so much for the warm welcome. It's fantastic to see you all and I'm so proud to be heading up such an extraordinary company, particularly today. The pace of innovation at Million Eyes in the last few years has been stunning. I have been with this company since the beginning –"

You have? Jennifer imagined the Wikipedia scribes scrambling to add this vague detail to her page.

"– and it's been a privilege and a source of awe and inspiration to watch it grow around me. In recent years our engineering teams have outdone themselves and in a moment I will be talking about the products and platform developments that I am personally most excited to share with you. But first I want to thank you."

Jennifer felt her lip curling, her frown deepening.

"All of you. Everyone here tonight and everyone watching at home. Million Eyes has changed the world. It has transformed the lives of every person on Earth but none of it would've been possible without you. You have helped us help you. Your support and your enthusiasm is the reason Million Eyes technology is in every home and office, every shop, cafe and restaurant, every school, every factory, every farm, every car, train and aeroplane. Because of you, Million Eyes… is everywhere."

Jennifer shivered, a chill skittering up her back. She grabbed the remote and switched it off.

If there was anything she was sure of right now, it was this – Toasty's new TV was going back.

22

August 30th 1997

"George! My old friend, what a wonderful surprise." Sebastien Touchard, a French waiter living in the centre of Paris, opened the front door of his modest apartment by the Seine to his English friend, George Langdon, who he'd not seen for years.

It was clear pretty quick that this wasn't going to be the happiest of reunions. George looked tired, pale, distressed. Beads of sweat glistened on his receding hairline. Granted, it was a hot day in a hot city, but Sebastien suspected there was more to it.

"We have to talk," said George, out of breath.

"Of course. Come in."

Sebastien showed George into the lounge. "Can I get you – ?"

"Nothing, thank you." George seated himself on the leather couch.

Sebastien sat in the chair opposite. "What is it, George? What's wrong?"

"Are you still a waiter at the Ritz?"

Sebastien had been at the Paris Ritz for ten years. It wasn't always a bed of roses, but the rewards far outweighed any unpleasantness. "Yes. Why?"

Still trying to catch his breath, George replied, "Diana. Princess Diana. She's staying there tonight, isn't she."

And these were the sorts of rewards he reaped – getting to serve extraordinary people like her. But what did George want with the princess? "Yes. She and Dodi Fayed are due to arrive sometime after four."

"Are you working tonight?"

"Yes. My shift starts at seven. George, enough with the questions. What is this about?"

"I need you to give her something."

"Princess Diana?"

"Yes."

"What?"

George reached inside his jacket, pulled out a small, ancient-looking book, handed it to Sebastien.

Sebastien frowned. The plain green buckram cloth binding was ripped in several places, exposing the boards beneath. The pages were stained and rippled. Much of the gold foil lettering on the front and spine had flaked away, leaving just the indentations from the blocking process. The words remained perfectly readable, however: *The History of Computer-Aided Timetabling for Railway Systems.* By *Jeremy Jennings.* Not a book – or author – Sebastien had ever heard of.

Sebastien looked at George. "You want me to give *this* to the Princess of Wales?"

"It is not as it seems. Open it. Open it to the last page of text."

Sebastien opened the book to the last few pages. He frowned. They were blank. He went backwards through the pages – all blank.

He looked at George. "I – I don't understa –"

"Keep going."

Sebastien continued flicking backwards through the pages with his thumb, eventually ending up at a page of text, less than two thirds in. He quickly thumbed through the first two thirds – looked like there was text on all of those. *What a waste of paper!*

"Read the last page."

Sebastien huffed and flicked to the last page of text.

```
George Langdon: Are you still a waiter at
  the Ritz?
Sebastien Touchard: Yes. Why?
George Langdon: Diana. Princess Diana. She's
  staying there tonight, isn't she.
Sebastien Touchard: Yes. She and Dodi Fayed
  are due to arrive sometime after four.
```

```
George Langdon: Are you working tonight?
Sebastien Touchard: Yes. My shift starts at
  seven. George, enough with the questions.
  What is this about?
George Langdon: I need you to give her
  something.
```

Sebastien blinked hard several times and shook his head. *Not possible. Simply not possible.*

He looked at George, whose eyes were wide and staring, thick purple shadows hanging beneath them.

Retraining his eyes on the page, Sebastien hoped he'd imagined what he'd just seen.

```
Sebastien Touchard: Princess Diana?
George Langdon: Yes.
Sebastien Touchard: What? [19-second pause.]
  You want me to give this to the Princess of
  Wales?
```

Damn. He hadn't. He looked up. "How can this be possible?"

George nodded to the book, and Sebastien's eyes were back on the page.

His words. The words he'd just spoken... *were typing themselves out.*

It couldn't be. It just couldn't be.

And yet, as Sebastien watched, blinking frenziedly, the words *Sebastien Touchard: How can this be possible?* were appearing on the page, letter by letter, beneath George's instruction to *Read the last page.*

Magic? What else could it be?

"It's not a book about computer-aided timetabling for railways," said George. "That's merely a disguise. It's a transcription device. One that is way more advanced than any technology that we have – or at least know about – today. It instantly transcribes any conversation in its proximity and can even identify the speakers."

Sebastien glanced at the page, saw that George's words were typing themselves onto the page, slammed it shut and placed it on the lamp table next to him. *That's quite enough of that madness.*

He stood up, walked over to his drinks cabinet, and poured

himself a cognac. He gestured with the bottle to ask George if he wanted one. George shook his head.

Sitting back down, Sebastien asked, "Where did you get it?"

"My grandfather's attic. He died last month and my mother and I decided to do a clear-out. There was a load of stuff up there belonging to my great-grandfather that nobody had ever gone through, including some items that he'd collected – and kept – from when he was a tosher."

Sebastien frowned. "A tosher?"

"It's an old English word for a scavenger in Victorian times. Toshers would rifle through the muck in London's sewers, looking for valuables that had been washed down from the streets above that they could sell."

"So you're saying your great-grandfather found the book in the sewer?"

"I can't be certain. My mother had never seen it before, and doesn't recall my grandfather – or great-grandfather – ever mentioning it. My great-grandfather was illiterate but I presume he at least saw that the book was somehow capable of writing itself. I suspect that's the reason he kept it, rather than selling it."

"But that's… surely that must've been over a hundred years ago."

"Yes."

"So you're saying the Victorians were secretly more advanced than we are today?"

"No. I'm not saying that."

"I'm confused."

George paused, leaned forwards, took a breath and said with a grave look, "Here is where it gets complicated."

Sebastien swallowed. He wasn't sure if he wanted to hear this or not. "I'm listening."

"*The History of Computer-Aided Timetabling for Railway Systems* is a real book. Jeremy Jennings is a real author."

"Okay…"

"The book was published in 1995. This device, disguised as a real book from 1995, was discovered by my great-grandfather a hundred years before it could've been."

Sebastien did a fast shake of the head. "George, what are you saying?"

"I'm saying it's travelled back in time. From the future."

"What? Don't talk nonsense."

George sat back in his chair. "Sebastien, if you can think of another explanation, I'm all ears."

He had nothing.

George nodded. "As I thought. I actually think its travels extend much further back in time than the 19th century. There are conversations in that book going back to the 12th century. I've read them all. Most are former protectors of the book talking about its importance. But not because of its power. Because of the very first conversation the book recorded."

"What conversation?"

"Look for yourself. Read the first few pages and you'll see why I've come here so urgently."

Sebastien picked up the book from the lamp table and, reluctantly, opened it to the first transcription.

Looking up, "Who are these people?"

George shrugged slightly, "I don't know."

Sebastien continued reading, stomach rolling with dread as the conversation between the two speakers took a startling turn. It became clear why George wanted him to give it to the Princess of Wales.

Sebastien felt his heart start to race. "This can't be real…" he said, struggling to wrap his mind around the enormity of it.

"I'm afraid it's very real," said George. "Million Eyes have infected my country. They have to be stopped – now."

Sebastien shut the book and downed his cognac. It was going to be a long day.

23

Sebastien got to the Ritz early – 6.30pm – in the hope that he could speak with Princess Diana before his shift started. He had to carve through flocks of paparazzi on the Place Vendôme, cameras trained on the Imperial Suite on the first floor where Diana and Dodi were lodged, waiting like vultures for the princess to risk a peek through the damask curtains.

He soon learned that preparations were being made for Diana and Dodi to leave again, which meant there was no time or opportunity for Sebastien to meet with her.

"Are they due to be coming back?" Sebastien asked the night duty manager, Thierry Rocher. Rumour had it they'd gone to Dodi's apartment near the Arc de Triomphe, but nobody in the kitchens knew where they were due to be spending the night.

Sebastien got a dismissive – "What's that got to do with you? Get back to work" – and was left to stew over the possibility that he'd missed his chance.

Fortunately they did return. Ever-increasing numbers of paparazzi had forced the couple to cancel their dinner plans and head back to the Ritz, so they were at least going to eat here; whether they were going to stay the night was still unclear.

Shortly before 10pm, looking stressed and beleaguered, Diana and Dodi entered the l'Espadon Restaurant where Sebastien was serving.

But he couldn't just go up to her in the middle of the restaurant, not with dozens of people already staring at her. He'd have to wait.

As it turned out, they were only in the restaurant for a few minutes. After serving another table's drinks, Sebastien looked over and saw that theirs was empty. He asked Matthieu, the waiter who'd attended them, where they'd gone. Matthieu said the princess looked upset, probably because everyone in the restaurant was looking at her, and had asked for their dinner to be served in the Imperial Suite. Sebastien wasn't surprised. He'd hate to be the subject of so much attention, so many gossipy eyes. Then again, if you marry a member of the Royal Family…

As soon as the l'Espadon Restaurant began quietening down, Sebastien ducked out, hoping his absence wouldn't get noticed by the head waiter, and made his way up the grand staircase to the Imperial Suite. Heart pounding, sweat collecting beneath his collar, he took a deep breath and knocked at the door of the suite.

The door opened and Diana greeted Sebastien with a smile so warm and radiant it momentarily put him at ease. Her beauty was mesmerising – striking blue eyes, silk-smooth pink cheeks, shining blonde hair coiffed and preened to perfection like always. She looked far cheerier than she did in the restaurant earlier, like she'd just been laughing.

And now Sebastien was about to ruin it all.

Returning her smile, Sebastien bowed and said, "Good evening, Your Royal Highness. My apologies for disturbing you so late."

"That's quite all right," she replied in that famously soft voice of hers. "But 'madame' is fine. The Germans took the HRH off me some time ago." She laughed, briefly.

Sebastien knew Diana's relations with the Royal Family were on the frosty side. Had been since her divorce from Prince Charles.

"I'm a waiter here, madame. My name is Sebastien Touchard."

Smile widening, Diana did a slow blink, nodding, "We're fine, thank you. Dinner was wonderful albeit late. But that's not the hotel's fault."

She thought his attendance was a courtesy. Oh, how he wished it was.

"Forgive me, madame, but I am here for a different reason."

"Oh?"

"It is, I fear, a matter of grave importance."

The brightness on Diana's face dimmed. She glanced over her shoulder and, in a moment, Dodi Fayed had joined her at the door.

"May I come in?" said Sebastien.

"What is this about?" said Dodi.

Sebastien glanced around, checking that the small carpeted foyer he was standing in was clear. It was but he lowered his voice regardless, saying, "Million Eyes, sir. It is about the computer company, Million Eyes."

Diana frowned. "What about them?"

"It would be best if I came in for a moment. I have something I need to show you."

"This is highly irregular, Mr Touchard," said Diana. "Where is Claude Roulet?"

Claude Roulet was assistant to the president of the Ritz and had been attending to Diana and Dodi's needs throughout the day. He had no idea Sebastien was here.

"Monsieur Roulet is engaged presently," Sebastien lied, "but I would be happy to fetch him for you. If I might just have a moment of your time before I do."

Dodi shook his head. "Absolutely not. Get out of here."

Sebastien swallowed hard, chest heaving, cold beads of sweat trickling down his lower back. "Forgive me, sir, but it is the princess's time I require, not yours."

Diana's eyes widened at Sebastien's boldness, which surprised even him. But then, he had no choice but to stand his ground. He couldn't leave till he'd given Diana the book.

"And what if *I* refuse?" said Diana, eyes shining with anger.

Sebastien shook his head. "Please, madame, you mustn't. They are planning something terrible."

Her expression instantly softened to worry. "What do you mean?"

"Let me come in. You have to see it for yourself."

Dodi shot forwards, shoulders hunched aggressively. Sebastien thought for a moment that the hot-headed Egyptian was going to hit him. "Who the hell do you think you are, you little – !"

Diana put her hand on his shoulder. "Dodi, *don't*." Dodi

pulled back reluctantly and Diana stepped aside, allowing Sebastien to pass and enter the room. She nodded to Dodi, "Close the door, please, Dodi." Despite his incredulous frown, Dodi did as asked. Diana looked at Sebastien, "You have five minutes, Mr Touchard. Tell me what this is about."

Sebastien unbuttoned his jacket, reached into his inside pocket and pulled out the transcription device. "*This*, madame," he said, handing it to Diana.

Diana read the title, "*The History of Computer-Aid* –"

"The title is not relevant. It is not really a book. It is merely disguised as one."

"I'm sorry?"

"Please, madame, open it to the last page of text."

He waited for Diana to find it, then watched the colour drain from her cheeks as she read a transcription of the conversation they'd literally just had.

"What is this?" she said quietly, looking up.

"A transcription device," Sebastien replied. "From the future."

Diana retrained her eyes on the page, saw their just-spoken words typing themselves out, and cupped her hand over her mouth in dismay.

"What the hell are you going on about?" said Dodi, and Diana handed him the book, open.

He shook his head. "What!"

"There are conversations in that book going back centuries. But not just… *back*."

"Do not speak to me in riddles, Mr Touchard," said Diana firmly.

"Forgive me, madame. Open the book to the first transcription, the first conversation it recorded, and you'll understand why I'm here."

Diana and Dodi read it together, both going paler by the second, Diana clutching her chest.

Afterwards, Dodi slammed the book shut and blared, "What kind of sick joke is this?"

"Sir, if this was a joke, do you really think I – a waiter – would be capable of it?"

Dodi looked at the princess. "Diana, this has to be a trick. *Has* to be!"

Diana didn't respond. She looked dazed and blinked

several times. A moment later, "Mr Touchard, where did you get this?"

Sebastien explained how his English friend, George Langdon, had brought the book to him just hours ago, how it was recovered from London's sewers by George's great-grandfather in the late 19th century.

Diana sat down in one of several duck egg blue Louis XVI armchairs that graced the Imperial Suite, rubbing her hands together nervously.

Sebastien approached her. "You should act quickly, madame."

Diana looked at him, a mix of confusion and anguish on her face. Then she looked at Dodi. "He's right, Dodi. We should go. Now."

"Darling, it's a trick," said Dodi irately. "It's ridiculous."

"Neither of us is qualified to determine that, Dodi. A threat has been brought to our attention and we need to act on it."

"So what do you want to do?"

"I have to get this book to the Queen. What happens next is up to her. Dodi, please arrange for a private plane to take me to Balmoral tonight."

Sebastien had seen it on the news. Balmoral Castle in Scotland was where the Queen and the rest of the Royals, including Diana's sons, Princes William and Harry, were spending their summer holiday.

"You're serious?" said Dodi. "*Tonight?*"

"Yes," said Diana, more sharply this time. "You read what was in that book. Just arrange this for me, will you?"

Dodi huffed, red-faced, "Fine. So much for salvaging the last night of our holiday."

As Dodi went to make a call from the Imperial Suite phone, Diana looked at Sebastien. "Thank you for bringing this to my attention, Mr Touchard."

That was his cue to go. He'd discharged his burden. It was in her hands now.

He bowed and turned to leave. Stopping at the door, he said, "Be careful, madame."

Diana gave him an uncertain smile, and he left.

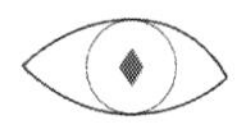

Sebastien's mind was spinning from the moment he left the Imperial Suite to the moment he got home later than night. His encounter with Princess Diana was replaying over and over like a TV commercial you can't block out. He wondered if she was already on a plane to Balmoral with the book, what the Queen would do when she saw it, what would become of Million Eyes once their treason was revealed.

He poured a cognac to help him sleep and took it into the bedroom. Just as he started to undress, there was a knock at the door.

Sebastien glanced at the clock. Nearly midnight. *Who on earth...?*

He approached the door, tentatively, and looked through the peephole. It was Frederic, the night manager for the building. Had something happened?

He opened the door. Before he could say a word, the right side of Frederic's head exploded in a red mist. *So quiet.* The gun was silent as air and Frederic's head blasting open made barely a hiss.

Frederic fell like a sack of meat and Sebastien's eyes were on the gun, now pointed square at his head.

His killer wore black, he thought – the last he ever had.

24

By midnight the number of paparazzi outside the front of the Ritz had doubled. Sporadic appearances from Diana and Dodi's bodyguards, Kes Wingfield and Trevor Rees-Jones, their chauffeur, Philippe Dourneau, and the Ritz's deputy head of security, Henri Paul, had given the paparazzi a sense that the couple would soon be emerging. This was, of course, what they were supposed to think.

With the arrangements almost in place, Henri Paul took a moment to slip into a restroom on the ground floor of the hotel, locking the main door behind him. He took out a silk handkerchief to dab the sweat on his face, leant against the mosaic-tiled wall and stared at the ceiling, taking slow, steady breaths.

"Shit, shit, shit, shit...."

Henri took out his mobile phone and, hands shaking, called 'Jane'.

"Mr Paul, do you have an update?"

Henri opened his mouth but swallowed his words. He paused, took a deep breath and said, finally, "Y-yes. Everyone is where you said they would be. Diana and Dodi returned to the hotel and have now decided to leave again – as you predicted."

"Good. And?"

Henri cleared his throat, not that there was anything in it. "I have set a plan in motion for Diana and Dodi to leave the hotel with as little attention from the press as possible. The Mercedes and Range Rover they have been using through the day will act as decoys and leave from the front of the hotel. Diana and Dodi will leave from the rear entrance in the Rue

Cambon in the Mercedes your people are providing. This will make it easier for you to" – he swallowed – "pursue." It all left a horrid aftertaste in his mouth.

"And you'll be driving our Mercedes, Mr Paul?" said Jane.

He swallowed again. "Yes."

"You sound nervous."

What a stupid thing to say. "Are you surprised?"

"Don't overthink it. All you have to do is head for the tunnel, wait for the engine warning light to come on, act like something's wrong and, once you're inside the tunnel, pull the car over. Then, before anyone knows what's happening, we'll advance on the vehicle, abduct the princess, and be gone. Piece of cake."

Did she actually just say 'piece of cake'?

Jane continued, "And I promise you, when this is over, you'll never hear from us again."

"Apart from when you wire fifty million francs to my bank account, you mean?"

"Apart from that, yes."

Henri hung up the phone. His fingers went limp and the phone slipped through them, crashing onto the tiled floor.

He'd thought that the money would make it easier. It didn't. He felt like he was standing too close to an inferno, his skin burning, his lungs filling with smoke. He couldn't breathe.

Princess Diana was the most famous woman in the world – and Henri was about to aid and abet her kidnapping.

Was he out of his mind?

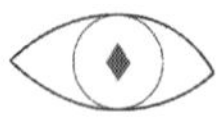

Outside the front of the hotel, two photographers – a blonde woman and a bald man – joined the back of the crowd just as the excitement among the press was starting to build. Both wore jackets and jeans, rode motorbikes and had big, expensive-looking cameras hanging from their necks. But these were just props. The woman and the man weren't photographers at all. They were Million Eyes operatives.

The woman, Lynn Forbes aka 'Jane', tucked her phone into her pocket after Henri Paul had hung up. She and her colleague, Alex Bradley, started round to the back of the hotel on their bikes. A couple of photographers followed, but most were expecting the princess to emerge from the main entrance and stayed put.

Stopping near the rear entrance in the Rue Cambon, Forbes took out her phone again, this time to call her boss, James Rawling.

"We're in place, sir," she advised. "The princess is leaving shortly from the rear entrance in our Mercedes in a ploy to evade the press."

"And Sebastien Touchard?" Rawling replied. "Has he been dealt with?"

"Yes, sir."

"Good. What about the evidence?"

"We've disabled all traffic and CCTV cameras on the scheduled route of the Mercedes. Simpson's in place at the mortuary and is going to swap the dead drunk driver's blood samples with those taken from Henri Paul at his autopsy. We've also arranged for a transport forensics expert to remove all evidence of the rigged brakes and seatbelts from the Mercedes. Subsequent reports will state that the brakes and seatbelts were functioning perfectly and all the passengers would've been able to put their seatbelts on. Everyone will see it as their fault for not wearing them."

"This forensics expert – is he Million Eyes?"

"No, but he's getting the money we've promised to Henri Paul. And I've threatened to kill his children."

"It looks like you have everything under control, then."

"Yes, sir."

"Thank you, Miss Forbes. I'm confident everything will go without a hitch. Actually, I'm starting to think it's pre-destined to go without a hitch."

"Er, I'm sorry, sir?"

"Never mind. Call me when the princess departs and I will be on my way."

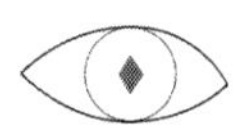

Diana and Dodi left the Imperial Suite and moved downstairs with Henri Paul and Trevor Rees-Jones to the hotel's rear entrance to wait for their car. Henri was sweating, still wondering if all this was worth fifty million francs. He took out his handkerchief to wipe his forehead.

"Are you alright, Mr Paul?" Diana asked.

"Yes, princess," Henri lied. "Absolutely fine."

"You're sweating rather profusely."

"Yes. It's… a warm night."

At 12.20am, the other Mercedes arrived. Henri and Trevor Rees-Jones led Dodi and Diana to the vehicle, immediately catching the attention of a small band of photographers gathered on the other side of the road, motorcycle engines coughing into life.

Here goes. Henri got in the car and switched on the engine. Diana and Dodi scrambled into the rear passenger seats, Rees-Jones closing the door behind them and hastening round to the front passenger seat.

As his three passengers clawed at the seatbelts, Henri drove away.

"Mr Paul, my seatbelt's not working," said the princess. Henri turned his head. Diana and Dodi were both struggling to buckle themselves in.

"Neither's mine," murmured Dodi.

"Or mine," said Rees-Jones.

That was odd. In his haste to speed away from the hotel without attracting attention, he hadn't even tried his own. He wondered if his wasn't working either. He took his right hand off the steering wheel, reached for his seatbelt, pulled it over his shoulder and plugged the metal tongue into the buckle, expecting it to click.

No click. The tongue jerked back out. He tried it again – it wouldn't fasten.

This was the Mercedes they had provided – why would it have defective seatbelts? That didn't make sense.

"Mr Dodi, I think I should pull over, check the seatbelts…" Henri murmured, thinking as soon as he said it that if he did, he might scupper the plan to kidnap the princess and screw himself out of fifty million francs.

He saw Dodi looking through the Mercedes' rear window. The motorcyclists who'd seen them were in pursuit, engines snarling.

"No, don't stop. Speed up," said Dodi. "They'll be all over us if we stop. So much for your fucking decoy plan."

The Pont de l'Alma underpass wasn't far. Henri just needed to get there. The engine failure warning light would come on, he'd pull the car over, and that would be that.

He sped up.

Despite Dodi's orders, Henri was forced to stop anyway – at the traffic lights at the corner of the Avenue des Champs Elysées. Like wasps to sugar, the motorcyclists swarmed the vehicle. A blitz of camera flashes rained down on the passengers. Diana buried her face in Dodi's jacket. The moment the lights turned green, Dodi hollered, "Go! Let's lose these bastards." Henri pushed the accelerator to the floor in a bid to outrun them, tyres wailing.

As Henri started his approach to the Pont de l'Alma tunnel, the engine failure warning light still hadn't come on. Should've done by now. Henri needed it as his excuse for pulling over. He noticed in his rear view mirror that a white Fiat Uno had joined the mob of motorcyclists and was following him.

Cameras flashed like fireworks.

Henri sped up. The speedometer flickered past sixty-five.

The paparazzi started falling behind, apart from two motorcyclists – a man and a woman – who matched Henri's speed with ease and swerved around to the left side of the Mercedes, passing by Dodi's window.

Here come the kidnappers.

Heart racing, Henri saw the two motorcyclists take sunglasses from their pockets and put them on. The man fished something from inside his jacket – some sort of tubular device. What were they doing?

The Fiat Uno pulled up next to the Mercedes on its right side.

They were surrounded.

Still no engine warning light.

Henri was moments from entering the tunnel, and it wasn't a long tunnel. He had to start pretending something was wrong. He had to start slowing down.

He was going to have to do it without the warning light. He had no idea what. He had to fake something – and quick. The only thing he could think of was pumping the brakes, making the car jolt suddenly and repeatedly, forcing him to bring it to a stop.

He took his foot off the accelerator and, with a deep breath, rammed the brake pedal.

Huh?

The car didn't jerk, or react at all.

Henri pressed the brake, gentler this time. There was no resistance. The car didn't slow.

"What the fuck?" He pushed the brake pedal to the floor, then thrust his foot against the clutch and lowered the gear.

Nothing worked. The speedometer was stuck at sixty-five miles per hour.

"Henri, what? What is it?" shouted Dodi from the back.

"They set me up!" Henri screamed.

"What?" gasped Diana, lifting her head.

The Mercedes and surrounding vehicles entered the tunnel. As they did, Henri yanked the steering wheel to the right, tossing his passengers against the left side of the car, in an effort to push the Fiat Uno out of the way.

The crunch and squeal of metal on metal rang out as the Mercedes swerved hard and struck the Uno. Didn't work. The Uno was slightly ahead and able to block Henri's escape. The pillars on the tunnel's central reservation rushed past the car in a soft blur. Dodi, Diana and Rees-Jones were all screaming at him, but he didn't register any words, their panicked voices blending into the noise of roaring engines, screeching tyres and Henri's own thumping heart.

Then, from both sides, dazzling explosions of light illuminated the whole tunnel and Henri saw nothing but white.

His head spun with the same thought, over and over. They lied. They lied. They lied.

Then a crack of thunder ripped through his head.

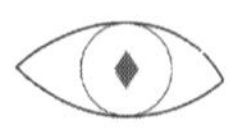

Bradley deactivated his flare. James Rawling in the Fiat Uno did the same. The blasts of light went out and Rawling sped up, hastening to the tunnel's exit. Bradley and Forbes slowed down, letting the Mercedes advance. They could see that Henri had lost control. The Mercedes careered towards the thirteenth pillar of the tunnel at high speed.

Forbes hit the brake, sucked in a breath and watched the Mercedes ram the concrete pillar, front half crumpling like paper with a boom so tumultuous that it rattled her brain in her skull. The vehicle ricocheted off the pillar, spinning like a toy in a rapid three hundred and sixty degree turn into the right hand lane. It hurtled into the tunnel wall with another dreadful crunch, spraying flecks of glass and chunks of metal everywhere, then rebounded slightly and stopped, mounting the kerb along the tunnel's right side.

Forbes and Bradley edged towards the crashed Mercedes, climbed off their bikes and walked towards the vehicle. Inside the car, they saw Henri, unconscious, head buried in an airbag; Trevor Rees-Jones next to him, face a fleshy, disfigured mess, but moving and murmuring; Dodi Fayed slumped between the two front seats, body twisted and bloody, unconscious; and Diana, Princess of Wales, in a crumpled heap in the passenger foot well, also unconscious.

Forbes thrust her arm inside the shattered rear window towards Diana. She reached inside her blazer, searching for the transcriber. Nothing in her right pocket, so she tried her left – and there it was.

Forbes grabbed the book and pulled it from her pocket. At that moment, Diana awoke. Her arm shot up and her hand clamped around Forbes's wrist.

Her grip was weak. Forbes yanked free with ease.

Forbes opened the book and read a few lines of the transcription that had caused Million Eyes centuries of damage. At last, they had it.

She handed the book to Bradley and retrained her eyes on Diana. The princess was dazed, eyes rolling, blood dripping from a three-centimetre-long wound in her forehead.

It was hard to feel sorry for her. All these royal cunts had such self-importance. It was time they realised they weren't any more special than anyone else.

"You… you won't… get away with this…" Diana choked, labouring to lift her head, voice barely there.

"We already have," Forbes replied coldly.

Forbes spun away from the car. Photographers were advancing on the scene, some instinctively snapping pictures of the wreck, others trying to assist the victims. Forbes and Bradley quietly extricated themselves from the rising commotion, returning to their bikes and making a quick exit.

They drove to a small, quiet side road. There, Forbes dismounted, made sure there were no nearby storm drains (strict orders from Rawling), and reached for the disruptor holstered on her hip.

Bradley handed her the transcriber and she placed it on the ground, pointed her disruptor and pressed the trigger. A shaft of bright green light skewered through the book and the ground, kicking up chunks of tarmac and blowing the book apart. Scorched slivers of paper and a few flakes of the binding were all that was left.

Job done.

"I think we deserve a pint," she said to Bradley as she got back on her bike. "Or two or three. What do you say?"

Bradley was staring ahead with a deep shadow of remorse on his face. "We've just assassinated Princess Diana. I think I'll go for something stiffer."

25

September 2nd 1997

Erica Morgan smelled sweat and something else – urine, maybe – as rotund American billionaire Arthur Pell leaned forwards and kissed her on both cheeks.

"You're looking mighty fine this evening, Erica," he drawled in his thick Southern accent as he helped her to her seat – one of those needless acts of chivalry that made her want to bring up her lunch. Still, there was plenty more she going to have to keep down tonight.

She smiled, brushed her silky black fringe from her eye and replied, "You're looking mighty fine yourself." She was lying, of course. Arthur Pell was a truly grotesque lump. "Have you lost weight?" Of course he hadn't. If anything he looked bigger than when they last met.

"A bit, maybe," Pell replied, voice as deep as a tuba, but that was probably because he had no neck, just a solid ring of fat that his round head bobbed on top of. "Don't wanna lose too much, though. The ladies love my love handles." He laughed, his fat face wobbling.

No, Arthur. They love your deep pockets.

Miss Morgan and Pell sat in Le Caprice, a swanky restaurant in Arlington Street, London. Last time they met she'd sussed him out. A crass, simple man who'd had fortune after fortune handed to him on a platter, the sort of man she could manipulate with some flirting, ego-stroking and a low-cut dress that made her boobs look giant.

After ordering starters, main courses and a bottle of champagne, Pell blared, "So, Erica, you got a man in your life?"

None of your fucking business.

"Oh, Arthur. You might have to get some champagne in me first."

His eyes crawled down her body. "I'm gonna get something in you."

She swallowed her gag reflex, forced a flirty grin.

The waiter arrived with bread and olives. Arthur shoved his sausage fingers into a brown roll, ripped a chunk off and tossed it in his mouth. He leaned back in his chair and mumbled, mouth full, "Come on, then. Give it to me."

Miss Morgan cocked a teasing eyebrow. "Give it to you?"

"Reasons why I should invest my hard-earned dough into Million Eyes."

She leaned low over the table to accent her breasts, her shiny black locks spilling over the tablecloth, and sunk her eyes into his. "Because Million Eyes will change the world."

As expected, his eyes kept straying to her breasts. "Big words. How so?"

At this wholly inopportune moment, Miss Morgan's phone rang. She frowned and fished it from her handbag. "I'm sorry, Arthur, do excuse me." She looked at the screen on the front. *Unknown number.* And underneath. *Unknown temporal variant.*

Someone was calling – from another time.

"Arthur, forgive me. I have to take this." She stood up and wrapped her silver and black brocade stole around her arms. Then she leaned towards Pell and said, winking at him, "I'll promise I'll make it up to you."

In his deep, lecherous voice, "You better."

She walked as fast as her tight blue gown and four-inch stilettos would allow, exiting the restaurant onto the pavement. Phone still ringing, she walked a little down the street to a quieter spot and finally answered, "Hello?"

A familiar voice replied, "Hello, Erica. It's me… *Erica.*"

"Excuse me?"

"I am *you*. I am you from the future."

She didn't know how to respond. Yes, Million Eyes had secretly invented time travel and Miss Morgan had had various conversations with colleagues across time, but never with *herself.* She knew it was feasible but it just seemed so incredible, so unreal, so *weird*. She couldn't quite believe it.

More to the point, if this really was her future self calling, wasn't it an enormous temporal infraction?

Finally finding some words, "What do you want?"

Future Erica's voice was thick with confidence, "I'm calling from a time when Million Eyes is the most powerful company in the world and you are its CEO."

CEO! Admittedly it felt good to hear that.

Future Erica continued, "Your dinner with Arthur Pell was a contributing factor to both those things."

"Then why are you interrupting it?"

"Because you need to know that there are people out there who want to destroy us, and that we've had to go to great lengths to suppress them."

It sounded grave but Miss Morgan couldn't help the not-really-pertinent questions darting through her head. How different was the future? What things had changed in her life? Was her wretched mother still refusing to die or had she finally kicked the bucket?

Future Erica noticed. "Erica? Did you hear what I said?"

She tried to focus. "What sorts of lengths?"

She heard her future self inhale. "I gather you've been watching the news the past couple of days."

"Yes. I've seen some. It's hard to avoid."

"Those lengths."

"Pardon?"

"Princess Diana's death. I ordered it."

Her heart stopped. "What!"

"Don't sound so surprised. This isn't the first time Million Eyes has had to orchestrate something like this. Diana had information she shouldn't have had and was on her way back to the UK to hand it over to the Queen."

This was huge. Massive. It sounded like Future Erica was hardened to things like this, the way she was minimising it. And clearly there was a good reason – that wasn't the issue. It was the scale of it.

"Erica, say something," said her future self.

Miss Morgan realised she'd been silent for several moments. "I'm just trying to process what I'm hearing… Are you telling me you've changed the timeline? That Princess Diana was never supposed to die?"

"It's complicated."

"Then uncomplicate it."

"There isn't time. The reason I'm calling you is to make you aware of what we've done so that you can protect us."

"What do you mean?"

"Diana was well-loved by the nation, the whole world in fact. She was one of the most highly publicised figures ever. As you are probably already aware, the outpouring of public grief following her death was unprecedented. The public became obsessed with her. Everyone speculated. Everyone looked for someone to blame. And everyone cooked up their own little conspiracy theory. Erica, it's your job to make sure that none of those theories and speculations get traced back to Million Eyes. You must observe the public and the authorities carefully and make sure our backs are covered. I'm handling the rest."

"I understand, but –"

"I have to go. Just listen to me when I say that the Mission is more important than ever. We can't let anyone threaten it. You're a good person, Erica, but don't hesitate to take extreme measures when you need to."

"Wait – is that it? Is that all you're going to give me?"

"Yes. If I tell you any more, I'll corrupt the timeline. And I've had quite enough of that for one night."

"What does *that* mean?"

"Let's just say there's been an incident. This phone call we're having right now is going to put an end to it."

"I don't understand."

"You will, Erica. You will."

Future Erica hung up.

Miss Morgan took some deep breaths, waited for her thumping heart to slow, then slipped her phone into her handbag and click-clacked back to the restaurant. A television in the bar area was showing the news and a bald Sky News presenter was giving the latest on Princess Diana's death, "Tests reveal that the man who drove Princess Diana to her death was more than three times over the French drink-drive legal limit…"

She shivered, but it wasn't the cold. It was the intimidating prospect that one day she would arrange the death of the most famous woman in the world.

She rejoined Arthur Pell. Their champagne had already arrived – she wished it was vodka. As she seated herself, the waiter came with their starters: scallops for Pell and chargrilled octopus for her.

"Problem?" Pell asked.

Her priority was this meeting. Future Erica had confirmed how important it was. She couldn't let herself be distracted, not now. She re-donned her flirtatious facade, all provocative grins and heavy-lidded eyes.

"I'm sorry, Arthur," she replied. "No, no problem. Just a little urgent business, but now I'm all yours."

He smirked, creepily, "Glad to hear it."

Miss Morgan tucked into her octopus. "So, where were we? Ah, yes. You want to know why Million Eyes is going to change the world."

26

October 13th 2021

Having reburied her feelings for the second time that day, Jennifer went back downstairs. She unfortunately had to pass the Million Eyes TV – or METV – still sitting in its box in her hallway. If Toasty hadn't paid a probably extortionate amount for it, she'd be tempted to take it upstairs and toss it out of the window, or stamp on it with the highest heels she could find, or find a hammer and bash the bloody thing to pieces.

But no, she kept her anger and distaste confined to a wordless glare as she passed it, softening her expression as she went into the kitchen. Toasty was making lasagne, or attempting to, for their dinner with Sarah. A wok of mince and vegetables was bubbling on the hob next to the pan of white sauce Toasty was stirring. Normally Jennifer would make a joke about her sketchy culinary skills right about now, but their fight earlier made that a risky move.

So instead, "Smells good, babe."

No reply. She was still upset. Jennifer walked over to her and slipped her arms around her waist. She didn't respond, just continued stirring.

"Toasty, I'm really sorry," said Jennifer. "I shouldn't have gone off like that."

"No, you shouldn't," Toasty muttered. "It's a TV, for fuck's sake."

Jennifer stepped back, unlooping her arms from her waist and standing next to her at the worksurface. "Yes, but I've told you I don't like Million Eyes tech" – she felt her voice and temper rise – "and you don't listen."

Damn. This was escalating again. Jennifer wasn't sure how

to stop it.

"Fucking hell, Vicks," Toasty snapped. "You need to get your head out of your arse. Million Eyes is everywhere."

A chill knifed through her as she remembered Erica Morgan's words from earlier.

"Everyone uses Million Eyes devices these days," Toasty continued.

Jennifer couldn't help but counter, "Willow's doesn't. We've got Uzu laptops and an Uzu TV in the staffroom."

"That's 'cause the guy lives in the past. Nobody rates Uzu anymore."

"I do."

Toasty huffed. Her cheeks were reddening. "You're so fucking stubborn. Does it not matter that *I* might want a METV? Or is it all about what *you* want?"

She deserved that. Where could she go next? The Uzu TV in their lounge was past its prime. The picture had never been great and now there was a weird shadow in the corner of the screen. She wanted another Uzu TV but it was – she had to admit – a dying brand. Now that Toasty was playing the selfish card, she needed a new reason for not getting a METV. *She just didn't like them* wasn't going to cut it.

Money. That was the only thing she could think of. METVs were still a lot more expensive than Uzus. If they stuck with their Uzu for now, they could spend the money on a holiday or something.

But she didn't get a chance to make the point because Toasty veered the conversation onto an even more contentious subject. "Is this to do with the baby thing? Is that why you're so uptight? Because you're freaking out?"

It wasn't, but it didn't help. "No. It's not."

"If you're that scared of the possibility of having a baby with me, I wish you'd fucking come out and say it."

Oh, how she wished she could.

"I'm not scared. I just –"

Saved by the bell. The doorbell rang before Jennifer was able to formulate an answer, which was good, because there wasn't one. Not one that would satisfy Toasty, anyway.

Jennifer glanced at the clock on the kitchen wall. If it was Sarah, she was fifteen minutes early. It was a bit of a mixed blessing. It saved Jennifer from a conversation she wasn't ready to have, but it also meant that Sarah was arriving right in the middle of a row.

Jennifer took a deep breath and tried to bring the conversation to a simmer. "That's probably Sarah. Look, Toasty, I love you, okay. I'm sorry for being a bitch and I promise we'll talk about everything later, when Sarah's gone. Okay? Let's just try and have a nice evening with our friend."

Toasty shrugged and did her *fine, I'll be civil but I'm not happy* face. That would have to do. Jennifer went to open the front door.

"Hey… you alright?" said Sarah. She had that wide-eyed, flat-smiled look of hers, suggesting that she'd heard some of their argument but wasn't going to pry (even though she secretly wanted to).

"Hey," said Jennifer brightly. "Fine. All good. Come in."

Eyebrows wilting in acceptance that she wasn't going to get the gossip there and then, Sarah came in. She was in a thin blue-grey cardigan and a mottled green, roll neck jumper dress over navy leggings and had two bottles of Pinot Grigio, one in each hand. It was their go-to tipple when they all got smashed together.

"I thought you might need these," said Sarah, now with a sympathetic look, handing the bottles to Jennifer and taking off her shoes. She was obviously referring to earlier at Willow's.

"Thanks, sweetie," said Jennifer, smiling.

"And yeah I know I'm early. Gloria came round again, shouting her mouth off at me. Just had to get out the house."

"What have you done this time?"

"Apparently I'm letting my cat poop on her chrysanthemums."

"Er – you don't have a cat."

"I know! The woman is batshit insane."

Jennifer laughed, gesturing with the bottles of wine, "Sounds like you need these as well."

As they started towards the kitchen, Sarah noticed the METV on the floor in the hallway. "You got a METV?" she said. "Thought you hated Million Eyes?"

"Don't ask," said Jennifer quickly. "Just don't ask."

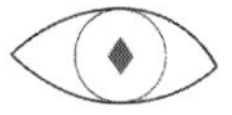

At dinner, Toasty put on a front for Sarah. They had a few laughs – the wine helped. It didn't get awkward until Toasty decided to talk Million Eyes with Sarah. Sarah, like many people, had a METV, a MEc, a MEphone, and a MEye – those virtual home automation assistants that everyone was obsessed with. She also had a MEcar X7, a sporty green driverless hatchback outfitted with Million Eyes software and the first car with a nitrogen- and oxygen-powered fuel cell. It ran on air, basically. Sarah mentioned how she hated using the Uzu laptops at work, how slow and inflexible they were next to Million Eyes – which didn't much help Jennifer with her argument. And Toasty kept talking about how Jennifer was refusing to give Million Eyes a go, as if she was goading her or something. It got to the point where Jennifer had to kick her under the table to shut her up, at which point you could cut the tension in the room with a machete.

"Sorry about tonight," Jennifer said quietly to Sarah after dinner. She was washing up and Sarah was drying. Toasty, now just trying to avoid Jennifer, was in the lounge watching TV.

Sarah smiled. "Don't worry about it, sweet. I've been stuck in the middle of worse domestics than that, trust me."

"Some of it's to do with, you know, the baby issue."

Sarah nodded. "I guessed that."

"I think we have a lot to talk about."

"Yeah. But do it sober."

Very good advice.

Sarah then said, "By the way, you can talk to me, you know."

Talking about it more with Sarah wasn't going to help Jennifer come to a conclusion, not when she could only talk about a fraction of what the real problem was. "Thanks. I know. But don't worry, we'll sort it." *Somehow.*

"No, I mean about earlier. We didn't get a chance to talk about, you know, when you got upset at the shop."

Ah. Jennifer knew Sarah would ask about that at some point. "Oh. No, I'm fine, absolutely fine." She forged a smile.

"Well like I said, you can talk to me, if you need to. You know I'm a damn good listener and talking's always better than bottling things up."

Not in this scenario it wasn't. In this scenario, Jennifer was the best bottler ever.

"You're a sweetheart," Jennifer said, "but it's not really something I like to talk about, you know? I dealt with it a long time ago and I guess I like to avoid dredging stuff back up. Just had a bit of a wobble earlier."

"I totally understand."

"Thanks for the offer though."

"Any time."

Sarah made herself scarce shortly after that. The uncomfortable atmosphere was hardly guest-friendly and Sarah probably thought she ought to give Jennifer and Toasty a chance to talk.

Not that Sarah's exit made a squat of difference to the lingering silence between them. Admittedly Jennifer didn't really try too hard to engage Toasty in conversation – not knowing what to say – but Toasty just stared glumly at the TV, not laughing once at *A Little Bit of Sick* even though it was her favourite show, which meant her thoughts were clearly elsewhere.

Jennifer was just starting to fall asleep on the other sofa when her phone vibrated. She tugged it from her pocket.

A text message from Sarah. Vicky, we need to talk. Urgently.

Jennifer blinked away her sleepiness and texted back. It was just gone 10pm. What's up? Everything okay?

An instant reply. No. You need to come round. Now. And please don't tell Toasty.

Jennifer felt her heart rate start to climb. Sarah, what the fuck's going on? And why can't I tell Toasty?

Because there's something you need to know about her. Something I've literally just found out myself.

Sarah, you're scaring me.

Just come round, Vicks. You need to know the truth.

27

Jennifer told Toasty she was going for a walk to the seafront for some air and got a quiet "K," Toasty's eyes not leaving the TV. Jennifer threw on a hoody and headed out, shivering as a cold blast of air swirled around her. She probably should've worn a coat as well, but it was only a five-minute walk to Sarah's, if that. She lived on Berkeley Way, a few roads down from Trafalgar Rise, in a two-bed terrace a bit smaller than Jennifer and Toasty's. Unlike Jennifer and Toasty, who were renting, Sarah owned hers and paid a mortgage, although her parents had covered most of the deposit.

Jennifer had this continually tightening knot in her stomach as she walked. Sarah had learned something about Toasty and Jennifer couldn't help but think it was to do with Million Eyes.

Jennifer trusted Toasty. It had taken a while but she did – implicitly. Had that trust been misplaced? Should she have stuck with her solitary life? Was trusting people again a mistake?

A low thrum of voices and music wafted from the Sticky Frog pub on St James's Street – otherwise the roads were dark and still. Jennifer was almost trembling, but not with cold, by the time she got to Berkeley Way.

She reached Sarah's house and walked up the short path to the front door.

Shit.

The door was open. It wasn't obvious from the street, but she could see now that it wasn't latched and hung slightly ajar. Sarah wouldn't have left her door open. She was OCD when it came to security.

Jennifer pushed the door gently and stepped onto the recessed coir doormat. Weak orange light limped around the hallway and up the stairs from a single low-energy lamp. She called softly, "Sarah?"

No answer.

She went further into Sarah's hallway, turned around the bottom of the stairs and saw the lounge at the end of the hall – pitch-dark. She passed the kitchen, also dark.

A moment later, voices. Jennifer was nearly at the lounge and heard muffled voices beneath her, coming from the basement. She listened for a moment, couldn't make anything out, but at least discerned that there were two voices. A woman and a man, judging by their pitch.

Sarah had a male visitor. Could this man be the source of the information about Toasty? Who could he be?

Anxiety pressing down on her belly, she started towards the basement.

Wait a minute...

Jennifer noticed that the door between the downstairs toilet and lounge was open. It was the only door Sarah hadn't opened when Jennifer first came round and got a tour of the house. Sarah just said it was a storage cupboard, which Jennifer thought was odd because it had a lock on it.

"Don't ask me," Sarah had said when Jennifer asked about the lock. "Maybe the previous owner was a serial killer and kept pieces of his victims in there!"

Jennifer laughed, "I presume you've checked for body parts?"

Sarah replied, "Yup. All clear. Just the hoover and boxes of Christmas decs in there now."

Now that the door was open, Jennifer could see inside.

And it wasn't a cupboard.

Confused, Jennifer stepped lightly towards the door, urged to take a closer look. The muffled voices continued below her, apparently oblivious to her presence.

She pushed the door wider and eased into what was clearly a whole other room, windowless and swathed in darkness, barely touched by the dim hallway light.

She stroked the wall for a light switch, found it and flicked it on. A much brighter bulb burst into light and made Jennifer squint. When her eyes adjusted, she looked around.

The room *was* being used for storage, just not the kind of storage Sarah had led Jennifer to believe. No hoover or Christmas decorations in sight. Shelves lined the walls from ceiling to floor and divided the middle of the room into a couple of narrow aisles. Each shelf was stacked with white boxes, all neatly placed, labels stamped in exactly the same place on every box – an eerie and uniform display. Jennifer tiptoed across old floorboards that could give her away at any moment. She scanned the boxes, read the labels. *Chronodes. Chronophones. Disruptors.*

She saw one labelled *Chronozine.* The third one with the *chrono-* prefix. Something to do with time, but it sounded like medicine.

She reached for the chronozine box and slid it off the shelf, breaking the symmetry of the room's lines and squares. It wasn't heavy. She set it down gently on the floor and crouched over it, lifting the lid. All the time her body was on high alert: muscles taut, eyes darting back and forth to the door, ears homed in on the voices in the basement, listening for any change in their location.

Inside the box was a batch of small plastic medicine bottles, all labelled *Chronozine.* Jennifer picked one out. It rattled – there were pills inside, or something like them. She unscrewed the cap and tipped the contents into her hand. Yep. Small, capsule-shaped, red pills.

Red pills.

A memory pushed its way to the front of her mind with a jolt. The deathbed confession of charcoal burner Purkis, saying that the man who killed William II had taken a red stone from a pot, swallowed it, then vanished before his eyes. The journal of Sir Lionel Frensham, detailing an encounter between Edward IV and an intruder with a pot of strange red pills. The woman who met with Gregory Ferro, told him about the man she saw disposing of a white Fiat Uno in the woods on the night of Princess Diana's death, a man who took a pill and disappeared.

Jennifer's chest tightened. She inspected the label. Like medication, there was a list of directions:

Do not use without a chronode. Take one tablet only. Wait at least 6 hours before taking a further tablet. If you experience dizziness, coughing, abdominal pain or nausea, consult the Time Travel Department immediately before further use. All time travel must be authorised by the Time Travel Department. Do not use chronozine unless it has been prescribed by the Time Travel Department.

It was them. Million Eyes. No question.

But that means…

No. No, no, no.

Sarah? A Million Eyes operative?

Jennifer tipped the pills back into the bottle and fastened the cap. She tucked it into the large front pocket of her hoody with her phone and house key, then replaced the box of chronozine on the shelf. She looked around at some other boxes. *Tachyon inverters. Cognits. Polaron relays. Thoridium.* It was sci-fi technobabble central in here. She wouldn't have been surprised to see a box of flux capacitors.

Her eyes settled on a box labelled *Covert transcribers*. She wasn't sure why that one intrigued her. Perhaps it was the word *covert.* She pulled the box off the shelf, set it down on the floor and looked inside.

Her heart skipped a beat. A queasy feeling rippled at the pit of her stomach. Her armpits felt hot.

The box was full of books, all copies of the same one. A book Jennifer had seen before – and tried to forget: *The History of Computer-Aided Timetabling for Railway Systems.* By *Jeremy Jennings*.

Gregory Ferro never learned why this book was so important to Million Eyes. So important that they were willing to rewrite history to get it back. Was Jennifer about to find out?

Fingers trembling, she lifted a copy from the box. For some reason the books were vacuum-packed in cellophane, or something like cellophane. She tried to rip it open with her fingers – too tough. She pulled her house key from her pocket and used it to stab the plastic – also not easy. Pushing hard she eventually made a hole at the top, but she had to dig all her fingers inside to tear it open.

Finally inside, Jennifer lifted the plain green cover.

What?

It was blank.

Jennifer flicked through the pages – all blank. She grabbed another copy. Also blank. Every page – empty.

What the fuck is going on here?

Stairs creaked. *Shit!* Her attention had waned from the voices in the basement – and now those voices were travelling up the stairs.

She kept a hold of the copy she'd taken and, faster than she'd ever moved, flung the lid on the box, shoved it back on the shelf, sprang at the wall to flick the light switch and bolted into the closest aisle between the rows of shelves, out of sight of the door.

The voices and footsteps got louder.

Jennifer could hear Sarah. She and her male visitor were about to enter the room.

Jennifer sucked in a breath and held it.

They came in. With a click, the light was on again. As they entered, the man was saying, "I remember my mother telling me about the coronation. My grandfather got the family a TV just so they could watch it."

For some reason they were talking about the Queen, although Sarah said nothing in reply.

Shuffling noises. Someone was moving one of the boxes.

Jennifer didn't move, didn't breathe. Sarah and the man were literally a metre from her, standing on the other side of the shelves.

"What?" said Sarah.

Oh God. She'd seen something. She'd noticed one of the boxes wasn't in the right place.

Jennifer squeezed her eyes shut.

"What is it?" said Sarah.

The man replied, "This is really happening, isn't it."

Okay, she hadn't noticed anything – yet. She was addressing the man.

"Yes, Finn, it is," she replied, although it didn't sound like her at all.

"Elizabeth II is going to be Britain's last queen."

Jennifer's heart stopped. What on earth were they talking about?

"Yep," said Sarah, "and it's about time too."

"But is Miss Morgan sure about this?" said 'Finn'. "We're about to assassinate Britain's longest-serving monarch."

Jennifer felt like someone had kneed her in the stomach. Did she just hear that right?

"What are you, a royalist?" said Sarah. "You know what's at stake here."

"Yes, I do. But surely there's a solution that doesn't involve assassinating her. She's ninety-odd, for God's sake. How dangerous can she be?"

"Very. The Queen might be past it physically, but her mind is sharp as anything. And you know she hates Million Eyes. She's been interfering with our work for years, undermining us at every turn. It's time we put a stop to it."

A bead of sweat dribbled down Jennifer's side from her left armpit. The blank copy of *The History of Computer-Aided Timetabling for Railway Systems* shook in her hand.

"Isn't there some way we can expose what she's doing?" said Finn.

"Not without exposing ourselves, no. Do you think the people of Britain are going to accept that Million Eyes has been secretly controlling their country since the 17th century?"

Jennifer swallowed hard. *The 17th century?*

"No. I suppose not," said Finn. "But… what about after? After the Queen is dead? Then what?"

"There's a plan in place. The government will move to abolish the monarchy and our uneasy alliance with Britain's capricious kings and queens will end. Million Eyes will take full control of Parliament and Britain will become a republic."

"I just think –"

Sarah snapped, making Jennifer flinch, "Frankly, Finn, you're not paid to think. You're paid to do as you're told. Can you do that or do I need to find someone else?"

Silence. Jennifer's shaky right hand, holding the book, froze. Her left hand, which had been twiddling with the cord of her hoody, clenched. Again she held her breath and didn't move.

Finn broke the silence, "I'm sorry, Miss Myers. Yes. I can do that."

Not being able to see her face, a part of Jennifer had been imagining – or at least hoping – that the woman talking wasn't Sarah at all, but someone else. After all, she sounded so different. So cold. So austere. Not like her friend. Not like her lovely, caring, hilarious friend.

But then Finn said *Miss Myers* and smashed the fantasy.

"Are you certain?" said Sarah. "I need to know I can count on you, or it'll be my head on the block as well as yours."

"You can count on me, I promise."

"I hope so. Just remember why we're doing this. With the monarchy out of the way, Million Eyes will be able to advance the Mission unimpeded."

The Mission? What in the world was the *Mission?*

"I understand, Miss Myers."

"Good."

Sarah spoke like she was role-playing, performing, pretending to be a fictional character who bore no resemblance to her. It was now becoming clear that the Sarah she'd known for over a year was the fictional character, their friendship the performance. None of it was real. None of it.

Jennifer *did* misplace her trust. Not in Toasty. In Sarah.

"You'll need these," said Sarah. More shuffling sounds. The swish of more boxes moving on and off shelves. *Please, please don't come round the other side of these shelves.* Rustling and clicking. "And this." Sarah was obviously taking things out of the boxes and handing them to Finn.

Then she said, "Okay. Come back downstairs and I'll fit you with a chronode. Then you'll be good to go."

They were leaving. One of them, probably Sarah, switched off the light, plunged Jennifer into darkness. She listened to their clacking footsteps, quietening as they left, turning to creaky thuds as they went back down to the basement.

Time to go.

Gently as she could, she tiptoed out of the room and across the hallway, slipped out of the still-open front door, let out a huge breath of relief – and ran.

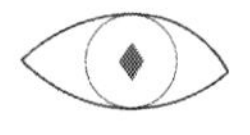

Ten minutes later, Sarah Myers and Dominic Finn came back up from the basement. Finn was fully briefed and had everything he needed to get started. As they went up the hallway so that Sarah could see Finn out, she wasn't expecting to find her front door wide open.

"What?"

She looked around, stuck her head in the kitchen, then the lounge, then the downstairs toilet, switching on all the lights. No one there. She paced around the hallway, looking for signs of an intruder, and saw that the storeroom door was open wider than she'd left it.

"Shit!"

Sarah burst into the storeroom. Finn followed. She switched on the light. Her eyes pored over the room, looking for anything out of place. Every box was perfectly in line with the next – apart from one. The box of covert transcribers.

Sarah yanked the box off the shelf, threw it down on the floor and flipped off its lid.

One of the transcribers was missing.

Sighing heavily, she straightened, felt her whole body tighten, turned and slammed her fist into the wall.

"What's going on?" said Finn.

Sarah didn't answer. She pulled her phone from her pocket and opened her home CCTV app, which was linked to tiny cameras at the front and rear of her house. Footage from five minutes ago showed Victoria Moore – her 'friend' – hotfooting it through the front door.

"Miss Myers?"

"Someone I know was here," said Sarah. "I don't know how she got in, but she was here. And there's a transcriber missing, which means she was in this room."

"Do you think… she was in here when we were?"

"I don't know. Even if she wasn't, the fact that she was in this room at all is enough."

"What do we do?"

She shot Finn a glare. "What the fuck do you think?"

28

Jennifer ploughed through her front door, which crashed against the wall behind, flakes of cream paint flying. She kicked it shut and bolted upstairs.

"Vicks?" Toasty called from the bedroom. "Is that you?"

Jennifer tripped over the rug on the landing as she thundered into the bedroom, breathless, strands of hair stuck to her clammy cheeks.

"What the hell's going on?" Toasty asked, jumping out of bed in just her pants.

She tried to catch her breath. "It's Sarah. She – she's –"

"She's what?" Toasty's eyes went to the book, still in Jennifer's hand. "What's that?"

Jennifer didn't know why she still had it. She remembered there was a bottle of chronozine in her hoody pocket too. What on earth was she going to do with them? She flopped on the bed, chest heaving, and tossed the book to Toasty. "It's – I don't even know what the fuck it is. It's blank. There was a whole box of them in Sarah's house."

"Sarah's house? What were you doing there? You said you were going down to the seafront."

Jennifer shook her head. "Doesn't matter." She remembered something that still didn't add up about all this – the texts. The texts Sarah sent her, asking her to come round, saying she'd discovered something about Toasty. Sarah clearly had no idea Jennifer was in the house, nor did it sound like she was expecting her, even though – also inexplicably – she'd left the front door open.

Frowning, Toasty opened the book, leafed through it quickly. "No, it isn't."

"Isn't what?"

"Blank. It isn't blank. Not all of it, anyway. Look."

Toasty handed the book back to Jennifer. *What the fuck?* The opening pages were now filled with text. But she could've sworn…

Jennifer read the text.

```
Dominic Finn: I remember my mother telling
  me about the coronation. My grandfather got
  the family a TV just so they could watch
  it. [11-second pause.]
Sarah Myers: What? [3-second pause.] What is
  it?
Dominic Finn: This is really happening,
  isn't it.
Sarah Myers: Yes, Finn, it is.
Dominic Finn: Elizabeth II is going to be
  Britain's last queen.
```

Jennifer remembered what it said on the box. *Covert transcribers.* Of course! They weren't books at all, not really. They were transcription devices, albeit futuristic ones – but nothing surprised her about Million Eyes anymore.

Jennifer handed the book back to Toasty. "Read it."

"Okay…"

Jennifer watched Toasty read, eyes squinted with confusion, cheeks reddening with growing horror.

"*What?* They're going to assassinate the Queen? Who are?" She looked at Jennifer for an answer.

"Keep reading."

Toasty resumed reading and a moment later her eyes snapped wide. "Million Eyes?" Her eyes darted through the rest of the text, then shifted to Jennifer. "What is this? Is this a joke?"

"I wish it was."

"But I don't understand. This looks like… like a transcript of a conversation. Why is this in here? In some book about computers and railways?"

"The book's a decoy. It's a covert transcription device. I just heard that conversation – about ten minutes ago – and the book transcribed it."

Toasty looked at her like she was mad. "Are you telling me

this book can, what, write itself?"

"Yes."

Toasty gave a mocking laugh. "I'm sorry – have I stumbled into *Harry Potter* or something?"

Jennifer grabbed the book off her and flicked to the last page of text. As she expected, the words Toasty had just spoken were typing themselves onto the page.

```
Toasty Clements: I'm sorry. Have I stumbled
  into Harry Potter or something?
```

Jennifer was about to hand the book back to Toasty so she could see for herself. She hesitated when she saw her own words recorded above Toasty's.

The book had identified her as Jennifer Larson, not Victoria Moore.

Fuck.

"What?" said Toasty, noting that Jennifer had gone quiet. "Is it recording what we're saying right now?"

Jennifer swallowed and shook her head, shutting the book quickly. "No. It's stopped."

Toasty started pacing around the room, breathing heavily and shaking her head in disbelief. "I don't understand."

"It's technology the public don't know about," said Jennifer. "Million Eyes have plenty of it, trust me."

"But it says… it says Sarah was saying those things. Sarah Myers. *Our* Sarah."

Jennifer shook her head. "I don't think she was ever our Sarah."

"But she was talking about assassinating the Queen. Bringing down the monarchy. And… what? Million Eyes have been controlling the country for *four hundred years*?"

"Yes. This transcript is evidence that Million Eyes…"

Hang on a minute.

Evidence. The transcript was evidence that Million Eyes had been controlling the government since the 17th century and were conspiring to assassinate the Queen to preserve their power. It was something that, if publicised, would devastate Million Eyes, which made it something they would try and retrieve at all costs.

This *was* the book Gregory Ferro was looking for. The

book that led Million Eyes to travel back in time and radically alter history.

Jennifer's mind raced. Did that make sense, though? All of that already happened, but the transcript had only just been made. How could it already be a part of history?

Wibbly wobbly timey wimey. The words of the Tenth Doctor had never rung truer.

"Vicks – what is it?" said Toasty.

"Ssshh. Wait. Let me think."

Alright, let's try and figure this out. If the book was already part of history, did that mean it was inevitable that it was going to end up in the past, chased across time by Million Eyes? Or could Jennifer, in theory, destroy the book right now and undo all of history as it now stood?

She couldn't destroy it, though. How could she? It was evidence of Million Eyes' treason, evidence that democracy in Britain was a sham. It was what she needed to get her life back from those bastards. She'd been devoid of ideas on how to deal with Million Eyes ever since she ran away. Now a bomb that could blow them all to hell had fallen right into her lap.

"Vicks, talk to me!" said Toasty.

"We have to get this book out in the open," said Jennifer. "I'm not sure how but the whole world needs to know about this."

"Shouldn't we give it to the police?"

"We can't trust the police, Toasty. I was told once that Million Eyes have people inside the police."

"Told by who?"

"That doesn't matter. The point is, Million Eyes have people everywhere. Finding out that Sarah's one of them has just proven that."

"There's got to be some explanation. I *know* Sarah. She's one of my closest friends."

"You thought you knew her. So did I."

"Vicks, no. I don't believe it. It's totally insane."

Jennifer took a deep breath. Should she tell her? Should she tell Toasty what Million Eyes did to her? Was it time she came clean?

Toasty deserved the truth. She shared everything with Jennifer, but Jennifer had always kept her at arm's length. On all her down days, when she missed her mum, her sister,

Adam, she just fobbed Toasty off. And Toasty knew she was being fobbed off. Of course she did. But she put up with it.

"Toasty, I need to tell you –"

A forceful knock at their front door cut her off. She glanced at her bedside clock – 10.43pm.

Oh God – Sarah.

Toasty had grabbed her dressing gown and was already walking out of the bedroom as Jennifer shouted, "No – don't!"

Toasty ignored her and carried on downstairs.

Jennifer waited for the sound of the door. Her heart thumped so hard she could feel every beat in her fingers and toes.

The clink of the latch was followed by a deep, blaring *crack*. A familiar sound. She'd just made the same sound herself ten minutes ago. It was the sound of the door swinging open fast and hitting the inside wall.

Silence.

She listened, heard nothing.

She waited. Dread snaked up her throat.

Shit! Footfalls up the stairs. She grabbed the transcriber off the bed and shoved it into her hoody pocket with the bottle of chronozine and her phone.

Hide. Hide. Hide.

She sprang into the en-suite, quietly closed the door and locked it. She picked up the cylindrical steel laundry bin and positioned herself behind the door.

She heard creaks. Whoever had just come up the stairs was in the bedroom.

Shit. A creak just outside the door.

She swallowed hard.

Oh God.

Someone was turning the doorknob – the lock held.

"Vicky?" Sarah's voice through the door.

Jennifer's instinct was to pretend nothing was wrong.

"Sarah? Is that you?" she replied brightly.

"Vicky, please can you come out."

"I'm just about to get in the shower! How come you're back? Where's Toasty?"

"Vicky, we need to talk now."

She didn't know what to say next. Sarah was here for the

transcriber – she knew that. And Sarah probably knew she knew that. And she was probably going to kill her once she got it.

"I'll be out shortly," Jennifer murmured.

"Come out now." Suddenly Sarah's tone was laced with fury. "I know about the book. Give it to me, and I'll let you go."

What a crock of shit.

No point playing dumb anymore.

Jennifer said nothing.

"I won't ask again," said Sarah.

Jennifer stayed silent.

A long hiss. The doorknob rattled. Metal scraped and whined. Somehow Sarah was slicing through the lock.

Jennifer lifted the laundry bin.

The noise stopped.

The doorknob turned.

The door opened.

Jennifer saw Sarah's hand, clasping a gun, appear around the rim of the door. Jennifer didn't waste any time and lunged.

The steel laundry bin thunked into Sarah's shoulder, slamming her into the sink. The gun escaped her grip and skimmed across the vinyl tiles. Jennifer plunged and grabbed it, then two hard hands clamped onto her shoulders and yanked her back. Jennifer fell through the en-suite doorway onto the bedroom carpet, the gun flung behind her.

Jennifer spun on the floor, saw the gun at the foot of the bed and sprang for it. Sarah dived for it too. Jennifer got to it first and, turning on the floor, swung hard as Sarah swooped over her. The gun met Sarah's jaw with a solid thwack and she hurtled backwards, thumping onto the floor.

Jennifer got to her feet and pointed the gun at Sarah, who'd risen onto her elbows, blood trickling from the corner of her mouth. "Don't fucking move!"

"What's going on up there?" shouted a male voice from downstairs. It sounded like the man Sarah was talking to at her house – Finn.

"Stay down there!" Sarah called to him.

Jennifer had never touched a gun before, but she'd seen plenty on TV. This one was silver, small, lightweight, had a sleek barrel with a sequence of recessed buttons, and looked a bit like the destructive ray gun used by that nurse to try and kill her two years ago. She had her finger over a pretty normal-looking trigger, and the gravity of Sarah's expression told her that it worked like any other.

"What the fuck, Sarah?" she said. "What the actual fuck?"

"Vicky, I'm your friend. You're not going to shoot me."

"You're kidding, right? *Friend*? Where's Toasty?"

"Downstairs with my colleague."

Jennifer called to her, "Toasty!"

No answer.

"Toasty!"

"She won't hear you," said Sarah.

Jennifer's stomach turned. "What have you done?"

"My job."

Jennifer felt a pang in her chest. "Stand up. Stand the fuck up."

Sarah got to her feet. Jennifer gripped the gun so tight it was like she was welded to it.

"Keep your hands where I can see them. Move." Jennifer gestured with the gun and steered Sarah onto the landing.

Sarah backed against the wall. Holding her aim, Jennifer gripped the top of the balustrade that skirted the staircase and looked down. A man – probably Finn – was standing in the hallway, slowly lowering a mobile phone from his ear as Jennifer and Sarah appeared on the landing.

At Finn's feet was Toasty, motionless on her back on the floor, mouth open, eyes open and staring blankly, shimmering blood spilling from her neck.

Jennifer clapped her hand over her mouth. *No, no, no, no….*

Her legs felt boneless. If she wasn't still gripping the balustrade, she would've fallen. Her right arm, outstretched and pointing the gun, wavered.

"W-what have you done…" she murmured.

"I told you," said Sarah. "My job."

Jennifer's breathing became convulsive – anguish, panic, fury overwhelming her. Her hand tightened over her mouth, her fingers bruising her cheeks. Hot tears swelled in her eyes.

At once, Sarah lunged, taking full advantage of Jennifer's distress.

She grabbed at Jennifer's arms, trying to wrestle the gun from her grip. Jennifer pushed back. They thumped onto the landing floor, knocking over a small lamp table as they grappled.

It all happened so fast. A blur of violence. Jennifer grabbed the chunky ceramic tealight holder that had rolled onto the floor when the table fell, and smashed it into the side of Sarah's head.

Sarah's thrashing arms flopped.

Jennifer swung again. *Thunk.* And again. *Thunk.* And again. *Crack.*

In the corner of her eye, Finn charging up the stairs was the distraction she needed to stop herself.

She spun towards him, gun raised, and pressed the trigger.

A shaft of green light burst from the tip of the gun and slammed into Finn's waist, tossing him backwards down the stairs.

Jennifer collapsed on her rear, shaking. Both hands released their weapons. There was blood everywhere – all over the carpet, all over her.

What the fuck had just happened…

Toasty!

A bolt of emotions launched her down the stairs. She leapt over Finn's body and dropped to her knees at Toasty's side. She tried to shake her awake. "Toasty! Babe, wake up! Fucking wake up – *please!*"

Toasty's vacant, empty stare persisted. Her limbs didn't twitch, her chest didn't rise. Her only movement was the steady stream of blood weeping into the carpet from the deep laceration across her throat. Jennifer checked her pulse. She couldn't feel anything.

No. Come back. You have to come back.

Tears blurring her vision, Jennifer pulled open Toasty's dressing gown and, straining to remember back to the first aid course she did at uni, interlocked her hands over Toasty's breastbone and began pumping her chest.

Jennifer knew she was dead even before she started compressions. She just wasn't processing it. Tears rained over Jennifer's hands and Toasty's bare chest. Before long, her arms went weak and she crumbled, sinking into Toasty's waist, which was still warm, and murmuring between sobs,

"Don't leave me."

"*Myers! Finn!*" a muted voice crackled.

Jennifer lifted her head from Toasty, looking with bleary eyes towards Finn's body, a heap at the foot of the stairs. The voice was coming from his direction.

"Myers! Finn! What's happening over there?"

Jennifer crawled towards the body, spotted the source of the voice – a mobile phone about a metre from where he lay.

Finn had been on the phone when she and Sarah came onto the landing. Looked like he never got a chance to hang up.

Sniffing and rubbing her eyes, Jennifer reached for the phone and breathed, "W-who is this?"

"Ah," a woman replied, disappointment in her voice. "You must be Victoria Moore. I take it Miss Myers and Mr Finn are dead then."

Jennifer tried to steady her breathing. She could hardly see for tears. Each time she rubbed her eyes, more came. "Y-yes."

"That's a shame."

Jennifer swallowed. "Who… are you?"

"Why don't you take a moment. Go have a cup of tea. Some of my people will be there shortly to explain everything."

Wait. I know that voice.

"Who *are* you?" Jennifer said again.

"I'm not sure that really matters."

Then, a snap of memory.

Erica Morgan. CEO of Million Eyes.

Jennifer gasped for breath. "You're Erica Morgan. You're the one who's responsible for all this." She looked at Toasty's bloody corpse. "You're the one who's just killed my… my…" Her voice broke. More tears fell.

"Now listen. I can tell you're upset and I'm sorry – I truly am – for your loss. But trust me when I say that the work we're doing is more important than you or your loved ones, or me or mine."

Jennifer felt a deep, hot fury rising from the pit of her stomach like a stirring volcano. "You mean… the 'Mission'?"

"Hmm. You've been eavesdropping on things that don't concern you." Her voice was sticky with condescension.

Jennifer's fingers tightened around the phone. "I know you're planning to assassinate the Queen."

"Yes, well, that'll be our little secret, won't it?"

"Not for long. I have evidence of what you're doing. I'm going to expose you to the whole fucking world."

"Oh, petal. Are you? I presume you're talking about the transcriber you stole. Fear not! My people will soon be there to take care of that. And you."

"Fuck you. You'll never find me."

Miss Morgan laughed coldly. "Of course we will. Why do you think we called ourselves Million Eyes?"

Miss Morgan hung up and Jennifer lobbed the phone at the wall, shaking all over, an ever-mounting pile-up of emotions crashing through her head. She tried to catch her breath, calm herself.

"You have to go."

A whispered voice. Again it was coming from the direction of Finn's body.

Jennifer looked over at him. Shit – he wasn't dead. His eyes were open, his left arm edging across the floor.

Jennifer looked up at the blood-splattered landing and Sarah's motionless legs. Her gun was up there. Jennifer had dropped it after she'd shot Finn.

Why the fuck didn't I keep a hold of it?

Jennifer got to her feet.

"You have to." Finn's voice was wheezy, strained. "You have to run."

What?

"Keep that transcriber safe," Finn continued.

Jennifer shook her head. "Why are you – ?"

"Who do you think left the door open for you?"

"That was you?"

His speech was becoming more laboured. "I needed you there… I needed you… to hear it."

"Was it you who sent those texts as well?"

"Y-yes."

"Why? Why me?"

"Because… because it's how it has to… be…"

"I don't understand. What am I supposed to do?"

"Run."

Finn's head flopped to the side.

Jennifer checked that the transcriber and the bottle of chronozine were still in her hoody pocket. They were. So was her phone.

She crouched over Toasty, stroked two fingers against her cheek and kissed her lips, whispering, "I love you."

Then she bolted up the stairs, grabbed Sarah's gun, flew back down, swiped the keys to Toasty's Mazda Dimension from the hall table, and hurtled through the front door.

She sprinted up Trafalgar Rise, along St James's Street, ran for a couple of minutes before reaching Elizabeth Terrace, one of the few roads in Kemptown where there were parking spaces. She spotted Toasty's Dimension and unlocked it. She dived into the driver's seat, tossed Sarah's gun onto the passenger seat, and started the engine.

The tyres wailed as she floored it out of Elizabeth Terrace. She had no idea where she was going. Out of Brighton. That was as far as she'd got.

As she reached the junction with the busy Old Steine thoroughfare, Brighton's Royal Pavilion sneaked into view through the gaps in the trees flanking the road, its onion domes and minarets lit up and glowing gold against the night sky.

As she turned right onto the Old Steine, a black Mercedes promptly overtook her, then swerved hard in front of her and stopped.

No, no, no.

She hit the brakes, lurched forwards. Sarah's gun flew off the passenger seat into the footwell.

She shoved the car into reverse and whirled round in her seat. Before she could move, a second black Mercedes pulled up fast behind her, skidding to a halt – tyres screaming, bright headlights skewering her eyes.

Fuck!

She was trapped.

Miss Morgan was right. They'd found her. They'd caught her.

The front doors of the Mercedes ahead of her swung open. A woman stepped out of the driver's side, a man out of the passenger side. Both were wearing smart, dark suits and brandished silver guns just like Sarah's. They approached Jennifer's car.

"Ma'am, please get out of the car," called the woman.

Jennifer glanced at Sarah's gun in the passenger footwell. Her heart sank. She'd never be able to reach it in time. As soon as she went for it they'd shoot her.

But…

Slowly, stealthily, Jennifer slipped her hand into her hoody pocket. The transcriber and her phone were still in there – as was the bottle of chronozine.

It was insane. She knew it was insane. But Million Eyes weren't going to let her live.

"Miss Moore, get out of the car now."

She had two choices.

Death or time travel.

She fondled the cap off the bottle, poked a finger inside, dug out a pill. The two Million Eyes agents were nearly by the car. Her hand flashed to her mouth and the pill was on her tongue.

She swallowed.

A loud, continuous hum pinched her ears. She felt sleepy, dizzy. She blinked. Suddenly there were people and vehicles everywhere, surrounding her car, and everyone and everything was transparent – like ghosts – and blurred together like countless photographs superimposed over one another. The two Million Eyes agents were lost in a throng of see-through people walking through see-through cars driving through see-through walls and buildings.

And it wasn't just cars. Horses, too. Horses pulling chariots carrying… wait a minute. *Romans?* Yes, Romans. The huge, red, horsehair crests arching over their bronze helmets were unmistakable.

Jennifer homed in on some of the other people, then appreciating what was an inconceivable collision of fashions. There were men in top hats and frock coats, women in coifs and pinafores, walking among men in shorts, t-shirts, flip-flops, women in jeans and crop-tops, and both men and women in sleek, skin-tight onesies with gills, bizarre jackets with triangular protrusions, and dresses that looked like a mesh of alien tentacles.

She looked up. *What?* The sky was filled with vehicles the size of cars whooshing through the clouds at high speed. And among them, large birds crossing at a far more leisurely pace.

Not seagulls – the birds you usually expect to see in abundance in Brighton – but pterodactyls.

It dawned on Jennifer what this blur of ghosts meant. Time. All of it. The past, the present, the future. All of it happening at once. All of it merged in front of her eyes.

She looked down. She was still in her car, but that was see-through too. She could see the road through the footwell, and she could see grass through the tarmac. She moved – she couldn't feel her seat. She felt weightless, floating.

Now what?

She looked up again and her attention lingered on two figures in the crowd of ghosts. Two men on horseback, cantering towards her, wearing chainmail and dome-shaped helmets, bearing swords and shields, and staring right at her. Medieval knights.

Could they see her?

As she watched their approach, they changed. Their hazy, transparent bodies sharpened, solidified. The humming eased and the ghosts around them slipped away.

Then she blacked out.

29

July 9th 1100

Thump.

Jennifer landed on her back against a hard surface. She opened her eyes, saw only brightness, white and hot in her eyes. She felt weak and tingly and her chest and throat were on fire. She squeezed her fingers, digging into cool soil. She sucked in a breath, wheezing. The painful heat in her throat and chest provoked a violent cough. After that, it started easing.

The intense whiteness dimmed, softening into a blue-green hue. Thicker patches of blue and green started to form, finally sharpening into sunlight pouring down from a cerulean sky through the leafy knots and weaves of a tree.

Jennifer sat up, felt like she was wearing a rucksack full of rocks. She took slow, deep breaths, rolled her shoulders, bent, stretched and rotated her arms and legs, trying to re-energise her stiff, weary body. The tingling eased, life returned to her limbs, and she was able to climb to her feet.

She looked around. She was standing in a lightly wooded area skirting a field of cattle and a smattering of barns and medieval-looking dwellings with thatched roofs and wattle and daub walls, the steeple of a small stone church peeking over the top of them. The village was framed to the north by green, forest-patched hills, to the south by a familiar-looking sea. A growing wind blew whorls of salt across the land that she could taste.

The ghosts were gone. So were the Old Steine Road, its houses and apartment buildings, the Pavilion, the Pavilion Gardens. All gone.

She'd gone back in time, to a fairly distant past it would seem.

Not ideal.

She looked up, drawn by the familiar caw of seagulls.

At least they weren't pterodactyls.

She reached inside the large front pocket of her hoody for the bottle of chronozine.

Her hand touched the transcriber. Still there, still safe. Her phone was still there too. She dug past them – no bottle.

Panic speared through her. "No, no, no, no." Her eyes combed the ground. She couldn't see it. She dived to her knees, scrabbling through dirt and grass and weeds. Nothing.

She stood, spun round, returned to her knees and repeated the search she'd just done.

"Shit, shit, SHIT!"

Could it have fallen out of her pocket?

When?

Jennifer's search was in vain. It wasn't there. *What now?* She plunged her hand in her pocket, pulled out her phone instead. She wasn't sure why, what it would achieve, but she did it anyway.

The phone was dead. The screen wouldn't turn on. She pressed every button she could. Nothing.

"Aaaarrrrghhh!"

A fierce caterwaul erupted from her throat and she hurled the phone forcefully at the nearest tree. Then she fell limply onto her back and stared up at the sky. Her stomach rolled, churned and convulsed and before long a fast torrent of vomit was snaking up her throat. She turned quickly onto her side and released it heavily into the grass.

She was stuck here.

Actually stuck here.

Approaching hoofbeats jolted her. She lifted stiffly onto her elbows. Two dark brown horses, ridden by silver men, cantered towards her.

She'd risen to her feet by the time the horses scraped to a halt in front of her. Both riders wore boots, stockings, knee-length skirts of silver chainmail, and pointed, dome-shaped helmets with protruding strips extending over their noses. They each carried a kite shield bearing different motifs, and a sword fastened at the waist by a leather belt.

Knights. The ones Jennifer saw, right before she blacked out.

The knight with a three-headed red dragon emblazoned on his shield looked her up and down and said something to the other, whose shield displayed a vulture inside a ring of fire. The words sounded French – she could gauge that much.

The vulture knight responded.

Definitely French.

The Normans spoke French.

If only she'd done French and not German at school.

The dragon knight spoke again, signalling the vulture knight to dismount his horse. He approached her, glaring eyes probing her every curve. He circled her, leaned, smelled her hair. Then he grabbed the shoulder of her hoody roughly and rubbed the purple fabric between his fingertips.

"Get your fucking hands off me," she barked, pulling away.

The vulture knight hissed a reply and yanked her back by her hood. He continued circling her, brushed his thick fingers over the thigh of her blue jeans. Another garment that would've looked super-strange to a Norman knight. Then he noticed the stains on the front of her hoody – Sarah's blood – and his eyes narrowed.

He inspected the large front pocket of her hoody, stuffing his hand inside and pulling out the transcriber.

He raised it, gestured to his colleague, then babbled something in French. The dragon knight held out his hand and the vulture knight passed it to him.

Should she run? Should she try to escape?

It wasn't like she could do anything with the transcriber anymore. They could keep it. That ship had sailed. The Queen was on her own.

And while they were distracted looking at it, she could slip away…

No, Jen. Don't be an idiot. They'll chase you. They have horses. And swords.

She waited, watched as the dragon knight flicked through the book and, frowning, found the transcription on the opening pages.

He showed the vulture knight. They wittered in French.

The two knights huddled around the book and went silent. They seemed to be reading it, although Jennifer knew they wouldn't be able to understand a word – it was all in Modern English, a language totally alien to two Norman knights.

But then the dragon knight gasped. And the vulture knight's face was rigid with the sort of horror you'd expect if he realised that the transcription was about murdering a future monarch of Britain.

Except he couldn't have realised it. Neither of them could. Why were they reacting?

Jennifer watched as they continued reading. If they couldn't understand the words they would've given up by now. And yet both their faces displayed the same pointed alarm that had probably seized her own features the first time she heard this heinous and treasonous plot being hatched.

They *did* understand. But how?

A moment later, the dragon knight shut the book and conversed with his colleague. Then the vulture knight faced her, grabbed her arm and pulled her roughly towards his horse, snarling something at her.

"Wait – stop! Let go of me!" she hollered, yanking back.

His grip was too strong. The dragon knight threw down a long rope, which the vulture knight used to tie her wrists.

Realisation struck her in that moment.

These two knights were probably about to take her to London and bring her before the king.

She knew which king. William II. The king killed for a book. History was coming full circle and Jennifer was along for the ride. Was this really her destiny all along?

She felt a twist of dread in her gut. They probably thought she was part of the plot. She urged, "Please, I'm nothing to do with this. I'm not one of them." She wasn't sure what she was hoping to achieve, given that neither of them understood her, nor she them.

Then the vulture knight got right in her face and barked a string of ferocious-sounding words, his hot, stale breath wafting over her, a couple of beads of saliva hitting her nose and cheek. And though she spoke no French, certainly no 11th-century Norman French, one of the words he shouted was obvious: "Traître!" *Traitor.*

The dragon knight kept hold of the transcriber. The vulture knight finished tying her wrists with the rope, then tied the other end to his saddle. He remounted and urged his horse into a walk – Jennifer had no choice but to follow or be dragged. The dragon knight brought up the rear, probably to keep an eye on her.

They went north, away from the sea, towards London.

She had to find a way to communicate. She needed to prove to William II that she was nothing to do with Million Eyes, or she was in for a rendezvous with the gallows.

But then she wondered if that would be such a bad thing. She'd lost her mum, Jamie, Adam – and now Toasty. The girl she loved, murdered by someone she thought was her friend.

She'd lost everything. Everything and everyone. And now she was stuck in this century forever.

She started seeing flashes of Toasty's face. Her dead stare. All that… blood. She wanted to be sick again. She gagged a couple of times, nothing came out. She had nothing left in her.

So she just sobbed.

30

October 13th 2021

Erica Morgan was in her office on the top floor of the gargantuan glass and concrete skyscraper that stood on Puttenham Lane in Central London, looking out of the window and blowing rings of cigarette smoke at the glass. Nicknamed the Looming Tower for its coarse, Brutalist architecture and intimidating appearance, the building had been Million Eyes' corporate headquarters since 1998, thanks in part to a substantial investment from billionaire Arthur Pell, whose statue graced – or more aptly *spoiled* – the gardens at the front. A condition of the investment, this creepy eyesore was forged from solid eighteen-karat gold provided by Pell, or so everyone thought. In reality, Miss Morgan had used the gold to buy another building in the city, then had the statue constructed from bronze and gilded.

Something was wrong. Miss Morgan hadn't heard from her operatives in Brighton in twenty minutes. She thumbed her silver Zippo lighter into life and lit cigarette nineteen of a twenty-pack she had opened less than two hours ago.

She picked up her phone to call Susan Hicks, who was coordinating the operation to kill Victoria Moore and destroy the transcriber. As she did so, Hicks called her. Miss Morgan answered, "Jesus, Hicks, take your fucking time down there."

"Miss Morgan, you need to raise the Shield."

A pang of dread. "What?"

"Ma'am, raise the Shield. Now."

Miss Morgan threw her phone down, tapped a few keys on her MEc and called the Time Travel Department. Deputy manager Rupert Whistler's face appeared on screen.

"Yes, ma'am?"

"Raise the Shield," said Miss Morgan immediately.

"But there aren't any scheduled –"

"Raise the Shield *now!*"

"Y-yes, ma'am." She saw Whistler nod to a couple of colleagues. A moment later, the main panel lights in Miss Morgan's office dimmed and the red pyramid lamp at the centre of the ceiling came on, giving everything in the room a crimson tint. The lockdown light. There was one in every room. Its purpose was to tell all staff that the Shield was up and the building was sealed. Normally the Shield was raised during time travel assignments, protecting everyone inside from potential changes to history, while the purpose of the lockdown was to stop staff from leaving the building and getting absorbed into an alternate timeline.

"Shield's up, ma'am," said Whistler.

"Thank you."

"Can I ask wh – ?"

"I'm not sure yet. I'll let you know as soon as I do."

Miss Morgan ended the call and picked up her phone. "Hicks, you still there?"

"Yes, ma'am."

"What the hell is going on?"

"I'm afraid Victoria Moore has travelled back in time."

Suddenly this mess with Miss Moore had got a whole lot worse. "What! How?"

"We were able to apprehend Miss Moore on the intersection of Marlborough Place and the Old Steine. But she had a bottle of chronozine. She took a pill before we got to her."

"Did she take the transcriber with her?"

"I… think so."

"Damn it, Hicks! What's her exact destination?"

"1100. Juuulyyyy theeeeee…"

Hicks' words became strangely distorted. Miss Morgan yanked the phone from her ear and glanced at the display. The call was still connected, no sign of any signal interference.

She returned the phone to her ear and heard, "Eeeeeaaaarrrr…"

"Hicks? What's wrong? What's happening?"

The call went dead.

Before she could call back, the floor quaked, vibrations travelling up her chair to her rear, tickling their way to her fingers. Soft at first, the vibrations rose quickly and were soon drilling through the floor and walls with an almighty, ear-pummelling roar, as if the huge skyscraper was trying to shake free of its foundations. Miss Morgan's chair shook violently – she braced her hands against the arms, teeth chattering, vision jittering. The lockdown light blinked, her laptop rocked across her desk and her mug skittered off the edge, smashing, cold coffee spilling across previously immaculate carpet tiles. Outside her office, yells and screams proliferated through the C-Suite.

Then it stopped, just like that. The light stopped blinking. Everything was still – like nothing had happened.

Oh no...

She stood and bolted out of her office into the open-plan area of the C-Suite. There for the night shift were five executive assistants, her PA, Lara Driscoll, among them. Her chief technology officer, Juanita Salazar, was also there. She hadn't actually been home in three days due to a big fuck-up in the Internet Services Department.

All six of them were at the windows and staring, lips parted in horror, across night time London. Miss Morgan joined them.

Jesus H. Christ.

Big Ben and the Houses of Parliament, normally beautifully aglow at this time of night, were gone. A smaller building stood in their place, cloaked in darkness. St James's Park, Green Park and Hyde Park had been swamped by buildings, and Buckingham Palace had been replaced by a football stadium. On the other side of the Thames, the London Eye, County Hall and a dozen other buildings were missing, replaced by an illuminated parade of skyscrapers and an enormous bronze statue – taller than some of the skyscrapers – of a woman with the head of a frog who bore a close resemblance to the Ancient Egyptian goddess of childbirth, Heket.

Miss Morgan pulled her gaze back to the immediate vicinity. The streets below, glimmering orange as they reflected the light from shops, restaurants, houses and cars, had moved and changed shape. And Miss Morgan's favourite

Starbucks on Puttenham Lane was now a topiary garden sparkling with fairy lights.

The only welcome change, from what she could see, was that the statue of Arthur Pell had been replaced by a fountain.

"Miss Morgan, this is bad," said Juanita Salazar quietly. "How could this have happened?"

Miss Morgan looked around at her employees. The executive assistants were back at their desks, some tapping away at their MEcs, others making calls on their personal phones. She heard Melanie Cox shout into hers, "Damn it, it's me. You know who I am. I'm your fiancé!"

Then she heard Anthony Graves shout into his phone, "Pick up the fucking phone!"

This had never happened before. Not on this scale, anyway.

Thank God for the Shield.

Miss Morgan projected over the jangle of shrill, panicked chatter, "Everyone, could I have your attention. Put down your phones and listen."

They did as asked and stared at her, features stiff with dread.

"I want you all to calm down," she said. "Look around. We're okay. We're all still here. The Shield is holding and whatever's happened to the timeline will have no effect on us while we remain in the building. Which means we can fix this. Alright?"

A few uncertain nods.

"Alright. Miss Cox, send a message to all departments. Let them know that we're handling this."

"Yes, ma'am."

She stepped closer to Lara Driscoll's desk. "Miss Driscoll, call Rupert Whistler in Time Travel and tell him to initiate a sensor sweep. I want a full report on the changes. I also want to know the status of the Shield and who else is on duty down there."

"Already done, ma'am," said Driscoll.

Not a surprise. While the others had families and friends they might've lost, Lara Driscoll – a former detective chief inspector – had none. It was useful, actually. Her lack of emotional ties meant she was always on task and never lost her cool in a crisis.

"Asha Wilkins, James Rawling, Parker Scott, Sheila Ruben

and Robert Skinner are all on duty tonight," said Driscoll.

Miss Morgan nodded. "Okay. Good."

"But they can't initiate a sensor sweep. Whistler says there's never been a temporal incursion of this magnitude and it's overloaded the sensor grid."

A few of the staff overheard. Melanie Cox shouted, "What does that mean?"

Miss Morgan replied calmly, "It means we can't tell exactly what changes have occurred beyond looking out the windows. But don't panic, because I'm pretty sure I know what caused this."

"Ma'am, there's something else," said Driscoll. "The Shield. Whistler says that, due to the scale of the incursion, the Shield's using up a lot more energy than normal to protect us from it. Which means it won't hold for long."

"What?" Melanie Cox's piercing voice once again. "The Shield's gonna fail?"

"Miss Cox, calm down," said Miss Morgan. "That's not what she said." Looking at Driscoll, "How long do we have?"

"Six hours. Max."

That wasn't a lot of time. It would have to do. "Plenty of time," she fudged for the sake of morale and Melanie Cox's blood pressure. "Now, what do we have on Victoria Moore?"

Still earwigging like a champ, Melanie Cox piped up, "Did she cause this?"

"Miss Cox, why don't you concentrate on what you're doing and let me handle this?"

Cox retrained her worried eyes on her screen.

Driscoll answered, "I did some digging before the incursion. It turns out we've had a run-in with Victoria Moore before. She changed her name to Victoria Moore two years ago, but she used to be Jennifer Larson."

"The girl who was working with Gregory Ferro? The one Robert Skinner was supposed to have killed?"

"Same night he killed Ferro, yes."

Miss Morgan dug her fingernails into her palms. She could see that Melanie Cox was trying not to react. "Can you access her file?"

"I'm afraid not. I was just about to retrieve it when the incursion happened. It's disrupted our access to the cloud."

"What about the paper file?" Million Eyes always kept paper files as back-ups, in case something like this happened, though the archives were bursting at the seams and discussions were ongoing on what to do about it.

Driscoll looked uncomfortable – more bad news. "It's... been misfiled."

Great. There was no way they'd be able to find a misplaced file in their labyrinthine and overflowing archives in six hours. So much for their back-up system.

"What about the paper file for Gregory Ferro?"

Driscoll's cheeks reddened. "I'm afraid we can't find that one either."

Miss Morgan smashed her palm against the nearest desk, which happened to be Melanie Cox's. The anxious analyst nearly jumped out of her skin.

Sucking in a breath, Miss Morgan said to Driscoll, "Skinner's working the night shift, isn't he."

"Yes, ma'am."

"Get him up here – now."

31

Robert Skinner had no idea why he was the one being summoned to Miss Morgan's office after such an enormous temporal incursion. He was only promoted to the Time Travel Department two months ago. Why not James Rawling?

When he exited the lift into the C-Suite, all the night shift staff were looking at him gravely. A couple of the executive assistants even shook their heads at him.

What the fuck is going on?

His heart was thumping as he crossed the C-Suite to Miss Morgan's office. The door was open when he got there and Skinner saw Anthony Graves lifting what looked like a coffee stain off the carpet.

The CEO looked up from her MEc, saw Skinner hovering in the doorway. "Get in here now," she snapped.

His heart sank. *I've done something.*

He tried to walk confidently into the room but ended up doing an awkward two-step jig to avoid tripping over his own feet. Miss Morgan looked at Graves. "Are you done?"

Graves smiled briefly, "Yep. All done."

Miss Morgan nodded, "Close the door on your way out."

Graves left and Skinner went to sit down in the chair opposite Miss Morgan's desk.

Her eyes widened. "Did I say you could sit down?"

He stopped, swallowed hard and clasped his hands together in front of him. "Sorry, ma'am. How can I help?"

"Mr Skinner, what do you see when you look around this room?"

He looked, eyed the circular Roman numeral wall clock,

with its sparse, skeleton frame forged from black iron and, beneath it, built into the plain, bone-white wall, the glass-fronted cabinet housing six glasses, six bottles each of Chase Vodka and Ridgemont Reserve Bourbon, all evenly spaced and symmetrical, labels facing outwards, with a small ice dispenser at the bottom. Skinner's eyes drifted to the adjacent wall behind Miss Morgan's desk, the 'feature wall' that had a 3D stone-effect wallcovering with Egyptian hieroglyphics that looked like they'd been carved into it. There was a single floating shelf on that wall, supporting three lever-arch files pressed between cubic, white marble bookends. Finally there was the black-tinted glass desk, dressed only with an ashtray, phone, coaster and MEc, free of all dust and blemishes thanks to probably obsessive amounts of polishing.

He wasn't sure what she was getting at, so he thought he'd simply say what he saw. "A… clock, a desk, a cabinet of –"

"Order, Mr Skinner," she interrupted. "You see order. Control. I don't like mess, never have. But do you know what I abhor? When my employees make a mess and don't clean it up."

He felt the blood rushing to his cheeks. *Oh shit.* But what? What had he done?

Miss Morgan continued, "You told me Jennifer Larson was dead."

What? She is *dead.*

Skinner remembered back to that tense night in the Guildford office when he was trying to write a completion report on an operation that wasn't actually complete. Even though he was having to doctor the report anyway (there was no way he was going to include his failure to properly check for Jennifer Larson's pulse after running her over or the fact that he'd secretly drafted in Katie McKinley to finish the job for him), he wasn't prepared to submit a report to Miss Morgan confirming Larson was dead till he knew for certain that she was. That big a lie just wouldn't stay secret, not from the most powerful woman in the world.

But then he remembered Katie McKinley phoning him and telling him it was done. Jennifer Larson was dead. Which meant the bitch fucking lied to him.

Feeling a solid fist of dread balling at the pit of his stomach, Skinner searched carefully for the right response.

"Y-yes. I thought she *was* dead."

"Well, she isn't. Which means you didn't make sure after you ran her down."

"I checked for a pulse. I couldn't feel anything."

"Then you're a fucking idiot, because clearly she still had one."

"I – I should've checked again."

"Yes. You should have."

"It was… I had to get out of there quick. I wanted to make sure I wasn't seen. It was a mistake. When the current crisis is over, I'm fully prepared to take the consequences." *And I'll make sure Katie McKinley does too.*

He took a deep breath. He knew he'd fucked up but surely there were more important things to deal with right now. Like restoring the timeline. Like restoring his wife, Karen. His two girls. He'd phoned Karen's number right after the incursion, got through to someone else. The likelihood was that, in this timeline, Karen was not his wife, and that meant Carly and Shannon had never been born. For all he knew, Karen had never been born either.

"Ma'am, if I may," he said carefully, "surely we should be focusing on what's happened to the timeline."

Miss Morgan shook her head with what looked like dismay. "Mr Skinner – we are. Jennifer Larson is responsible for what's happened to the timeline. She stole some chronozine and travelled back in time, minutes before everything changed. What was it you were saying about consequences?" She gestured towards the window and the radically altered cityscape below. "There are your fucking consequences."

"My God." The ripples of guilt through his body made his stiff posture waver, his head dip and shake. He gripped the top of the chair he was standing behind, for support. "I – it's my fault. My wife, my children – they're gone. Erased. And it's my fault."

"Yes, it is. And you're going to fix it. You're going to clear up your mess."

He stiffened. Yes. He could do that. He could fix this. He *had* to fix this, if he ever hoped to see his family again.

He returned both hands to his sides and stood straight and determined. "Yes, ma'am. What do you want me to do?"

"I learned from our operatives in Brighton that Larson went back to the year 1100. July 1100. But that's all I got before the rewrite took effect. So I don't know when in July. The safest course of action would be to send you back to the end of June with enough time to get to Brighton so that you can be there when Larson materialises. When she does, kill her immediately. I have approximate coordinates for where she'll be; these are being sent to your phone."

So he had to go and just wait for what could be weeks for Larson to appear? *Great.* "I understand."

"Good. Now listen carefully because killing Larson is only part of it. More important than that is destroying the covert transcription device that she has taken with her into the past."

Trying to hide his uncertainty, "Okay."

"This transcriber is disguised as a book called *The History of Computer-Aided Timetabling for Railway Systems* by Jeremy Jennings. Not only is it highly sophisticated future technology that does not belong in 1100, but the first conversation the book transcribed contains some very sensitive information. My belief is that everything that has happened to the timeline is because of that transcription."

"What information?"

"What I'm about to tell you is strictly level one clearance. Understood?"

He swallowed. It was above his own pay grade. "Yes, ma'am."

"In the here and now, Million Eyes is preparing to carry out a high-profile assassination. The *highest*-profile assassination. The Queen herself."

"The Queen? Why?"

Miss Morgan shook her head. "You don't need to know all the details. Just that the Queen is a problem that needs dealing with. The transcription is of a conversation between two of our operatives discussing plans to assassinate her and bring about the abolition of the British monarchy. As I'm sure you can gather, such a transcription would have a devastating effect on our rise to power, hence my theory as to the cause of all this."

"Y-yes, ma'am. Although…" He was confused. How could a Modern English transcription do damage in 1100? Was this really his fault or was Miss Morgan barking up the wrong tree?

Maybe this incursion had nothing to do with Jennifer Larson…

"What?" Her glare intensified. Skinner felt a strangling heat beneath his collar.

"I'm just… wondering. How a book with Modern English writing in it could be… damaging. No one's going to understand it in 1100. Nor many centuries after that."

"It has an inbuilt translation matrix, Skinner. Anybody who reads it will understand it."

Oh. Damn. Still looking like his fault, then.

"You'll also need to recover the chronozine she has taken with her," Miss Morgan continued.

He nodded, "Yes, ma'am."

She looked at something on her MEc screen. "I understand that you're fully trained to time travel – but you've not actually travelled before."

"Yes, that's correct."

"Alright. Report to Dr Ruben first. She'll fit you with a chronode and a cognit. Once you've done that, report to Rupert Whistler. He's in charge of Time Travel tonight."

"Understood."

"And there's something else I need you need to understand before you go. Something critical."

Another nervous swallow pushed its way painfully down Skinner's dry throat.

"Larson has altered history. That means the timeline is in a fragile state right now. We can change it back, but – and this is a big *but* – the fragility of the timeline means that any changes *you* make when you go back will be permanent. If you screw with the timeline even further, we can't undo it."

"So you're saying I get one chance to apprehend Jennifer when she arrives in Brighton."

"Yes. And if you fail, you can't nip back to before she arrived and try again. If you go back to fix your own mistakes while you're already there fixing hers, you'll cause a temporal earthquake that could very well destroy us all. Understand?"

Not really, but he got the gist of it: *don't fuck up*.

"I understand."

"Good. Then get moving. The Shield will only hold for" – she pointed at the clock – "five hours, forty minutes. After that, we're done. We all get absorbed into the new timeline.

You need to fix this fast."

Feeling hot and shaken, Skinner nodded, turned and left Miss Morgan's office. The steely glares of the C-Suite staff were on him again. Now he knew why. By the time he entered the lift he was all but shitting himself. It wasn't just the fate of his wife and daughters that now rested on his shoulders. It was the whole bloody world.

Then, as his lift descended from the C-Suite to the Time Travel Department, a knot of anger made his thoughts turn to something else: all the horrible things he was going to do to Katie McKinley once the timeline was restored.

32

Half an hour after Skinner left her office, Miss Morgan got a call from him saying he'd arrived in June 1100. She waited for him to call again. Another half-hour went by. If Time Travel had configured the temporal alignment on Skinner's chronophone correctly, weeks should've passed for him by now. Had he done it? Had he apprehended Jennifer Larson? Had he recovered the book?

She continued to wait, having now swapped coffee for vodka, checking the clock every minute and burning her way through another pack of Marlboro Reds.

When she couldn't wait any longer, she picked up her phone and called him. "Mr Skinner, what's going on? Why haven't I heard from you?"

"Ma'am, I – I think I know where the book is."

Her heart skipped. "You think? What do you mean you think? I already told you. Larson has it."

"She did. She doesn't anymore."

"You mean she's already there?"

"Yes."

Miss Morgan felt every muscle in her body tighten. Both of her fists were balling. "Mr Skinner, you were supposed to go to Brighton, wait for her to materialise, and take the book from her the moment she did. Are you saying you haven't done that?"

"There was a problem. I wasn't able to get to Brighton in time." As though he'd foreseen the furious tirade of abuse that was coming his way, he said quickly, "But I have everything under control."

Grinding her teeth, "Oh, do you?"

"Yes. I'm posing as a lord called Walter Tyrrell to get close to the king, William II, and there's talk of a bizarrely-dressed traitor currently imprisoned in the Tower of London on William's orders, who no one can communicate with. It has to be Larson. Which means the king has the book."

"Are you telling me that Larson, the book *and* a bottle of chronozine are all in the possession of the King of England?"

"Currently, yes."

"And what is your grand plan to put this fucking mess right?"

"Kill the king. He's just invited me to attend a hunt in the New Forest, on August 2nd. The day William II dies."

Miss Morgan shook her head. "What are you saying?"

"According to history, William II dies while hunting, on August 2nd, shot by an arrow apparently meant for a stag, and fired by Walter Tyrrell – *me*."

"So – what? You're saying all this was *meant* to happen?"

"It would seem so, yes. And it's possible that this one act – my killing the king – will restore the timeline."

Miss Morgan wasn't going to get into the temporal physics. "What about the book and the chronozine?"

"I'll keep searching for the book. But the chronozine... I don't think we need to worry about that. I think Larson must've lost it on her way through the Chronosphere. Otherwise she would've just taken another pill and travelled in time again. She wouldn't have let herself get captured."

A fair assumption, but an assumption nonetheless. In any case, they were out of options. Any changes Skinner made now were permanent and couldn't be undone. He had to keep moving forwards, stop Larson from impacting the timeline some other way.

Now came a twist in this tale. It seemed Robert Skinner was *supposed* to kill William II. The funny thing about time travel was that not every change to the timeline actually changed it. Some were already a part of it to begin with. Predestined to happen. Dictated by fate.

Honestly, it all gave Miss Morgan a fucking headache.

"Fine," she said. "Do what you have to do and keep me updated."

At least Skinner seemed pretty sure of himself. What else could she say?

The future was in his hands.

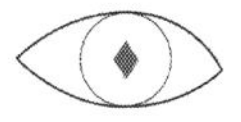

Fifteen minutes later, Miss Morgan was puffing on a new cigarette and sipping her second vodka when Lara Driscoll was at her door.

"Ma'am, I have something I think you should see," said Driscoll as she entered and laid a piece of paper on Miss Morgan's desk. "It's a printout of one of Gregory Ferro's blogs. Göransson in Archives has been going through our Information Security files, looking for the papers on Ferro and Larson. He hasn't found them yet but this printout was loose in one of the filing cabinets. It obviously fell out of the Ferro papers at some point."

Gregory Ferro had started out as one to watch, but not stress about. He wasn't the first person to make claims about time travellers messing with history, and since he hadn't linked anything to Million Eyes or anyone working for Million Eyes, he wasn't much of a threat. Miss Morgan was happy to let the Information Security Department deal with him and stay out of it.

Of course, everything changed when Ferro started delving into the death of Diana, Princess of Wales. That's when Miss Morgan took over the operation. And when the traitorous Stuart Rayburn breached security, learned about Million Eyes' role in Diana's death and decided to tell Ferro everything, that was it. Ferro had to go. Miss Morgan had made a promise to herself (literally) that she would not let anyone trace the princess's death back to Million Eyes.

She read the blog. Ferro talked about having laid his hands on a 14th-century history of England by Simon of Stonebury, which described the rumour of a plague doctor who interrogated victims of the Black Death about a *book with a strange title* during the autumn of 1348. All the victims were surnamed Godfrey. Apparently this doctor was also seen talking on a strange device and disappearing into thin air. Ferro wrote: Just like the man who killed William II.

The book with a strange title. Of course. It had to be the transcriber. Nobody at the time Ferro was being watched would've known this – the transcribers disguised as Jeremy

Jennings' unspeakably dull book only went into production a few months ago.

And while she knew at the time that Ferro's conspiracy theories were about things that Million Eyes hadn't done yet, it hadn't occurred to her that she'd one day have to *rely* on his theories as a source of intel.

But hey, that was time travel for you.

"Thank you, Miss Driscoll," said Miss Morgan. "Leave this with me. Tell Göransson to keep looking."

"Yes, ma'am."

Driscoll left and Miss Morgan immediately called Skinner. "Report, Mr Skinner."

"The king is dead," Skinner replied quietly. Miss Morgan could hear the twitter of birds in the background. "Did it work?"

Miss Morgan looked out of her window. "No. Nothing's changed. You presumed wrong. Killing William II had no effect."

"Then I'll continue searching for the book."

"Yes, you will."

"I'll have to lie low for a while, change my identity. I think the king's chief minister, Ranulf Flambard, might know –"

"No, you're done with 1100. I've just been reading one of Gregory Ferro's blogs. He found evidence of a plague doctor who interrogated victims of the Black Death about a book with a strange title and could make himself disappear. I think that could very well be you, which means, by the same logic you were using when we last spoke, that's where you're supposed to go next."

"Are you ordering me to make another jump?" He sounded reluctant.

"Skinner, *time* is ordering you to make another jump."

"When?"

"Autumn 1348. That's all I know, so go to the start of September of that year. Ferro's blog says that all those who were interrogated had the surname 'Godfrey', so it stands to reason that William II or whoever was doing his bidding handed the book to someone with this name in an attempt to hide it from us."

"So shouldn't I stick around here, find out if Ranulf Flambard was the one who – ?"

"We don't have time to debate this. I just told you, you're supposed to go to 1348, so *go*."

He sighed. "Yes, ma'am. I'll take care of it."

Hanging up, Miss Morgan left her office and walked across the C-Suite to the office of chief technology officer Juanita Salazar. "Juanita, what's the ETA on getting access to the internet of this new timeline?" Finding out more about the new world outside headquarters would've been invaluable to the effort to restore the old one.

"We hit some snags but we're almost there," said Salazar. "Should be about fifteen minutes."

Miss Morgan looked at the clock. Just under four hours until the Shield failed. "Let me know the second we have access."

"Of course."

Miss Morgan started back to her office, stopping as she detected Melanie Cox behind her. She recognised the sound of her walk – small strides, fast footsteps.

She turned and faced her, "What is it, Miss Cox?"

"Miss Morgan, please can I ask what you're doing about the incursion?"

"No, you may not."

"I'm sorry, Miss Morgan, but I feel that we all have a right to know exactly what you're doing to fix this."

The audacity of it. "You have a right to know exactly nothing about anything until I am ready to tell you. And at this moment I don't have the time or the inclination. So get back to what you were doing." She turned and continued towards her office.

"Miss Morgan, please!" Cox wailed. "The Shield's going to fail in less than four hours – I want to know what's going on!"

Miss Morgan stopped again and faced her, silent.

"I – I'm sorry." Cox's face was crimson, her hands trembled and the glint of tears was in her eyes. "Please. Please just tell us what's happening. How can you expect us to work under these conditions? I don't even know if I'm alive or dead out there, or if I was even born at all. When I finally got hold of my fiancé, he had no idea who I was. Called me a crazy bitch and hung up the phone."

"That's normal, isn't it?" shouted Anthony Graves, smirking, from across the room.

"Fuck off, Tony," said Cox. "Look, my point is, if you

want us operating at optimal capacity, you have to give us something. Please. Just something to reassure us and put our minds at ease."

Highly strung Melanie Cox had worked in the C-Suite for the last year. Her anxiety issues were tiresome but, annoyingly, she was also Million Eyes' most talented analyst.

Miss Morgan stepped towards her, got right in her face and said gently, "Miss Cox, I want you to take a breath and think very carefully about what you do next, because if you challenge me once more, I'll have you escorted to the Room so fast your face will turn inside out. Is that clear?"

Cox visibly swallowed, paling instantly, and gave several small, frightened nods.

"Good. Now what I suggest you do is turn around and go back to your desk and we'll forget this."

Cox turned and scuttled over to her desk like a mouse, and Miss Morgan carried on to her office.

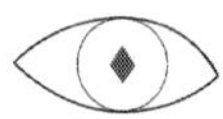

Not long after, Lara Driscoll was at Miss Morgan's door again with another printout from Ferro's blog that had been misfiled. Thank God for shit archive staff.

In it, Ferro mentioned having learned about the recently discovered journal of Sir Lionel Frensham, one of Edward IV's courtiers, and the pertinent section read:

> I spoke with the Bodleian Library, which now has possession of Frensham's journal. They told me that the journal references an incident that occurred in June 1482, namely an encounter between Edward IV and a mysterious intruder who broke into his bedchamber and interrogated him about a book.
>
> I'm heading up to Oxford tomorrow so I can study Frensham's journal in detail and find out if this book was *The History of Computer-Aided Timetabling for Railway Systems* by Jeremy Jennings. I highly suspect that it was, and if so, then Edward IV's intruder was another time traveller.

"Fuck me," Miss Morgan whispered. It was now all but certain that the book Ferro had been chasing was the one Jennifer took with her to the past. And she suspected that Edward IV's intruder was not *another* time traveller at all, but the same one. Robert Skinner's next stop was Edward IV's bedchamber in June 1482.

She called Skinner.

"Yes, ma'am?" he said, sounding fatigued.

"Report, Mr Skinner."

"Nothing yet, ma'am, but I will find it. I just need a bit more –"

"Please don't say *time*."

She heard him swallow. "I promise, I *will* find it."

"No, you won't. Not there, anyway. You're done with 1348."

"What do you mean?"

"I have a new lead. I've found evidence, courtesy of Gregory Ferro, that the 'Godfreys' – whoever they were – may have returned the book to the Royals. And this information tells me that you're due to pay King Edward IV a visit in June 1482 and interrogate him about it."

Skinner sighed. "You want me to jump again?"

"Yes. Was that not clear by what I just said?"

"I – er – yes. It was. I just…"

"What is it? Spit it out."

He paused, then, "Nothing, ma'am."

"Good. Get it done, Mr Skinner."

She hung up.

Moments later, Juanita Salazar informed her that they had gained access to the internet of the altered timeline. Now she could find out what was really going on out there. She told Salazar to give her – and only her – access. She didn't want everyone distracting and worrying themselves googling their alternate lives.

She immediately connected her MEc and tried to navigate to Google. She ended up at a search engine called 'Spoggle', so it looked like either Google had been erased or had undergone a desperately ill-conceived name change. She 'spoggled' her most important consideration: Million Eyes.

Spoggle brought up nothing. Million Eyes' official website and social media pages – gone. All the sites for their products, subsidiaries, and subsidiaries' products – gone. All the recent news articles about Million Eyes winning nine awards at the Vantage Point Innovation Awards – gone.

Wait. There was an entry for Million Eyes on something called Omnipedia, which looked like this timeline's version of Wikipedia. She clicked the link.

> Million Eyes, originally known as Thousand Eyes, was an English secret society founded sometime in the 10th or 11th century. Its goals are unclear, but it is believed by most modern scholars that it wanted to control the monarchy and government of England.

Not good. Not good at all. Miss Morgan swallowed hard and took a drag of her latest cigarette.

> Very little is known about Million Eyes, its members and what they did. What is known is that when James VI of Scotland succeeded to the English throne as James I in 1603, it sought an alliance with the king to attain a direct influence over the government. James was immediately presented with evidence that Million Eyes was planning to destroy the monarchy at some point in the future and, in consequence, a large number of its members were arrested, tried and executed for treason. James subsequently passed an Act of Parliament banning Million Eyes.

It appeared from the rest of the page that nobody knew what this 'evidence' presented to James I was, but it didn't take a rocket scientist to work that out.

The book. The transcription. Miss Morgan was right about what effect it would have on Million Eyes' rise to power. Thanks to that transcription, Million Eyes never rose to power. Centuries of hard work had been erased from history.

She called Skinner.

The phone rang and rang. Where the bloody hell was he?

Finally, the call connected. "Why did it take you so long to answer?"

Silence. "Skinner?"

No one answered, but she could hear breathing.

"Mr Skinner! What the hell are you doing?"

Finally, an answer. "What sorcery is this?"

Shit. Not Skinner's voice. "What? Who is this?"

"You are speaking with King Edward IV of England. What is your name, madam?"

Fuck! How could he have got hold of Skinner's phone? She pounded her desk with her fist, "Jesus!"

The king took her curse as an answer. "You dare to impersonate our Lord Jesus Christ? You must be one of Satan's apostates."

She played along. Since her chronophone had a translation matrix allowing her to communicate with non-English speakers without having to learn the language – including medieval kings speaking archaic forms of English – there was a chance she could get through to him and find out what had happened to Skinner. "Yes. That's right. I am. And I have great power, too. So I suggest you do as I say or I will release a plague of" – she thought quickly about what would sound most frightening in the 1400s – "cats upon you."

A pause. The king probably didn't like the sound of that, but held firm nonetheless, "I am not afraid. I serve the Lord, and Him alone. Whatever power you possess is no match for Him."

"Don't be so sure. Where is the owner of the device we are using to speak?"

"You mean the man I just killed?"

No! She gritted her teeth. "*Fuck!*"

Skinner had failed. He'd failed and fucking got himself killed. Now she'd plummeted right back to square one.

She felt a stab of guilt. She was the one who tasked him with this, even though he'd failed once before. She should've seen this coming.

She hit a sequence of buttons on her phone and transmitted a feedback surge across the phone line. The effect would've distorted the chronoton energy in Skinner's phone and displaced it in time. She couldn't leave a medieval English king with a chronophone.

That being said, Skinner had a bottle of chronozine with him. Where was that now? Presumably he would've kept it on him, which meant Edward IV might've got his hands on it. She could only hope that he'd be none the wiser about its capabilities.

Wait a minute.

Glancing back at the Omnipedia page for Million Eyes, still displayed on her MEc screen, she noticed something.

The wording had changed…

> Million Eyes was an English secret society that amassed great power in the Parliament of England shortly after James VI of Scotland succeeded the English throne as James I. It maintained this power until it was found to be plotting against the throne in the late 19th century.

Now it was the 19th century?

How could this be?

She read further. The subsequent paragraphs had changed too…

> Million Eyes' exact motives are unclear. It is believed the group was initially founded in the 10th or 11th century. After James I came to the throne, Million Eyes sought an alliance with the king to attain a direct influence over the government. James I agreed to grant an undisclosed number of peerages to high-ranking members of Million Eyes (although their affiliation with Million Eyes was kept secret).
>
> Million Eyes' influence in Parliament grew over the next few centuries. Then, in September 1888, evidence was presented to Queen Victoria via an anonymous informant (revealed years later to have been Mary Ann Nichols) implicating Million Eyes in a plot to destroy the monarchy of Britain and completely take over the government. As a result, Million Eyes members of both Houses of Parliament were exposed, tried for treason and imprisoned. Queen Victoria subsequently passed an Act of Parliament banning Million Eyes.

She stood up and walked over to the window.

Everything had changed again. Had it changed back? No. The bronze statue of Egyptian goddess Heket and the parade of skyscrapers were gone, but a couple of unfamiliar towers still remained. County Hall and Buckingham Palace were back and the royal parks were green again, but the London Eye, Miss Morgan's regular Starbucks and the statue of Arthur Pell were still missing. And although the Houses of Parliament had returned, there was no sign of Big Ben.

Actually, the lack of Big Ben was the most disturbing change. If the timeline had been restored up to 1888, Big Ben was already built by then, which suggested that, in this timeline, someone or something had destroyed it.

Miss Morgan hurried back to her desk and continued reading the Omnipedia page. As before, whatever this 'evidence' presented to Queen Victoria consisted of was unknown.

It had to be the transcription. Had to be. Somehow the path of the book had changed. No longer did it make its way to James I and lead him to block Million Eyes' rise to power in Parliament. That all still happened as it was supposed to.

Now it was Queen Victoria who was responsible for bringing down Million Eyes.

How?

Of course. Me. It was my fault.

Miss Morgan had changed the path of the book by sending Skinner to retrieve it from Edward IV. Steered it out of James I's hands and into the hands of some woman called Mary Ann Nichols.

So Skinner's journey to 1482 to confront the king wasn't pre-destined.

Or was it?

Fucking time travel. There were times when she really hated it.

But, even though she'd altered the path of the book, she hadn't stopped it. It still ended up in royal hands, and Million Eyes was still erased. All she'd done was delay its erasure to 1888.

She needed to move quickly. Three hours, ten minutes left till the Shield failed.

She remembered Driscoll telling her that James Rawling was working the night shift in Time Travel. She called Driscoll from her MEc, "I want James Rawling sent up to my office immediately."

33

When the lanky and strange-looking James Rawling crossed the C-Suite and entered Miss Morgan's office, Melanie Cox felt a twist of angst in her gut. Why was he getting involved? Where was Robert Skinner? It wasn't fair of Miss Morgan to keep them all in the dark like this.

"Why do you think he's here?" she whispered to Lara Driscoll as Rawling closed Miss Morgan's door.

"That's none of your business, is it?" Driscoll said like a teacher to a naughty schoolchild. "Did Miss Morgan not make that abundantly clear when she threatened to send you to the Room?"

Oh shut up you brown-nosing bitch, Cox thought but would never say. She wasn't sure why she asked her, to be honest. Driscoll had her head so far up Miss Morgan's arse she was surprised she could see for shit.

Cox had chewed off all her fingernails while she waited for answers that just weren't forthcoming. How Miss Morgan expected her to concentrate when potentially her whole life had been changed, perhaps even erased, she had no idea.

Enough was enough. She wanted answers and she'd waited long enough. She got up, walked over to the office of Juanita Salazar, the CTO, and knocked at the door.

"Come in," said Miss Salazar, looking up briefly from her MEc as Cox entered. "Ah, Miss Cox, have you calmed down after your little outburst earlier?"

She had, but she stood by everything she said. She just should've phrased it differently and, well, not shouted. Shouting at Miss Morgan was never a good move.

"Y-yes, ma'am," said Cox, swallowing.

"What can I do for you?"

"I, er… I'm sorry to disturb but I wondered if you knew why Miss Morgan has summoned James Rawling to her office?"

"I didn't know she had."

"So she hasn't told you what she's doing about the incursion?"

"No, Miss Cox, she hasn't." There was an irritated edge to her voice. Cox couldn't tell if it was because Miss Morgan had kept her in the dark too, or if she was similarly annoyed with Cox for prying for answers.

Cox pretended not to detect any irritation. "Doesn't that concern you, ma'am?"

Miss Salazar looked at her, frowning. "We're all concerned, Miss Cox. The whole world has been rewritten."

"Exactly!" said Cox, a bit too excitedly. "That's what I've been saying. And we don't have a clue what's being done about it."

"We know Miss Morgan is trying to restore the timeline. We've already seen changes."

"Yeah, okay, so Buckingham Palace and the Houses of Parliament are standing again, and that giant Egyptian statue is gone, and some of the streets are back where they're supposed to be. But scattered changes here and there – surely that means she hasn't managed to nail what caused this. Otherwise she'd be able to restore everything all at once. Wouldn't she?"

"Miss Cox, why don't you get to the point?"

"I'm sorry, Miss Salazar, I don't mean any disrespect. I'm just… I'm struggling to just sit here and have absolute trust that Miss Morgan can fix this singlehandedly without any input from the rest of us."

"That's how she works most of the time. She keeps her own counsel."

"Yeah, and she's been criticised for it before."

"Who told you that?"

"People talk, ma'am. The point is, this situation is entirely different. All our lives are at stake here. She should be consulting us. And what worries me is if she's enlisted Rawling, it means Robert Skinner's failed."

"We don't know that."

"I just wondered if you could... if you might just consider... talking to her. Just to find out what's going on." She glanced at the clock on the wall of Miss Salazar's office. "Because in three hours, the Shield around this building is going to fail and, if Miss Morgan's not on top of this, all of our lives will change permanently."

"That might not be a bad thing for some of us."

Cox couldn't tell if that statement was directed at her. She knew everybody thought Ian, her fiancé, was a nasty, abusive drunk, but they only knew the half of it. They didn't see him when he was tender, when he brought home yellow roses for her every Monday, when he massaged her feet at the end of a hard day's work, when he made her breakfast in bed at the weekend and bought her jewellery and beautiful dresses just to thank her for being her. He loved her and, for all his flaws, she loved him too.

Right now, all of that was gone. Everything they had together, good and bad, had been pinched out of existence. Screw what anybody else thought. She wanted him back.

"I'm sure all of us have things in our lives that we want back," said Cox. "If we get absorbed into this new timeline, they'll be gone forever, or worse. Some of us might not even exist in the new timeline. Some of us might never have been born."

Miss Salazar sighed heavily. "I'll consider talking to her, but I'm not promising anything."

Cox gave a polite smile. "That's all I ask. Thank you, Miss Salazar."

Miss Salazar nodded and Cox turned and left, closing the door behind her and returning to her desk.

Ten minutes later, James Rawling exited Miss Morgan's office. As he closed the door, Cox caught a glimpse of her face, which – alarmingly – wasn't displaying the usual confidence and poise that had always seemed an unwavering trait of hers. In fact, she looked anxious, even panicked. Two emotions Cox had never seen or expected from her.

Miss Morgan was in charge – but was she in control?

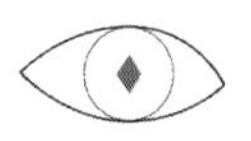

Miss Morgan had briefed Rawling as succinctly as she could on what had happened with Robert Skinner. In terms of his mission, there wasn't really much she could give him: Go to August 1888. Find Mary Ann Nichols, the woman who gives the book to Queen Victoria in September. Get the book back. Prevent Million Eyes' downfall. Save the future.

Simple.

She'd looked up Mary Ann Nichols on the internet of the new timeline. Nichols had an Omnipedia page, a brief one. It just said that she was once a prostitute, stumbled upon evidence of a plot by secret society Million Eyes against the monarchy, managed to get the evidence delivered personally to the Queen thanks to one of her regular clients' connections, and was given money and a house in the country by the Crown, so she could live out the rest of her days free from squalor.

Shortly after Rawling left her office to get ready to go back to 1888, Juanita Salazar was at her door. "Yes, Juanita, what is it?"

"I'm sorry to intrude, Miss Morgan, but I wonder if I might get an update on what's happening regarding the incursion?"

Not you as well. "When I have something concrete, I will let you know."

Juanita persisted, "Yes, but if you told us what's going on, we might be able to help."

"I have everything under control, thank you, Juanita."

"What happened to Robert Skinner?"

"Juanita, did you hear what I said?"

"Miss Morgan, forgive me, but I really think –"

"That's enough. I said I will let you know when I have something concrete."

"But I –"

"Juanita! The last thing I want to do is send my CTO to the Room, but I will if you force me to."

The interfering old crow relented at last. "I – I'm sorry."

"Okay. Now please let me get on."

Juanita left. Miss Morgan was starting to get tired of being questioned. They should all have known their place.

She refocused, continued researching the new timeline's internet, looking for anything that might help her and Rawling stop the trail of that damned book.

Half an hour later, Rawling called to say that he'd arrived in 1888. Exactly fifteen minutes after that, which Miss Morgan was sure of because she'd been staring unblinkingly at her wall clock, Rawling phoned in with an update.

"Yes, Mr Rawling?"

"I've found the book, ma'am," he replied.

"You have it?"

"Not yet. A man called John Snider has it. I'm pursuing him as we speak."

"Do you know how he got it?"

"Yes, ma'am, I do. He took it from… from Edward V and Richard, Duke of York."

Miss Morgan knew those names. The Princes in the Tower. The ones who went missing in 1483. She now knew why.

"So they had Skinner's chronozine. Edward IV must've given it to them. And the book."

"Yes, ma'am."

"Where are the princes now?"

"Gone. They used the chronozine to travel in time again."

"To when?"

"Out of temporal radius."

"For fuck's sake." She paused, took a breath. No point losing her cool over it, not when time was gaining on her. She sighed, "One problem at a time. Just get that book back, Mr Rawling. We have less than two hours till the Shield fails."

"Yes, ma'am. Understood."

She hung up.

She kept checking the Million Eyes Omnipedia page while she waited for Rawling to call back.

Nothing had changed – yet. An unknown number of Million Eyes-affiliated members of Parliament were still tried and imprisoned thanks to Mary Ann Nichols passing the book to Queen Victoria.

One hour, forty-seven minutes left of Shield power.

Fifteen minutes later, Rawling phoned again. "I have the book."

Though Miss Morgan felt like punching the air, her composure held firm. It was way too early to celebrate. "Good. Destroy it. Destroy it now."

"Yes, ma'am. Then what?"

"Wait for my call."

"Yes, ma'am."

She hung up, stood and approached the window, waiting for Big Ben, the London Eye, her regular Starbucks, and the horrible statue of Arthur Pell at the foot of the building to return.

Woah. Her vision blurred as she watched. Everything – all the buildings below her – went fuzzy and were… moving. A kaleidoscope of hazy shapes and lights roving about indiscriminately. She felt woozy, unsteady, and her latest cigarette dangled loosely from her fingers, eventually slipping through them and landing on the carpet tiles, still lit.

She looked down. The carpet tiles, the cigarette, her black, leather, buckle-up ankle boots weren't fuzzy at all.

She returned her look to the illuminated cityscape. It wasn't her eyes. It was the city itself that was blurry, like she was looking at it through a lens that wouldn't focus.

It made her dizzy. Spasms of pain bit at her temples. She had to look away and rub her eyes.

A moment later, she opened her eyes and looked through the window. Everything was in focus again.

In focus – and different.

Most of the cityscape looked as she remembered it. The London Eye was back. The streets below were in the right place. Her eyes searched for Starbucks.

Wasn't there. But it wasn't a topiary garden anymore. Now it was a strip club, judging by the large neon-lit contour of a scantily clad woman in the window.

Still no Arthur Pell statue.

Still no Big Ben.

She looked at the clock. Less than an hour and a half left of Shield power.

Looking down, she saw that the smouldering ash at the tip of the cigarette was singeing the carpet tile it had landed on. No time to worry about that. She stubbed it out with her boot and hurried over to her desk.

The Omnipedia page for Million Eyes was gone. She navigated to Spoggle, ended up at Google. Running a search for Million Eyes, she found that Wikipedia was back too, and there was a page for Million Eyes. But there was no active Million Eyes website and most of the results were either pages on computing history sites or articles with titles like *The Million Eyes Scandal* and *Million Eyes: The Greatest Corporate Conspiracy in History.*

Feeling her whole body tighten, Miss Morgan clicked the Wikipedia page…

> Million Eyes was a British computer company headquartered in London, England. In 1997, it was at the centre of one of the biggest corporate scandals of the 20th century, which ultimately led to its collapse.

So things had moved on quite a bit. Rawling had basically restored the timeline up to 1997. She read on.

> Million Eyes produced software, personal computers and consumer electronics that were particularly popular in the UK in the 1980s and 1990s. On August 30th 1997, evidence brought to Diana, Princess of Wales, implicated the company in an elaborate plot to assassinate Queen Elizabeth II. Diana personally presented the Queen with this evidence on August 31st. Subsequently, all of Million Eyes' senior management team were investigated, prosecuted and convicted of treason and conspiracy. Sales plummeted after the scandal and the company was finally dissolved in 1999. It was during this time that rumours spread that Million Eyes was controlling the government and that its computer business was just a smokescreen hiding its political endeavours, although these claims have never been substantiated.

The page went on to talk about the trials. Alongside the text were mug shots of all the Million Eyes executives who were prosecuted.

"Oh my God," Miss Morgan murmured aloud when she saw her own. She was twenty-four years younger and actually looked worse than she did now. Pale, gaunt, tired, no makeup, her normally stunning black hair dishevelled and matted with grease.

Her name, under the mug shot, had a link. She went to

click it. *Don't, Erica. Why torture yourself?* She stopped and clicked away from the page. Time was ticking away. The details of her alternate self's downfall were not important. Stopping it was.

Diana, Princess of Wales, was the next – the *final* – obstacle to be removed. Since 1997, Miss Morgan had known that at some point in the future, Million Eyes would travel in time and assassinate Diana, but she didn't know when or why. Now she knew why, and when was *now*.

She phoned Rawling. "Mr Rawling, are you still in 1888?"

"Yes, ma'am," he replied quietly. "Shall I return to the future?"

"No."

"Is the timeline still…?"

"Fucked? Yes."

"What do you ne – ?"

"Where's the book?"

He hesitated.

"Rawling, I know you failed to destroy it. So where is it?"

"I was attacked by the man who stole it, and it… it fell into a drain."

She rolled her eyes. Time itself had dictated that her employees act like cretins. "It fell into a drain."

"Yes, ma'am. So it's as good as destroyed."

"No, Rawling, it isn't. Someone has it. Fortunately for you I know who."

"Ma'am?"

"Diana, Princess of Wales. Now is when we take her out and this is why. Based on what you've just told me, someone is going to recover the book from London's drainage system between 1888 and 1997. On August 30th 1997, that someone is going to hand the book to Diana in Paris, who will deliver it to the Queen the next day – unless we stop her."

"Should I not try and retrieve the book from the drainage system in 1888? Surely that would be a much easier undertaking."

"Possibly, yes. But Diana's death is part of the timeline we're trying to restore. We're *supposed to* assassinate her."

"Er – I see."

"I don't understand it either. I just know this is how it has to be."

"What are your instructions?"

"Go to the start of July 1997. That'll give us two months. Go to Paris and coordinate the operation from there. Get operatives from Million Eyes' Paris branch to assist."

"I understand."

"Call me when you arrive and I'll give you more details on what needs to happen. And we need to readjust the temporal alignment on our phones so that, from my perspective, we're speaking every five minutes."

"Five minutes? Isn't that somewhat r…"

"Risky? Yes. But it's a risk we have to take. We have very little time left."

"Yes, ma'am."

She hung up, and the clock ticked past 4.19am.

One hour, seventeen minutes left of Shield power.

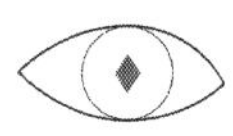

Melanie Cox was watching the clock. Had been since Juanita Salazar's failed attempt to get some information out of Miss Morgan. One hour, eight minutes remained until the Shield failed and still they knew nothing. Yes, London looked *almost* the same as it did before, but there were a few major differences, which meant they were still stuck in an alternate timeline.

The knot of dread in Cox's stomach was growing. She and Ian were supposed to get married next summer. Would she ever see him again?

Yes. Yes, she bloody would. She wasn't going to let Miss Morgan screw her out of her happily ever after.

Patience expired, Cox got up and walked over to Miss Salazar's office. This time she didn't even knock. She just burst in.

Miss Salazar, staring out of her window, faced her with a stunned glare. "Miss Cox, wha – ?"

"We have to do something," said Cox. "We have to do something *now*."

Miss Salazar didn't even argue. "What do you have in mind?"

"You need to get Miss Morgan to tell us what's happening.

Insist on it. If she refuses, relieve her of duty and order her to tell you."

Miss Salazar's eyes widened. "Relieve her? She's our CEO."

Cox felt her voice rise. "I don't care. We have an hour and six minutes until the Shield fails and I'm not confident she knows what she's doing."

"What's going on?" Anthony Graves came into Miss Salazar's office. "Are you talking about Miss Morgan?"

"Yes," said Cox. "Miss Salazar's going to relieve her of duty and order her to tell us what's happening, so we can help."

"I am, am I?" said Miss Salazar.

At this point, Cox didn't care about professional etiquette or that Miss Salazar was the CTO. "Unless you're happy to have your existence completely rewritten or even erased when the Shield goes down – yes."

"I'll support you," said Graves to Miss Salazar. "There's still time to send a bunch of us back in time to fix this, rather than relying on James Rawling, who's shadier than a weeping willow."

Reluctantly, Miss Salazar nodded.

"Good," said Cox. "I'll talk to the others."

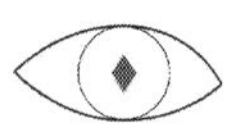

Everything was in place. Miss Morgan had been liaising with Rawling, but there wasn't time to micromanage the operation, so she just gave him the salient points of what he needed to do to orchestrate Diana's death, and left the detail up to him.

Every five minutes, Rawling called with updates. With an hour left of Shield power, the latest was that Henri Paul had been recruited to drive the rigged Mercedes, Rawling had secured a white Fiat Uno to collide with the Mercedes in the Alma tunnel, and arrangements had been made to disable all CCTV along the route and cook the forensics.

A lot now rested on Rawling's shoulders. Did she have absolute faith that he'd pull it off? Not completely, no. Not after he'd let the transcriber fall into London's drainage system. But if Rawling failed, she wouldn't have long to regret it.

There was a knock at the door to her office.

"Not now," she called.

The knocker was impudent enough to open the door anyway.

Looking up, "I said, not now!"

Juanita Salazar was at the door, Melanie Cox next to her, Anthony Graves, Eve Tambara and Norman Higgins standing nervously behind them. Everyone except Lara Driscoll.

"What the bloody hell is this?" said Miss Morgan.

"You need to tell us what's happening," said Salazar. "Right now."

"You don't give me orders. All of you, get back to work."

"No," said Cox.

Miss Morgan was incensed. "No?"

Salazar took a breath and said, "We're not convinced you're going to fix the timeline before the Shield fails. You need to tell us what you're doing so that we can help. All five of us are willing to travel back in time and do what needs to be done."

"That would do more harm than good."

"Explain that to us," said Cox, unbelievably brazen.

"I'm not explaining anything." She felt her anger rise from a simmer to a boil. "How dare you come in here and challenge my authority? Get the fuck out of my office – now!"

Cox and Salazar exchanged some kind of knowing look, like they'd planned for this.

"Then I'm sorry, Miss Morgan," said Salazar, "but I hereby relieve you of your duties."

"I beg your pardon?"

"Graves, Tambara, restrain her."

Graves and Tambara charged into her office. Miss Morgan launched to her feet. She knew she was going to have to give them something.

"Wait – stop. If you do this, the operation I am coordinating will fail, the timeline will remain as it is, and we'll all get absorbed into it as soon as the Shield goes down."

"Obviously we don't want that to happen," said Salazar. "So tell us what this operation is."

"We don't have time!"

"Just give us the fucking headlines!" yelled Cox.

You little cunt. I should've hauled your arse to the Room when I had the chance. They weren't giving her much choice. If Rawling's operation failed because of this, it'd be on their heads. And there'd be no chance for hindsight.

"Alright. Rawling is –"

Her phone rang.

"Is that Rawling?" said Graves.

"Yes!"

"Answer it, and put him on loudspeaker," said Salazar.

Miss Morgan picked up the phone and tapped loudspeaker. "Is it done? Is Princess Diana dead?" She gave Salazar a piercing look as she said it. The five mutineers exchanged stunned glances.

"Yes, ma'am," said Rawling. "It's done."

"And the book?"

"The book is destroyed." More confused glances from the mutineers.

"*Actually* destroyed this time?"

"Yes, ma'am. It can no longer harm us."

"Good. Finish up there and wait for my instructions. There's one thing left I need to do. If I don't call, assume it didn't work and headquarters has been absorbed into the altered timeline."

"I'll wait for your call."

She hung up. She looked at the clock – forty-nine minutes left – then at the mutineers. "If you traitors are satisfied I've got this, I need to make a phone call."

All five of them looked humbled, defeated, pathetic. They meekly left her office.

Lighting a new cigarette, Miss Morgan tapped a familiar number, one she'd not seen or heard for a while, but remembered well.

"Hello, Erica," she said to her younger self, who'd just interrupted her very important dinner with Arthur Pell in 1997 to answer the phone. "It's me… *Erica*."

She explained to Young Erica that she had just orchestrated the death of Princess Diana and tasked her with making sure it never got traced back to Million Eyes.

After hanging up, she closed her eyes, clenched her jaw and took a deep, long breath as she went to click the

Wikipedia page for Million Eyes.

Please, please, please.

She opened her eyes.

> Million Eyes is a British multinational technology company headquartered in London, England, that designs, develops and sells computer hardware and software, consumer electronics and internet-related services. It is the world's largest technology company by revenue and total assets and its current chief executive officer is Erica Morgan.

A sigh of relief blew past her lips. "We're back," she whispered, a proud smile easing across her face.

She googled Million Eyes to make sure. She found that the top stories, ahead of the company's many websites and social media pages, were all about Million Eyes winning nine awards at the Vantage Point Innovation Awards.

She got up and went to the window. As expected, Starbucks and Arthur Pell's ugly statue were back. And although she was getting tired of looking at clocks, she was very pleased to see that the world's most famous one – Big Ben – was standing again at the north end of the Houses of Parliament, proudly overlooking the city.

Normally the Time Travel Department would be able to confirm that everything was back to normal with a sensor sweep, but since the network had been overloaded, the internet and the view from the windows would have to do.

From what Miss Morgan could see, everything looked good.

She poured a shot of bourbon and sat down at her desk. First she used her MEc to video-call Rupert Whistler in Time Travel and tell him to begin deactivating the Shield. With thirty-seven minutes of power left, it could now be recharged. Then she used her phone to call Rawling and tell him to return to the present. Finally, after stubbing out her latest cigarette, she left her office and announced to the C-Suite that the timeline had been restored.

As everyone started checking in with loved ones, Miss Morgan walked over to Lara Driscoll's desk. "Miss Driscoll, please send security up here immediately."

A couple of minutes later, two security guards with disruptors stepped out of the lift, drawing worried gazes as they crossed the C-Suite to Miss Morgan. "Please escort everyone here, apart from Miss Driscoll, to the Room," she said, loud enough for them all to hear.

Not surprisingly, they erupted.

"What?" screamed Melanie Cox. "No – you can't. We're sorry!"

"Really sorry!" shouted Anthony Graves. "We were doing what we thought was best – for all of us. But we were wrong."

"Erica, don't do this," pleaded Juanita Salazar. "You need us."

I don't need people I can't trust.

"No! Please, no!" Cox started running towards the C-Suite lift.

Her chances were spent. One of the guards looked round at Miss Morgan. She gave him the go-ahead with a nod.

He raised his disruptor and, before Cox had reached the lift, fired. A bolt of green light slammed into her back, sent her hurtling into a couple of empty desks with a crash.

Silence fell over the C-Suite and Salazar, Graves, Tambara and Higgins froze, their eyes locked on Cox's lifeless body, flopped over one of the upturned desks. It was enough to get them to submit. Without protest, they accompanied the two security guards to the lift.

Miss Morgan walked over to the windows and looked pensively across the restored cityscape. It was over. In an hour or so the sun would rise, and nobody would be any the wiser about the catastrophe Million Eyes had spent the night averting.

Lara Driscoll came and stood next to her.

"I think I need a holiday," said Miss Morgan softly.

"You deserve one."

Miss Morgan looked at her and nodded, "Thank you, Miss Driscoll. Your loyalty means a lot."

"Don't mention it, ma'am. So what now?"

Miss Morgan smiled. Some words from her childhood sprang to mind. She had systematically wiped from her memory most of the Bible passages her mother had subjected her to, but there was one, just one, that she'd always rather liked, and, right now, was apt. Her mother had read it to her when she came home from school one day, bruised and bloodied.

"Our bricks have fallen down. So we will rebuild with hewn stone. Our sycamore trees have been felled. So we will plant cedars in their place."

Driscoll frowned. "What's that, ma'am?"

"Just something I heard as a child. It means that what happened here tonight will make us stronger. And it means that if anyone tries to –"

Hang on a minute.

"Tries to?" said Driscoll.

Miss Morgan didn't answer.

At the top of Puttenham Lane was a hotel, Puttenham Plaza, that looked… different. Bigger. Maybe two floors taller.

She was probably remembering it wrong, but she had to be sure. She darted over to the nearest computer and googled *Puttenham Plaza.*

"Huh?"

Puttenham Plaza was owned by business magnate Roger Kimble, and Google had just brought up a photo of Kimble shaking hands with Donald Trump in 2016.

But Donald Trump had been languishing in jail since 2012, after being convicted of fraud and money laundering and getting a twenty-year prison sentence.

Miss Morgan read the caption with the image: *Donald Trump with Roger Kimble, one of Trump's biggest backers for the presidency.*

What? The… *presidency*?

She googled Trump: *Donald John Trump (born June 14, 1946) is the 45th and current President of the United States.*

"*Fuck!*" she cried. "I missed something!"

Hillary Clinton was president, not Donald Trump. Miss Morgan jumped on the nearest MEc to call Time Travel. "What's the status of the Shield?"

Whistler replied, "Deactivation in four – three –"

"No, abort deactivation!"

"W-what?"

"The Shield – do *not* deactivate it! The timeline's still corrupted!"

"Ma'am, it's too la –"

34

October 26th 2026

Adam Bryant sat down with his girlfriend, Izzy, to watch the final episode of *Eastenders*, which had been refusing to die with dignity despite years of terrible ratings. Finally the BBC had thrown in the towel and apparently the final episode was going to feature a terrorist attack that would destroy Albert Square and kill off the entire cast, which was the only reason Adam had agreed to watch it.

He popped the cap off Izzy's beer and handed it to her. "Cheers babe," she said as he opened his. "So, how was it?"

"Really good," he replied. "Everyone seems really sound." He'd just been promoted to the software development team at Million Eyes headquarters. Today was his first day in the role.

"Did you get to meet Erica Morgan?"

"Nah. I doubt I will. Too low down the chain."

"Depends how far you want to go up it."

"True." There were times when Adam wondered if Izzy – an astrophysicist for the British Republic Space Agency, or BRSA – wished he was as ambitious as she was. Honestly, 'ambitious' was never a word he'd used to describe himself. He just loved computer science.

Eastenders started and the rest of this conversation would have to wait till it was over. Things never ended well when Adam talked over Izzy's shows.

Two minutes in, his phone rang.

Izzy blew an irked sigh and said, "Pause," to the TV. *Eastenders* froze just as the terrorists were about to murder Ian Beale. "Who the hell could that be when the last ever episode of *Eastenders* is on?"

Stretching to grab his phone off the coffee table, Adam

smirked, "Someone with better taste."

In jest, she flipped him the finger.

He looked at his phone. *Private number calling.* He answered, "Hello?"

A woman's voice said, "Is this Adam Bryant?"

"Who's asking?"

"We need to talk, Mr Bryant. I have information you need to hear."

A strange way to start a sales call, if that's what it was. An effective way, perhaps, since it triggered a further question from Adam, "What information is that?"

"It concerns Queen Elizabeth II. I have evidence pertaining to her death. Evidence that confirms she was murdered."

Well he wasn't expecting that! "I – *what*?"

"It's true. The evidence consists of letters recently excavated from the grounds of Cawston Manor in the New Forest."

Weirdly enough, Adam was just thinking about the Queen the other day. Probably because it was the fifth anniversary of her death, and royalists held a vigil outside Windsor Castle to mark it – he saw it on the news. Hundreds of people laying flowers, wreaths, cards, pictures and Union Jacks at the gates of the castle, with many kneeling in prayer.

It reminded him of the day her death was announced and the wave of public hysteria that followed. For a few days the country just ground to a halt. And there were people who refused to believe it. She was very old, yes, but she'd been photographed in public just a couple of days before and looked fit and well. To Adam, it was perfectly believable that a woman that old could just die peacefully in her sleep from natural causes. But there were thousands of conspiracy theorists – Liz Truthers, the media called them – who suspected foul play.

For many people, the most tragic thing about the Queen's death was that she wasn't just the country's longest-serving monarch. She was its last. The government dissolved the British monarchy after her death. Adam avoided politics wherever possible, so he didn't know the ins and outs, only that despite nationwide protests, the United Kingdom of Great Britain and Northern Ireland – the UK – was no more. In its place, the British Republic – the BR.

Adam figured that was why there were so many conspiracy theories – even more, perhaps, than after Princess Diana died. People didn't want to let the monarchy, the Royal Family and many centuries of history go.

Still, why would a Liz Truther have called him?

"I think you've got the wrong number," he said.

"I know for a fact I haven't."

Well, that was sinister. "I'm hanging up now."

"No, don't. This is important, and I don't have long. This line is secure, but only temporarily. In a few minutes, they'll be able to trace it."

"Who is this?"

"My name is Dr Samantha Lester, but that won't mean anything to you. The person who wrote the letters – her name will."

Adam swallowed. "Who?"

"Jennifer Larson."

All the breath vanished from his lungs.

"Who is it?" said Izzy. "Are you okay?"

"Are you – are you still there?" said Dr Lester.

Adam had not heard his former best friend's name in a long time. A million questions fired through his head. None turned into words.

"Mr Bryant," Dr Lester continued, satisfied he was still there, "I had Jennifer's letters dated. They're over nine hundred years old. Nine hundred years old and written in Modern English. They're real."

"Adam, tell me what's going on," said Izzy, but her voice sounded miles away.

Dr Lester explained, "Jennifer wrote in them that she was a time traveller from the future, stranded in the past, and I believe her."

Finally, Adam found his voice. "H-how did you find me?"

"She talked about you. You were her best friend."

Adam felt a tear form on the brim of his right eyelid and squirm free, wriggling to the corner of his mouth.

"I'm sorry, Mr Bryant, but I must hurry this along. There are serious matters to discuss. We need to meet."

Adam sniffed. "What matters?"

"Million Eyes, Mr Bryant. We need to talk about Million Eyes."

ACKNOWLEDGEMENTS

First and foremost, I must thank the person this book is dedicated to: Vicky Ward. Vicks, this book only exists because of your faith in it. I was ready to chuck it out and move on till I sat down with you, ran through the plot and you told me – shit, you have something here. I stuck with it because of how excited you were by it. As a result, you became my muse, with an ear always willing to be bent. So thank you. I hope I've done you proud.

Thank you everyone at Rushmoor Writers for listening patiently to the entire book over two years and helping me refine it. Your (sometimes brutal!) feedback has nurtured me into a better writer. I must also thank Anthony Self, Ross Jeffery and Tomek Dzido at Storgy Magazine, whose constructive feedback at a late stage in *Million Eyes'* development helped me make real improvements and produce a much stronger book.

Mum, Dad and Katie, your unwavering pride in me and my writing means the world to me and has always kept me going. Matt Pamplin, you clever bastard, those *Million Eyes* trailers you produced are bloody awesome. And to the truly wonderful circle of friends and family I'm so lucky to have in my life, thank you. Never underestimate the power of your encouragement.

Last but certainly not least, I have to thank the fabulous and super-dedicated team at Elsewhen Press for believing in *Million Eyes* and being so enthusiastic about it throughout the publication process. (It was particularly fun creating the *Million Eyes* website with you, Pete!) I was wondering if I might never make it in the traditional publishing industry when Elsewhen's acceptance letter landed in my inbox. And for us struggling authors, there's nothing more motivating or satisfying than getting your first endorsement from a publisher.

Elsewhen Press

delivering outstanding new talents in speculative fiction

MILLION EYES: EXTRA TIME

C.R. BERRY

Twelve time-twisting tales.

Million Eyes: Extra Time is a compilation of short stories set in the universe of C.R. Berry's time travel conspiracy thriller trilogy, *Million Eyes.*

The stories act as an introduction to the Million Eyes world, exploring themes that are central to the trilogy and offering a unique insight into its time-travelling villains. They focus on side characters who (mostly) do not appear in the trilogy while revealing clues to key storylines in all three books.

Many of these stories are inspired by conspiracy theories and urban legends you may recognise.

Think of these tales as a bit like the mini-episodes you get with TV series – Star Trek: Short Treks, Lost: Missing Pieces, and Doctor Who's many prequels, mini-adventures and 'Tardisodes'.

While the stories in Million Eyes: Extra Time can stand alone, you'll notice that a number of them are strongly linked and follow a loose chronology. The author's advice is that you read them in the order that they are presented.

Available for free download in pdf, epub and kindle formats
Visit bit.ly/Million-Eyes-Extra-Time

SmartYellow™

J.A. Christy

SmartYellow™ is the story of a young girl, Katrina Williams, who finds herself on the wrong side of social services. After becoming pregnant with only a slight notion of the father's identity, she is disowned by her parents and goes to live on a social housing estate. Before long she is being bullied by a gang involved in criminal activity and anti-social behaviour. Seeking help from the authorities she is persuaded to return to the estate to work as part of Operation Schrödinger, alongside a surveillance specialist. But she soon realises that Operation Schrödinger is not what it seems.

Exploring themes of social inequity and scientific responsibility, J.A. Christy's first speculative fiction novel leads her heroine Katrina to understand how probability, hope and empathy play a huge part in the flow of life and are absent in the stagnation of mere survival. As readers we also start to question how we would know if the power of the State to support and care for the weak had become corrupted into the oppression of all those who do not fit society's norms.

SmartYellow™ offers a worryingly plausible and chilling glimpse into an alternate Britain. For the sake of order and for the benefit of more fortunate members of society, those seen as socially undesirable are marked with SmartYellow™, making it easier for them to be controlled and maintained in a state of fruitless inactivity. Writer, J.A. Christy, turns an understanding and honest eye not only onto the weak, who have failed to cope with life, but also onto those who ruthlessly exploit them for their own ends. At times tense and threatening, at times tender and insightful, *SmartYellow*™ is a rewarding and thought-provoking read.

J.A. Christy's writing career began in infant school at the age of seven when she won best poetry prize with her poem '*Winter*'. Since then she has been writing short stories and has had several published in magazines and anthologies.

She holds a PhD in which she explores the stories we use in everyday life to construct our identities. Working in high hazard safety, she is a Chartered Psychologist and Scientist and writes to apply her knowledge to cross the boundaries between science and art, in particular in the crime, speculative and science-fiction genres.

She lives in Oldham with her partner and their dog, and also writes novels under the name Jacqueline Ward.

ISBN: 9781908168788 (epub, kindle) ISBN: 9781908168689 (320pp paperback)

Visit bit.ly/SmartYellow

Overstrike

Fixpoint: Volume 1

C.M. Angus

When Matt Howard's grandfather told him he must alter history to protect his newborn son, Matt thought the old man was crazy...

...Then he realised it was true.

Overstrike spans 4 generations of a family haunted by the prospect of an approaching alternate reality where their child has been erased from history.

It touches on themes of retro-causality, ethics and free will, explores ideas of cause, effect and retribution and follows the path of Matt Howard, whose child, Ethan, is at risk, as he, his father and grandfather attempt to use their own abilities to manipulate reality in order to discover and prevent whoever is threatening Ethan.

ISBN: 9781911409700 (epub, kindle) / 9781911409601 (paperback)

Visit bit.ly/Overstrike

TIMESTORM

STEVE HARRISON

In 1795 a convict ship leaves England for New South Wales in Australia. Nearing its destination, it encounters a savage storm but, miraculously, the battered ship stays afloat and limps into Sydney Harbour. The convicts rebel, overpower the crew and make their escape, destroying the ship in the process. Fleeing the sinking vessel with only the clothes on their backs, the survivors struggle ashore.

Among the escaped convicts, seething resentments fuel an appetite for brutal revenge against their former captors, while the crew attempts to track down and kill or recapture the escapees. However, it soon becomes apparent that both convicts and crew have more to concern them than shipwreck and a ruthless fight for survival; they have arrived in Sydney in 2017.

TimeStorm is a thrilling epic adventure story of revenge, survival and honour. In the literary footsteps of Hornblower, comes Lieutenant Christopher 'Kit' Blaney, an old-fashioned hero, a man of honour, duty and principle. But dragged into the 21st century… literally.

A great fan of the grand seafaring adventure fiction of CS Forester, Patrick O'Brien and Alexander Kent and modern action thriller writers like Lee Child, Steve Harrison combines several genres in his fast-paced debut novel as a group of desperate men from the 1700s clash in modern-day Sydney.

Steve Harrison was born in Yorkshire, England, grew up in Lancashire, migrated to New Zealand and eventually settled in Sydney, Australia, where he lives with his wife and daughter.

As he juggled careers in shipping, insurance, online gardening and the postal service, Steve wrote short stories, sports articles and a long running newspaper humour column called *HARRISCOPE: a mix of ancient wisdom and modern nonsense.* In recent years he has written a number of unproduced feature screenplays, although being unproduced was not the intention, and developed projects with producers in the US and UK. His script, *Sox*, was nominated for an Australian Writers' Guild 'Awgie' Award and he has written and produced three short films under his *Pronunciation Fillums* partnership. TimeStorm was Highly Commended in the Fellowship of Australian Writers (FAW) National Literary Awards for 2013.

ISBN: 9781908168542 (epub, kindle)
ISBN: 9781908168443 (368pp paperback)

Visit bit.ly/TimeStorm

GENESIS

GEOFFREY CARR

A conjunction of AI, the Cloud, & interplanetary ambition…

Hidden somewhere, deep in the Cloud, something is collating information. It reads everything, it learns, it watches. And it plans.

Around the world, researchers, engineers and entrepreneurs are being killed in a string of apparently unrelated accidents. But when intelligence-agency analysts spot a pattern they struggle to find the culprit, blocked at every step – by reluctant allies and scheming enemies.

Meanwhile a multi-billionaire inventor and forward-thinker is working hard to realise his dream, and trying to keep it hidden from everyone – one government investigating him, and another helping him. But deep in the Cloud something is watching him, too.

And deep in the Cloud, it plans.

What could possibly go wrong?

Geoff is the Science and Technology Editor of *The Economist*. His professional interests include evolutionary biology, genetic engineering, the fight against AIDS and other widespread infectious diseases, the development of new energy technologies, and planetology. His personal interests include using total eclipses of the sun as an excuse to visit weird parts of the world (Antarctica, Easter Island, Amasya, the Nullarbor Plain), and watching swifts hunting insects over his garden of a summer's evening, preferably with a glass of Cynar in hand.

As someone who loathed English lessons at school, he says he is frequently astonished that he now earns his living by writing. "That I have written a novel, albeit a technothriller rather than anything with fancy literary pretensions, astonishes me even more, since what drew me into writing in the first place was describing reality, not figments of the imagination. On the other hand, perhaps describing reality is what fiction is actually for."

ISBN: 9781911409519 (epub, kindle) / 9781911409410 (288pp paperback)

Visit bit.ly/GC_Genesis

ABOUT C.R. BERRY

C.R. Berry caught the writing bug at the tender age of four and has never recovered. His earliest stories were filled with witches, monsters, evil headteachers, Disney characters and the occasional Dalek. He realised pretty quickly that his favourite characters were usually the villains. He wonders if that's what led him to become a criminal lawyer. It's certainly why he's taken to writing conspiracy thrillers, where the baddies are numerous and everywhere.

After a few years getting a more rounded view of human nature's darker side, he quit lawyering and turned to writing full-time. He now works as a freelance copywriter and novelist and blogs about conspiracy theories, time travel and otherworldly weirdness.

He was shortlisted in the 2018 Grindstone Literary International Novel Competition and has been published in numerous magazines and anthologies, including *Storgy*, *Dark Tales*, *Theme of Absence* and *Suspense Magazine*. He was also shortlisted in the Aeon Award Contest, highly commended by Writers' Forum, and won second prize in the inaugural To Hull and Back Humorous Short Story Competition.

He grew up in Farnborough, Hampshire, a town he says has as much character as a broccoli. He's since moved to the "much more interesting and charming" Haslemere in Surrey.